Zeal

Zeal

A Memoir of My Early Years in Greece and America

Tolly Kizilos

Published by Lulu
www.Lulu.com

ISBN: 978-0-557-59171-8

Printed in the United States of America

To our three sons, Peter Justin Kizilos-Clift, PhD, Paul Taito Kizilos, JD, and Mark Alexander Kizilos, PhD, for doing the best they can in life, the academy, their professions and avocations and to our grandchildren, Justin, Jamie, Joshua, Olivia, Andrew, Jason and Alexander, in the hope that they will do even better.

Good character is not formed in a week or a month. It is created little by little, day by day. Protracted and patient effort is needed to develop good character.

Heraclitus

To exist is to make a difference.

Empedocles, interpreted by Apostolos Pierris

I have learned that success is to be measured not so much by the position that one has reached in life as by the obstacles which he has had to overcome while trying to succeed.

Booker T. Washington

One's country is the country where one fares best.

Greek Proverb

Contents

Prologue   13

Part One: Childhood in Athens and Eleusis

1. The Desire to Achieve   19
2. The Fever and Fear of War   27
3. Grade School Rebel with a Cause   32
4. Guilty of Sickness?   43
5. The Art of Random Reading   46
6. My Father's Side of the Family   52
7. Hard Times for My Father   57
8. The Treasure Behind the Wardrobe   61
9. Bombs and Brutes   66
10. Uncle Paul Was My Best Friend   73
11. Uncle Gerassimos Dodges a Bullet   78
12. Hunger, Cold and the Archangel Michael   81
13. But for One Hot Potato   91
14. Small Business but No Monkey Business   97
15. The Noose Tightens   102
16. The War from the Stoop of Kortessis   107
17. The Gestapo Arrests My Father for Sabotage   115
18. You Can't Lick a Lollipop Forever   117
19. Mother Visits a Prophet   119
20. The Outsiders of *Neos Kosmos*   121

21. Sins, Miracles and the God Who Loves Us   131
22. Wheeler-dealers and Free Lunch Seekers   138
23. The Alcazar Stalemate   142
24. My Mother and the Arvanites   151
25. Mourning for a Hero   156
26. Barba Vassos in History and in My Mind   161
27. Civil War in Athens: Chronicle of a Nightmare   169
28. My Sister, Vasso, Is Born in the Rebellion   180
29. A Summer in Eleusis with Grandmother Marigo   185
30. Short Circuit for Goodness Sake   190
31. Summertime Dangers and Adventures   193
32. Grandma's Strong Presence   199
33. My Impressions from Orestes' Words and Ways   209
34. City, Marsh and Sea Adventures   215
35. Pointers for Life and Love from an Old Tar   223
36. My Father and the Bohemians   229

Part Two: High School Years in Athens

37. Life at Varvakeion Model High School   237
38. My Father and I   244
39. Mother and I   251
40. Striving for Excellence in High School   257
41. Guideposts for Life from a Physics Teacher   262
42. The Heartaches of Adolescence   274
43. Class Consciousness and College Lore   284
44. Foray into the Fulbright   288
45. Coincidence or Providence?   292
46. More Gifts from Above   306
47. Emancipation by Confrontation   310
48. All Aboard for New York   315

Part Three: College Student and Steelworker in the U.S.A.

49. Hot Dogs or Bust   324
50. The Greeks of Darbury Room   327
51. MIT for Dummies   336
52. The Psychopathology of Our Exams   343

53. Coping with Loneliness   347

54. Chess with Checks and Balances   354

55. A Fool's Errand: Photoshoot for a Roadkill   358

56. Light Bulbs Make Good Hammers   362

57. On the Road to Augusta   366

58. The End of the Beginning   370

59. Steel Town Blues and Highs   373

60. But for Luck or Providence   380

61. Slim Takes the Stage   385

62. Struggling with Chaos   388

63. Love and Laplace Transforms   392

64. Decisions that Count   398

65. The Pursuit of Excellence in the Family   408

Epilogue   417

Chronology   421

Photo Album of the Family of Tolly Kizilos   425

Prologue

I have enjoyed a good and long life, most of it here in America, but I was shaped by unusual experiences in Greece, and I felt I owed it to my family and especially my grandchildren to recount for them the story of my formative years. After all, they know nothing of the culture of my youth, and there will be no one around to tell them anything about their heritage from my side of the family after I'm gone. Some parts of my character are, no doubt, the result of my genes; others were shaped by the way I dealt with family and friends, in the culture and the history I was in. Some of my ways, I believe, are the result of coping with the violence, the sadness and the deprivations that haunted my early years during the Big War, as well as experiencing the joy of surviving in one piece while trying to do my best and thriving.

I also wanted to compile a more coherent summary of the events and the people that critically affected my life. Among the people who influenced my thinking as I was growing up are, of course, my parents, but also my grandparents and some uncles and aunts. These ancestors are the roots from which I came, both genetically and culturally.

This account of my early years in America includes the beginning of my own family's story, as I meet Betty, fall in love with her, marry her and we start thinking of having children. The story stops when I was still a college student and most of my adult life was only a possibility. I don't have to write about that, because it is a life in America and our children and grandchildren know it and may tell their own stories someday. I couldn't part from this work, however, without a brief summary of what I think as "the family years." I wanted to leave behind a few remarks on the way we tried to bring up our children. Our family is, I believe, not only a gift from God, but also the best and most enduring achievement Betty and I have. A dynamic family doing good things in the world became the focus of our efforts. Our family is the thing that matters most.

Having attained no great heights of knowledge, power, fame or wealth, I have neither secrets to bequeath on getting any of the above nor heroic deeds to relate; but I do have some stories to tell for those who care to reflect on the ways that experiences shape character. We can all learn as I have learned from people who live with irrepressible confidence and zest for life, those who risk peril for a cause or those who live in fear of the unknown. The reader will have to discover any wisdom a story may contain; but the message is that we add depth to our character when we reflect on our experiences: we become aware of things that were unnoticed at the time and revise our understanding of events; we marvel at the unpredictability of existence and the complexity of all that happens around us; we gain self-confidence from having done our best under the circumstances and use our mistakes to launch our ships into the future. I hope this memoir becomes a vehicle for the reader's own exploration.

All my life I have been a fierce competitor, trying to get to the top while playing fair and being open about it. Sometimes I broke the rules openly and took my punishment; sometimes I took risks that paid off and other times I was set back. I came to understand that our control over events is limited. Luck, coincidence and God's Providence hold sway over us. It took me a long time to find out that winning lasts only until the next loss, but trying to do my best endures; winning is always dependent on what others do, whereas trying to do my best is always under my control. It was sweet to win, but losing would have been intolerable, if I hadn't done my best.

I am not writing the history of my early life here. I'm dealing with memories not documents and consensus on the facts. Memories pass through consciousness and we try to capture them, cobble a collage out of them and give shape to our past and meaning to our present. We have some memories that have attached themselves to our lives without making any sense to us. We haven't come across some memories since the event that created them, while we have used others time and again to give meaning and context to the present. My mother's candlelit face by the old RCA radio in her kitchen as she listens to the Greek Orthodox vesper service comes to me when I think of her with a sense of sweet sadness; and then, an image I had not recalled for decades and have no idea why I think of it at all arrives and I see a few violet, flower petals and a dead golden scarab stuffed in a shallow, dirt hole in the ground, under a piece of glass. Children made these artistic memorials, called "phaneromata" or "revelations" and competed as to who had created the most beautiful. The fresh smell of pan-fried mullets still wafts in the air whenever I want a reminder of life's little joys, and terror comes like a shadow as I hear the staccato bursts of a machine gun rip apart the night. Memory adds feelings to the senses to etch its horrors and its marvels to the soul.

There is a mysterious randomness to memory that makes me wonder, why does *this* little bit of insignificance come into focus now, rather than *that*? I see the shoes I wore for a long time as a child. One of the new cleats the shoemaker put on the soles of these shoes was slightly twisted and sticks out in my memory; but why do I remember that and not a thousand other things that happened that same day, or the days that followed that quick glance? Memory does not respect time: it can account for five minutes with a thousand words and only ten words for a year or a decade. Remembering for this work has been a humbling process.

Out of respect for facts, time and organization, I have provided a brief Appendix with an accurate chronology that is incomplete as all chronologies are bound to be. It dates some of the events in my story and the early times of our family.

The names of the people in these stories are usually factual, especially the nicknames, but on occasion fictional, to avoid offending anyone. With some exceptions made for the expression of my gratitude, I have avoided giving last names to the people I write about, since their actions rather than their identity are the focus of this work. The stories are told the way I remember them, and others who were present, may remember them differently. That's OK with me. The story of the past comes in many versions, all different, and all true.

When my memory was too weak to cut through sixty years of time, and the story I wanted to tell was significant but vague at best, I went ahead and made up the deficit. If paleontologists can reconstruct links to Homo sapiens from a jawbone or a shinbone and a molar, why can't I tell a story from the scant bits and pieces I remember? So, I set sail for Ithaca.

Part One

Childhood in Athens and Eleusis

1 • The Desire to Achieve

Human beings seek recognition of their own worth, or of the people, things or principles that they invest with worth. The propensity to invest the self with value, and to demand recognition for that value, is what in today's popular language we would call 'self-esteem.' . . . It is like an innate human sense for justice. People believe that they have a certain worth, and when other people treat them as though they were worth less than that, they feel angry. Conversely, when people fail to live up to their own sense of worth, they feel ashamed; and when they are evaluated correctly, in proportion to their worth, they feel proud. The desire for recognition was first described in Plato's *Republic*.

Francis Fukuyama, *The End of History and the Last Man*

I was born in Athens, Greece, on May 10, 1935, which puts me in my seventies as I tell my story. I was told early on that this happy event took place at "the best clinic in Athens, the clinic of Dr. Mayakos." Given the fact that my parents were hanging by the skin of their teeth from the middle class step of Greece's socioeconomic ladder, this expensive and, perhaps, prestigious birth in a clinic for the children of the rich and famous was recounted proudly to me when I was a boy by my mother, and gave me a vague sense of being privileged by association, "a special boy," as my fiercely egalitarian wife would put it many years later, with half shut eyes, raised eyebrows and a slight shaking of her head. It was a kind of boost to my ego, I suppose, and lasted just long enough for me to take some chances that paid off later in life. In time, this vague awareness of being privileged, even though I sometimes went about with a hole in my shoe and patches on my pants, grew with encouragement from my parents. They gradually came to believe that I could carry their dreams of greatness to reality, and so, loaded them, ever so gently, but oh, so firmly, on my shoulders. I never caught on to what they were doing until I was an adult. Of course, they never did.
I felt strong and part of some unspecified elite group. The catch was that I had to justify this feeling of belonging to an elite group by outstanding performance and worthy achievements. Since I wasn't born to bluebloods, or the privileged rich, and never was or thought I was a genius or even smart enough, I had to work very hard and squeeze into the only elite group that had open membership for ambitious young

people at the time: the aristocracy of intellectual achievers. I had to achieve distinction in the schools I attended and gather the knowledge and the resources needed to achieve further educational goals, either at home or abroad, so that I could choose a job I liked and do some good in this world, later in life. I note here that this rather legalistic and unusually clear formulation of my life goals, complete with the way of attaining them, was in fact driven into my psyche. That's how it was from an early age, perhaps when I was only six or seven years old. There was a time, when I was twelve or so that I imagined being rich and famous, but I never let it become a goal. If I happened to strike it rich, I certainly wouldn't turn that down; but I never planned doing anything for the sole purpose of making money. I wanted to become an engineer and invent all sorts of devices as Thomas Edison had done, which would make life better for people everywhere and gain the approval of society and God. I had a plan to make something good happen, and I wanted others to recognize me, if I managed to pull it off.

I learned early on that there were always people who weren't trying hard enough to play the games going on in the neighborhood streets; the same was true in school and at work. Some people in the neighborhood had what it takes to reach the top in the field they chose to compete in, be it math or soccer or auto repair, but they didn't care to do the work to get there. Others did their best, but couldn't do well because they chose to do the wrong thing. I admired people who had a gift and used it to advance, and was angry with people who either didn't take advantage of their gifts or refused to recognize that they were laboring in the wrong field and never tried to change it. It seemed like a great waste, and I never liked waste. Here I was squeezing every drop of brainpower I had, to stay at the top of the class and there was Kostas who could solve math problems in his head faster than anyone I knew, but would forget to do his math assignments. And what about Nikos, who could play on the piano any song that anyone asked him to play, but never bothered to learn how to read music in class, or apply himself to excel in anything? There was a time when I wanted to be a first class runner in the 100 meters distance and I gave it all I had; but I had to recognize that excellence in running wasn't in the cards for me. I had to learn that I could still enjoy running without expecting to win competitions. I was angry with people who could do well but didn't try, and admired those who excelled and those, who used whatever gifts they had, to produce the best work they could, even if it wasn't first rate.

I saw myself as a fierce competitor for the few rewards that could be won in open, face-to-face, long-term, open competition, in the field that the Greek society valued most: education. I focused on being the best all around student I could be at the top high school in Greece, and made it. But this preoccupation with academic distinction, inculcated to some extent by my parents, made me think, sometimes, that I was a cut above the common folk. As I gained experience in life and understood better the people around me, my feelings toward the "common folk" changed. I stopped seeing the "common folk" as inferior to those who excel, when I realized that I too was part of the crowd more often than I cared to admit. Just because I could do certain things better than others, it didn't follow that I was above others in every task I had to pursue and most certainly not, as a person. Human beings are too complex to be defined by anyone for anything they do. Any evaluation of persons is unfair, even though measurement of the output of students, workers, leaders, musicians, ballplayers and others is unavoidable and often necessary, if society is to develop and use effectively its resources. A human being is always more than what he or she does, even when that is done with excellence. I learned this and many other lessons, not in the top schools I attended, but as a laborer in the steel mills of East Chicago, Indiana, where I clocked several summers of work, as a college student. Change of heart comes from experience and change of mind by reasoning. At times I have had to use both to transform myself.

As I look back now, I see that many of my achievements became reasons for even greater expectations for achievement, followed by the ever-increasing anxiety of not fulfilling them. I had enough intelligence, perseverance and creativity to excel at the time. If I didn't, I might have ended up in some loony bin or I might have given up all ambition to contribute in any way. Later, when I found myself studying at MIT, probably the top engineering school in the world, I was giddy with delight on those occasions that I received the average grade! But, by then, I had discovered that I could exist without standing alone at the top of anything. There were many aspects of life to explore, and I was getting ready to do so from any level of the pile.

If everyone strives to do their best for themselves and others, then everyone will be exceptional at something, given the great number of things to do in the world. Conducting one's life with an eye on the best – the *ariston*, in Greek – creates a society of excellence, an aristocracy of the gifted, no matter what their gifts might be. There are no "common folk" when people care about doing their best for themselves and their fellows. We are not endowed with aristocracy, either by inheritance or by genetics; we become aristocrats by just doing the best we can with whatever we have.

So, I should say that I wanted to be in the class of people who are trying to do their best, rather than in the class of people who do enough just to get by. I would never stop searching and testing myself to find where my gifts could be applied to produce a useful result after a satisfying process. The problem with my own situation wasn't the intellectual elitism that I was urged to pursue, but the distortions in the origin of that motivation and the limited fields to which my pursuits were directed. In short, it is hard to do your best when you are thrown into an arena you didn't choose freely and are playing the game not only to please yourself and improve the world, but also to make your parents or others happy, or proud, or more loving. I can remember my mother bragging that when I grew up I would become a civil engineer. I was given to understand that this was the best that a person could be in our world. I deviated marginally when I decided to become a mechanical engineer, instead. I think I would have done a lot better as a philosopher, or a theologian, or a writer. But, then, I would have never pleased my parents, who thought that words were not where glory and wealth are found, and I would have never been able to come to the United States. No Greek bureaucrat believed that the United States had anything better to offer in philosophy or theology or literature than the motherland of philosophy, tragedy and foundational theology; they allowed hard currency to leave the country only for study in professions needed most in the country, like engineering. But, more importantly, no one was giving scholarships for philosophy or theology abroad. So, I remember drawing houses on the dirt with a stick outside our little apartment in Hymetus, a not so prosperous suburb of Athens, at the feet of Mount Hymetus, where I spend the first few years of my childhood, under my mother's loving and ever mindful care. She was telling me what great things architects and civil engineers can do.

My father found a good white-collar job in the largest munitions company of Greece, the *Kalykopoieion* (or "bullet-making place") of the famous or infamous tycoon, Athanasios Bodosakis. The plant where he worked was located in Hymetus, also. There are a few more scenes that come to mind from my life there, bizarre, disjoined, random, but they are significant because they tell me what I was learning from the world before the age of six, the time when we moved out of there.

My parents didn't like our home because it was on the ground floor and thought it was too cold and wet for my alleged rheumatism. Also, the landlady was too weird for them to put up with. I don't know this for sure, but I do remember that my mother didn't trust the landlady, a short, older woman with huge breasts and an enormous belly because she never lost a chance to interfere in our family's affairs. But more than that my mother worried that the landlady would feed a tiny bit of dried and ground up piece of human excrement to us in a cup of coffee, or a cookie, or some other treat she would offer us, because in Asia Minor, the land where she came from, such an accomplishment brought good luck to the one who achieved it. I was under strict orders from my mother to eat nothing the landlady offered me. I was to take the offering, thank the landlady politely, put it in my pocket and give it to my mother when we were out of the landlady's sight, so she could dispose of it without offending the landlady. Well, this and other maneuvers my parents had to perform in order to continue renting there, must have been weighing on them and, combined with my sickly disposition, which was partly attributed to the cold and the dripping moisture of the apartment walls – a favorite urban legend at the time – gave them more than enough motivation to move. Also, my father was doing well at his job, and they might have decided to upgrade their house.

I was a frail child and, somehow, the word rheumatism hovers in my memory, though I cannot be sure that I had been clinically diagnosed with rheumatism or some sort of joint disease, loosely called "rheumatism." I know that my knees were hurting, and I was in bed a lot of the time. I was taking a medicine called *salicilat* and listening to stories my mother read me while I lay in my crib. I had a book about a little dog that jumped into a burning building and saved a child. I cannot tell whether I also had a toy dog, but I have the image of a little toy dog plowing under the heavy blankets of my parents' bed and emerging out of them with a doll in its mouth. I thought this was a worthy and noble deed and admired the little dog enormously because of its heroic achievement. I also had a rubber ball but couldn't play with it in our small apartment with fragile vases and frail tempers around. One of my uncles gave me a tricycle, but I couldn't ride it as fast as I wanted, because there was nothing but bumpy, dirt streets all around us. The desire to ride bicycles, however, persisted, and followed me throughout my early life. It was also a desire that on one occasion, as I will explain later, put me in harm's way.

The last toy I remember from that apartment was a little steam engine, with a boiler, a flywheel and some kind of magneto that could light a flashlight bulb. I know that it was smaller than a breadbox, fire engine red with a bright brass wire for a railing around all the moving parts, and beautifully constructed. I can still smell the red and gold paint. It had a sweet smell, the same as most toys of the time, probably from the lead they contained, and I loved it. I was always asking grownups to make my steam engine work, but no one ever did. Was it unsafe? Were the instructions on the box hard to follow? I'll never know. I can only remember turning the flywheel with my index finger and making the bulb flicker. Perhaps, I became a mechanical engineer out of an unfulfilled desire to make that little steam engine work.

One sunny day, as I was playing outside our apartment, I heard a couple of neighbors talk about a teenage boy, who was caught by the harbor police inside an ocean liner's hull. They were discussing the poor boy's desire to go to America, and lamented the abrupt end of his dream. One of them said that even when they were dragging him out to take him to the police station, he kept shouting that he would try again until he found a way to go to America. The boy said, "Never give up." I think that I can still imagine what I had imagined when I first heard the neighbors talking, more than 65 years ago: a little rascal, wriggling like a fish out of the water, yearning for its element. I felt the desire of that boy to fulfill his dream, and I wanted to make that my own dream as well. And, as it turned out, I did.

I have a few more vivid memories from our stay in the Hymetus apartment that have endured the passage of time, perhaps, because of the fear, or the amazement, or the excitement I felt at the time. One of these memories came with the apprehension and wonder of the spectacle of bonfires. It was dark, the evening of "Saint John's Day," and I remember bonfires up and down the street near our house, and people jumping over them. I remember the shadows of people growing large on the walls of nearby houses and dancing around and shrinking down low following the dancing flames. People were laughing; people were howling. It is the custom on Saint John's Day to jump over bonfires in the streets of Athens, for fun, for show, for good luck in the coming year. No one knows why fires, jumping and Saint John have come together on that day to make this a rite, but I know that somewhere, lost in the depths of time, there must be a story that makes the legend last. I wanted to jump, but I was only five years old at most, too little to leap over the fire. Suddenly, somebody grabbed me, held me up on his shoulders and jumped with me over the fire. The flames leaped high, but we went over them. We jumped over the fire three times for good luck. I was afraid but being high above those flames gave me a thrill I would always remember.

The fires and the children's shouting were joyous, but they didn't last long. It was 1940 and Mussolini and Hitler had already started their murderous campaigns in Europe. Soon, we would see the buildings burn and hear the thunder of exploding bombs, followed by the thudding boots of goose-stepping Nazis. The killers were bringing their nightmares once again to the motherland of tragedy. Greece was next on their agenda of conquests, and we had to fight them to the death, to submission, to humiliation. Damned steel of armor flattens the daring of men and rolls over their guts. I had to grow up fast. There was no victory in the cards.

On the day we were moving out, I was outside our house while my parents were loading our meager possessions on the back of a little truck my father had been given by the company, along with a driver, to help us move. I was transfixed on what was happening across the street from our house. A man was changing the shoes of a horse, and I was fascinated. He was a farrier, an *"albanis,"* my mother told me, and the word still rings in my ears with anticipation and change. I know that it was the first time I had ever seen a horse being shoed. It was the first time I heard of such a thing. I crossed the street, moved in close to the scene and watched the man shave off pieces of the horse's hoof, afraid that at any moment the horse would be hurt, and in a frenzy of pain kick and stomp to death the poor farrier. But the horse took it, and didn't even move when the man drove spikes through the metal shoes and into the horse's hooves. There was no evidence of discomfort, no kicks, no angry neighing of a horse in pain beyond endurance. I sat there and marveled at the expertise of the man. Sometime later, I heard that in the old days, the farrier also doubled as a blacksmith and a kind of a dentist who pulled the teeth of people with horrible toothaches. I was in awe. Perhaps, this is the reason I remember this scene so well. What a strange profession this was! And why were we moving now that there was so much more to learn? My respect for dentists then and later for my father in law, who was a dentist, may have had something to do with that scene.

My mother was calling for me to say goodbye to our landlady and her daughter. Reluctantly I went back and walked up to the landlady and tried to shake her hand. It was not to be. She drew me close to her ample bosom, the quivering flesh of her arms was wrapped around me and she squeezed me and kissed me, over and over again. I took it as a martyr would. And as she let go, she slipped a chocolate cookie into my shirt pocket. "Good bye," I said. "Goodbye," we shouted as the truck moved away. I gave my mother the chocolate cookie, but I wished that I had tasted it and found out once and for all whether that cookie was bad or my mother thought it was. And what if it had a microscopic piece of shit in it? Doesn't everything good in this world have at least a bit of evil in it? Or, taking another tack and using my mother's frequent admonition to me whenever I complained about being sick with a virus or a bug of any kind, I should have told myself, "You are bigger than that bit of crap; it cannot hurt you."

We left the Hymetus house and came to *Neos Kosmos*, sometime in 1940. *Neos Kosmos* means New World, though it was as new as the rocks of the Acropolis across the way and as worldly as any working class suburb in the old world. *Neos Kosmos* became my home throughout my childhood years, until I left for America, immediately after graduating from high school. I wasn't aware how lowly and poor *Neos Kosmos* was until I was well out of it, and people from Athens I met in America, rolled their eyes when I told them I grew up there. There were a couple of times when I wanted to tell the privileged Athenians who acted that way, "I was born at the clinic of Dr. Mayakos; where were you born, buddy?" but prudently I bragged about the street smarts and the competitiveness my rough neighborhood bestowed on me. After all, I was an aristocrat also, but not of the kind with inherited privilege!

Our small, two-bedroom apartment on the second floor of one of the three robust buildings in the neighborhood had more class than our previous roost. For starters, we now lived "upstairs." The entryway stoop had three spacious white marble steps and an imposing ironwork-and-glass door, electrically operated with a buzzer, and a winding marble stairway. There were three apartments altogether in the building – two upstairs for the owner's family and for us, and one downstairs, occupied by an elderly lady and her older daughter whose only distinction in my mind was that she was divorced, though the word meant nothing to me at the time, and ten years would have to pass before I heard of another person being divorced – that one, some distant uncle on my father's side – and grasped the seriousness of the situation for single parents, evil stepmothers, orphans and whatever followed the stain of divorce at that time. My mother would humor the old lady, who wanted to stay young and beautiful at all costs and was intent on accomplishing all that with lipstick, face creams and powders of all kinds. Our apartment had a balcony, a long though a bit narrow balcony, overlooking the street. It was from this balcony that my mother carried out her self-imposed public relations responsibilities. She became a key link in the communications network of the neighborhood, and helped us survive some of the dangers of the Nazi occupation and the Civil War that followed. It was also from this balcony that my mother tried to oversee and control my movements and my behavior as I explored the streets and went through the trials and tribulations of growing up without losing body parts, my mind or my soul, in the swirls of violence of wartime Greece and the free-for-all opportunism that succeeded the Nazi occupation and the civil war.

2 • The Fever and Fear of War

War may sometimes be a necessary evil. But no matter how
necessary, it is always an evil, never a good. We will not learn
how to live together in peace by killing each other's children.

Jimmy Carter

In October 1940, the Italian dictator Benito Mussolini and his Fascist
army demanded passage through Greece and threatened to invade our
country. The Greek government responded with a resounding "NO," and
Mussolini, or *el Duce*, as he was affectionately called by his followers,
attacked Greece. That historic "NO" is commemorated with a huge
illuminated sign of "*OXI*." It appears up on the Rock of the Acropolis
and shines like a beacon of freedom every October 28th, the day this
refusal to capitulate was delivered to Mussolini, and the Second World
War begun for us.

For me, the war began when my mother and I heard the word "war"
in the radio and rushed out to the balcony of our apartment to see what
was happening in the neighborhood. She asked an old, scrawny man on
the street below to tell her what people outside the Alcazar Theater were
saying about the war. I was standing beside her and saw him stumbling
in his drunken daze under our balcony. He was proclaiming the glory
that would come to Greece after we won this war. I remember staring
down at that little bundle of babbling turns and twists and feeling sorry
for him. He turned his head skyward to respond to my mother's insistent
query, mumbled "glory to the army," then lost his balance and collapsed
on the ground like a bag of bones. It seemed that he was bigger, more
real, lying flat on the ground than twisting and turning on his feet.

A couple of people ran up to him to help. My mother took off and
raced downstairs. I ran after her, eager to see what would happen. "He's
plastered," said one of the two men who were trying to revive the old
drunk, moving his head from side to side and slapping him lightly on the
cheeks. "So damn early in the day," the other chimed in. My mother bent
down and got ready to take over the rescue operation, when the old man
regained his dazed, rambling senses and made some sounds as he tried to
sit up. "Just a bump on the head," one of the men announced, and wiped
a trace of blood from the back of the old man's head with his
handkerchief.

"Glory be to Greece," the old fool mumbled.

My mother stood up, grabbed my hand and surveyed the street around us with a penetrating gaze. There was worry in her dark sparkling eyes and her furrowed forehead. "There will be trouble," her eyes conveyed the grim foreboding. "Stay sober, grandpa, and make Greece proud!" she wished the old man as we headed back up to our perch.

The Greek army was mobilizing. There was excitement all around us. Young men and women were joining the army in droves. I remember Kyr-Argyris, the candy and tobacco storeowner, saying that there were "trainloads of people going north, and the recruits were hanging out the windows and doors of the overflowing trains and there were a some accidents – hands and heads sheared off."

I wanted to be in the army. Why couldn't I be in the army someday? I could feel the wind blowing on my face as the train sped north, toward Thessaly and Macedonia and Epirus, the northernmost reaches of our land, and then into Albania, where the Italian army was stopped. Some people were ready to celebrate victory. My father, always cautious and measured in his ways, didn't like what was going on. He saw clouds closing in. He wanted my mother and me to be extra careful out in the streets. He became concerned about scarcity in food in the months ahead. My mother was on top of all the news from the neighbors, the radio and the newspapers. She was the hub of communication gathering and dissemination for the neighborhood, tracking the moves of the enemy and helping others cope with the sadness of loved ones leaving for the front, or consoling women who were left behind with nothing but kids and poverty.

I became afraid of ever sticking my head out of train windows like the recruits had done. One word, one look, one move and the way you used to look at the world could be forever changed. No imaginary heads or arms out of imaginary train and bus windows for me. I wanted to stay healthy so I could fight our enemies some day at sea. That is what my uncle Vassos had been doing, and that is what I wanted to do. Dreaming of fighting for freedom was exhilarating. We had learned from cradlesongs and stories that the history of modern Greece was told in three words, "Freedom or Death." The men and women who liberated our land from the Ottoman Turks taught us to fight for freedom, and that's what we were doing now.

My father wasn't drafted. He had served in the army before he got married, when he first came to Athens from his hometown in Aigion in the 20s. He had been a translator of English and French for the army back then, because he had picked up some foreign languages in the business high school he attended in Patras, the district capital, near

Aigion. Now he was needed at the Bodosakis munitions company in the production of machine gun and rifle bullets and artillery shells for the Greek army. He showed me a red metal badge pinned on the backside of his lapel and said that it allowed him to enter the secret places in the plant. After that, I would look regularly at my father's badge, when his coat was hanging on the back of his desk chair at home. It was a solid metal button, red with a white bar in the middle, a thing of beauty, and I admired my father for the work he was doing for our country. My mother let the neighbors know in general terms about the service my father and his coworkers were performing for the war effort, but he never discussed his work, and none of us knew anything specific about it. There was a lot of talk in the neighborhood streets about guns and bayonets and flags and bullets, but my father never cared for guns, never talked about them and never owned or used one, as far as I know.

He was now a supervisor of the materials section at the plant. He took me along once and showed me the huge presses that shaped bullets out of brass "buttons," which were cut off from long brass rods. I liked the smell of the lubricating fluids that kept the rod and the saw blade cool. We also visited the underground secret shelters of the factory, where, I imagined, they stored ammunition, huge long tunnels, well lit, apparently impenetrable. Inside the plant, he wore his red, round, security badge on his lapel, and I had a green visitor's badge on and held my father's hand proudly. He introduced me to people he worked with, and they all were very welcoming as they explained what they did. I must have been less than seven years old because after that the Germans were running the factory and there was no way I could have been there.

When I visited the plant again the war had been won, but the plant was in decline. My father talked about "peacetime conversion," when the plant was making cigarette lighters out of the unused rifle bullet shells they had in stock, and desk lighters out of larger machine gun shells. They also manufactured toys out of the wood ammo boxes used for storing shells. The products, I think, were too well made and too expensive; the market for them was very limited and the ventures bombed. In time, the plant went back to munitions production for NATO, but there was no excitement then, no national emergency to support, just the business of war. My father was promoted to Section Head of Materials and Transportation Services.

Almost from the start, the war against the Italian army dominated all discussions. There were always rumors of battles won and enemy losses, followed by verification or correction of the events. Saint Mary's bells would toll, celebrating a new victory at Tepeleni or Argirocastro or some other newly mentioned city in Northern Epirus that had become part of

Albania some centuries ago. I had a map and followed the fighting up in the mountains of Northern Greece and Albania, and celebrated every victory as we pushed back the Italian invaders. They said that it was deadly cold up in the mountains of Albania and our soldiers were freezing even as they were winning, and that we were in the right because we were defending our land, not trying to conquer someone else's land, as they were doing. The horror of the war and its consequences were upon us, even though no one in the neighborhood, except for my father, I suspect, seemed to know it at first.

We started covering the windows with blankets to make sure the city was dark and the Italian planes couldn't find their targets. There were a lot of jokes about the Italian soldiers' lack of courage in battle. The newspapers were reporting that all our soldiers had to do was chase the Italian soldiers yelling the word "AERA," which means "wind," and the Italian soldiers would run for their life. The newspapers were having a ball ridiculing the fascists with cartoons. There was a cartoon of an Italian soldier singing arias to a busty Victory Lady while she drives her big bare foot on to his face and crowns a Greek soldier with laurels. It was never as easy as that, but Mussolini's army was no match for the ill equipped but indomitable Greek soldiers protecting their land. I have always wondered if the Italian newspapers were having as much fun ridiculing our soldiers and us. Perhaps, we had more reasons to ridicule them, since we were the ones who were wronged. And we were courageous because we were fighting for our lives whereas they were in this war of choice for conquest and power and greed. We learned the hard way in the invasion of Turkey in the 20s that the victimized people have the advantage and it was proving to be very true now.

Uncle Paul, my father's younger brother, was called to serve in the army, and my mother was busy knitting socks and sweaters for him and for other soldiers up at the front. Uncle Paul wasn't a warrior by profession like uncle Vassos, but he was willing to fight and die to defend Greece from those who were bent of enslaving it. My mother liked Paul like a brother because he was considerate funny and understood women's feeling and dreams, like most artists do. Her way of standing beside him was to remember her sitting on her straw chair for hours on end knitting. She could carry on a conversation looking straight at you while her needles blazed past each other in total silence. I envied her skill at knitting and tried to learn how to do it myself, but her expertise was awesome, and I never went very far. Every two weeks or so we would pack boxes with these woolen socks or gloves or scarves she had made, along with figs, raisins, walnuts and cigarettes and other things that soldiers needed and mail them to my uncle and other soldiers at the front. Well, I did have a special spatial talent packaging the most stuff in a box.

Soon after the war began, the Greek Prime Minister Ioannis Metaxas, who had refused passage through Greece to Mussolini's army with his unequivocal "NO," died under mysterious circumstances. Some people said that he was pro-German, which he was, and he wasn't really the one who refused passage to the Italians, so "they" killed him. Others said that he wasn't murdered at all, but he ate some spoiled octopus, and that's what killed him. There wasn't a lot of mourning for him. Metaxas was just another dictator, after all, and no one seemed to miss him. Most people were relieved that he wasn't leading the country during these difficult times for the nation. But, for some reason, I remember thinking and wondering about this man's death, even though I was only a child. The intersection of the mystery of death and the octopus was too vivid to forget. The truth, of course, is that I didn't know what really happened to him, until years later, when I read that he died of "a phlegmon [inflammation] of the pharynx which subsequently led to uncurable [sic] toxaemia," or toxemia. Clearly, this sentence was literally translated from the Greek. We have no way of knowing whether the translator or the diagnostician or both were sympathizers of Metaxas or not, so I cannot say that the mystery of his death is solved. The point of this brief aside is that the reality I describe in this story, and perhaps in any other story, is not a compilation of facts and figures, but a tapestry woven from my experiences, including hopes, dreams and fancies as well as facts. I believe that this is what we do as we try to explain what happens to us and search for ways of coping with whatever shapes our futures might take.

3 • Grade School Rebel with a Cause

"I am not bound to win, but I'm bound to be true.
I'm not bound to succeed, but I'm bound to live up to what light I
have."

Abraham Lincoln

My parents were believers in God and Jesus Christ and were friends of
the local priests. My mother embroidered a beautiful tablecloth covering
for the church altar and my father was the treasurer of the church for
several years. They respected the priests' views on many issues and
trusted their judgment, but they weren't frequent attendees of the Sunday
liturgy. They taught me to pray and ask Jesus for help in times of great
need, but didn't try to resolve life's issues without engaging their God-
given abilities. "Along with Athena's help, use your own resources," is a
common saying in Greece. My mother kept many of the fasts and
celebrated the feasts, but I don't think my father believed in fasting. My
parents' friendship with the priests was probably the main reason they
sent me to a small private school, owned by the neighborhood priest,
Father Haralambos and his wife, The United Pedagogical Grade School.

Most of the teachers were lay people, both men and women, except
for the fifth and sixth grade's combined class, which was taught by
another priest, Father Constantine, or Papa-Kostas, for short. I'm sure
that my father must have got a good deal on the tuition to this private
school to be able to afford it for both myself and later for my sister. Most
of the teachers were big on discipline, but they were also caring and
knew their stuff very well. Papa-Kostas was a judgmental, authoritarian,
who believed that his way of teaching was best for his students. He
wanted us to succeed and would use all his resources for that end. He
tempered his autocratic style with humor and a healthy desire to explore
whatever subject came up in class. All teachers were determined to
pound the fundamentals into our heads, one way or another.

I believe, that I got a first class primary school education, which
includes a good start in critical thinking and problem solving as well as
understanding the basics of ethical and responsible conduct. By the time
I graduated from that little grade school I had a good grasp of the Greek
language and children's literature, the history and geography of the
country, and I could deal with decimals, fractions, analogies and all the
basics of arithmetic. I also knew a lot of orthodox theology and church

history because all these were subjects we had to master before advancing from one grade to the next.

From the start, I was a good student, combining several ingredients of success: hard work, adequate smarts, imagination and the ability to use good judgment in taking risks. My way of learning was to ask questions, lots of questions, about every aspect of any topic, and study hard, even though I would usually start late, and leave a lot of things for the last minute. In class, there were times when I knew I ought to remain silent, but felt I owed it to myself, the class and the teacher to speak out; and there were times when I knew I should have kept my mouth shut, but didn't and paid for it one way or another. Inquisitiveness was sometimes perceived to be disrespect, or disobedience, or rebelliousness, and was punished by additional work or beatings with a wooden ruler on the palms.

After awhile, I found out that I wasn't only one of the top students, but also the class pest. I know this because there were some periods of time when I was on the dock getting punished practically every day for all sorts of infractions, and the teachers sent reports to my parents regularly, praising my academic performance but regretting my disruptive behavior in class. My father had a standard response: "Thank you for your efforts to instill excellence in my son, but I recommend stricter discipline to correct his disruptive behavior." I was the most restless student in class, and was punished when I stepped over the line, but never because I hurt anyone or because I was in any way unethical or unprepared. I knew my parents didn't like the distinction of having the most rebellious son in the school, but I sensed, as kids, somehow, always seem to sense, that having such a smart and sassy kid didn't dismay them. Besides, wasn't my uncle Vassos, the captain of a submarine who was admired by everyone in the family, a rebel all his life?

The teachers, feeling justified by my father's encouragement, would renew their efforts to crush my rebelliousness, but to no avail. I would raise my hand, and ask my question before the teacher called on me. And if the teacher asked the question of someone and he or she didn't have a quick response, I was there with an answer that was usually right on and out of order. These moves were unacceptable to the authoritarians in the school, and I would be called to the front of the class for disciplinary action. I would be asked to stretch out my hand, palm up, so the teacher could land two, four or whatever number of hard strikes with a square oak ruler, with a square inch in cross section and two feet long, raised sometimes over the teacher's shoulder and powered by whatever human strength that teacher possessed. Miss Ioanna, my third grade teacher, was one of the most competent, strict and cold-blooded wielders of the ruler that I ever came across. The strikes were particularly painful if the ruler's edges had thin strips of steel – inserts to preserve the integrity of the corners – and the teacher wanted to leave two parallel, red marks on the skin of a student's palm. In the sixth grade, when the teacher was Papa-Kostas, the rod whizzed through the air and the strikes he delivered were hard enough to make me wince and act more defiantly than ever. Papa-Kostas, the teacher, was a midsize, burly, black-bearded man with shoulder length hair, who really intended to straighten out any student that broke the rules, especially the top students in his class, upon whom he rested his excellence as a teacher and his duty as a servant of God. His blows hurt, especially if the ruler struck a finger bone, which was rare, but not unheard of, given that most hands were trembling with fear and hurt, and floated in space, as the transgressor of the rules tried to take a glancing blow, which would count, but wouldn't hurt as much, and ended up taking a blow on a thumb, or a little finger, both being the most vulnerable parts of the hand and hurting more than any blow on the palm. Even the teacher winced, if he or she struck a knuckle. It was like telling the teacher, "Do you see what you have done? You came close to maiming a little child. Shame on you!" But, we all understood that discipline was necessary and even desirable to maintain order and act responsibly and learn. We never believed that discipline was unfair.

And, there were times when even Papa-Kostas would forget about enforcement and focus on the substance of any curveball of a question or a sneak attack on his opinion, delivered on the run but revealing a point of view that seemed to have never crossed his mind before. I was good at doing that because there were points to be scored on those occasions, and I felt justified and any punishment that might be administered worthwhile.

When other students asked questions I listened with the same expectation of revelation that I had for my questions. Because I found myself in this unusual situation of exploring under a more-or-less benevolent dictatorship, I have generally fond memories of my teachers and my student life. I always knew that Papa-Kostas admired my guts and respected me as a person, so his harsh ways were born without lasting resentment. I had several friends in class and was always included in the games we played in the schoolyard and beyond. So, overall, in spite of the strict enforcement of rules by my teachers, and especially by Papa-Kostas, I feel that they did right by me. I felt free to play by the rules or not, and that feeling empowered me to be the kind of person I wanted to be. They were teachers who cared about me and showed it many times by answering my questions or praising my work. Later in life, when I became the father of three boys, I found that the hardest thing I had to do with them was to punish them for breaking the rules and say "no" to them, at times. This reward and punishment regime I went through, taught me that sometimes you have to take the risk of being punished or even being ridiculed, so you can learn what *you* want to know, and act the way *you* want to act rather than learn what the teacher or the boss or the authorities want you to know and conform to the rules of conduct without exceptions.

Taking the risk of speaking my mind when most people remain prudentially silent has always been my way of doing the best I can in the search for answers to real problems. But, as I was getting ready to make the transition to high school, I realized that I needed to become more deliberate in my actions. I felt that sometimes I let my impulsiveness take over and acted in ways that caused me discomfort and regret. I would no longer be a pest. I needed to be bold and take risks, but I had to stop kneejerk reactions to the views of others. I set out to train myself, to postpone gratifications of all sorts. I remember practicing the art by placing a piece of chocolate in front of me as I studied and let it stay there for hours before I decided to eat it. When I had just enough money to buy my favorite Eskimo ice-cream bar, I would purposely skip it and save the money for another day. It took me a couple of years of saving the money I earned singing carols to buy the chess set I had wanted ever since I was seven or eight, and seen my cousin Omiros play chess with a friend of his. I applied this control of my impulses to all sorts of situations and got to be good at it. And when I had it down to a science, I felt free to be impulsive or cautious at will.

In spite of my rebellious way, my parents believed that I was responsible and exceptional. They trusted my ability to know and do the right thing, but didn't trust me to choose and do what they wanted me to do. As some of my teachers wrote in my report card, "Apostolos is disobedient." Somehow, I never took that very seriously.

My parents always coddled me, giving me more and better food than they ate, paid great attention to my progress in school and sought the best possible care when I complained of the slightest ache or pain. They overlooked my various transgressions, but never relaxed their vigilance for safe and proper conduct. My mother had many ways and means of finding out where I had been and what I had been doing. She was a master networker, before networking was conceived. She talked to my friends and their parents about all sorts of little things, always fishing for details on my conduct. People liked to confide in her and my friends were easy pray for the clever ways she had for picking their brains. When I disobeyed her rules to stay safe and took a tumble or two on the gravel pits, or climbed barefoot the mounts of broken glass from beer bottles to collect bottle caps for gambling in the streets, as I did a couple of times, my mother knew and threatened to let my father know of such daredevil acts, but she never did. I usually would present her with arguments that convinced her that I had thought about all the dangers she was dreaming of and had come up with solutions that made sense. The glass from broken beer bottles rattling in trucks and being dumped and moved around by backhoes and being bleached by the sun was never sharp; it just couldn't cut your feet. "Mom, do you see any cuts here?" I asked her raising the soles of my feet up, so she could inspect them.

When I came home with a bruise or a scraped knee because I got into a fight, my mother would invariably blame me for the deed and never saw me as the victim. Somehow, it would never occur to her that some bully in the streets could get the best of her precious son. Ergo, I was the perpetrator of all misfortunes in the streets of *Neos Kosmos*. I was, indeed a fierce defender of all my body parts, but never an attacker. Once, I got into a fight with Vouss, one of the older and tougher kids that hung around the neighborhood and played in the streets with us. He was built like a tank. He was much too strong for me to tackle and I found my head being squeezed between his knees. I remember the utter silence I felt because my ears were completely plugged up. I tried to wiggle out of the lock but he kept pushing me down and squeezing my head. And, then I did something I had never done before and would never do again: I sensed a moment when he eased his hold and I slid my head just enough to get my teeth around the tendons at the side of his knee and bit him. He howled and let go. I stood up and we stared at each other fuming with fury.

"I could have squeezed your head like a lemon," Vouss said glaring at me as he rubbed the side of his leg, close to the knee.

"And, I could have taken a chunk of flesh out of you," I answered.

Andonis stepped in between us. He was the only person who could command Vouss' attention. "We are all friends here, right?" he asked, his eyes focusing on Vouss or me sequentially. "Shake hands and forget the fight."

No one moved. There was no way I would move, and, I was sure, hell would have to freeze over before Vouss would. Andonis walked toward me and took my hand in his and held it so I had to follow him for a couple of steps as we approached Vouss. Andonis took Vouss' hand and joined it to mine. "Friends?" he asked.

Our hands stirred, and we shook our heads.

"Friends?" Andonis shouted turning his head first toward me, then toward Vouss.

"Friends," we mumbled.

My friends thought I was crazy to tangle with Vouss. They thought that I had suffered a lapse of reason, instant insanity. I didn't mind it one bit. To come out even from a scuffle with Vouss was no mean feat.

This incident, somehow, escaped my mother's detection apparatus. But if she had found out, I know she would have accused me of acting with savagery against a boy, who played fair and never used his choppers to bite another boy. I would protest my innocence even as she burst out with her retort: "Forgive me, Lord, for I have raised a cannibal!" But, deep down in my gut, I knew that my mother would have been proud of me, even if I ate Vouss alive.

My parents must have felt that I could take care of myself if I got into any scrapes in the streets, but they protected me from harm as much as they could, just the same. I hadn't demonstrated that I could follow rules, or that my behavior had inspired a lot of trust in me, but they had to take a chance because there was no other way. They showed their trust in my judgment by giving me the key to our home when I was a mere eight-year-old child and the world was dangerous, full of desperate people. That brass key opened some very heavy doors. Now, I could come and go home as I pleased. I had to lock the door when I left and never miss. My father was at work and my mother would scour the countryside of Greece trading shoes for food, or shopping in the queues for groceries, while I read my books and pamphlets and did my assignments, which often included writing a hundred times the same phrase that expressed regret for disrupting the class, or for breaking some other rule in school. When I had finished my obligations and, sometimes, before that, I would take to the streets to find my buddies and have fun playing. I would get back home when my mother started bellowing my name from our balcony like a Muslim muezzin calling the faithful to prayer from his minaret. She had a mighty powerful voice that woman, and whenever I heard her calling, I would run as fast as I could so that I could stop the utter embarrassment I felt having my name echoing in all the nooks and crannies of the neighborhood. Why was I the only boy whose name was heard regularly in public spaces and other people's homes? What secret ways had other mothers found to call their young ones home? I felt crushed because she didn't trust me. But, then, why should she?

I would run as fast as I could to reduce the number of dreadful calls from the balcony, stand under the balcony and protest that one call would have been enough.

"Why are you persecuting me?"

She would always find reasons to defend her practice. "I've been calling you for ten minutes now. Where have you been?"

The older I got, the more resentful I became and the less willing I was to debate the issue with her. Many years later I found out that my mother was the only parent who had to have proof positive that her son was accessible and accounted for, twenty-four seven. She needed to know that I was all right and wasn't going astray. Was it because she didn't really trust me, or because she couldn't bear the thought of something happening to me, while she wasn't looking after me? Later, much later, while in college, I would read a little psychology and learn about a mother's love, and how too much of it can choke a child rather than protect and nourish it. I bet that if I could have had a heart-to-heart talk with her and explain what I knew, she would have understood and gone deep into the subject. She would have no desire to disprove the experts, but she would have tried to find a way to fit exceptions for her special boy into any theory. She was an explorer, and would have asked a lot of questions, but would have understood. She would have understood that she didn't need to be my alarm clock every morning throughout my teenage years, and that she didn't need to carry my drawing board throughout Athens when I forgot it at home, or to tie the laces of my shoes when I was thirty years old. But, that was my mother – a woman whose mother love had no bounds. She was hard to overcome because she gave everything she had, and asked for nothing in return. That's not an easy person to have so close to you, after you leave your childhood behind. She would have understood, but I don't know if she could have changed. I am an old man now, but her voice calling my name still echoes in the alleys of my memory: T-o-o-o-o-o-o-l-y-y-y-y-y-y!

In the sixth grade, I sat on the outside of a four-seat school-desk with the other three top students in class. We often thought that we were in a boat and would rock back and forth battling waves, or that we were in a car travelling on bumpy roads in the countryside. When I became too obnoxious for the others, they would squeeze me out of my seat, and I would have to reclaim it with a running start up against them. One of them, Yannis, was a little gentleman and was liked by everyone; next to him sat Sotiris, a real operator, who should have become a secret agent rather than waste his time becoming a top-notch architect, which he did, after being expelled from the top high school in the country for a prank. Next to me sat Kefàlas, who was a hard worker, likable and cooperative, with a good head for practical things, who ended up becoming a manufacturer, somewhere in Central Europe.

The Nazis and the Fascists left us alone in school, but when the Communists came and were running things in the neighborhood, they made us sing the communist *Internationale,* and started giving us some indoctrination that they hoped would incline us to join the youth organization of the party. I remember that most guerrilla soldiers had beards, carried machine guns that hang from their shoulders and called each other "comrade" in the streets. After the government wrested control from them, and the Truman Doctrine was implemented in 1947, we sung the Greek National Anthem and learned a lot about American sailors and American people. I remember clearly that I was in a cub scout meeting when someone burst in the room and announced with a joyous cry that uncle Truman, leader of the free world, had decided to help Greece fight the communists. The Greeks wanted nothing more than to befriend Americans in uniform, and the kids would flock around the sailors from the fleet that docked in the port of Piraeus as if they were groupies following movie stars.

Later, Greece became one of the great supporters of the Korean War effort, fighting next to Americans. Immigration to America was an opportunity most Greeks considered a godsend. The word "nylon" came to symbolize the latest advances in technological progress and became the "cool" thing to have or be in the Greek Fifties. America was admired as the savior of Europe for its inspiring constitution, its helping hands of AID and USIA, and its Fulbright Scholarships and Grants of all kinds; America was the hope of the world through its leadership in founding the United Nations with the life-sustaining agencies of UNRA and UNESCO; and America was the guarantor of a future through the NATO alliance which was committed to the defense of the free nations in Europe.

Right after our liberation from the Nazis and for several years after that, we were crazy for all things American. Women would "kill" for a pair of nylon stockings; men for Gillette razors and Lucky Strikes; and we, grade school students, were into K-Rations that were distributed at the school. We didn't know English, but it took only a day or two to figure out that the best box of food to get was the blue one with the word "Dinner" on it; after that came the green box, which was for "Lunch," and the least desirable one was the reddish box for "Breakfast." A free market grew out of these preferences: everybody wanted blue boxes and very few wanted reddish ones. In two or three days there was a market valuation for every color box you wanted: three "greens" for two "blues" and three "reddish" ones for two "green." Capitalism was in full swing among the street-smart school children of a more or less free Greece. Everyone wanted blue boxes with ham or corn beef and little crusty apple pies and delicious little chocolate bars and other delicacies, rather than crackers and egg salad and beans with some pork fat. And everyone knew how to calculate the relative value of any two kinds of boxes in an exchange. If it weren't for the fact that the breakfast box contained corn flakes and peanut butter, things we had never tasted before but got to like a lot, its market value would have been even lower than it was. So, we came to like the Americans, because they brought us freedom and were generous in helping us survive when our country was down. I dreamed of going to America someday and doing my best to excel.

Many years later, in 1967, the American government of Richard Nixon alienated the Greek people by siding with a Greek dictatorship rather than support the freedom of the people. The American government needed the Greek air bases to guard NATO against an attack from the Soviet Union. The friendship with American soldiers and tourists, and the admiration for all things American faded away. It didn't have to be that way. It would take years to rebuild the relationship between the two countries, which is based on values that are at the roots of the Greek culture and the American Constitution.

The last two years of grade school were among the most intense. In a class of about thirty students, the four boys I mentioned and one girl, Maria, were competing fiercely for first place. All the boys were friends, but when it came to solving problems, answering questions, reciting lessons or responding to any challenge the teacher gave us, we held nothing back within the rules of ethical conduct. As for Maria, she was too good looking to escape our dreamy ogling in class and too serious or too shy to befriend, so we left her alone. I never heard what field she pursued, but I bet she became a doctor or a lawyer, two of the fields that were open to Greek women long before they were opened to American women.

Papa-Kostas wasn't only a demanding teacher and a strict disciplinarian but also a man who enjoyed lively exchanges of ideas with students. Unfortunately, he didn't know that his approach to education could frighten some of the more timid souls in class and, perhaps, cause them to perform poorly. I didn't mind the harsh discipline or being put on the spot, but I'm not sure others felt the same way. And, I might have learned more about obeying authority than I did by fear. Most people, I think, learn to obey first and then rebel. I was a rebel at the start, and chose to become more obedient when I left Papa-Kostas' class and entered high school.

Even so, I didn't rebel in Papa-Kostas' class the one time I should have done so. It happened when Papa-Kostas decided to punish Krokas, the poorest, most troubled kid in the class. Krokas was big for his age, but clumsy and slow. He seemed unable to learn much. He was scruffy, and a repulsive odor emanated from his nose that forced you to stay away from him. Anyway, no one had much to do with Krokas, and he was usually left to himself. Everyone suspected that he was a church charity case and tolerated him. Papa-Kostas had tried to get him to learn every way he knew how, but had no success. So, when Krokas did something in the back of the room that disrupted the class for the third or the fifth time, Papa-Kostas decided to punish him in a way he had never used before and no one had even imagined he would ever resort to. He took out two pebbles from the ceramic pot that held a plant by the window, and ordered Krokas to kneel on top of them in front of the class. We all winced, and I felt a great scream arise in my mind, but I said nothing. I thought that this was torture, and I wanted to protest, but I was as inert as stone. Krokas took the punishment without showing pain, but I knew he was in pain and was angry with the priest. Fear must have tamped down my anger, and I was left with the shame that comes when we fall short of the expectations we have of ourselves. I thought about this failure of my own courage and vowed never to repeat it. The coward knows when he fails and makes up all sorts of reasons to prove that he was wise in doing nothing. Sometimes I wonder what happened to Krokas. I never spoke to him, either before or after his humiliation, but I have thought of his courage and his dignity in taking his punishment more often than I have thought about many other things that seemed important back then.

I often gave a voice to what others wanted to say but didn't want to risk saying it. Later in life I tried to understand why it was so hard for me to be more obedient in grade school. It is possible that I had some kind of behavioral dysfunction, but I don't think so. As I matured, this rebelliousness was appropriately channeled and became disciplined inquisitiveness, probing, exploration and, most of all, an impulse to dig in until the hidden was revealed. In math, I would labor to solve classic problems; in literature, I wouldn't close the book, until I also understood the theme, the reason for the existence of the book and its connection to other, similar books. In class, I asked questions until I had some answer to the why of a battle, or the cause of a famine, or the reason God might have had for asking Abraham to sacrifice his son, Isaac. In a class on religion, I asked once professor Keramidas what the difference was between morality and lawfulness. He said that lawfulness was doing the right thing because you were afraid of being "caught by the pincer of the prosecutor," whereas morality was doing the right thing because you chose to do the right thing. I also asked some questions that were ridiculed by the professors and had to sit down as my classmates laughed at me.

In later years, when I was a manager in a large corporation, I spoke out for fair treatment of others in the workplace, argued with executives for changes in company policies to improve work life. These actions made me feel that I was doing something worthwhile. I have always been the person who asks questions, and when asked, I answer questions as openly and passionately as I can. Often, I feel that if I don't explore the assertions a speaker has made, or I don't defend a weaker opponent in a conflict, I am negligent; I feel as if I have let Krokas down again. Deception, dissembling and political chicanery make me angry because they render me mute when the need for challenges is so great. I want to be face to face with the person who abuses the truth and challenge him or her with the truth. When I heard for the first time upon coming to America, the expression, "You have to stand up and be counted," I felt that I had found an old missing shoe that fit me perfectly and would always be pleased to wear. Once or twice, I even thought that I would put on my gravestone the words "He stood up to be counted." But, even though I tried, I don't think I managed to do so every time there was a need; therefore, I cannot.

And, my motives haven't been as noble, as it may appear: I always wanted to earn recognition from people that I respected. Wanting to win, to excel, to stand out and be recognized have always been important to me, and I've been willing to work hard, and compete fairly to achieve them. I've always wanted to become better than I was. I'm neither selfish nor unselfish; I am both at the same time.

4 • Guilty of Sickness?

In my early school years I remember spending a lot of time indoors. We had no yard to play safely in, and it took a little while before I could learn to find my way in the streets around our new apartment. Besides, I remember being sick a lot with earaches and colds and just being scared of catching a cold. My parents believed that a person who sweats and is then exposed to the cold *would* catch a cold, period. Because of this belief, I was terrified of being caught sweating outdoors in the colder months of the year, especially by my father. If my father saw me flushed from playing in the street, he would call me to approach him, and then he would slip his finger under the collar of my shirt to test for sweat. Detection of sweat was followed by an angry rebuke on the spot, in the middle of the street, sometimes with some of my friends stunned and staring at us. He would then order me to go back home to change my shirt and stay inside for the rest of the day. I was a teenager before I felt strong enough to resist the sweat inspection, but the fear of catching a cold because I had been sweating never really left me. I lived with the fear of being sick. If I ever caught a cold, or had a running nose or sneezed a couple of times, or I couldn't stifle a cough or I had to declare that I had an earache or a fever I would be terrified. My father's scowling and rising anger usually followed any of these signs of sickness. His reprimand would follow, including accusations of disobedience, violation of the procedure of changing undershirts and confinement and disregard for the feelings of worry I caused my parents.

My mother would usually find some excuse, like a change in the weather, or a terrible epidemic running up and down the street and making many children sick and so on. Then she would make the disease the villain instead of me and go on the attack against it with frantic action on several fronts: first she would give me an aspirin for the fever, if fever was detected – heaven forbid –and then she would begin the appropriate treatment. If my ear was hurting we were all troubled because it was a persistent problem in my early years. My mother would heat up a piece of ceramic roof tile, pour some vinegar over it to get it steaming hot, wrap the tile in a piece of flannel torn from some discarded flannel undershirt of my father's and place this burning, steaming brick on top of my aching ear to reduce the pain and heal it. Then she would begin praying to "dearest Jesus" and to Saint Spyridon, who was the patron saint of people suffering from earaches. The heat seemed to help at first, but after awhile the discomfort from the hot pad was worse than the earache. Nevertheless, a little burn was only a temporary evil, whereas an ear infection was the real McCoy and, in the years before penicillin, could kill you.

After the initial shock of having a sick son, my father would come around, sit down beside my mother close by my bed, holding my hand. He would feel my forehead, as if he couldn't believe that I was struck down, take out his old steel pocket watch with the chipped porcelain face, the only *Tavannes Watch Co.* watch I've ever seen in my life, a watch I still have around as a precious memento, take my wrist and count silently my pulses. I would await anxiously the verdict, knowing not if it would fuel his anger and start the chain of accusations again, or elicit a look of understanding, support and solidarity in defeating the disease, this enemy that threatened our peace. I learned that he was never angry after the initial outburst. He couldn't laugh and forecast a great tomorrow as my mother could, but love and the assurance of his presence softened his face and I could feel his strength pulling for me. He wanted to know when the fever and the pain let up, and I was no longer in distress. He just couldn't take my pain. Only my mother took it all in without flinching, always talking about the better day that would dawn tomorrow with the help of "dearest Jesus," and one of the saints she would ask for help.

Fighting the disease meant that I had to go through many types of quasi-magical, quasi-medicinal therapies, often including the application of heated glass cups on my back, or *vendouses*, in Greek, which were supposed to bring the blood to the skin surface, thereby improving circulation and dropping the fever. I never had to be bled with tiny razor cuts to which *vendouses* were applied, causing blood to ooze out of the patient's back into the glass cup – a remnant of the medieval medical practice against diseases of all kinds. My mother was good at administering the dry *vendouses*, but never had anything good to say about the bleeding ones. And if the coughing were bad, my mother would start boiling eucalyptus leaves in a pot and I would stand over it, with a blanket covering my head and the pot and breathe the vapors, which seemed to quiet the cough. So, we fought colds and earaches and coughing with whatever tools we had and our faith in Jesus and his agents.

There were however three times when I was sick and my mother's medicinal aids didn't work. On these occasions, my father had to carry me on his back and in busses or taxis several miles from our neighborhood to the downtown office of an ear specialist for a procedure to relieve the infection, the swelling and the pain. The doctor would puncture the eardrum, and I would scream in pain. Until I broke my arm many years later and felt unbearable pain for a week because the bones weren't set right, this pain of drilling into my eardrum, this *parakentisis* (near-puncture) that the ear doctor had to put me through was the worst pain that I had ever experienced. After the first procedure, when the suffering was burned in my memory, any subsequent earache depressed me because of the possible ordeal I might have to go through to get rid of it. After the doctor drained the fluid the world seemed warmer, more inviting, and my father was all smiles and greetings with the doctor and the nurses. He would pick me up and carry me on his back for the return trip home by any means available, including piggyback. My mother was never more than two feet away from me. She was by my father's side, usually holding my hand.

Beside the ordeals I have talked about, I remember at least a couple of details from most of my childhood illnesses. I don't know why, but I was kept in the dark, without any kind of light, when I had the measles; I was rubbed under my ears with black, oily soot from the back of a frying pan for a cure of the mumps; I barely escaped being cut by Kyra-Nota, the neighborhood shaman, under the lip, inside the mouth, with a razor, as a cure for jaundice, which is called "the golden" in Greece, because of the yellowish skin one develops during the illness. Oh, I remember the sick days and the cures, the pain and the sweet recovery. My parents were overjoyed to see me grow stronger after every illness and expressed their joy with all sorts of treats. I remember that broiled steak and mashed potatoes with olive oil and lemon was always a sign that the worst of any illness was over. Such memories make me ponder the struggles of growing up with parents that are fumbling and stressed out, but also loving and protective. How do they do it? How did we do it?

Every illness comes with stress, and everyone is joyful when the fever breaks, or the rash fades, or the operation is successful. Do the children know that we love them with all these deficits of effort and inability to will pain away? I knew that my father would get the best health care for me because he always asked everyone he knew who was the best doctor and would take me there on his back, no matter what; and I knew that my mother's hand was always there to hold onto, night or day, to strengthen me along with her prayer whispers from which the name of "dearest Jesus" was audible every few seconds. We tried to do the same for our children but, in spite of the advances in modern medicine, the effort is never enough.

5 • The Art of Random Reading

Books let us into [the authors'] souls and lay open to us the
secrets of our own.

William Hazlitt

When I was a little boy I spent a lot of time turning the pages of the
dozen or so books we had in the house, and looking at whatever pictures
I could find there. Sometimes I drew my own pictures on top of those in
the books with colored pencils. One of these books was the best Greek
cookbook of all time, called the *"Tselemendes,"* and I loved looking at
the roasted lamb leg, the chicken with red sauce over spaghetti on a huge
platter and the few pictures of colored torts built like towers on glossy
paper. I didn't know until much later that Tselemendes was the name of
the best chef in Greece, the Julia Child of Greece; I thought
"Tselemendes" meant "cookbook." This book and a pamphlet with the
"Lives of the Saints" were my constant companions. Many years later,
when I transported a few memorabilia from Greece to America, I made
sure to include the *Tselemendes*, and still have it here with me to this
day. I couldn't find the "Lives of the Saints," but that is one book I read
many times over when I was in the early years of grade school as part of
my prayer regimen and I could leave behind without forgetting its
essentials: the saints were exceptional people devoted to Christ, standing
by to help with their special prayers to Christ and their gifts those who
were in trouble. I didn't know for quite a long time that one need not
approach Christ through intermediaries, or that the saints, being human
rather than divine, cannot help or save anyone with their own gifts. Like
most Orthodox Greeks, I didn't know that Christ himself invited each
and every one of us to go directly to him with anything that troubles our
hearts, or with any other requests we have, and ask for his help. I wasn't
used to reading the Bible, so I didn't know what God said to us, as
distinct from what the saints or the priests said to us. It took me many
years of exploration and my wife's example of prayer directly to Jesus to
find out that, if one wants to know the truth, he must go to the Bible and
use his head and his heart to discern from it the word of God. I don't
think that reading the "Lives of the Saints" did me any harm, because I
learned the history of many good people, some of which gave their lives
for the glory of God. Nevertheless, I'm sure I would have been more
enlightened, if I had known about the word of God straight from his
Book.

My hunger for learning intensified when I started school. My parents must have thought that the public schools around us could not prepare me adequately for whatever good things they thought I was destined to do later in life, so they enrolled me in the small, private school, owned by Fr. Haralambos, the local priest. It was located in our neighborhood, and as I found out later, it provided me with an excellent primary education. We had no gym, no cafeteria, no gathering hall, no library and no musical instruments, but we did have one eight-by-eight bathroom for all one hundred and fifty or so students, and a few tattered maps for the teaching of geography, history and religion.

The school did possess one treasure, however, which I coveted fervently; it was the Pyrsos Encyclopedia in twenty-four volumes, kept at the Principal's office. When I was in the fifth or sixth grade and I was desperate for the knowledge of facts, I tried to gain access to it by stealth, but they caught me and told me that it was "for teachers only, not students." The set was locked in a bookcase with a glass door, and I often fantasized about picking the lock and getting to it, though I felt that I could never steal a volume, even if I could find the bookcase unlocked and no one in the office.

The strength of this little school was due entirely to its dedicated teachers. They knew their stuff very well and were determined to have us learn. They held us responsible for learning what they taught and administered punishment to enforce their directions. They did what they thought was best for us without fear of displeasing parents or being sued for their strict discipline and for demanding good performance. At times, their authoritarian ways ignored individual differences and didn't help some students learn, or even hurt some students, but in spite of their ignorance of child and educational psychology they gave most students satisfying experiences to guide them later in life. I know that my friends there and I used that education to achieve our goals later in life. I think that no philosophy or system of education can ever be best for all the students, but some students will benefit a lot and some will suffer some, while most students will learn enough to move forward. But, an educational system, which emphasizes the teachers' love for teaching and rewards teachers for their results, is essential to learning. Learning happens and results are achieved when students are excited about doing their best and behave responsibly toward others and themselves.

As I mentioned, we owned very few books at home and never an encyclopedia. My father and my mother subscribed to a newspaper and a magazine or two, but they didn't buy books. They just couldn't afford it. I don't know how, but my father, had discovered a source of old magazines, mostly children's magazines, advertising and explanatory pamphlets and portions of books from someone or somewhere at his workplace, and often brought home some of these for me. It was a thrill to dig into this ad hoc collection of written materials and find all sorts of facts and stories. Occasionally he would find weekly issues of an encyclopedia-in-the-making and was sure to bring those to me, knowing how I craved to read about historical figures and events.

I remember waiting for every new bunch of materials he brought, always hoping that I would find the continuation of an article on dirigibles I had started reading, or the conclusion of the battle of Gaugamela waged against the Persians by Alexander the Great in the previous installment, so I could close the circle of learning, though that was seldom the case. It was there that I first learned about the Athens of Pericles and Luther's protest and Erasmus in a beret, Sigmund Freud and the Vandals. I can see in my mind their lithograph portraits in oval frames, or scenes from their lives to this day. Because of this discontinuous supply of encyclopedic information, my knowledge of some historic events and famous people was a bit spotty for a long time. I remember, for example reading about Freud's Oedipus complex, but never discovering from the pamphlets what exactly it was. It was a puzzle even after I read Sophocles' *Antigone* in High school and became familiar with Oedipus and his abominable deed.

I learned that Luther defied the Pope, but I never had a chance to continue my reading and find out why and with what effect. A little knowledge might have been worse than no knowledge at all for an adult, but for a child in grade school it was just fine. Perhaps, that article on Luther I read when my world was limited to my neighborhood gave me a glimpse of the larger concerns people had in other places and at different times and predisposed me kindly toward this great reformer. Perhaps, this is the reason I never believed that his followers were "pagans," as some Orthodox believers called Lutherans and many other non-Orthodox Christians. Good thing too, since Betty, the woman I fell in love with and have been married to for more than half a century or so, happened to be a Lutheran! Was this just a hint for the providential help I would get in my life? I don't know, but I believe there are mysteries that exist in every human life, and they taunt our reason with unanswerable questions. I'll mention more of them as I cover the story of my life.

Later, in my high school years, when I was studying French at the *Alliance Française* School, I found a fellow student whose father had a terrific library. I had to walk a couple of miles to get there and borrow one book per week, but I managed to read several books that way, including some novels of Jules Verne, and let my imagination fly beyond the scattered materials I had available from my father's accidental collection. Captain Nemo became the hero who inspired me to seek adventures in learning and exploration. When I was a junior in high school, I used my weekly allowance and some of the funds I collected singing Christmas Carols to subscribe to the New Encyclopedia of *Helios*, published, I think, by the very prestigious *House of Hestia*. It was a great encyclopedia, published in magazine form, about 30 pages every other week, and I could read it whenever I pleased. But I had to confine the satisfaction of my intellectual curiosity to subjects starting with the early letters of the Greek alphabet. By the time I left home for America, the Encyclopedia had reached the letter E, *Epsilon* in Greek, which is only the fifth letter of the Greek alphabet. Even so, there is plenty of information one can absorb, reading articles about topics that begin with one of the first five letters of the alphabet.

I tried other ways to get hold of books to broaden my knowledge and expand my imagination, but I was never able to get hold of a complete encyclopedia in Greece, because there were no school libraries around. I tried once to get into the National Library of Greece in downtown Athens, but the guard demanded that I produce a college student's identity card, and since I had no such card, he refused to let me in. I told him that I just wanted to *look* at books, not to borrow any, but he wouldn't budge. It seemed to me that there was a conspiracy to keep me away from books. I resented this much more than I resented not being allowed to see movies with what we would call an R rating today. The Ancient Greeks established the greatest library of the known world in Alexandria, Egypt, but they didn't have a Benjamin Franklin to give every citizen of the country access to books through local libraries. Since I couldn't get access to many of the books I wanted to read, I would visit the best bookstores in Athens as often as I could, open the books I wanted to read and smell their paper. It was like trying to satisfy my hunger for a steak by frequenting the best restaurants.

This unfulfilled desire for having an encyclopedia that I could call my own, so I could access it at will, became an obsession. Some years later, when I was a starving college student in America and had to scrounge for money from friends for weekend meals because they were not included in the prepaid room and board fee for the college cafeteria, I actually bought the Encyclopedia Britannica with monthly payments and no money down. I had no place to display the twenty-six glorious volumes in my room, but, from time to time, I would open one of the two cardboard boxes in which they came, the one with the volumes beyond the letter K, pull out a volume, admire it, smell it, read a bit of it and slide it back in its place in the box. I kept up the payments for several months, but I had to give up the set and return it to the company when my budget for food could take no further stretching. It was one of the more painful things I ever had to do, and the only failure to pay a debt I ever had, but it was unavoidable. I don't like the order of things in the world, but hamburgers have priority over encyclopedias.

Somehow, this urge to absorb information, discover ideas and form opinions about all sorts of people, things, concepts and events was and still is part of my makeup. It may be that demand, not supply, is the key to at least some aspects of learning: if one wants to learn, he will find the resources and track down the sources, no matter how limited the access may be. Information is the raw material out of which one forms knowledge by using judgment and intuition; and knowledge is the stuff out of which wisdom is extracted by discernment. Now that there is Internet and Google, anything one wants to know is within reach. And, I reach to place what is out there inside me. But, many young people don't, and that troubles me. Information left in the Internet isn't yet ready to make knowledge out of it; it has to be taken in and owned before it can be used.

Years later, when my three sons were growing up, I wanted to transmit to them the hunger for knowledge from books that I had felt. They weren't as hungry as I had been. There were many libraries around and plenty of books in the house to choose from; and there were all kinds of interests to satisfy any taste they had: all kinds of sports with facilities and equipment and coaches; music classes with instruments, bands and orchestras and teachers; they could participate in debates and make speeches; they had opportunities to act in plays and create their own bands and plays; they could get together with friends and play complex table and computer games requiring problem solving; there were movies and TV to learn about the world to feed the imagination and entertain. Because they weren't hungry for books, I thought that they were falling behind in their encyclopedic knowledge and their critical thinking and problem-solving skills. I was slow in adapting to the changed world I had found myself in. I didn't give up trying to direct their attention to books. I would get books that I had yearned for when I was their age and assign monetary incentives for reading them, especially during the summer vacations. They nibbled at the bait and sometimes bit, but I never felt that they were hooked on books. I was learning from them that there are many ways to acquire information and form knowledge. But books, in some form or other, will always be important to learning because they can anchor information for awhile and have it ready for launch to a different destination when the time is right. I tried using the TV shows the boys liked to steer them into the origins of the shows: stories of lasting value. I would point out that *Startrek* of Gene Rodenberry had some of the same building blocks as the Odyssey of Homer, that it was the story of the struggle of man against other beings, if Clingons, the Bork and the Ferengi could be seen as Cyclopes, Lastrygonians or the Lotus eaters. Didn't Captain Kirk owe part of his identity to Ulysses, given his stubborn pursuit of goals, his inventiveness and his courage? Wasn't Captain Kirk's devotion to the Federation and his yearning for the Earth similar to Ulysses' devotion to the cause of the Achaeans and his longing for Ithaca? I wanted them to grasp the fact that books connect people to their culture, their history and each other. The Greeks, of 2500 years ago wanted the same things we do, had values similar to ours and told stories like the stories we tell today. The more the world changes, the more ways we find to express the essence of our humanity. I don't know the effect of my efforts to instill the knowledge of enduring values in my sons; I don't even know which of my efforts helped or hurt them; but I did what parents, I believe, ought to do: the best they know how for their children.

6 • My Father's Side of the Family

I see my father slogging up the dirt road with his bulging black briefcase full of the account books he keeps for his small business clients and hugging a bag of groceries. I'm about to spray a shower of dry peas at Kefalas with my copper-tube blowgun, but I stop and run up to him and take the bag of groceries from him. I can tell he is sweating and I am afraid he may want to feel if I am sweating also. But this time he doesn't check me behind the neck with his finger. He just trusts me. Besides, this time, I am not sweating, and he lets me have the bag. It is late evening and he's been working several jobs since early morning with only a three-hour break for lunch and a brief siesta. He has been walking for miles, sometimes because there is no public transportation to where he is going and sometimes to save the bus fare. Work, saving and hoping for a better lot for his children is what my father does, what he has been doing all his life. Hard work and hope for a better day, is what all the Kizilos have been doing ever since I can remember.

The Kizilos clan had settled for a long time in the mountains near Acrata, mostly in the village of Versova, the modern Chryssanthion, which can be found with a little effort in the Google maps. Nobody knows what the clan name was back then. They were Moraites, people of the Moreas, which is another name for Peloponnesus, the landmass, below mainland Greece. There are stories of dare-do during the years of the Turkish occupation, accidents and crimes and misdemeanors that villagers talk vaguely about as they remember the Kizilos family. And there is the legend of a warrior, killing a brute of a Turkish soldier with an arrow that had a bullet tied at its tip. The Turks chased him all over the mountains of the Peloponnesus to no avail. He was probably a redhead, because "*kizil*" means "red" in Turkish, and the name stuck. "Kizil; have you seen Kizil?" I can hear the Turks asking the villagers up and down the mountains as they tried to find him and hang him. Everyone got to know Kizil and his family, but the Turks never caught him. The villagers knew who he was and the name for him and his family, the Kizilos name, stuck. Years later I found that the name is also related to the longest river in Asia Minor (Kizil Imak, or Red River), and there were many Greeks living in these lands, who later came south, to Greece. One thing worth noting is that my father insisted on spelling our name with a long "ee" ("eta" in Greek), which would have been translated as "Kizelos," in English. He would have me tell teachers who misspelled our name as "Kizylos" or "Kizilos," to correct it. I wanted to avoid the phonetic ambiguity of my name and I settled for Kizilos when I came to America. Thinking about the title of this Memoir, however, I realized that my father wanted the name to be derived from the Greek word "zelos" which means "zeal," in English, not the Turkish "kizil." It is fortuitous that my name, at least in Greek, reflects one of the most pervasive characteristics of my life: ZEAL!

Some of our distant relatives immigrated to America around 1913, according to Ellis Island immigration records. One of them was also named Apostolos Kizilos, probably a cousin, but I didn't know of his existence until recently, when I found his name in the archives of Ellis Island. Several members of the family, besides my Turk-hunting, redhead ancestor, were a bit wild by nature – playful, fun loving and aggressive enough to survive the rigors of the mountains and the oppression of the Turks. Some of them immigrated to Australia, but I know only a couple of them personally. Panayis Kizilos was the only other Kizilos in America when I arrived. He was a cousin of my father and had worked in the restaurant business, I believe. I was going to spend some time with him in Washington DC, but he died before I arrived so I never got to meet him. His wife gave me his gold watch and a cigarette case as mementos, which I still have around to this day. Consequently, as far as I know, anybody named Kizilos in America is a member of my immediate family.

My grandfather Apostolos left his village up in the mountains for work as a shoemaker in the nearby city of Aigion, around 1900. I thought that my grandfather was the toughest member of the family. He was stocky but quick in his movements and loud in his talk. He was expressive and said what he had in his mind without softening it. You always knew where you stood with him. Grandpa married Ekaterini Chryssicopoulou, my grandmother, and they settled in Aigion to work and raise a family. He started working as a shoemaker at someone else's store, but when he had saved some money he opened his own shoe store and never regretted it. His store had a great reputation for sturdy, quality footwear among the countryside folk, who came to buy shoes and boots and slippers from miles around Aigion, because they trusted him. All their sons worked, helping at the store. Years later, the store passed over to my father's brother, Paul, who was a talented shoe designer and extended the store's clientele to the more affluent people of Aigion. Later the store passed to Paul's son, Marios. The store was in business for the better part of a century and would still be a going concern if a severe earthquake hadn't damaged it in the 1990's.

Besides being a craftsman, my grandfather was a lifelong cantor at the Orthodox church of the Holy Trinity in Aigion, and could read byzantine music. Several other members of the family had some musical talent. My uncle Paul played the mandolin and his son Elias studied music and became a symphony conductor in France; my cousin, Nikos, the son of my uncle Gerassimos, was the music director for the classical music station in the National Radio Station of Greece for many years. Perhaps, our children and grandchildren inherited some of their musical talents from the Kizilos family though there are genes from other family members mixed with these to establish a correlation.

I remember my grandfather singing hymns and teaching me to accompany him with a steady hum, as it is done in the Orthodox churches. And, I remember him debating politics with his friends. He was a staunch royalist and defended the king and the royalist party with everything he had. I remember him laughing and raising his glass of *retsina* for a toast with his friends when I was visiting in Aigion; and I remember him filling our little apartment in Athens with his teasing humor and his cheerful presence. Grandpa Apostolos didn't do "sad!"

I remember one winter night in particular when my parents, my sister and I were trying to get warm in one of the rooms we could afford to heat at our apartment, when there was a knock at the door. My mother jumped up and went to the door. She opened it and stood like a pillar of salt looking at my grandfather, standing at the door and clutching a suitcase in each hand.

"I know what you guys are thinking," the old man said with his playful smile beginning to surface with mischief. "You're thinking, 'Welcome, horse manure!' Isn't that right?" My mother let out a cry of protest and a joyous welcome and pulled him in.

"We didn't expect you," my father mumbled and pulled out the best chair we had for his father. We spent a couple of the most pleasant hours I can remember, joking and laughing and listening to the old man tell us the stories of everyone we knew in Aigion. He was always full of life, his bright eyes, quick, restless, laughing at himself and the world.

"Stop worrying, Petro," he would scold my father, who could always find something wrong or something unfinished, that needed attention. Grandfather was always ready to play and we did, tickling and teasing each other and counting the beads of his *komboloy* while he tried to throw me off, until we had exhausted the energy we had and we wanted to sleep. I remember that when he tickled me, his hands dug into my ribs with so much energy, that I felt I had to defend myself. I think he wanted to find out if I could take it, if I was strong enough to take care of myself in the coming storms of life and when I pinched back hard, he was very pleased.

"Welcome anytime, grandpa."

The old man was a connoisseur of Greek food, especially meats. He always bought the best cuts and urged everyone he knew to never economize on food. My father felt the same way, and in time, so did I. My grandfather, however, was a bit extreme. He paid a lot of attention to the lamb he brought home for the special celebrations on Greek holidays. He would bring the meat home, usually half a baby-lamb and the "plug," and hang them from two hooks by the kitchen door until my grandmother cooked them. He even brought a lamb plug to our kitchen once and hanged it from our kitchen door, driving my mother nuts and making my father growl at the extravagance. The old man laughed and joked and by the middle of that dinner had smoothed everything out to the delight of everyone. I have heard that his anger was explosive and he ran his store and his house like a despot. In spite of these flaws, however, I liked the old man for the love of life I saw emanating from him. He was a dynamo and enjoyed living. I got to know him well when my mother and I spent a few weeks at my grandparents' house in Aigion at the start of the war and later, when I visited my grandparents during summer vacations.

By contrast, my father was the most austere member of the family. He spent a lot of time worrying about the future and missed a lot of life's joys. My father, however, tried to be as considerate and supportive of his wife and children as he could, and I don't think I could say the same for my grandfather. It didn't seem that he helped my father when he needed his support, and there were times when I thought that grandma Ekaterini acted like a servant in her own home. She was afraid of the old man, but I cannot say whether the old man made her afraid or she was afraid to be free. My grandfather's exuberance and abundance of expression could make anyone withdraw to a defensive posture.

Grandma Ekaterini was a stoic, peasant woman, who had worked hard all her life to bring a little extra money for her family. While my grandfather labored to escape from the lot of the wage earner and become owner of his own business, she worked as a washerwoman. She took whatever came her way with a smile and never complained. She was as quiet and accepting, as my grandfather was volatile and restless. Everybody thought she was a saintly woman, beyond the meanness of the world.

My father was very close to his mother and took her side on all issues. I didn't get to know her very well, but grandma Ekaterini struck me as a person with few ambitions. Only a few essentials mattered to her, and she had no desire for more of anything. I would watch her dip a dry piece of bread in a glass of water and eat it with relish as it it was a delicacy served by a French chef. She was content with what she had and couldn't be disappointed at missing out on the good things in life. I don't think she cared much about my top performance in school or the things I was after, like achievements, recognition and contributions to society; and I was sure she would love me as much if I had no such ambitions and no record of excellence.

For a long time, her sympathetic round face with slit eyes and thick lips struck me as the face of the quintessential oriental, wise, old woman, who knew a lot but said little. She also looked more like the old Eskimo women one encounters in old National Geographic magazines, than the peasant women who toil in the fields of the Greek landscapes. She was a very good cook and her specialty of fish *savoro* was legendary in the family for as long as I could remember. She was always good to me and her calm, quiet way raised a question in my mind whether the pursuit of "better" and "more" in life is the only way to seek happiness. She gave me a hint to another way of being, but I didn't consider it seriously for a very long time.

Only once, grandma Ekaterini disappointed me, and it was a good thing because I might have come to believe that she was a real saint. I had been a guest at grandma's house longer than was expected, and the poor woman was beginning to think that my father had left me on her household for the entire summer. She knew my father well, and might have thought that this was one of his self-interested plans. She was probably tired of taking care of a spirited teenager and was missing the peace and quiet of her household. She complained to my grandfather about my father's plans and asked him if he knew when I might be planning to leave.

My grandparents didn't know that I was in the next room with the door open and overheard their conversation. I felt that they didn't want me there and I wanted to leave right away. I was too young to appreciate the problems a teenager's prolonged stay might pose on an older woman's strength and peace of mind. I had never thought that grandma had expectations of peace, tranquility and relaxation in her own home! I thought she was beyond all that, as all saints are, and suddenly I found that she had some human needs that make up happiness, like everyone else. From that time on, her image in my mind was a little more human, i.e. a little more selfish, and much more understandable. There are limits to everyone's tolerance, and if you keep testing them, intentionally or clumsily, as I had done, you'll bump into them. I wish I had understood what happened at the time, but I didn't. I would have been less disappointed and kinder toward her. I also might have been more tolerant of others when they tested my limits.

7 • Hard Times for My Father

My father, Peter Kizilos (Petros Kizilos, in Greek) was born in 1905, in Aigion, a coastal city, but never had much to do with the sea and didn't care for it. One of his standard warnings when I was about to leave home to visit my grandparents was, "Be careful because the sea at Aigion is treacherous and you can drown in the downdrafts." He was the oldest of four children, all boys. His two surviving brothers were Paul and Gerassimos. He also had another brother, Stavros, who died before I was born.

When he was in his early teens my father worked at the shoe-store, helping with chores and sales. In time he found out that his father bought string for making shoes one spool at a time. This gave him an idea. He managed to save some money from the tips customers gave him and bought a box of spools wholesale. When his father needed a spool of string, he would sell it to him retail and pocket the difference. This is elementary for us, living in the twenty-first century and in the heart of the free enterprise system, but for a young boy living a hundred years ago in the boonies of a country just waking up from hundreds of years of Turkish occupation, it was a revelation. Saving and making a little money became a guiding principle in my father's life. As he carried it to extremes, saving became an obsession.

He left home in Aigion to study in Patras when he was fourteen or fifteen years old even though he was dirt poor. His father either didn't have any money to send him, or he didn't see the value of doing so. He was hungry much of the time, but he persisted. He told me that his landlady was a kind old woman who took pity on him and gave him a bowl of soup from time to time. He also told me that there were times when he had nothing else to eat but collard greens. He would put the collard greens in a copper pan filled with water and heat them over the blue flame of an alcohol burner. The water could never boil, so he ate the warm collard greens practically raw with some bread. He finished a commercial high school in Patras, having studied bookkeeping and foreign languages, and came to Athens in the late twenties to find a job and make his career. But first, he joined the Army and served as a translator. From the pictures I have seen of him from that time and the few stories he told, these were some of the happiest years in his young life. When he completed his military service, he joined the accounting department of a dealership for a large tire company, I think Goodrich, in Greece, if I recall correctly the name on the rubber-rimmed ashtray we had in the house for decades.

Later in life I learned that my father had been going through some very hard times with his career and his finances in the years following my birth. He was apparently caught in some kind of a stock market bubble and lost the house he had received as a dowry from my mother's family. (He regretted this loss greatly and wouldn't rest until he managed to build a new house for my mother, twenty years later). Then the company he was working for went out of business, and he lost his job. He applied for the franchise of another tire company in Athens (I vaguely recall that it was a franchise of the Dunlop Company) and, as far as I know, he was granted the franchise, but balked at the risk he would have to take, and didn't follow through. I think, he regretted that decision, because the people who got the franchise became very successful; but his cautious approach might have been a blessing in disguise, because he didn't do well under stress, and wouldn't have fared well with a business of his own. Business is a line of work that always requires an overoptimistic outlook and the ability to take risks, two qualities that my father did not possess. These life reverses left scars on him and, together with an early childhood of extreme deprivation, limited his world to the point where he hardly ever did anything spontaneously or took a chance on anything, especially when it came to money. He prided himself for his economical approach to all things, but others might not have been as generous judges of his ways and called him a miser. One thing became clear to me, however, as I grew up under his guidance: he was tight with money and didn't like taking risks to experience new situations in life. He stayed pat most of the time and, as a result, missed out on some of life's enjoyments. He came close to travelling to America to see us, but he never took the final decision, as my mother did. It is true that doing things his way, he benefitted others in the family, but he overdid it, because he turned a good thing into a burden.

His "economizing" and risk aversion were made poignantly clear to me from watching my father's unique way of "playing" the National Lottery of Greece. Lottery vendors used to carry lottery tickets on poles and sell them usually to older people sipping their coffee on sidewalks, outside the thousands of coffee shops, or *kafeneia*, of Athens. My father would call one of these vendors and buy a ticket from him. Then, he would check the numbers of four other tickets and write them down. When the results of the drawing were announced a few days later, my father would check all the numbers of the tickets he had written down as well as the ticket he had bought, to find out if they were losing numbers. Then, he would immediately announce that he had won an amount equal to the cost of the tickets he hadn't bought. Winning something by being "economical" and not paying for tickets that ultimately proved to be worthless was a thrill for him. I have no idea what he would have done, if one of the numbers he jotted down, but didn't own, turned out to be the jackpot winner. Fortunately that never happened.

One of my sons, many years later, said to me that a lottery is a product which is guaranteed to fail; after all, a ticket "works" only once out of a million or a hundred million times! Yet, unlike his grandfather, he still buys a lottery ticket occasionally, and so do I. Besides, as another of my sons, who knows his statistics says, "buy only one ticket because that changes the odds from zero to something positive, but you don't need to buy more than one ticket because that doesn't change the odds of winning so dramatically. My father had done just that! But, my father had largely lost the ability to be foolish, careless and spontaneous. He had forgotten how to play because playing was unpredictable and unproductive, even dangerous in his early life. It was sad to see him so preoccupied most of the time with facts and figures. "I wish I could stop thinking for a while and stare at the world with an empty head," he told me once. Yet, he didn't think much of people who seemed to be at peace with whatever troubles they had. I know that if somebody told him "Don't worry; be happy," he would have thought him to be an airhead.

I tried to get him to read, learn how to draw or collect things, but nothing was of great interest to him beyond keeping up with the tax code and saving or investing his savings. It seemed that his fears were often related to money, never to the real big issues of life. Perhaps, he had solved the "other" issues, but couldn't do the same for money. One time, many years later, when I visited him and my mother in Greece with my own family, I was sick and in pain. I was going to enter the hospital for an operation to fix the wrist I broke running down a mountainside in Portaria, a little mountain village near Volos, in Central Greece. The unbearable pain I had put up with for a week was payback for the elation I felt being almost airborne in my descent down the mountain. I told him how thrilling it was to fly downhill, and how scared I felt to go under the knife. He looked at me puzzled, thinking, always thinking how to solve a problem.

"I'm afraid of dying on the operating table," I blurted out the words to show him that I was troubled.

"It'll be fine," he said.

I was surprised. "Aren't *you* afraid of dying?" I questioned him, feeling that he still didn't grasp the despair I felt.

"There is nothing to fear from death," he said with uncharacteristic calm and certainty. He was so utterly convincing that I believed exactly what he said. I remember this interaction with great clarity because it showed me that my father had thought about some things that went beyond facts and figures and made some wise decisions.

I'm no longer afraid of dying. Going under with anesthesia though is another matter, altogether. And, I hope, the end is without prolonged pain and the anxiety of modern medicine's procedures. Perhaps, I am more afraid of death than I thought I was.

8 • The Treasure Behind the Wardrobe

Acute, life-threatening crises, then, can justify lies to save
innocent lives; and prolonged threats to survival suspend the
efforts to evaluate lies told in self-defense.
Sissela Bok, *Lying: Moral Choice in Public and Private Life*

As the war against the Italians dragged on, it became clear that the best
we could achieve was a stalemate. The Italians were held back on the
mountains of Albania, but they could not be defeated. Italy was, after all,
four or five times more populous than Greece and had the backing of the
Nazis behind it. The war's hardship started to become apparent in
Athens. Suddenly the number of amputees we saw in the streets
increased so much that you could hardly walk a couple of blocks without
seeing someone in crutches or on a wheelchair with a leg or legs missing.
The word was that soldiers were losing feet and legs from frostbites and
the gangrene that followed due to the severe cold and the poorly made or
worn out boots they were using. That's when the value of the woolen
socks my mother was knitting became clear to me. After the war, the
government compensated these veterans for their sacrifices, by giving
them loans to buy newspaper and cigarette kiosks. Soldiers became small
businessmen, whether commerce was in their blood or not. It was one of
the many unintended consequences of that war, as there are always in
any war. The enemy we see is never the enemy that causes us the most
pain. Broken bodies, broken hearts, broken homes and broken souls are
the enemies we never saw and never fought against.

Closer to home, we felt the scarcity of food when the rationing of
most staples was imposed. Bread, butter, meat, potatoes, beans, olive oil
and other staples could only be bought with the proper coupon, in the
amount allotted, after waiting on long queues for endless hours outside a
store that had something to sell, hoping all along that it didn't ran out
before our turn came. There were some foodstuffs still available, but the
war made them scarce and, therefore, very expensive. Things would get
worse, but we didn't know it at the time.

My father, being both inclined to assume the worst outcome of an
uncertain situation and the first to plan meticulously for that, decided at
some point, that things would, indeed, get much worse, with food
becoming very scarce, and we started hoarding whatever food we could
save, behind our big bedroom wardrobe. All we had to do to create a
makeshift storage place, that no one would ever think it could be a
pantry, was move the closet from its flat position against the wall to one

where its backside formed the third side of a triangular space, the other two sides being formed by the walls of the room. If we saved enough food, we could avoid starvation and survive. But, our ability to stash food was limited and the risk of hoarding food could become very high. Nobody was supposed to know about our stash behind the closet. Father was very clear and very explicit about that. He predicted that hoarding food would become a crime some day soon, and anyone caught would end up in jail. My mother, went along, though her natural inclination was to take care of today and let tomorrow take care of itself. She was the optimist and her intuitive approach to problem solving discounted planning and the future. I could never decide how hidden this makeshift pantry was, and its existence was an ever present threat in the back of my mind.

A couple of years later, during the Nazi occupation, when the German soldiers established themselves in Athens, boots pounding the streets and guns dangling from their leather belts, the law against hoarding was announced along with severe penalties for transgressors. The smell of leather wafting off the German soldiers is embedded in my brain, and to this very day, if I smell it, I look for a German soldier to appear from somewhere. I was terrified that we would be discovered with a hidden stash of foodstuffs and be thrown in some dungeon forever. I even thought that they might go easier on us if we had our foodstuffs out in the open, rather than in that makeshift pantry my father had contrived. But, my father had a definite view on how we would deal with the coming famine, and my mother went along because she understood the logic but hated the situation it imposed on us. I never had any say in the matter, other than tremble when the wardrobe was moved in or out. I suspected my father might be hiding the stuff from unexpected visitors to the apartment, who might squeal to the authorities, rather than from a routine inspection by Germans looking for a hoard of foodstuffs in our humble abode. He was probably right. It is hard to trust anyone whose life or his family's life hangs on squealing.

We started with a couple of cans of pork and beans, some wheat in a sack, a bottle of olive oil and a couple of precious tin cans of corned beef. The cans of corned beef were from Argentina, a bit of information on the cans that raised Argentina's image in my mind for all time. When we wanted to add to our supplies, or had to dip into them, we would slide the entire closet out a few inches and my mother or I would squeeze in to move the food in or out of the vault. Once the job was finished, we would all push the wardrobe and slide its edge back against the wall to hide our treasure. I know that my father hated to ever get things out of there, and my mother hated to reduce the present quantity of food and stash things in there, to be used at some distant future she could not taste or smell. Thus, any movement of the closet, no matter what the reason, always came with resentment of one of my parents or the other. If these emotions were openly expressed, as it happened sometimes, verbal skirmishes between my parents erupted and I headed for the kitchen. This tug o' war between my father's worry about future catastrophes and my mother's strong preference for a better life here-and-now was evident in most aspects of our family life. They were two very different people: mother was the grasshopper and father was the ant. I was somewhere in between the two of them, so I couldn't decide if the risk of being caught some day was worth the risk of starving to death. Or, whether enjoying the present day was better than getting by some distant tomorrow. Later in life, when I could afford it, I would try to own two of everything I needed, or used a lot. That's when my wife started calling me Tolly-Two-Sheds, from having built two sheds for our lake cabin when one might have been enough. One thing was for the here-and-now and the other was for the time when things went awry. Or, to be more explicit: one for mom and one for dad. I'm still not sure, but there must have been one for me somewhere in there.

Rumors of a German invasion began to terrify the population. My mother prayed for peace, and my father worked harder to increase the provisions we saved for the coming disasters. Beside his regular job, my father kept the books for four or five small businesses. He would get up at five in the morning walk about a mile to the bus stop to catch a bus and get to his regular job, and come back home after two-thirty in the afternoon. (After the war, the company provided a car to give a ride to my father and a couple of other managers and he was very thankful for that.) He would eat his lunch and have his traditional siesta nap, for an hour or so. At four-thirty or five, he would leave for his bookkeeping jobs in downtown Athens. After that, he would stop to buy any kind of food, wherever he could find it. He was usually back at home sometime between seven or eight. He was tired, often disheartened by the news and had little to say. One thing that animated him and made him laugh was the occasional great buy he made at some grocery store, or the find of a stash of foodstuffs he discovered at some distant corner of Athens and how he bought a sack or a bundle of it at a great price. My mother would hug him and congratulate him for his superb sense of unearthing bargains. That would be a good evening.

The Germans couldn't wait any longer for the Italians to take Greece. They needed to get through Greece and, from Crete, vault to North Africa and reinforce Rommel's army, the Africa Corps, which was fighting against Montgomery. A sort of panic took hold of Athens when German fighters started dropping bombs on the port of Piraeus and my mother's birthplace, the port city of Eleusis. We watched the air battles from our balcony, rooting for the Greek gunners and hoping that the flack would hit one of the enemy aircraft. I never witnessed a hit, but there were some distant flashes from ground explosions. Eleusis was bombed and there were some casualties, but no one we knew. My father couldn't leave his job at the munitions plant, but he thought that it would be safer for my mother and me to go south to his birthplace in Aigion, on the northern shore of the Peloponnesus. We would stay with his parents until the situation with the German invasion was resolved.

We took the train to Aigion. It was my first trip on a train, my first trip outside Athens, and I remember the excitement and the anticipation. We were going on a trip to strange places, mythical places, far into the lands of wonder. We were speeding in the countryside, nature in its green calmness engulfing us. And, then, the planes came diving down on us, and machine guns were crackling all around us. "*Stuka*" someone said. I had heard enough about *Stuka* planes spreading death with their machine gun fire and bombs on our cities and I was afraid. The train raced toward a nearby tunnel and managed to enter. It stopped and we scrambled out of the train and sat down low by the rock walls. It was pitch black and we felt the utter helplessness of bomb blasts outside the tunnel. It was as if a beast was trying to enter our cage and devour us. And then there was silence. Bodies seemed to rise up from the floor in the dark. I tried to imagine that we had stopped outside the tunnel to enjoy the beauty of spring in the countryside. There were no planes, no bombs, no darkness pushing us against the rocks and the rails. Just green leaves of trees and flowers, red poppies and anemones.

I didn't know it yet, but soon after that, I learned how to squeeze through the crack of reality's nightmare and enter a makeshift triangular little shelter I concocted with the folding door that separated our bedroom from our living room. When I had enough of darkness in this claustrophobic campanile, I would climb up inside to the top and poke my head up near the ceiling and recite prayers and slogans facing the wardrobe's mirror. Sometimes we must make do with the illusion of safety and victory till dawn shatters all pretensions.

After the planes left, there was only the noise of people shuffling in the darkness as we worked our way to the other side of the tunnel. The bombs had blasted out some rocks and blocked the tracks. We waited for a long time until busses finally arrived nearby, and we were picked up for the rest of the way to Aigion. By the time we got to my grandparents' home, my mother and I were exhausted. I was hungry, and they gave me some bread, cheese and dry raisins to eat. We settled as well as we could and waited for whatever evils the world would bring. I was given access to three things and made them my toys. I spent a lot of time rearranging the wax fruits on a platter that my grandmother had as a dinner table decoration; I also found a small empty revolver, which I learned how to assemble and disassemble and would have never thought at that tender age of shooting; and I discovered my uncle Paul's mandolin in a closet, which I was allowed to take out and strum at will provided no one was sleeping. I was beginning to get acquainted with my grandfather and my grandmother. It would take awhile before I got to know them.

9 • Bombs and Brutes

They wrote in the old days that it is sweet and fitting to die for one's country. But in modern war, there is nothing sweet nor fitting in your dying. You will die like a dog for no good reason.
Ernest Hemmingway

Uncle Paul had been a soldier, fighting the invaders at the front, but we didn't know where he was after the German invasion and the collapse of the army at the front. Uncle Gerassimos was a coast guard noncommissioned officer near Aigion, but didn't live at the home of my grandparents. So, my mother and I would be the only guests of the old couple. We were looking forward to the tranquil atmosphere of a home overlooking the Gulf of Patras that joins the Ionian Sea some miles away.

My grandfather was a light sleeper and took his siesta on the first floor under my room, which had some very creaky floorboards. I couldn't walk around when he was asleep because he would wake up and bang the ceiling with a broom, or shout at me to go to sleep, if the thuds didn't work. If I needed to go to the bathroom I had to tiptoe along a predetermined path to avoid any major creaking, though, the floorboards being what they are couldn't be trusted to provide me with a safe passage. Sometimes I wouldn't risk the trip because I was afraid. I just lay in bed and stared at the wax fruits as I assembled and disassembled the revolver till I fell asleep.

Every day the German planes would fly over us and drop their deadly cargo of bombs. Grandpa said that they were after factories and cargo ships docked offshore, but occasionally a bomb would stray and strike houses in the city. We could see the smoke rising from various parts of town. There were sirens of fire engines and people would run to help with the fires or to see and report what damage was done. We would gather on the ground level of the house every time the sirens sounded the alarm, and crawl under beds and wait for the thudding to begin. A couple of older women in the neighborhood, who lived alone in flimsy houses near us, Calliope and Koula, would rush into our house and scramble under the beds, also. The only person who refused to crawl under a bed was my grandfather. He fancied himself a tough guy, and in many ways he was. But, I suspect that he just wanted to believe that no matter what the Germans did, they wouldn't be able to make every Greek bow down to them. I always thought of him as a kind of wild man, and I wouldn't have been surprised to learn that he was one of the first rebels against the

Nazi occupation. In later years, remembering those days, he would reminisce and joke about the two women who came for shelter at his home: "The worst thing about these bomb raids," he would say with a sparkle in his eyes "wasn't the bombs exploding close by and the fires they set in the city, but having to endure Calliope's fat butt sticking out from under one of the beds!"

One day we heard that one of the bombs struck the Church of Holy Mary, the cathedral of Aigion, which was partly sculpted out of a rock in the hills above the sea and was called *Tripiti*, that is "hollowed out" because of this. It was said that the bomb pierced part of the rock above the dome of the altar and was lodged there without exploding. Immediately, many people pronounced this unusual event a miracle, and flocked to the church to pray for the city and their loved ones. The church became known for this miracle to all the towns around Aigion. When the topic of the miracle of the bomb was raised in a discussion, grandma Ekaterini would raise her eyes up at the icons and higher up, at the sky, and whisper prayers in awe, as she crossed herself.

I would hear many such stories about miraculous events, especially during the occupation that followed the war. Sometimes, I tried to see for myself whatever was supposed to be happening. Over the years, I've had plenty of time to think about miracles, providential action and other supernatural events. I never had any problem believing that miracles are possible. I mean that, if one believes in an omnipotent God, who created the universe and is present in his creation, it is foolish to doubt the possibility of miracles. But, to believe in any one particular miracle, I require some personal experience, some kind of verification. So, for example, I believe that I have been the recipient of extraordinary help by providential action, but I cannot prove that particular events in my life were providentially done, or prove to the satisfaction of others any miracle that someone else reported. I believe that God intervenes supernaturally in the world, and humans call these interventions miraculous, sometimes without proof other than their personal experience. So, I don't know if the bomb that pierced the ceiling of St. Mary's dome above the altar in Aigion was just a dud that happened to fall on a very solid, rocky roof, or a bomb held back from exploding by the power of God.

I mention this event because it relates to my story in an unusual way. I have no memory of this happening, but I was told that when I was about four years old and while staying in Aigion, sometime before the war, I happened to be walking from my grandparents' house to grandpa's shoe store, holding my mother's hand. Suddenly, I let go of my mother's hand and ran toward an abandoned house. Before my mother could reach me I had fallen into a deep stairwell and was unconscious. I remember nothing of this accident or of being there. They tell me that I was completely out of it for some time. My parents and grandparents prayed for my recovery and dedicated the customary silver image of the body part that was hurt, in this case a boy's entire body, as it is done for such occasions. They took this silver offering, the size of half an iPhone with half the thickness of a dime and hang it up before the icon of the Holly Mary in that same church. As I said, I was out when they took me to the hospital and when all these things were happening, so I have no memory of what happened; my relatives, however, believe that I could have died in that fall, or I could have been left with a damaged brain, or ended up a paraplegic, yet, miraculously, none of these things happened. I got well and everyone was thankful to God and the doctors, and so was I in later years, when I was told of this. As my friend, Fr. Anthony says, the question that always looms in the mind of the faithful is: providence or coincidence?

Though I was too young to know much about the war, I sensed that things weren't going well for Greece. The bombing stopped, but no one was laughing. The Germans were winning. Our defeat seemed inevitable. The Greek army fought the Germans valiantly for three weeks and then succumbed, unable to hold back Hitler's panzers. Winston Churchill praised the Greek soldiers when he said, "Some say that the Greeks fought like heroes; instead we should say that heroes fight like the Greeks." Historians praise the effort of the Greek Army, because the three weeks of resistance it offered fighting the German army were very valuable to the Allies. Hitler was forced to delay the reinforcement of his army at the eastern front, in Russia, thus giving the Allies time to organize a defense. History records that the Germans came to the rescue of their Italian allies by invading Greece on April 6, 1942, and Greece surrendered on April 27. We heard that the Germans had occupied Athens and were barreling down toward us in Aigion and throughout the Peloponnesus. We were crushed. The loss of a country leaves its inhabitants with a broken heart that seldom mends.

And so it was that I saw German soldiers for the first time riding on big motorcycles and trucks and speeding past the little house of my grandparents. We stood still at the roadside, numbed by the awesome sight and the terrifying roar of these chariots from hell. Then, some of them stopped, soldiers dismounted, jumped out of trucks and clutching machine guns underarm scrambled and took positions in doorways, stairwells, and around corners, while the rest of them sped ever forward beyond our part of the town. There was no hope of freedom now. We were slaves, just as the songs from the Turkish occupation said we were in the past, before our liberation from the Ottoman Turks in 1821. Even I, a mere child, sensed the ominous change that hang above us like a heavy cloud. We didn't know then what the word "occupation" meant, but it wouldn't take us long to find out. The reason I remember the mood and the images of the times is because these things lasted long after the Germans were gone and the war had ended. As Greeks, we knew well our history of occupation by the Turks, and before that by the Romans and the assorted Europeans who followed them. But we didn't have the experience of being occupied. The adults were trying to look calm and composed, but I knew they were afraid of something sinister and unfathomable. In time we would learn that occupation means deprivation of most things people value in life – safety, food, water, shelter, electricity, medicines, free speech, travel, due process of law and the rest of freedom's fruits. It was a terror that seemed to go on and on without a hint of ending. Would this last a year? Five years? A millennium, as Hitler had planned for his Third Reich? The last time it happened in Greece with the Turkish occupation, it lasted four hundred years! We would exist, but how would we live? Everything became scarce, and basic trust among people soured and turned to suspicion, uncertainty, anxiety. Without trust humanity loses its civilized veneer and dons the devil's mask. The evil of occupation and the hatred of the enemy can slowly turn to self-hatred and fratricides, as it eventually did in Greece. More human beings had to shed their blood to blot out the planned millennium of Hitler. They had to die to shrink that monster's millennium into less than four miserable years.

I would go with my grandfather to the shoe store and listen to the shopkeepers who stopped by, as they talked in whispers. They didn't seem interested in selling their wares or complaining about poor business. They didn't even discuss politics, normally, the lifeblood of all Greek discussions. They were always talking about the still missing soldiers of our army. They were lamenting the loss of the war and the loss of public buildings and houses and anything that the Germans took a fancy to and occupied and used for their quarters or for other needs they had. The same topics were discussed in the stores we visited on the way back home. Someone at the coffee shop, said, "Greece is lost in the garbage heap of history." Everybody cursed him. The Greeks resented the fact that their victory against the Italians was stolen from them. We had lost, but the Greek army with its dilapidated equipment and dwindling supplies was no match for the German panzers and the vast resources Hitler had devoted to it. The men in the coffee shops and the taverns argued with vigor about the reasons for losing the war; some consoled themselves by the knowledge that we managed to push back "the Julia Division," the second best division of the Italian army; but the wounded pride of most Greeks could not be healed by reason. What were these men thinking of? It took the combined might of the greatest nations of the world to subdue the Axis forces of Germany, Japan and Italy. We never had a chance of winning this war on our own. But standing our ground with our friends in America and England we couldn't be losers for long. But, no one was up to celebrating, yet.

In later years, as a teenager with a record of excellence in high school, I would visit my grandparents in Aigion for a couple of weeks during summer vacation. I would go to my grandfather's shoe store every day and try to be helpful, as instructed by my father. My grandfather was always trying to teach me how to take care of shoes in the store window by dusting them, tilting them this way or that, changing them "to suit the customers' tastes," he would say, though I never could figure out how he knew that. Then he wanted me to learn how to stack shoeboxes that arrived at the store by mail, and even how to welcome customers to the store and find out the right size shoes for them. I felt some obligation to work handling new shoes and stack boxes, but I dragged my feet, totally repulsed by any kind of work that required contact with used shoes or feet. My reluctance to handle worn shoes and feet irritated the old man, but I was undeterred. I couldn't imagine myself as a salesman, stock boy or anything else associated with the shoe business. Then, he gave me the broom and asked me to sweep at the back of the store, just to be useful with something. I obeyed reluctantly, but let him know with my surly face that I wasn't happy with that kind of work either.

When I wasn't busy inside the store, I would stand by the entrance and watch the people go by. There was a coffee-roasting store next door with a coffee roaster turning most of the time. The aroma of the coffee was sweet and mysteriously cheerful. I wasn't a coffee drinker back then, but I came to love the smell of coffee. The owner, Souren, was a jovial Armenian-Greek man, a good friend of my uncle Paul, who never tired of answering my questions about his business and the locals. Beside coffee, he sold all kinds of sweets and sometimes would treat me to some candy or a piece of baklava and tell me stories from his childhood in Armenia as he sipped a cup of his special brew of coffee. He listened patiently to all his customers, who told him about their troubles and their pains or raved against the government or some politician's misconduct without ever disclosing his own political affiliation, which might have alienated some of his friends.

Sometimes before special days, like holidays and market fair days, our store would be full of customers and I had to get out of everybody's way and go outside and watch the river of humanity flow by. I would find myself entranced by the street sights, the sounds and the entangled smells of people, their animals and their wares. People were in a hurry to get things done, with carts pulled by donkeys and mules loaded down with merchandise; others used bikes stacked with cases of tomatoes or eggplants on the rack behind the biker and struggling to squeeze through moving carts and pedestrians. Once in a while a tricycle truck loaded high with cartons or live lambs or cages of poultry would try to get through the crowded street, the driver honking a horn and shouting angrily at everyone around, edging everybody just inches away from the bumper and himself. The perfume of coffee wafting from Souren's roaster, mixed with the tantalizing smells of kebabs and the new goatskins drying on pallets outside tanning stores. I could see whole lambs and goats and parts of cows hanging from hooks at the butcher shop and huge braids of garlic bulbs outside the dry goods store. When fishmongers laid down their flat baskets from their heads to rest for a moment, I could see the fish shine like silver leaves torn from a mythical tree and arrayed for viewing in a secret rite.

When I wasn't needed at the store, I would cross this street of floating humanity and its works and go to my uncle Paul's domain: the workshop. It was there that shoemakers made the various kinds of shoes customers asked for by special order. Uncle Paul was a talented shoe designer and loved his work. After the war ended, he expanded the business into upscale shoes, and many women ordered their shoes from his store rather than shop at Patras or Athens. To make the fashionable shoes he designed, he had to hire the best shoemakers around.

I spent many hours watching these craftsmen make shoes. I studied the way they built the shoe from the strong rough, wooden base and the sloppy looking top leather pieces, stretching the leather around the wooden forms and nailing it temporarily to them, then tucking it under the sole, sewing it to the sole with waxed string and curved needles and onward to the details inside and the heel outside to the finer shape and the finished product, down to the polished sole and leather top. I liked these workers and made friends with them. They were friendly people and very good at what they did. And they knew who was the best craftsman in the shop and respected him, even though no one had ever designated him as an expert. I admired them for making things they were proud of. My uncle wanted quality, distinctiveness and class in shoes, but my grandfather wanted durable shoes of any shape and form that his peasant customers would buy. There were many battles between my uncle and my grandfather and they got worse with time. I sensed the tension and tried to stay out of it, but it wasn't easy. Sometimes, obeying one and not the other was a sign of siding with one against the other. I had to be careful and managed to stay out of their way most of the time. Even my father, who was respected by all in the family for his reason and impartiality, was unable to stop the bickering between them.

My grandfather got sick and died before I left Greece, when he was in his mid-seventies. Uncle Paul took over the business and the store thrived for many years. When I visited him on a trip from America, he was as always welcoming and friendly. My wife and children went on a camping trip with him and his family and they were as enthused with him as I had always been. He died many years later in his mid-eighties.

10 • Uncle Paul Was My Best Friend

It is not so much our friends' help that helps us, as the confidence for their help.

Epicurus

After the collapse of the Greek army, soldiers were more or less abandoned up on the mountains of northern Greece. They had to walk for many miles at times, before they could hitch a ride on one of the rare trains still running, or on a truck going south toward Athens and beyond. I remember the night my uncle Paul came back home from the front. I was awakened in the middle of the night and told the news. I wasn't sure it wasn't all part of a dream. His overcoat and uniform were dirty and torn and hang on his body like rags on a scarecrow. He had to stay in bed for many days, because his feet were full of blisters from walking for miles on rough terrain. He was weak and barely able to talk. My grandmother was crossing herself all the time, thanking God who had protected her son from frostbite, capture and worse.

A few days after his arrival, uncle Paul started to move about and talk. One evening I heard a sweet melody coming from the mandolin I had strummed on before he came, and followed the sound to my uncle Paul's room, and saw him sitting on the side of his bed, playing it. He just turned toward me and smiled without stopping. I sat down on the floor and listened. I was entranced. I had never seen or heard anyone play an instrument before. I wished that I could play like him. When the song ended, he called me by his side, pulled out of his shirt pocket a metal badge shaped like a shield and gave it to me. "I got this for you from the front. Keep it to remember me and the war we won and then lost," he said. "I got it from a uniform I found in the battle field." He pointed to the writing stamped on the metal. "The soldier who had it must have been in the Julia Alpine Division of the Italian Army." I took the medal and stared at it. It was the most unimpressive medal I ever saw. It was just a piece of brass in the shape of a heraldry shield, and its surface was dark like an old penny with the insignia of the Italian Division, named "Julia," on it. I kept it for many years as a reminder of the hard times we went through and to remember my uncle Paul's mandolin playing. Later that night, he told us stories from the war zone, stories of courage and pain and loss. After that, we sneaked into the secret room, where my grandfather kept a radio, and the adults heard news from the BBC. Radios were banned and my grandmother nagged him to give it up, but the old rebel wouldn't listen. No one was smiling after the news, so I knew that our side wasn't doing well. Someday they would, but not yet.

One day I was watching the sea in the distance beyond, searching for a sailboat. I also kept my eye on the street under my bedroom window in case any kids came by. I saw a small group of Greek soldiers trudging uphill toward our house. They looked sick and walked with great effort. They had no rifles or guns and their uniforms were torn and dirty like uncle Paul's had been. They just dropped down on the front yard of our house and stayed down, totally motionless. I got scared, thinking that they may die right there and then. I ran into the house to warn my grandmother. My mother and uncle Paul were helping my grandfather at the shoe store. My grandmother wanted me to calm down. She went out, talked briefly to the soldiers and then came back inside. I ran up to my room and watched down at our yard. When she reappeared, she held a plate and passed it around, offering to each soldier a slice of bread. They thanked her and wolfed down what she had offered. Then, she brought water out to them, and they drank it all and thanked her. After a while they pulled themselves up and went on their way. I went inside and asked grandma what she had offered to the soldiers.

"Just bread sprinkled with a little salt," she said without looking at me.

"Salt?" I shouted. The word bounced in my mind and was cast out in disbelief. I couldn't understand why anyone would offer salt to hungry men.

"We got nothing else, today," she said. "Nothing!" And after a moment's delay, "Besides, people need salt to go on."

Later that day, at dinner, there was something else, some beans or broccoli and some salted sardines to go with a slice of bread, something to keep us alive. I didn't hold it against her.

The occupation of Greece had come with a vengeance for all of us. We had lost our freedom and we were hungry. We would stay hungry and cold and sick and fearful for several years. But, at some point during those bleak years, it dawned on me that, if the freedom that can be taken away is gone, one could still think and imagine and pray. One was free in some other way, and no one could stop that without killing you. There was a good reason to stay alive.

Uncle Paul and I were friends and spent many days and evenings fishing and laughing ourselves to tears. Uncle Paul had a terrific sense of humor and, I thought, he could have become a comic actor. He told stories from his life so vividly and with such humor that you couldn't help but change your mood and go with the flow. He was also a mime and knew what mannerisms and gestures characterized a person best. He would pick one trait out of all the things that give a person his or her identity and recreate that person with cunning accuracy and ingenuity. But more than that, uncle Paul could make a comment, an observation, or just give me a look of a certain kind and I would just lose it and have to hold my belly laughing.

He and I would go fishing from the piers of Aigion's harbor after he got done with work. We would prepare our bait and our rods and reels and start casting. Sometimes my line would get caught on the bottom, and he would catch me trying to get it loose again.

"We are not paid to dig up the bottom of this harbor, nephew; we are here to catch our dinner," he would say without taking his eyes off his line, as if his concentration upon the task was a matter of life and death in contrast to my cavalier attitude.

"We are in the wrong spot, uncle Paul. I told you there is trouble here," I would protest. I couldn't take it with a straight face.

"I hope you hooked some nice garbage, there," he would tease me.

"I think I got an octopus. They never let you go." I would try and pretend that I was concerned and trying to free my line, but it wouldn't last, and I would break up in a spasm of laughter and screeches.

And there was the time when we were alone on the pier and I caught a fish by the belly as I was reeling in my line. I lifted up my rod with the fish still on the line, and uncle Paul caught a glimpse of it and called out to the public at large, anyone out there who might listen, even though there was no one around but the two of us.

"This boy is killing innocent bystanders in the sea. They don't swallow his bait; they don't even bite that boy's bait; but he tracks them down, chases them with his deadly tools and guts them before they have a chance." I started laughing, and he saw that I was having a good time and went on. "This boy is not a sportsman, ladies and gentlemen – he is a hunter of innocent creatures, that's what he is!"

By the time he got done, I was rolling with laughter on the concrete blocks of the pier. I was never able to explain how this connection between us worked, but it was a wonder at the time and for the rest of my life. Ever since I was a little boy, uncle Paul made my days shine.

Uncle Paul had no higher education, no intellectual interests, no lofty career goals, but he wanted to be the best shoe designer he could possibly be and applied himself to that endeavor with a passion. More than anything else however, uncle Paul was a good man, who knew how to be a great friend. He was the kind of person who made you feel good about yourself when you were with him. He made no demands upon me, except when it came to fishing. He wanted me, for example, to make sure that I prepared the bait – a mixture of bread dough, olive oil and mashed herring – exactly as he taught me. Of course, there were times when I screwed up the proportions or the consistency of the ingredients, and the bait would be too hard to shape into little balls, or too runny not to dissolve in the water. Uncle Paul would mumble about the incompetence of the elite Athenian boys and the flaws of the bright and I would laugh again, and he would shout at me that I ruined his fishing night, and I would again fall down in tears and laugh and laugh and laugh. And after a while, he would grin at me and say, "I hope you're enjoying yourself now, because your belly will be empty tomorrow." And then, he would lay down his rod and reel and sit at the pier with feet dangling over the water and answer my questions about whatever topic was bothering me at the time.

Uncle Paul hated tangled lines, but it was dark when we were down at the pier and, sometimes, his line would get tangled, and he would cuss and fume and try to untangled it, which was more frustrating for him than finding a needle in the proverbial haystack. I knew that a comedy skit had begun, and at first, I would try to restrain myself and pretend to mind my business but continue to track his progress, and choke the chuckles that started to come up sporadically and tamp down the gathering outburst. After a few attempts at restraint, I would explode and laugh my heart out to the total consternation of uncle Paul.

"You see! That's the kind of friendly response I expect from Attila the Hun, nephew! Don't you have any compassion for your kin and kith? Shame on you, Attila!" And he would mock me with an Attila face and a gorilla stoop. He wouldn't stop untangling or tangling his line, but he would go on, as if he was the victim of a bully. I knew he was having fun. "OK, Attila; one of these days your line will be a mess and then I'll dance a jig for your agony." And the frivolity would go on until it was time to get back, eat whatever dinner grandma had prepared for us, and sleep the sleep of the contented. And, by the way, when my line did get tangled up, or my hook got stuck on the bottom, the first thing uncle Paul did, after a brief comic interlude, was to drop whatever he was doing and help me untangle it or free it.

When he got engaged to Ritsa, his childhood sweetheart, the three of us would go on daily excursions. I would go swimming and then sunbathe for a time or get a line in the water and try to fish far from the crowd. Sometimes I would give up and stay with the crowd and ogle at the girls who splashed the water as they ran playfully to the deep water. "I hope you are enjoying the view, young man," uncle Paul would tease me, "but you got to catch your dinner, if you want to partake of food." I would shake my head in agreement, and continue my vigil. After all,

Paul and Ritsa were back some distance whispering sweet nothings to each other, why shouldn't I take a break from the search for food? Noon would come and we would eat together the goodies that Ritsa had prepared for us, and meet other people and talk and joke and the day would pass and we'd get back in the boat and head for home. Many happy days with pleasant memories went by that way. I will never forget the gentle heart of uncle Paul. No one else from either side of the family gave me so many pleasant memories as a gift. And, he never asked for anything in return. I believe he just enjoyed my company.

Uncle Paul and Ritsa were married and lived a quiet contented life in Aigion. They grew very old together and, I believe, that they were in love throughout their lives. They had four children, Apostolos, Katerina, Elias and Marios. Apostolos became a merchant marine captain; Katerina married in France and became a nursing supervisor there; Elias is a conductor of an orchestra in France, and Marios was at the shoe store until it closed and he went to France, in search of work.

11 • Uncle Gerassimos Dodges a Bullet

Power is when you have every justification to kill someone, and then you don't.

Oskar Shindler

Gerassimos, the youngest surviving brother of my father, started as a rebel of sorts, who cared more about having a good time than working hard to build a career. He got a job as a policeman and later joined the Coast Guard as a noncommissioned officer. During the Nazi occupation, when guerrillas were harassing the Nazis in the countryside around Aigion, a German army squad arrested him. The Germans had a retaliation policy, which authorized the taking of hostages at random and executing them. He was one of about a dozen hostages held in retaliation for the murder of a German soldier. He had done nothing wrong but he found himself sentenced to death.

"We were set up against a stone wall with hands tied behind our backs, in the middle of nowhere," uncle Gerassimos told us. "The Nazi squad lined up before us and took aim. We were finished," he went on, emotion breaking his voice. "But something happened. A car showed up on the road, a couple of hundred feet ahead of us, and a German officer stepped out and stared at us standing up against the wall. The firing squad held their fire. The officer talked to the squad leader pointing at us, and the squad leader snapped to attention clicking his heels and saluted the general. 'Yavol, Herr general!' he shouted loud enough for everyone to hear. The general got back in his car and drove away. They untied our hands and told us to go home," uncle Gerassimos said. "It was a miracle," he added and crossed himself. So did my grandmother and the rest of us.

The ordeal was traumatic and uncle Gerassimos broke out with eczema pustules from the stress all over his body. He had to stay home for months, recovering. He said that their release from the edge of the grave was a miracle and, as far as I know, he believed it. "It was no coincidence, I tell you; it was a miracle," he would insist whenever he told the story and some challenged his explanation. He would sigh with relief and add, "May be that general was an angel who came to our rescue." When he recovered, he knew that he had to decide what to do with the rest of his life. He had drifted long enough and now was time to work hard and use whatever gifts he had to better himself. But, the time of the occupation wasn't a good time for making plans. He stayed in his job and tried to make the best of it.

After Greece was liberated, uncle Gerassimos was still at his post in the Coast Guard and he would have probably stayed as a non-commissioned officer longer, if my father hadn't pressured him to rethink his career goals and motivated him and helped him to go to the University and study Law. I remember him studying at our house and going over and over the tenets of Justinian's Roman law, which governed Byzantium and forms the basis for much of the European legal system.

Uncle Gerassimos was a dandy of sorts and quite a ladies' man in his early years, but under my father's supervision and encouragement he found the motivation to study intensively and pursue more ambitious career goals. Sometimes he would tell my mother some of his past adventures with girlfriends to explain how he missed opportunities to get the education he wanted, and I would overhear the discussions. He seemed to know a lot about women, but I never heard of a great love that he had in those early years. I liked him, but we weren't close friends. He was a bright, sharp looking man and required me to wear my best clothes before he would offer to take me with him for a stroll in downtown Athens. In fact, I don't remember if he ever agreed to take me with him, because I never had clothes that could pass muster.

After Law School, uncle Gerassimos attended the Coast Guard Academy, which required such a Law degree for admission, and became an officer, eventually becoming the harbormaster of Patras, one of the largest ports in Greece. He eventually retired as a commander, practiced law for a few years and wrote several books, both fiction and nonfiction.

While a cadet at the Academy, he met Irene, a fine lady, who taught Home Economics and English at one of the best girls' schools in Athens, and they married. Irene had a Master's degree from the University of Montana and spoke fluent English. She was a friendly and warm person, who loved America and became one of Betty's best friends, even though we met her only a few times in our visits to Greece. After his marriage to Irene, Gerassimos became a good family man, and with Irene, they had two children, Nikos and Evangelia. Nikos was always an intense and very caring person. He studied philosophy, worked in the classical national radio station for a few years and became a high school teacher and a counselor in later years. Evangelia was a sweet young woman, patient, bright and studious, who came to America and studied briefly in college. She is another relative who visited us here in America. She eventually became a translator of literary works in Greece, translating the Lawrence of Arabia tome into Greek. Like many young Greeks who wanted to use their skills and talents but couldn't do so in Greece for lack of opportunities, Evangelia left the country for Germany, where she married a German architect and, I think, she is now teaching English in a

German high school. She is another example of a Greek who adapted to survive and thrive abroad.

12 • Hunger, Cold and the Archangel Michael

Hunger is insolent, and will be fed.

Homer

One of the most humiliating things for the defeated Greeks was having Italian soldiers patrolling the streets and acting like they owned the place. Of course, they did own Greece. Hitler decided to give part of Thrace and most of Macedonia to Bulgaria and the rest of Greece to Mussolini, for Italy's "vital space," as he put it. Even Greek children knew that the Italian army did not defeat us; we lost to the mechanized power of the Nazis. And, as we found out after the occupation, "the philhellenic German military attaché advised the army command that minimal German forces could hold Greece, provided there was no occupation by Italian forces." It is documented that "from Hitler downwards there was nothing but admiration on the German side for the way the Greeks had fought."

So, the Greeks accepted the Germans as occupiers because they had won the war, bur never the Italians, even though the Italians, as we found out later, cared more for the wellbeing of the Greeks and tried harder to feed the population of Athens than the Germans. The Italian soldiers probably sensed the contempt of the people and responded more harshly than they would have, if we had shown them some respect. There were many incidents of Italian soldiers beating Greek men for their lack of respect, shown by name-calling and foul gestures. And, there was the issue of Italian soldiers getting a reputation for womanizing. Unlike the Germans who kept mostly to themselves, the Italians were looking for contact with the women and in the process incurred the resentment of men. War invents all sorts of torments for every participant.

I remember an occasion that illustrates some of these points. Sometimes my mother had to help my father buy shoes or leather from downtown Athens, and she would drop me off at Pinio's place. Pinio was born and raised in the same area as my mother, and they were good friends. Pinio and her husband were wine makers and their place was filled with barrels of wine which they sold mostly wholesale to restaurants but also retail to the customers who stopped by for a drink or two and sandwiches at their place. While my mother was out working, Pinio's daughters, two fun loving, teenage girls, never tired of teaching me how to play chess and other table games, as they babysat me. My mother would come after she had finished her work, and we would both eat something and then head for home.

One evening, as I was sitting down with my mother eating a sandwich prepared by Pinio, an Italian soldier came and sat down with us. He seemed like a pleasant fellow and eager to exchange a few words with my mother and me. I don't remember what he did that yanked my rebellious streak, but remember getting behind him and striking him once at the back of his neck. The man was startled and turned, grabbed me by the arm and was about to hit me when my mother held his hand and started pleading with him to let me go. He was angry and reluctant to let go, but in the end he yielded and freed my arm. He stood up and left, spouting all sorts of nasty things at us. My mother hugged me close to her and gave me her standard admonition: "Whatever came into you?" she kept asking. "He has a family, a *bambino*, like you," she said as if that would explain his behavior. But I wasn't buying it. The Italian soldier was too friendly, and I had heard so many times that Italian soldiers could not be trusted with women. I never told her that I wasn't going to put up with anyone who hit on my mother, but that was what I felt; I struck a blow against the enemy.

As the occupation dragged on, people resorted to unconventional ways of satisfying their hunger. Bread was undergoing many alterations as various strange grains and other substances like carob bean flour and corn with lupine normally used for animal feed along with seeds found only in the head bristles of brooms before the war, replaced wheat and was used for a concoction that bore a vague similarity to bread, without ever tasting like bread. That "black bread" would get hard quickly and then crumble into some kind of dry dust, as you tried to eat it. The few times when we could get corn used for animal feed we made "bobota" out of it, but it was just another tasteless, odorless food which looked like cornbread, but tasted nothing like the cornbread made from high grade fresh corn. Eating meat became questionable because people were killing horses, and later, dogs and passing them for beef or goat meat. Milk was getting thinner, as it was watered down to increase profits and keep more customers satisfied with something rather than give them nothing.

With widespread scarcity, people started improvising for things that were missing with things they had never used for that purpose before, as when they started converting automobiles, trucks and busses to *gasozen*, which allowed vehicles to burn wood rather than gasoline. This, in effect, turned the internal combustion engines of automobiles to small steam engines with a water boiler producing steam that moved the pistons. These "engines" left behind them clouds of black smoke, broke down often but moved people from one point to the next in the bleakest years of the occupation. I cannot forget the time when I was in one of these converted busses, returning home from the countryside after a day's excursion with my class. Suddenly, the bus stopped. A few minutes later the driver who had been trying to fix the problem came back in and announced that we had run out of water. He waited for us to digest the meaning of his words. "We need water to get moving again," he said and looked around from face to face. No one moved. There was no water around. "If anyone wants to pee, now would be a good time to do it." Several of us boys volunteered to pee in the gasozen boiler and save the day. The bus resumed the trip home, powered now by urinated steam, but it took me awhile to get used to the fact that urine could be so valuable.

I sat at the marble stoop of our front door as the sun went down, counting into the thousands, so that time would pass unnoticed, and I could run upstairs and eat a slice of bread with a few drops of olive oil sprinkled on top of it. Most of the time, that was my mother's portion of the daily rations of four or five ounces of bread each, since I had already eaten my portion by noon and was still unbearably hungry. Sometimes there were beans from our stash and a couple of sardines, other times some spaghetti, also made from strange tasteless grains; but some times there was nothing other than collard greens with drops of olive oil, a piece of cheese and some olives. I remember one night my mother had found an egg from a neighbor's hen and served it fried to me for dinner. It was a rare treat, but we had no bread to scoop up the yoke, which was for me the most important thing about eating a fried egg. I used a couple of slices of an onion to pick up the egg yoke from the plate and I never forgot how precious bread is.

My father had insisted on using olive oil from a small bottle that had a cork with a tiny hole in it, so that oil would drip but never run. My father didn't set a specific limit on the number of shakes one could use and, therefore, the number of drops one could get from that bottle, so I would shake and shake until he raised his eyes and started to pay attention to the process. This controlled dripping was another one of his conservation methods that my mother couldn't stand but had to follow judiciously, because she recognized that they were designed to keep us alive, if the occupation lasted a decade or more. Never had food tasted better than in those dark and difficult days.

As food supplies became scarcer and prices skyrocketed, my grandfather and uncle Paul started a cooperative effort with my parents to make some extra money selling shoes beyond Aigion. My father bought shoes from the wholesalers in Athens and carried them home on his back. Then, we packaged them in boxes and sent them to Aigion, for my grandfather and my uncle to sell. As food became even scarcer, my parents resorted to bartering shoes for food on the countryside. She would load herself up with shoes, find some friendly truckers from Eleusis, climb up on top of whatever load they carried and head for the villages, perched up in the open air and the elements. When the truck stopped, she would try to sell the shoes for whatever staples the villagers had available. She brought home olives and olive oil, beans and lentils, and one time a head of cheese, which we had to cut in pieces and keep in a large terracotta urn filled with brine so it could last a long time.

During my mother's travels I was alone at home. I would spend my time reading and playing. Sometimes, when I was done with my schoolwork, I would put on a robe and a cape as a bishop of the Orthodox Church does, fastening with safety pins my mother's gold embroidered table runners and pillow coverings to look as regal as a bishop does, and I would sing the liturgy of Saint Chrysostom in front of the wardrobe mirror, making all the appropriate moves for censing, blessing and sprinkling of holy water. Every time my mother was gone I prayed that she would return to us unharmed. She always did. In the evening, we would gather in the bedroom, and she would tell us stories about the people she had met. My father always wanted to know how she managed to get a good deal on the items she bought, and what plan she had for bartering more shoes in the area. She would relate how she was able to travel on top of the trucks, holding onto ropes and truck sideboards. She would tell us whether this trip was more comfortable than the last one, whether the truck driver had a co-driver or had a seat in the cub for her, and how she managed to get through the various checkpoints that the axis soldiers set up to catch saboteurs and black marketers. Her bright smile, her quick wits, her ease in social interactions were all that stood between starvation and us.

One night, a very cold winter night, my parents started a coal fire in the hibachi we had for cooking outside the house. The wind was howling and the north wall of our bedroom was like ice to the touch and dripping water when I breathed near it. Nobody knew anything about insulation back then. The wet walls made me fear that my father might think the place was unhealthy like the previous house in Hymettus, which was supposed to be bad for my rheumatism, and decide to move again. The heat from the hibachi couldn't have raised the bedroom temperature more than a couple of degrees, but the hot coals were a welcome sight and did provide some warmth sitting close by. We all wore a couple of sweaters, and it took a lot of maneuvering to move from this bedroom to the other, colder rooms in the apartment. I slept with a couple of heavy blankets and used a chamber pot at night, rather than venture a trip to the bathroom without any heat and, sometimes, without any lights. I remember listening to my parents' rhythmic breathing and feeling peaceful and secure.

That night I was awakened by my mother's screams. She was shaking my father, trying to wake him up, but he wouldn't move.

"Open the door," she ordered me.

I jumped and opened the door, terrified.

"Open the window!"

I didn't know why. It sounded crazy, but I obeyed.

I approached the bed and saw my father's ashen face. His arms were hanging down his sides. I started shaking him, screaming at him to get up. My mother slapped him on his face. My head felt heavy, pain pounding like a hammer. Blood was throbing in my temples. My mother jumped out of bed and opened another window to get a breeze. The cold wind rushed inside. I breathed the icy air with lust. I felt cold but my head was clearer. My mother took the hibachi out of the room cursing the coals, until the sizzling water she poured over them drowned her anger.

We managed to wake up my father and helped him sit up. He was babbling. We turned him over, tried to lift him. I don't know how, but we forced him to stand up next to a chair for support. Then he took a few steps. He felt sick, and we helped him to reach the bathroom. A faint light, from a flashlight with a dying battery was turned on, and for a moment, I watched him from the back. We didn't want him passing out again. My mother told me to wait outside. As long as I could hear him breathe and cough and move, I wasn't afraid. Terror was in the stillness of his sleep, in the stealth of the darkness, not in the sounds of sickness. We helped him back to bed. After awhile, some color returned to his face, and his eyes became calm, focused. We shut the windows and the bedroom door again. I went beside him and watched him breathe and felt a surge of joy. We had won this round. My mother was putting cold, wet compresses on his forehead, which is what she always did when headache struck for any reason. He placed his hand on my head and smiled at me. Then, he turned toward my mother and smiled at her. "Try and get some sleep. It will be fine now," she pleaded and smiled back at him. She leaned over him, removed the wet compress and kissed his forhead. After a while he fell asleep, but my mother kept her vigil by his side. I went back to my bed, thanking God for having kept us alive. The cold, somehow, seemed very friendly now. As long as I felt cold I knew no one would die.

The next day, I learned all about carbon monoxide poisoning. My mother swore never to allow the use of the hibachi for any reason inside the house again. She straightened my hair that morning with more than her usual tenderness and told me a strange story of how she came to be awake just in the nick of time to save us all. She was asleep, she said, dreaming that her cousin, Michael, was riding his motorcycle and was headed straight for her, as if to run her down. She said that Michael did, in fact, own a big motorcycle, and its noise had made her afraid in the past. But Michael had never tried to run her down, as he appeared to be doing in her nightmare. "Stop! Stop!" she screamed at him, but he kept coming at her like Death himself. Only at the very last moment did Michael veer off, and, out of her wits, she woke up. Then she felt her aching head and smelled the hibachi coals, felt sick and screamed, seeing the deathly, still body of my father next to her.

"It was the Archangel Michael, who woke me up!" she said with an unusually quiet tone of voice. "Michael wasn't trying to run me down; he was trying to wake me up! He saved us all, thank God!" And she crossed herself in the way of the Orthodox.

All the horsemen of the Apocalypse were out to get us, but God was also present, extending his powerful hand over us. My mother believed that there was much more to reality than what we see with our eyes. I did also, but I was always looking for verification of what I believed, and that's not easy to come by.

As the food supplies dwindled, more people were dying in the streets from starvation. The black market was one of the few ways to get food. But becoming involved in any way with the black market was a sure way to being hanged in public by the Nazis. My parents decided it was too dangerous to continue bartering for food, and my mother's traveling days ended. We had to focus on finding food around us. Soup kitchens for children were set up in schools and factories, and we had to wait patiently our turn for a bowl of bean soup and a slice of bread

Some kids with even less food from home than I had, needed more than the soup kitchens could provide. They watched the shopkeepers put out their garbage and rummaged in the cans for anything that could be eaten. Finding the rind of a lemon was like hitting the jackpot. I had never thought much about lemon rinds, but one of the garbage connoisseurs told me that they had vitamins, good for a healthy body. He also told me that there were some German soldiers, who found it entertaining to throw their leftovers to barefoot children in the street and watch them fight over them. They would point to the one who managed to get some chicken leg or the leftovers of a steak and cheer him on, while jeering the losers.

The German army sucked off most of the food the countryside could produce, leaving the rest of us to die. When they needed money, they just printed it and used that worthless paper to possess whatever precious things we had left. The bread ration in the winter of 1941-1942 in the Athens-Piraeus area, normally 406 grams per day in peacetime, averaged between 84 and 137 grams that winter. "Although Hitler himself had gone to pains to pay tribute to Greek heroism and to assure the Greeks that he respected their classical heritage, Axis food policies made it only too obvious that the victor was willing to see the Greeks starve," writes D. M. Condit in the document quoted below.

I remember seeing a horse-drawn cart from city hall going by and picking up the dead from the streets and from inside houses. I saw the body of a young woman being brought out of a house near us. They tossed that young woman's body into the cart, on top of other bodies as if it was a sack of potatoes. Sometimes people buried the dead out in the open fields without reporting the deaths, so they could continue using their food coupons and collecting their portion of food and bread. And for every dead person there were a dozen others sick, limping or freezing in the streets. There were reports of people dropping off and dying in the streets of Athens. Sometimes, a passerby would fall down and stay down. Sometimes, others would stop and minister to these hapless souls, and other times they would look down and walk away, as helpless to act as the fallen. Statistics from a study of the US Department of Defense show that in the winter of 1941-1942 infant mortality in the Athens area, according to the Germans, rose from 6 to 50 percent. Some Greeks estimated that of every ten children born during that time, only one lived more than a month, as reported in the USA Department of Defense Report AD 272833, "Case Study in Guerrilla War: Greece During World War II," by D. M. Condit. The mood of the population grew darker, and a horrible thought began to take hold of our consciousness: the Nazis didn't care if we all died. Death came without a reason; it came because we were Greeks.

Yet, the struggle to survive went on. The inflation skyrocketed. You needed a bundle to buy a loaf of bread and a suitcase full of bills to buy a pair of shoes. The price of a newspaper climbed from two drachmas to thousands of drachmas in one year, and by the time the war ended, four years later, it cost 25,000,000 drachmas to buy a newspaper. People realized that survival was worth all the possessions they had. There were stories of people selling their homes for five gallons of olive oil. The

Germans wanted to find others to blame for the scarcity of food and found black marketers to be suitable scapegoats. They hanged several from posts in public places to discourage the practice and show the people that they were looking out for their interests. The people hated the black marketers, but they knew that the siphoning of food by the occupiers was the main cause of their misery, not the dozen or so black marketers the Nazis hanged from posts.

So, alternative foods began to appear, foods that might fill the stomach for a while and not kill you in the process. People discovered carob beans and *pasteli*. Carob beans had always been around, food for pigs under normal circumstances, but now became a much-coveted staple. There were people selling carob beans from burlap sacks on just about every street corner of downtown Athens. The trick was to find the vendor who sold the least hardened carob beans, because these, not only tasted better, but also had a honey-like liquid drop inside them. When you found one of those specimens, you had found the essence of wartime culinary delights. *Pasteli* was a concoction like a candy bar, made from sesame seeds bonded with syrup. Occasionally the ship Kourtoulous, chartered by the Red Cross to bring some foodstuffs – flour, sardines preserved with salt, beans and such – to Athens from Turkey would arrive, and the people had a few more things to eat. "In December 1942," writes the chronicler, Christos Christides in his book, *Years of Occupation, 1941 – 1944, Testimonies from a Diary*, "because of the supplies allowed to come in the Kourtoulous, the allowed portion of bread at any store was increased from 4 ounces per person to 5.3 ounces and there was no day without bread." It must have been quite an achievement at the time. Another food that was found acceptable to eat in great quantities was dandelions. They grew wild everywhere, and people would pick them and boil them and eat them with a few drops of olive oil and any lemon juice one could squeeze from the "house lemon." I call it "the house lemon," because a lemon would stick around for a long time, being squeezed and crushed and mashed and get beat up and poked before it was finally garbage and could be discarded. And sometimes, instead of disposing it, there would be a few bites taken out of it, "for the vitamins," someone would say.

There were long lines outside grocery stores, butcher shops, bakeries and any other place where rumor had it that food was being sold. People waited their turn, but vigilantly, which means that they were always trying to cut corners and move a little closer to the distribution point, if nobody stopped them. They knew that whatever goods were for sale would run out before all the potential buyers were satisfied, and they tried to make it before the cutoff point was reached. You had to be alert, ready to defend your position and nip in the bud by protest, by push and shove, or elbows and knees any attempt by anyone to get ahead of you. And you had to make sure no one was attempting to get in line by "tangential attachment," which started with a greeting of someone on the line, progressed to discussion of news and other pleasantries and ended up with the newcomer attaching himself or herself to the person greeted, usually, way ahead of where the greeter would have had to stay in the queue, if he or she had any sense of fairness and civility left in that world of urgent need and deception. When firm attitude and minor bodily contact didn't stop the forward advance of some overbearing customer, there were threats of serious engagement with shouting or a display of fists and holds and locks, until others intervened and calmed down the would-be combatants. But, there was also banter humor and griping on the line that made time pass more tolerably. And every few minutes the rumormongering against the traitors in the government, the black marketers from hell and "the horn-bearing Germans" would begin again, the words bursting out like steam from the relief valve of a boiler that reached its pressure limits. And so, our common suffering became our bond.

As if the waiting, the jostling, the hunger and the helplessness were not enough burdens to carry, there was also the manipulation of the shopkeeper to worry about. To buy a pound of meat from the butcher, a rare find to be sure, you had to also buy a couple of pounds of bones "good for a fine, healthy soup," the butcher would whisper to your ear, as if letting you in on the secret of life; or to buy half a pint of olive oil, you had to also buy a pound of onions with huge dried up tails that weighed at least as much as the part of the onion one could possibly use for human consumption, or enough rotten potatoes to use for fertilizer for several tomato plants in one's home garden. Monopoly, even temporary and only local monopoly, was gouging everyone since hardly anyone could afford the bus fares to go from one neighborhood to another shopping for the best buys. I waited many hours on such lines, holding my mother's hand and, later, alone, and I saw and heard many of these events happening around me. Besides, incidents on various lines, as people waited to shop for groceries, became the topic of discussion whenever women with their children got together to talk about the state of affairs in the neighborhood.

During those days of lean cows in Athens, funerals were good for us kids. Somehow, people always managed to send off their loved ones with a generous serving of kolyva, which consist of boiled wheat grains with plenty of sugar frosting and candied almonds, as is the custom in the Greek Orthodox Church. We would fight over our portion of a handful of kolyva and attack anyone who dared go after a second serving before we did. Kolyva was the only sweet we could get in those days of great scarcity and grief, and we blessed the dead from the heart and the belly.

13 • But for One Hot Potato

Gentleness is the antidote for cruelty.

Plato, in *Phaedrus*

The best political weapon is the weapon of terror. Cruelty commands respect. Men may hate us. But, we don't ask for their love, only for their fear.

Heinrich Himmler

When German soldiers appeared in the streets, the kids would run for cover and the adults would bow their heads down and look busy with whatever they were doing. Rumors of arrests for black marketeering, for espionage, for stealing from the "protectors of the homeland" and other offenses and crimes would sweep the neighborhood and intensify the fear that weighed down our lives. The newspapers always showed photographs of those who had been found guilty of crimes against the people, hanging from poles or set up blindfolded against walls waiting for execution. The Nazis called themselves "protectors of the Greek people" and were quick to blame five or ten crooks every once in a while for the famine devastating Athens, rather than tell us that they were the ones sucking off the lifeblood of the population. The crimes reported were always such that the people would be satisfied with the punishment: stealing foodstuffs from public warehouses, gouging people with exorbitant prices in selling olive oil, bringing to market spoiled legumes, selling dog meat and calling it goat meat and other such violations hated by the starving citizens. Some believed the propaganda, but most were silent and fearful with their fury at the conquerors. Some thought that there were people out there who sabotaged the occupation forces but when they were caught were branded as black marketers instead of being celebrated as heroes.

There were rumors that people were taking to the mountains and starting to organize a resistance movement. Most of the rebels were communists or leftists; some were royalists and right-wingers and organized separately. The newspaper I was now able to read was full of stories about victories of the Axis forces and defeats of the Allies. I learned the word "propaganda" from the neighbors' whispers as they talked about the large, gaudy and ever present newspaper pictures. The most widely available news magazine of the Axis forces was called *Synthima*, which means Password, in Greek. I spent a lot of time reading that propaganda rag because it was cheap and we could afford it. That's when I started cutting out pictures from the magazine and learned the German uniform insignia as I had learned all of them for the Greek army and navy ranks. I also learned the names of all the allied and German aircraft used in the war – the *Spitfire*, the *de Havilland*, the DC-3 or "*Dakota*," the *Stuka*, the *Yunkers* the *Fokker* and the rest. After the victory of the Allies, I threw away the Nazi insignia and learned all the insignia for the American armed forces, studying the pamphlets my father brought home from work. I learned the German insignia for the American ranks to pass the time, but learning to recognize the American insignia, especially all the various types of sergeants and generals, made feel closer to Americans, if that was possible after the brutality we had suffered under the Nazis.

All of us were careful not to provoke any German soldiers in any way while playing in the streets. We were afraid of them but we didn't know exactly why. I was too young to know how the Nazis robbed and killed innocent civilians, but the evil was in the air around us, and even children could smell it. Later, many historians and chroniclers documented the brutality of the German military during their occupation of Greece. Mark Mazower in his book, *Inside Hitler's Greece*, based on hundreds of supporting documents, recounts some of the events that show the hatred these people had for the people they enslaved. I paraphrase below his description of some of the atrocities committed by the solders of "the master race" as the occupation went on and the people started to resist. I do this to show that the deprivations my family and I had to put up with were nothing compared with the horrors many other Greeks suffered.

> In the middle of the main square of Komeno, a village in the flatlands of the Arachthos estuary, in western Greece, some yards from the *kafeneion*, 317 villagers, who had nothing to do with the resistance, were killed, in August 1943. Among the victims were seventy-four children under ten, and twenty entire families. The killers were highly trained regular soldiers from one of the elite divisions of the German army, the fearsome Wehrmacht.
>
> In June 1944, in one of the worst atrocities of the entire war, a Waffen-SS unit on patrol against the guerrillas entered the village of Distomo and ran amok, massacring several hundred people in their homes. A Red Cross team which arrived

from Athens a couple of days later even found bodies dangling from the trees that lined the road into the village. The SS commander Fritz Lautenbach claimed that his troops had been fired upon with mortars, machine guns and rifles, but the German Secret Field Police agent, Georg Koch, had accompanied the troops that day and revealed that this was untrue.

In Kalavryta, a town in northern Peloponnesus, the Wehrmacht troops shot 696 Greeks and burned twenty-five nearby villages. (Greek Government sources, as reported in the USA Department of Defense Report AD 272833, "Case Study in Guerrilla War: Greece During World War II," by D. M. Condit, state that 1770 villages lay in ashes by the end of the occupation in 1944). The massacre was done according to the reprisal policy laid down by the German authorities . . . Near the beginning of the occupation the German Command had issued precise quotas for reprisals: 50 to 100 hostages were to be shot for any attack on, or death of a German soldier; 10 if a German was wounded, and so on. In practice such horrific guidelines proved unworkable, but the tenor of the order was adhered to. As early as December 1942, Field Marshal Keitel had issued the reprisal policy, which included the following: "The troops are therefore authorized and ordered in this struggle [against the Resistance] to take any measures without restriction even against women and children if these are necessary for success. [Humanitarian] considerations of any kind are a crime against the German nation . . ." The massacre at Kalavryta horrified even the German Ambassador Neubacher. He had the German consulate general report from the scene and demanded an investigation by the Theater Commander. "It is much more comfortable," he wrote to him with some irony, "to shoot to death entirely harmless women, children, and old men, than to pursue an armed guerrilla band . . ."

News of the Kalavryta massacre reached Athens and horrified the population. I was a child then, but the word "Kalavryta" brings chills down my spine. And the atrocities went on with Klissoura, and Lamia and Haidari and many other towns with massacres and destruction under the monstrous regime that was touted as the best hope of mankind.

We all knew that something terrible, something inhuman was going on at Haidari and were afraid of the word. Haidari was just a few miles outside Athens and we all heard whispers about the terror waiting for people in there. I remember kids shouting in anger "I'll take you to Haidari and show you," as if they were threatening a monster with hell.

"If there was a place in Greece where terror was refined and exploited to the full it was in the SS-run camp of Haidari," writes Mazower. "In part a transit camp where Indian soldiers, Jews and others were held before they were sent north, out of the country, Haidari also housed prisoners awaiting interrogation at the SS headquarters, as well as hundreds of hostages who were selected for mass executions. It was from Haidari, for example, that at dawn on 1 May 1944, 200 hostages were taken for execution at the firing range of Kaisariani, a suburb of Athens. Though there were other camps and prisons around the country, none acquired Haidari's reputation. Terror as a policy "was due in no small measure, to its commandant, Sturmbannfuhrer Paul Radomski, who had brought the murderous values of the Eastern Front to Greece. Constantine Vatikiotis who was arrested by the SS and ended up in Haidari describes in a postwar statement, how Radomski introduced himself to the prisoners: 'upon arriving at Haidari, during the afternoon roll-call [of 26 October 1943] the Governor called the interpreter and handed him a paper; he then ordered the unhappy prisoner, who stood next to me, a Jewish army officer, to advance toward him. After lashing the prisoner's face with a whip, he turned to the interpreter and told him to read aloud the written order.

The interpreter read as follows: The Governor of Haidari, Major Radomski, will personally execute before you the prisoner named Levy, for attempting to escape on the day of his arrest. Beware! The same fate awaits you in such a case. A shudder of horror went through us all. The terrible Governor then proceeded to carry out his threat. He drew his revolver and fired at the unhappy man, who crumpled to the earth in a bloody heap. His German assassin then ordered us to remove him. But, before we had had time to lift the man, the Governor fell upon us and began to lash at us with his whip. Then, tearing his victim out of our hands, he fired at him once more and ordered us to remove the man's shoes. They were new, and consequently, a good prize.

Of course, not all German soldiers were killers. My father continued to work at the munitions plant, which had been converted to a maintenance depot for aircraft engines headed for Rommel's army in North Africa and used to say that the Germans left you alone, if you did your job and obeyed their rules. The officers occupying my maternal grandmother's house and my uncle Doctor's and aunt Katina's house in Eleusis, were also said to be ordinary people who missed their families back home. But, I am fortunate because my own experience supports the view that neither nationality nor ideology can destroy most person's humanity.

I recall the time when mother and I were going to visit my mother's friend, Pinio, and a strange thing happened to us on the way there. As we were passing by a fenced yard where German soldiers had their barracks, we saw a giant stirring something with a ladle in a black kettle over a fire. We stopped to watch, and I wondered what marvelous food might be in that steaming kettle. The giant turned and saw me hanging from the wire fence. He smiled, and my mother motioned to him that I was hungry. She first pointed at me and then, bunching her fingers together, she pretended to devour whatever they were supposed to hold, including their present nothingness. The man was a soldier, wearing the trousers of his uniform, held by wide suspenders, but having only a khaki long-sleeve undershirt. He dug into the black cauldron with his ladle and brought up a huge steaming hot potato. He smiled looking at us and came toward us slowly, swinging the cradled potato to cool it. He stood behind the fence and forced the potato through the grid with his hand and the handle of the ladle. My mother and I caught the crumbling pieces in our cupped hands on the other side of the fence and thanked him. The potato was still hot, but we were hungry and we blew on the pieces and tossed them from one hand to the other and ate what could be eaten without burning our mouths. The soldier pointed at me and said something in German that we couldn't understand. Then he reached into his back pocket, and pulled out of his wallet the picture of a woman and a child about my age. He pointed to the picture and then to himself several times to indicate togetherness, and my mother gave him the sign of approval for the wonderful family he had.

"Heinrich," he said pointing to the child in the photo.

"Tolis," my mother said, tapping me on the head. Tolis is my Greek nickname before one of my English teachers Americanized it to "Tolly," when I was getting ready to leave for America.

We thanked him several times and he kept saying that it was nothing, raising his huge hands up by his shoulders and waving them at us, as if trying to erase the writing on some imaginary blackboard with wide sweeping strokes. We were still eating the potato pieces as we walked away. "Nice man," my mother said. "He must miss his wife and son." I looked at her incomprehensibly. I couldn't imagine a "nice" German soldier at the time. Potato-man was one of "them." And they were here to starve us and kill us. Yet, the potato was as good to eat, as it was hard to handle, and didn't seem to make any difference where it came from. But, I couldn't quite fit it in the morality of the universe I knew, and that was a good problem to have.

14 • Small Business but No Monkey Business

For what does it profit a man, to gain the whole world and forfeit his life?

Mk. 8:36

The struggle for survival was becoming intense. It seemed that everyone who wasn't a soldier had become a beggar or a trader of something; everyone was cutting corners and improvising. My uncle Orestes (I'll have a lot to say about him later in my story), who was a poet, a master of ceremonies at a variety theater and a filmmaker, was trying to survive and like everyone else was using his wits for business purposes because poetry didn't sell in times of peril. The trouble was that his business judgment was stunted, and that's putting it mildly. One day he and a couple of helpers arrived at the house while my father was at work and started unloading breadbox-sized cardboard boxes from a car parked outside our building. They carried the boxes to our bedroom and stacked them behind our wardrobe. My mother told me that "uncle Orestes is in business selling saccharine." She said that the idea was to sell saccharine pills now that sugar had become very scarce and people craved for something sweet to put in their coffee. Uncle Orestes was apparently trying to corner the market in sugar substitutes and make a bundle.

When my father came home from work he sensed that something had changed but had no idea what. He kept asking how everything was, and how did the day go, until finally he pulled out of my mother the fact that "Orestes had left some boxes for us to store behind the wardrobe." I know he must have been ready to explode, but he held back his anger. My mother was trying to point out that our sugar needs would be taken care of for years to come, but he was in no mood for a cost-benefit analysis. He slid behind the wardrobe and saw all the boxes neatly stacked up and exploded. They left little room for stacking additional provisions, but that was the least of his worries. He came out of the hideout incensed and slapped the wall with his palm. He wanted no part of this. He didn't like the double jeopardy this maneuver of the poet was creating for us. Hiding food for the family was a violation of the rules, but being caught for engaging in black market deals would be a criminal offense, punished by years of jail time or worse. And, what would happen if one of Orestes' co-conspirators in business squealed, and the Gestapo got wind of it and came knocking at our door? "Does he want to put us in Haidari?" he asked rhetorically my mother. He demanded that she tell her brother to take back his merchandise as soon as possible.

My mother protested that such a sequence of events was improbable, but she stopped short of saying that only paranoids come up with such things. She had done that on other occasions to no good end. My father was too angry to carry out a debate on the subject. She always expected the good consequences of people's actions, but had trouble anticipating their foolishness, their greediness and their malice. She wanted to help as many people as she could, whereas my father wanted to protect his family above all else.

The boxes stayed with us for a few days and then, Orestes sent his associates who took them away, much to the relief of my father and the embarrassment of my mother. I heard from one of the relatives that the saccharine business was a total flop. I wasn't surprised. I had tasted one of the saccharine tablets left for the house and it repulsed me. It had a bitter aftertaste and would have taken a mighty imagination and a shoe leather palate to make sugar out of it. I also know for a fact that uncle Orestes was never rich, though a lot of money passed through his hands after the war. Sometimes he had a lot of money to spend and other times he wanted to borrow a few drachmas to live on. I learned early on that the life of the poet came with hardship.

My father was the supervisor of a sizable department and was in a position to hire a good number of people for the needs of the company. It was very hard to find a job anywhere, so he did his best to hire people who were hard workers and had large families to support. Since we lived in a neighborhood with a lot of people from the island of Santorini, they knew that he could hire people and came to our house asking for a job. One of the people my father found a job for was Kyr-Andonis, from Santorini.

A year or so after the occupation began, even my father felt that he had to start a business and earn some extra money. He asked Kyr-Andonis, if he wanted to earn some extra money selling raisins. Kyr-Andonis had a large family to support and needed the extra cash. He agreed, and my father hired him and started teaching him the elements of selling, which were as mysterious to my father as to Kyr-Andonis.

I got to know Kyr-Andonis well because he hang around the house a lot when the business got going. He was a nice man with a huge reddish moustache, thick reddish hair that stuck out of his worker's cap and a jovial smile. He was friendly and seemed always ready to help with chores. There were many peddlers in the streets of Athens at the time, all trying to make a few drachmas selling various foodstuffs and escape death.

My father decided to go into business selling raisins. Raisins had always been plentiful in Greece, but they became very popular during the lean years of the occupation because they provided a lot of calories at low cost. Since our relatives in Aigion could find high-grade raisins at a good price in the surrounding villages, he figured we could make a decent profit buying them by the sack and selling them by the coffee cup, which was the usual way of selling raisins at the time. He had a wooden tray made for Kyr-Andonis, with a belt to carry it around the neck that held it waist high, and filled it with "blond" *Soultanina* raisins he bought from the villagers around Aigion. He calculated the price he could charge for a cup of raisins to make a decent profit; then he set a goal of selling a tray a day, and Kyr-Andonis was off peddling merchandise in the busier streets of Athens.

Every evening after the day's sales, Kyr-Andonis would stop by our house and give my father the money he had collected. Then he would report on the streets where he made most of his sales, tell my father if the raisin peddlers were increasing or decreasing and what should be done with the price per cup to keep the product moving. My father would pay him and he would leave, while my father reconciled the amount he had received for the raisins with the amount of the raisins sold. Everything was always in order, so he would close his books, relax and talk about the benefits of running a business.

But, reports started to appear in the papers that the police were catching some raisin peddlers who were short-changing their customers by lining the bottom of their cups with many layers of paper. You thought you got a cup of raisins, but instead you got three quarters of a cup or less because the cup was shallow. My father became suspicious when he couldn't reconcile the money Kyr-Andonis collected and the raisins he said he sold. There were more raisins left after a day's sales than there should have been left otherwise. My father cautioned Kyr-Andonis to be careful and always be straight in giving his customers a full cup of raisins. He cautioned him to never raise the price per cup because that could jeopardize the business. Kyr-Andonis protested that he wouldn't even think about cheating or making business decisions on his own, and how could my father possibly suspect such things. Didn't he trust him? Now, I have no knowledge of the details, but I think, my father couldn't convince himself that Kyr-Andonis had never inserted a little folded paper inside the measuring cup to shrink its capacity, and sell fewer raisins than he was supposed to sell. He thought that Kyr-Andonis was selling more cups with the same total product and pocketing some of the difference. Or, was he perhaps selling fewer cups at a higher price and keeping some of the money, without having to sell as many raisins? There were many scenarios for possible misdeeds, and my father was good at constructing them. Kyr-Andonis couldn't calculate exactly how many raisins were sold and what the remaining amount should be, so, my father reasoned, he was being generous in leaving behind more raisins than he should have left while keeping some of the revenue.

My father was born for measurements and calculations and he knew when something wasn't exactly right. What would happen if the police arrested Kyr-Andonis and found out that he was my father's employee? Who would believe that poor Kyr-Andonis wasn't directed by his employer and boss to cheat? My father was a crackerjack bookkeeper and knew more about business law than most lawyers did. He knew he would be liable and it could cost him his freedom and his livelihood. If the Germans got wind of it he could end up in Haidari. I bet that my father already saw himself doing time for fraud in a dungeon. He just couldn't take it. Perhaps, Kyr-Andonis never cheated and the relationship was dissolved because my father imagined that Kyr-Andonis was cheating his customers or would succumb to the temptation and cheat. I can see my mother trying to reassure him that nothing was or could go wrong. The fact is that the enterprise ended quietly, and my father went back to his work routines in peace. He never accused Kyr-Andonis of anything, so there was never any rift between them.

Kyr-Andonis had a daughter, Stassa, back home, in Santorini. He asked us if we could give her a job as a nanny and maid at our home. My parents knew how hard it was for him to support the large family he had and they agreed to give her a home and build her a trousseau, which she wanted to do very much.

Stassa came and lived with us for a couple of years. She cared about me as if I was her little brother, and we had a lot of fun playing games and competing. She had the same kind of helpful attitude as her father and was always helping my mother with the housework. In spite of my mother's close supervision, she managed to meet a soldier at a nearby park where we used to go and play ball, and she fell in love with him. I was upset when she told us that she wanted to get married. I couldn't appreciate the attraction of love compared to the job of taking care of a little boy.

We had a couple of other nannies over the years, girls from poor homes staying with us and helping with housework. One of them that I remember was Martha. She wanted to be in the movies and was hoping to start as a singer at my uncle's variety theater, but I don't know if she ever did. While at home, she used her time to collect pictures of movie stars from any magazine she happened to find. "Movies" wasn't my thing, but I helped her with the cutting and the pasting of hundreds of American movie star pictures and could rattle off the names of them all. She and the other nannies we had were fine people, but Stassa was the best friend I had among them.

Sometime later, Stassa gave birth to a baby, and she and her father wanted me to be the godfather. I didn't know exactly what a godfather was, but I followed the instructions and the little baby was baptized. A year or so later, I heard that Stassa's baby died. I was very distraught when I heard that. Somehow, I got it in my head that my anger at her leaving us was bad luck and caused the baby to die. I didn't know that I loved Stassa like a big sister and wouldn't admit that I was hurt. I didn't want to ever baptize another baby.

15 • The Noose Tightens

STRIKEBREAKING: During the workers' strike in June 1943, the Germans fired on the crowds gathered on Panepistimiou Street and arrested many hostages. A girl who was hit and fell in front of a tank was crushed beneath the tracks as the driver deliberately started forward.
Phokion Demetriades, Title of a drawing, in *Shadow over Athens.*

The Nazi occupiers were relentless in choking us with draconian laws and orders, starving and brutalizing us so we could have no taste of freedom. The Resistance from both the Left and the Right was growing as the Communists and the Royalists organized and started disrupting the occupation army's operations, even as the rulers were hell-bent on tracking them down and destroying them. They restricted electricity and cooking gas and made running water scarce. They restricted our freedom of movement by reducing the number of busses, trolleys and trains for every damage they suffered; arrests were made at random and people were punished by harsh jail terms or execution, according to their reprisal orders. Starvation became the reality of our daily lives and the wardrobe stash became our lifeline. As freedoms were taken away and suffering increased, we all became "the enemy" to the German and Italian soldiers. They looked at us with suspicion, as if we were all conspiring against them and planning their demise.

Sometimes one of the kids in the neighborhood would bring news of someone we knew, who died or was arrested or had an accident and all the evils we knew would get a face and threaten us. One of the guys who brought us news from all parts of Athens was Little Beggar. He had no other name for us. He wasn't a regular in our gang, but he wasn't a stranger either. He was one of several older kids who hung around us and joined us in the street games we played as often as their chores and occasional jobs allowed. No one knew where his home was, or if he even had a home, but we knew that he had no one to look after him, or anyone to help him. We thought that he had a sick mother to take care of somewhere in the slums of the city, but no one knew for sure. Unlike the rest of us, he appeared and disappeared in our neighborhood, and no one knew where he came from or where he went after he left us. Little Beggar had to do it all by himself. He sold cigarettes in boxes of one hundred to anyone who wasn't particular about the brand he smoked. People, who didn't want to wait in interminable queues for the cigarettes they needed to satisfy their addiction, often turned to itinerant vendors like Little Beggar. He had a reputation for being a very shrewd businessman. In addition to selling cigarettes, he sold whatever else people wanted to buy from the stash of junk he found scavenging the streets of the rich and the powerful in Athens. I think that people secretly admired his scavenging prowess and envied the fruits it yielded. He comes to my mind in pale colors, looking perpetually frail, sad and sick. But we didn't pity him. We knew that he was a sly fox, a formidable opponent to anyone who crossed him, using all his skills and talents to defend his possessions and his territory and survive in the jungle we were in. He wasn't a regular in our gang, but he wasn't a stranger either. He was one of several older kids who hang around us and joined us in the street games we played as often as their chores and occasional jobs allowed.

The rest of us spent a lot of time playing in the streets to forget the cold and the hunger. There were two classes of games we played with all the energy, cunning and imagination we could muster: the first class included war and ball games with clear winners and losers, to prove, I think, to ourselves that we were involved in some kind of struggle, like the war we were in, yet without suffering all its horrors; it was as if we were trying to immunize ourselves against the disease of war by getting inoculated with war games and intense competition; we played ball games, including soccer and handball, with balls we made out of stuffed stockings because balls filled with air were never available during the occupation; when a ball has no bounce at all, the only way to get it off the ground was by skill, so we got to be very good at dribbling; in the second class of games, we gambled with fervor for marbles, wooden spinning-tops, bottle-tops, cigarette box-tops, candy wrappers, shrapnel pieces, bullet shells, even inflated almost worthless paper money and whatever else we managed to create a market for by trading. We were on our toes when we played games. We calculated the odds, checked for signs of cheating, read faces and gauged behaviors for fear or aggression. We formed alliances with those we trusted and clashed with others. We took risks to win or lose according to our abilities, as we wanted to do in the real world but couldn't because the Nazis had the power and were ruthless. Sometimes we won and counted our wealth in hundreds of bottle caps or millions of candy-wrapper-drachmas and felt like rich and powerful people we thought felt in the real world. Perhaps, we played games that satisfied the desires of our dreams – power, wealth, freedom – with whatever goods we had available and reduced the limits of our wretchedness.

We were always on the lookout for soldiers. If we were scattered in the streets chasing one another or playing odd-or-even games for marbles or beer bottle caps and saw soldiers approaching our turf from the main avenue, we would just freeze on the spot we happened to be at until they left, or make a dash for the stoop of Kortessis and wait there, speaking softly to each other until the storm had passed.

We didn't know if anyone's parents or other close relatives were involved in the resistance, but we imagined all sorts of heroic acts about those we had heard of. Anyone against the occupiers was a patriot at that time, whether they were communists or the right-wing supporters of the king, which in time evolved into the security battalions and the X party, all of them considered fascists. My father, ever so cautious, never showed his political preferences because he didn't trust those who might gain power some day to respect them. He kept his views to himself, no matter how enthusiastically my mother showed her friendly face to all sides so we could survive. However, my father knew that the enemies were totalitarians internal and external, left or right, and made no bones about it.

One night he came home with broken glasses, a torn jacket and scratched hands. My mother screamed with alarm when she saw him. I stared at him as if he was a stranger I had never met.

"A German soldier shoved me out of the way on Stadiou Street and I fell down," he said, holding back his anger. Then, his fury overwhelmed him and he exploded: "The damned beast kicked me after I was down. He stepped on my glasses, smashed them and moved on like he had just stepped on a cockroach."

I watched him, and knew from watching kids lose games in the street that he felt impotent and angry. I felt sadness roll over me, like a black cloud.

"They are monsters," my mother supported my father's outburst with fervor. "They'll pay for it!" she went on, "I heard that George, Kyra-Chryssoula's son, has joined the guerrillas." My father glanced at her with apprehension. That's not what he wanted to hear. "He is a captain, already," she went on.

My father frowned. That kind of talk could land you before a firing squad, he meant to say and neither my mother nor I had any doubt about that. If she hadn't quit her harping on the virtues of the communist resistance, my father would have diverted his anger at the German soldier by pointing it straight at her.

She left the room and came back with a wet towel and started dabbing gently the scratches on my father's hands and face, lifting up the sunken room. "Nothing serious here; I'm glad this monster just went on his way and let you be. Glory be to God for all his blessings."

A few moments later he felt good enough to open the black bag he always carried with him and reveal the find he had made – a package of beautiful, white flour spaghetti. "Top quality," he bragged. My mother was elated and ready to cook the stuff, but he held her back.

"Where did you find it?" she asked.

"Some Catholic nuns were giving out food at the Eye Clinic, by the University. I had to wait in line for an hour and a half, but it was worth it."

She looked at him with her most congenial look. "We can have some of it tonight," she said. "We need some change in our diet."

"Too much meat and sweets," he said. Mother laughed.

"But only some of it," he mumbled. "The rest is for the crypt!"

The cataclysmic, rainy day was always coming. No matter how hard the day was, my father was sure that there was another day lurking in the future that would be worse. My mother always thought that today was better than yesterday and a little worse than tomorrow would be. I think I take a little more after my father, while wanting desperately to be a little more like my mother. Anticipation of problems is rationally the best approach for coping with evils to come, but it can also snuff out the enjoyment of living, which happens only in the here and now. My parents occupied the extremes on the optimism scare, which are always problematic; but I can't complain that they didn't provide me with a range of options.

The significant thing about living in extraordinary times is that you learn how to cope in new ways, even as your familiar world is breaking up and you change the rules you live by. Cheating, lying, pretending, cursing and all the other transgressions we shy away from in a civil society become useful and are tolerated in perilous times. A kind of uneasiness enters your awareness and you become alert to any change in the environment, ready to get away from it or to take advantage of it. You become suspicious of other people; you attribute selfish motives to them for doing what they are doing with little or no proof of wrongdoing, because you believe that you are less likely to be caught off guard and suffer irreparable harm. You become fearful of those in power, but you also feel the assurance of friendship's bonds with others who are as afraid and helpless as you are. I haven't summed up the gains and the losses, nor do I think such a summary would mean much without the experience of it, but the point is that adversity is both taxing and rewarding to those who live with it. As one learns to cope with the difficulties of a harsh world, one begins to celebrate the small victories one scores, even though they would be nothing to talk about under normal circumstances. It seems that people living under harsh conditions are, mercifully, not as desperate as observers at some distance imagine. I believe that God grants stamina, endurance, peace and satisfaction with life, perhaps, even joy, to those who are in dire need and ask for help to do their best. My memories of the days that I lived in fear, with hunger and cold are never without contentment for the little victories I scored, and never without a feeling of blessedness for surviving in one piece.

16 • The War from the Stoop of Kortessis

You have to learn the rules of the game. And then you have to play better than anyone else.

Albert Einstein

Every day after school, most of the kids in the neighborhood hung around the stoop of Kortessis to talk and play games. There was always some kind of competition, measuring ourselves against others, trying different ways of playing a game, honing our skills, learning how to gauge an opponent's desire to win and showing off our knowledge of facts. But we also formed bonds and created teams that last forever in our minds. We pretended to be ancient or modern heroes, explorers or movie stars, great soccer players and runners. I knew that Thomas Edison had invented the electric light bulb and others could rattle off the battles of Alexander the Great or describe the game won by one of the five Adrianopoulos brothers who composed the front five of the Olympiakos soccer team when he lost his pants before he fired the winning shot in the final game of the Greek tournament one year. We invented new ways to do familiar things and after a game was over we would discuss all that happened, evaluating the moves, criticizing and praising one another as if we were obliged to elect the princes and the bums of the day. That's how we learned to create little explosions with a tiny bit of a chemical found in an everyday product and using a key and a piece of string, or two flat pieces of marble underfoot with a kick from the side; that's how we learned how to make candy with sugar and milk, or sugar and lemon in a frying pan; or fly kites that carried razors in their tails and could cut the string of other kites in an air battle.

Sometimes we couldn't get along with each other and we split up in two camps and made war, throwing rocks at each other. I never thought what would happen if someone was struck with a rock on the head, and I cannot recall anyone else bringing up the issue. Did we believe that eyes couldn't be plucked out? That a rock striking a vulnerable part of the scull couldn't end it all for someone? We just did what the world was doing – we split up and had comrades and enemies like everybody else. The two sides had their headquarters in the basements of two houses across the street from each other, and most of the projectiles landed on plywood-boarded windows. We'd spend days on end preparing for war, which meant gathering rocks and finding empty tin cans which we filled with crushed rock, pebbles and dirt, and pounded them shut, to form lethal, steel-encased projectiles that could be stacked in piles and hurled against the enemies at will like rocks, hurting or maiming the enemy.

There was time devoted to training – who would do what in the heat of battle, and who had the right to give orders to whom, and who should throw what at whom and when. Andonis was the oldest kid, three or four years older than the rest of us and the *de facto* General and leader of our gang, fittingly named Warriors. We had many meetings before we decided by majority vote to take the name Warriors. Kefalas (literally, the Big Head, in Greek) and I were lieutenants trying to make captain. Spirto (literally "Match," in Greek, but metaphorically "Bright"), was Kefalas' younger brother and had been designated sergeant, only because he was a year younger than Kefalas and me. He had a thing about communications and was always working with some tin cans or paper cups connected with string to transmit the sound of words. Some kids were convinced that they heard a message, but I never heard anything other than some scratching noise. A couple of years later, however, Spirto with Andonis' help, did manage to put together a galena radio receiver that we used to get the news and some barely audible songs. It was illegal to have unregistered radios during the occupation, and we were both scared and thrilled to be able to break the tyrants' laws. Yannakis was the only private we had. We teased him for his clumsiness and sometimes called him Kalamata because he had a black, olive-sized birthmark on his cheek like a Kalamata olive. He was a wonderful private: good-natured, obedient, slow to anger and deliberate in his actions. He was the first guy you'd want to befriend in time of peace and quiet, and one of the last guys you'd want to have on your team in the heat of battle. His mother was always welcoming the gang, and in cold days she invited us inside their house to play board games, like Bingo and Tombola. We also enlisted Andonis' sister, Katie, as our nurse with the rank of lieutenant. She was a very proper girl, but she wasn't sexy, so no one was ever fighting over her, though everyone was her friend. I remember her straightening out some cotton, a few strips of adhesive and a little bottle of green rubbing alcohol on the shelf of an old cabinet. She proudly called these items her "medical supplies," but I cannot recall any occasion when she had to use any of that stuff taking care of casualties.

Some other kids who lived further away joined our gangs occasionally for games, sports or fights. We sometimes included Stellian, who seemed to be perpetually looking up at the sky, was clumsy and slow. No one knew anything about autism back then, but we could see that Stellian wasn't all there. The kids around him were divided into protectors and detractors. I couldn't stand people who made fun of him, but I wish I had fought more openly for his dignity, rather than put up in silence with the ridicule some kids heaped upon him. Quarreling with my friends was hard to do back then. But the time when I could risk their disapproval and put up with alienation wasn't too far away. Finally, I need to mention that we always wanted to have among us Goose and Little Beggar, both of whom were sharp and street smart and always tried to push beyond the rules we set. Goose was a few years older than most of us and had some kind of a job selling fish for a relative of his, but he would show up at the stoop of Kortessis and tell stories that kept the rest of us in pins and needles. I have already talked about Little Beggar, probably the most ingenious kid around, who managed to feed his sick mother and himself by his wits. His eyes could see behind his back and his hands could slip into your pocket and lift out whatever you had there before you could even see him near you. His main job was scavenging and begging in the streets of downtown Athens, mostly among the German soldiers, and trading whatever he could get his hands on for whatever he could get from people who wanted to buy. This lasted until the Germans gave him a job shining boots and his future was set for a while.

His presence has always haunted me because I could never stand being close to him, or look at his face, though I always envied him for his freedom of action, his adventures and his getting so many things done against all odds. I couldn't stand that kid, but I admired him just the same. He was the best at what he was doing, and that was always a worthwhile achievement in my mind, but he did some things with deception, and that was repulsive. Goose and Little Beggar brought us new ways of solving problems, inventing things and ways of surviving and kept us in touch with what was happening in downtown Athens and other neighborhoods.

The gang across the street called themselves the Rebels, and its regular membership had several kids, among them Beanpole, easily the tallest guy in the neighborhood, whose family lived on the first floor of the house across the street from the stoop of Kortessis, and the Abyssinian, a wild and fiercely competitive kid with olive, swarthy skin like his father, whose family occupied the second floor of the same house. It was rumored that his father had been a rich merchant in Ethiopia before Mussolini attacked Abyssinia or Ethiopia. They had come to Greece as refugees after they lost their business in the war, and we suspected that they were hiding. No one knew how rich or how famous the family was, but the topic came up when we had our regular gossip sessions and he was absent. Beanpole was a good salesman, always trying to recruit new members for his gang. He would sit on the stoop of his house and sing for hours some cryptic words, like "*Watch and Net, You Come and you Get*," that no one knew what they meant, as if they were the key to the meaning of life available only to those who joined the Rebels. Koula was the third regular member of the Rebels and easily its most aggressive fighter, according to those of us who planned wars, and had played games running, jumping and tackling with her. Everybody thought that she was a Tomboy, because, back in those days, girls with a fighting spirit and skills for playing hard were making everyone uncomfortable. We never figured out if Koula was asked to join the Rebels or forced them to take her in. However she became a Rebel, one thing was clear to everyone: if you ever called her Tomboy to her face, you could have your eyes scratched out of your skull. She was pleasant to look at and walked with a flowing movement of her body like a cat, her short brown hair stuck to her neck and cheeks. She was a little older than me, and I never had much to do with her, but she was a presence in most things we did.

Vouss was the most powerful guy in the neighborhood and when he visited the Rebels on occasion, we avoided provoking them. Vouss means Bull in Greek, and must have acquired that moniker because he was short and stocky, with a body without a neck, just a broad back joined to a big head, which was always slightly bent and pointed forward for action. He had stubby, powerful arms with muscles so well built that they prevented his arms from contacting his sides. I never heard his real name and never asked. I don't think anyone knew. But we all knew that Vouss was also short for *Voukephalos*, (Bucephalus) the ferocious horse of Alexander the Great.

The Devil could bite you, if you ever got into a fight with him and he was losing. He joined in sometimes for games and sports, but he couldn't be counted as a regular member of the Rebels. He was dirt poor and spent most of his days selling papers in downtown Athens or scavenging for food. I remember that he lived with his family in a shack, a block from our home, and his face was raw with pimples and boils and red blotches that made you want to avoid contact with him at all costs. Andonis had warned us that he might be the secret weapon the Rebels had in hand-to-hand combat. Did he think of him as a biological weapon of mass intimidation? I don't know, but the one time that I had a no-holds-barred fight with the Devil and his face was up against mine for a second or two, the contact kept me awake several nights waiting for the onset of a staph infection. It didn't happen; but I kept away from the Devil after that, though I never stopped worrying about his and his family's wellbeing.

Most of our battles began with fierce name-calling, shouted through improvised bullhorns and ended with lobbing the deadly tin cans we had stockpiled in the gang's basement bunker. Since everyone was behind concrete walls or protected by plywood that covered broken windows, not much damage could be done. But, there was always a chance that somebody would get caught out in the open and get hurt. Absent that, the thudding of the projectiles was enough to keep us motivated for war. At some point, one side would raise a green flag and emissaries would be sent out and start negotiations for a truce. The rest of us would come out of hiding and engage in endless debates during the negotiation and after, with post mortems about the damage each gang had inflicted upon the other, the causes of the conflict and the reasons for reconciliation. Any evidence of a new scratch on a wall or a bit of chipped cement was enough to make a team proud of its performance. I remember that I claimed hits on the enemy's wall to show my effectiveness as a warrior officer deserving of promotion to the rank of captain, but I had no proof and I never got the promotion I felt I had earned. Kefalas did the same thing, and Andonis refused to choose one of us for a promotion and risk breaking up the cohesion of his army. I admired how he managed to say "No" to both of us and never alienate us. It was part of being a leader, I thought, but never understood how it was done. I was about ten years old when I decided that I didn't like being a leader. The role required the ability to mitigate, to sooth, placate and avoid confrontations – all behaviors that curtailed my freedom to express outside what I felt inside. For some reason, I felt that it was immoral to hide inside things that matter and show nothing to those outside.

When we had enough with the improvised tin can "grenades," we started making wooden "rifles" and wooden swords to chop up the enemy to pieces, or use copper tubes and dry peas as peashooters. The "rifles" were actually slingshots with the elastic band stretching across the length of a piece of wood, cut out in the shape of a rifle. The leather part holding the rock and attached to the rubber bands had a wire loop behind it, which was held in tension by a nail driven into the upper jaw of a clothespin. The clothespin was nailed down to the wooden gun, roughly at the position where the trigger would be in a real gun. All one had to do is set the sling, aim in the direction of the enemy and squeeze the clothespin down. When the jaws of the clothespin opened, the wire loop would slip out of the nail that held it in tension and the rock would be hurled out, propelled by the energy stored in the elastic band. We also had plain slingshots, of course, but they were old technology and they never looked anything like rifles. When we got tired of throwing bombs we would come out in the open and go at each other with our wooden swords or the peashooters. I cannot remember anyone getting seriously hurt from these mock battles, though a few hands got whacked in various sword fights.

We teased each other, we called each other horrible names, we tried to stick each other with the wooden swords, and we fired pebbles and canned rocks at each other from a distance, but we didn't really want to hurt anybody. We wanted the to be at war and we wanted to find out who won a fight, or prevailed in a battle, or dominated the other camp. We knew we were kids, and we imitated the adults around us without deluding ourselves into believing we were adults. We fought these battles like monkeys do, trying to intimidate the opponent into submission without drawing blood. Perhaps we were wise enough to think that the adults around us ought to behave like monkeys, not bloodthirsty humans. On those occasions that we couldn't contain our justly felt anger and exploded at one another, we fought with our bare hands. I was in many fights, sometimes against an older kid, and I fought with everything I had, but never with a weapon. We were wise enough not to trust ourselves with weapons when we were angry.

One day we heard that Goose had an accident. It had something to do with a grenade. Goose was always careful; he thought about what he was doing; it couldn't be anything very bad. Then we heard that he was in the hospital, and we knew that it was very bad. Nobody went to the hospital unless something terrible had happened. We found out that his arm was blown away when he found a real grenade and tried to take it apart. We wanted to make sense of what had happened, but we couldn't. Goose was a couple of years older than me, with plenty of street smarts; how could he have committed such a blunder? Had somebody tricked him and caused that grenade to explode? But, who could outsmart a sharp, streetwise kid like Goose? Was this some kind of payback for a grudge? Who would want to maim a dirt-poor kid? Goose was a very angry guy and hated the Germans who killed his father in the war. Could it be that he was trying to blow up some Germans and something went wrong and blew a piece of himself up, instead? Everybody tried to pass it off as an accident, so Goose wouldn't be arrested and executed. It was hard to explain what happened because we lived when everything that seemed to be harmful was possible.

We didn't see Goose for a long time. One of his co-workers said that he didn't want to talk about what happened, that's why he hadn't shown up in the neighborhood. We thought he'd never come back, because he was ashamed of his missing arm. Secretly, I think, all of us had no desire to see him without his arm. But we didn't know Goose very well. One day, a couple of months after the accident, he did show up at the stoop of

Kortessis with his stump in full view, and acted as if nothing much had happened. My eyes were fixed on his amputated arm and I couldn't escape the irresistible horror. We forced ourselves to act normally and celebrate his return as if he had been on a vacation, a long trip to the tropics. Not only was his arm gone, but also one side of his face and one eye were mangled. We tried to be nice to Goose, but he didn't like nice; we tried to be indifferent, but he became quarrelsome and wanted more of everything that we tried to share with him; the gentle Kalamata asked him if he was in pain and he lashed out at him; we tried to treat him like everybody else, and he grew silent and moody and said nothing for a long time. We could find no way of dealing with his loss. It would take us years and other horrors before we could do that. And, still, to this very day, when I see someone with a missing arm, my first thought is Goose, a very demanding person, someone difficult to deal with and requiring special effort to avoid conflict, someone trying to rebuild his missing part with odds and ends gathered from others.

If we didn't devote ourselves to training for war or fighting one another or hiding from the Nazis when they were on the prowl, we spent our time gathering bullets, shrapnel, and other war materials for two reasons: we wanted to have the best array of armaments around and we wanted to gamble with shrapnel and bullets in the street games that were always going on. Each bullet and piece of shrapnel had its own value and could be traded for other such items or for money, sometimes. One bullet from a Mouser rifle was worth three Luger pistol bullets. Italian carbine bullets were the cheapest. Shrapnel with orange hues, imprinted on it from the chemicals at the explosion, was usually worth more than a similar size piece that had no color on it. Shrapnel with orange hues and very few or no jagged edges was like gold because you could carry it in your pant pocket without fear of tearing it up.

When I was in second grade, my father took me along on a business trip to another plant of the company in Lavrion, near the ancient Greek silver mine, at the southern tip of the Attic peninsula. While he was in a meeting, I left the building where I was asked to wait for him, and wandered outside in some open fields. I came upon a mountain of bullet shells – a mountain of them! I climbed on top of it and surveyed the landscape of war. All around me in piles of gold I saw brass rifle shells glittering in the afternoon sun, and beyond, mountains of artillery shells, helmets, rusting rifles and stacks of metal bars and tubes. I stared with awe at the quantity of war materials strewn all around. I wondered if winners of wars had such piles of bullets also, or used them all subduing the enemies they defeated. I recognized my chance and took it. I gathered many shiny rifle shells for the games we played back home and stuffed them in my pockets. I got back before my father's meeting ended and I reported that I had found a mountain of rifle shells around and wanted to keep a few of them to play with. My father was stunned at my bold public move and couldn't decide whether to be embarrassed and give me a thrashing or take my side for demonstrating exemplary guts and entrepreneurship deserving congratulations. I told the director of the plant stories about our neighborhood war games and he was very impressed. He cautioned me to be very careful with bullets and showed me how to tell if a shell had been fired and was therefore totally safe, or not. He was so pleased by my interest in war materiel that he gave me a Greek army helmet in mint condition and . . . a real, honest to goodness bayonet in mint condition! I could hardly take my eyes off the sparkling blue-black steel blade and the wooden handle. My father was silent, but I knew he wasn't very comfortable with my maneuvers. He didn't want me to have any of the instruments of war, but he couldn't quite find a way to turn down the gifts of a delighted, higher-level manager without risking offending him. Cleverly, I promised to him that I wouldn't play in the street with the helmet and the bayonet, just show them once or twice to my buddies, so they know that I have some special weapons and may be qualified to advance to the rank of captain. I could tell that he was cornered and he let me keep the stuff. With my pockets full of shells, wearing a helmet and carrying a bayonet, I waddled behind my father.

It didn't take long for me to become the envy of the neighborhood. I told everyone about my military equipment, but showed it only to my fellow Warriors at a brief visit to our home. Unfortunately, my father's cautious nature didn't allow for public displays of weaponry, so I refrained from street exhibitions of my armor. I spent a lot of time, however, marching inside the house, wearing the helmet, with the bayonet hanging down from one of my mother's wide leather belts. I also jury-rigged a couple of homemade bandoliers full of shiny rifle bullet shells and strapped them around my shoulders like the guerrillas wore up on the mountains. It was quite a turnaround from pretending to be a bishop to pretending to be a Greek warrior. I also gambled a lot with my rifle shells in the streets. Some kids hated me because the plethora of shells I created flooded the market, dropping the value of everybody's shell hoards. Times were imposing their own style and ethic upon me and, perhaps, upon the population at large. Soldier, gambler, clergyman – I was a Renaissance man before I had even launched my boat! But I never made captain.

17 • The Gestapo Arrests My Father for Sabotage

The resistance to the occupation had begun to organize from the day the Germans entered Greece, but after a couple of years of suffering under the Nazi yoke, it had grown and had began to inflict casualties on the occupier. The German army responded swiftly with brutal reprisals as I have already reported. The army would descend upon a neighborhood, blockade the streets and arrest anyone who happened to pass by. As soon as a "blocco" was set up, the word would go out and people would try to get back to their homes some other way, if possible, or stay away as long as they could. The streets would be deserted, and fear would grip the people in the neighborhood. Some of the people arrested at random were executed; others were shipped to Haidari or out of the country to concentration camps, which were vaguely known as "work camps" back then. My mother would enter a tormented vigil every time there was a "blocco" and my father wasn't at home. And I would start reading incessantly the little pamphlet my mother kept in the house with the "Lives of the Saints." I read and reread that pamphlet, believing that nothing bad could happen to us as long as I was reading and praying.

And then, the Gestapo arrested my father at his workplace. I wasn't old enough to grasp the implications of this misfortune, but I remember being very fearful when I saw how disturbed my mother became. My mother tried to see him, but they wouldn't allow prisoners any contact with anyone. She was either gone downtown to the Gestapo headquarters on Koraee street waiting for hours on end to find out why he was arrested and what needed to be done to get him out of there, or she was at home crying and praying. She told me that my father was doing fine, but I couldn't make myself believe her. She said that something bad had happened at work, some sabotage and the Germans wanted to find out who did it. They threatened to harm everyone they had arrested, unless somebody gave up the saboteurs. We visited aunt Sophia's house, and talked with her and the other relatives who gathered there for mutual support. As far as I could tell, my mother insisted that my father was innocent, and had no knowledge of any saboteurs. But, in my mind, deep down in my gut, I believed that my father was involved in heroic actions of sabotage against our hated enemies, and they would get it out of him by torturing him before executing him. I already had my father down as a hero of the Greek nation, with a crown of laurel leaves on his head.

As my mother had hoped, the Germans found out that my father had nothing to do with sabotage and let him go a week after his arrest. He came home looking thin and worn out. He had been subjected to countless hours of interrogation and was tired. We took out of the back of the wardrobe one of our most precious cans of corned beef from Argentina and my mother used it along with some of the spaghetti my father had bought from the Catholic nuns to make a memorable dinner. We gave thanks to God who brought my father back home alive. I didn't appreciate fully how unlikely that outcome was until later, after I read accounts of torture imprisonment during the German occupation of Greece. But, it must be said that the Germans were fair judges in this case.

18 • You Can't Lick a Lollipop Forever

Some days, my mother would take me with her to my aunt Sophia's house where my cousin Nondas Laskos and I would play war with lead soldiers for hours on end. Before he left Greece for North Africa, just as the Germans were entering the country, his older brother, Agis, had left him his entire collection of lead soldiers, including elaborately built fortifications sculpted on the limestone wall at the rooftop terrace of their house. Agis is the nickname for Agesilaos, and he was named after our uncle Agesilaos, who died in a naval ship explosion shortly after he finished the Naval Academy of Greece, in the early 1920's. Some say that it was Agesilaos' death that gave my uncle Vassos the dose of fatalism he showed at crucial times in his life – a fatalism that set aside reason and drove him to extreme actions, both foolish and heroic. The only thing I remember about Agis from those days is that he sent a letter home, telling his family that he was in Africa, in a place where the heat was so unbearable that he could fry eggs on a pan without building any fire under it. Agis became a successful merchant in Zimbabwe, but he lost most of his business in one of the wars there and was forced to return to Greece.

My cousin Nondas and I were good friends, which meant that we fought often and reconciled just as often. His mother, aunt Sophia, was married to my mother's older brother Yannis, who was a cheese merchant in Athens. They lived in one of the busiest and noisiest neighborhoods of Athens, called Psiris, which means "lice-infested." It was a grand flea market of a neighborhood, and if you weren't alert at all times, you were bound to lose your wallet or your watch or your shirt. Nondas and I would venture out in the streets of that world of sharp-witted, ever-ready-for-a-scam world, and visit various shopkeepers to find out if they had any bargains for our families. Nondas was always on the lookout, but I wasn't as street smart as he was. After the occupation, when the market was full of merchandise for sale, I remember the rich smells of cheeses and cowhides, of dry goods and grains and vegetables of all kinds and I long for these things as they were, before we sanitized them and packaged them into their optically appealing, plastic tastelessness. Sometimes, I think, the progress of civilization is measured by the reduction of smells in favor of pleasing sights of plastic.

There weren't many things I enjoyed more than going to visit my cousin Nondas, in downtown Athens. Nondas was his nickname for Epaminondas Laskos, and he was named after our maternal grandfather. We were the same age and on warm days we could stay on the roof of his house for hours, playing with his lead soldiers, competing on jumping and strength and arguing about everything that was dear to us. And there were always people coming and going at aunt Sophia's house, some sophisticated university students, friends of his sister Maria's, others plain folk from the countryside doing business with my uncle, or visiting my aunt from her hometown near Thebes. And, even in the darkest years of the occupation, there was always some food on the table at aunt Sophia's, including the almost extinct sight of cheese, and plenty of good discussion, which fascinated me.

My mother knew how I enjoyed these visits, and when she wanted to give me a treat she would take me there. I remember particularly one sunny spring afternoon as she held my hand and we walked along noisey, crowded streets downtown Athens, toward aunt Sophia's house at Psiris. With my free hand, I held the lemon-flavored lollipop she had just bought me. Looking at its yellow crystaline surface, sparkling in the sun was almost as delightful as sucking on the sweet lemon candy. It was a rare treat to have any kind of sweets in those days, and that knowledge added to the pleasure I felt as I walked, oblivious to my surroundings. Everything was right, and there was no need to worry about anything that day; no one could spoil this magnificent afternoon.

Suddenly, there was commotion behind me, a rush of wind to my right. Someone bumped me, and a shadow snatched the lollipop out of my mouth. I saw a scrawny figure in rags running up ahead, a small head with dark closecropped hair with a couple of shaved spots. I didn't see the face of the thief. And I never let out the scream that the sudden loss whipped up inside me. The afternoon in the sun was shattered, but I was too stunned to shout in protest. I don't remember if I cried, but I didn't want to talk or even think about the incident. It defied explanation in my mind and that made it dangerous. I could not accept that peace could be broken and joy could be stolen so abruptly without having done anything wrong without warning and a chance to fight for them. It was an event that put a dent on my ability to trust people. A lifetime has gone by since that lollipop was snatched away from me, probably by an urchin who was trying to stay alive and needed it more than I wanted it. But, I cannot forget the loss I felt, the emptiness that filled me that sunny afternoon. For a long time, I was suspicious of any feeling of joy that might delight my heart. And, even now, on rare occasions, I have to deal with that suspicion every time I start to feel good and relax. I recognize it like a face from the distant past and go past it, to let the good feeling stay. But, the memory cannot be wiped out and, sometimes, I stay locked in the past with suspicion lingering on. Then, my eyessee a threatening black spot floating in every image.

19 • Mother Visits a Prophet

Several women from our neighborhood, including my mother, discovered a lady prophet somewhere downtown Athens and attended her gatherings regularly, once a week. I started to hear a lot about Madam Zoe and her predictions, as well as her explanations for the suffering we were going through. The women must have found her words soothing, hopeful and even inspiring, because my mother always seemed happy when she came back home from one of those meetings. Unlike the view of the Church which attributed our suffering, partly to the satanic actions of the Nazis and partly to our sinful ways, Madam Zoe believed that we were going through a stage of trials and tribulations in order to emerge a stronger and more glorious world.

One evening, my mother came back from one of her sessions pumped up. Her face was beaming with joy and started talking excitedly to my father, who had just returned home after working at his part-time jobs as a bookkeeper for a shoestore and a lumberyard in addition to his regular job. He looked like the world had spat on his face, but he didn't interrupt her as she told him what had transpired. She said that Madame Zoe had prophesied the liberation of Greece by "a blond race from the East."

My father was changing his sweaty undershirt for a fresh one, as he usually did. When his head reappeared on top of the new undershirt, he turned toward my mother, looked at her with his tired eyes, and said with disgust, "The Russians!"

"Liberation!" she protested without hesitation.

Without missing a beat, "Communists!" he growled. And the argument picked up speed and spoiled one more peaceful evening. Ironically, wasn't even close to being a communist, and my father was no rightwinger, at all. But these arguments happen anyway.

As far as I was concerned, my parents always had trouble understanding each other. I learned from them that one's point of view shapes meaning more than the facts. My mother would see the bright side of things, no matter what the facts were, and my father would see the darkness that lurks on the "other" side of things, no matter what the facts appeared to show. I found my father's assessment of the facts in greater agreement with my experience at that time, but I always consoled myself by allowing that there must also be a bright side that may break through at any time. For me, that was hope. And, we were looking everywhere for it, especially in those bleak days of the occupation.

I wanted my mother's view of the facts to be true, but I was often disappointed to discover that it wasn't. We hoped that our armies would win, but they didn't; we hoped that the conquerors being citizens of Germany, a highly advanced culture, where the classics were celebrated and arts and sciences were valued, would treat us like fellow human beings, but they didn't. Word was out that these Germans were burning the books of the Classics in Leipsig, their own center for classical studies. I remember trying to sort out, as a boy, whether Leipsig was a good or a bad place and being unable to decide – Leipsig! And we hoped that our friends, the Allies, would come and stop these barbarians from enslaving us and starving us, but for a long time, they didn't. We had hoped too many times, but our hopes had not made a difference. It took a lifetime of living to learn that hope is a state of mind, and cannot be weighed up against facts; it took a lot of living to learn that hope isn't expectation, and that it is good for a human being to hope, but not to confuse that with having expectations.

I'm still learning how to hope without expectations, but I slip up and find out that reality isn't kind to one's dreams. Hoping for liberation doesn't bring it about. We had to fight for our freedom. And, that's exactly what was happening all over Greece as the occupation draged on: people were going to the mountains to organize and fight; and our armed forces, having regrouped in the Middle East, were beginning to fight along with the Allies for all of us, hoping that one day soon, we would be free. We were all waiting for something to end the war. "A blond race from the East," ethereal angels from Heaven, our fighters with bullets or the Americans who, finally, did set us free.

20 • The Outsiders of *Neos Kosmos*

Always fall in with what you're asked to accept. Take what is
given, and make it over your way. My aim in life has always
been to hold my own with whatever' s going. Not against: with.

Robert Frost

Soon after the Nazis occupied Athens they started looking for stranded
British soldiers. Thousands had been left behind when the British
expeditionary force pulled out of Greece in a hurry to escape the rapidly
advancing Nazi jaggernaut. The Germans tracked them down, and when
they found any, threw them in trucks and carried them away, God only
knew where. Two such British soldiers, freezing, in tattered civilian
clothes, passed through our neighborhood, handcuffed and shackled in a
German army truck. The driver parked outside Barka's tobacco store and
went inside. Several haggard Greek men and children gathered around
the truck to shake the prisoners' hands or touch them and give them
whatever gifts they could find in a hurry – a piece of bread, a half-empty
cigarette pack, a few dry figs, some raisins, a cookie. . . The British
soldiers took the stuff, gave many thanks, made the V sign for victory
and lots of thumbs up. Those who spoke a few English words were eager
to express the goodwill of everyone there and thank them for their help
in the war. They wished them good luck wherever they might be taken.
When the driver came out of Barka's store and saw the gathered crowd
behind his truck, he lunged at them, shaking his fists and cursing them.
The crowd dispersed, but not without shouting vile curses at the German
soldier.

My mother had warned me against displays of friendship toward any
Brittish soldiers, aware that such displays were common all over Athens
and that the German authorities were furious and kept issuing harsh
orders forbidding any contact with British soldiers, whom they called
"saboteurs," before they were captured, and "spies" after their capture.
Even when the punishment was 5 years of hard labor for aiding and
abetting British soldiers, the demonstrations of friendship continued
unabetted. On retrospect, I think that this was the first sign of rebellion I
saw. Others would follow.

It was a few months after the occupation that a strange beggar appeared
for the first time in our neighborood. He was a blind man in a white
smock, like street photographers used to wear in the old days, a white
cane and dark glasses. His face was ruddy, and he wore a worn out

worker's cap. He didn't show any sign of awareness of his environment as he swung his cane left and right in front of him and periodically shook a tin cup with coins to announce his approach and solicit help. But, the most peculiar thing about him, the thing that caused us to imagine all sorts of stories about him, had to do with his periodic shouting of a single, mysterious word, at the top of his lungs, in a sing-song voice. Every few steps, he would tap the ground with his cane and let out what appeared to be a double burst of a single word: "Eema . . . Eema . . ." The word "aema," or "hema" means "blood" in Greek (as in the word *hemophilia*), but the way the man pronounced the word was unusual, it had an accent, and the context of his saying it required some uncommon interpretation. Why was he shouting "Blood . . . Blood" in Greek with an accent? The reddish complexion of the man, his strange attire, his total unawareness of his surroundings and the way he pronounced the one and only word that he was ever heard uttering, created an aura of mystery about him. Besides, no one knew where the man lived, where he came from or where he went after he went past our turf. Many people asked him questions to clarify his situation, but the only response they got was that same double burst of "Blood."

His existence demanded an explanation, and we struggled to come up with one over many heated discussions at the stoop of Kortessis. Andonis thought that the man was a shell-shocked peasant from the northern part of Greece, probably Salonica, where light skinned, blond Greeks and red-headed Armenians are not rare; Kortessis thought that the man was not blind, but rather a lunatic, who probably escaped from the asylum at Daphni, the only asylum we had ever heard of, just before the Germans took over; Vouss, Little Beggar and Goose, the three guys with the most street smarts, who knew more about deception than all the rest of us put together, were convinced that the beggar was a run-of-the-mill con man, who happened to hit upon a clever scheme to extract sympathy, attention and money from the softies of the neighbourhood.

"What do you think, Chinaman?" Kefalas asked me. Kefàlas knew that he was risking a fight every time he called me that, but he just couldn't resist.

"The man is a Brittish spy," I said after a moment's hesitation.

Kefalas shook his huge head in disbelief. "Dream on!" he sneered.

"Well, what do you think, Kefalas?" Antony asked pointedly.

Kefalas cast a quick condescending glance at him. "Greek deserter pretending to have shell-shock!" he shot back, as if the answer was a no-brainer. He hated being called names as much as I did.

We turned Eema-Eema's story over and over again, and in the end we decided that the only thing he could be was just an unfortunate beggar trying to survive. At least this was the public consensus of the group. Some of us however were convinced that the man was a spy and we should never say that in public because there were always traitors around who wouldn't hesitate to give him up to the Germans for a loaf of bread.

Eema-Eema would visit the neighbourhood two or three times a month for all the years of the occupation, collecting a few coins here and there and whatever else the soft-hearted women of the neighbourhood and the children co-conspirators could spare. We felt sorry for him and were proud of him but never knew for sure what to feel or think about him. We followed behind him as if he was the leader of a procession and chased away anyone who might bother him in any way as long as he was in our turf. Eema-Eema disappeared after the liberation. No one saw him ever again; no one had any idea what happened to him. In the end all of us, regardless of our publically stated view of the man, were secretly hoping that he was a British spy hiding under the nose of the Nazis. We hoped that he made it back to England, but we feared that the Nazis got him and executed him. His howling cry for blood was never forgotten. It was the triumphant cry for revenge we all dreamed about for the suffering that Hitler and his vassal, Mussolini, inflicted upon all of us. We created a legend, and it sustained us.

One day, Kefalas came running out of his house and announced to all of us gathered at Kortessis' stoop that Bourèka's prize hen had hatched a freak chick overnight. We all knew that Bourèka kept several hens for eggs and for an occasional batch of chicks, so the news of something having to do with chickens and Bourèka wasn't strange. But, a freak chick? What on earth was that? We laughed at him and called him Kefalas to his face, and watched him turn red with rage. It wouldn't be the first time Kefalas exaggerated, just to be taken seriously. He had told us that he had seen the beautiful Stella, the daughter of Kyr-Andreas, the Math teacher, with a German soldier one night in the park, which no one believed anymore than we believed in the laughing ghost, which, Kefalas insisted, occupied the deserted house at the end of the field that we called *Alana*. But, this time, Kefalas managed to restrain himself. He calmed down after his brief outburst and bent his head down, thrust his hands in his pockets and walked away, kicking rocks on the street.

"I told you the truth," he said. "You'll see . . ."

Next day, the whole neighborhood knew that there was supposed to exist a freak chicken among us, but no one had actually seen it. Some said it had two heads, others said it had the head of a snake, and a few talked about four legs. I was afraid. What did that sign signify? Did this qualify as a miracle? What evil will befall us after that? I was also curious about the little freak, but I didn't dare go to Boureka's basement and see for myself, because I didn't want any ill omen to be transferred to me. Besides, I argued with inventiveness, what if it were one of Kefàlas' fibs? I would become the laughing stock of the neighborhood. But, I didn't have to wait long before my curiosity was satisfied. That same afternoon Little Beggar, who joined us only when he wasn't begging from the Germans or working for them or rummaging the better neighborhoods of Athens for junk, showed up, as usually with a plan.

He announced that anyone who wanted to see the freak chick could do so at a cost of two thousand drachmas, or equivalent goods. He hang a cardboard sign on the wall fence outside a yard, located near Vouss' place, to inform everyone the business he was in: "Freak to View." Inside the yard there was an abandoned outhouse, a little shack really, and Vouss was posted there, ready to collect the price of admission and keep the peace.

Some paid with four marbles to get in, others with six beer bottle caps, all foreign brands, and I paid with a piece of shrapnel with a beautiful orange streak from the explosion which created it. It was medium size and smooth, which gave it higher value because it fit in pants' pockets without tearing them up and had the look of an arrowhead, valued by most collectors and gamblers in our turf. Vouss was also the arbiter of bartering and asked Little Beggar's advice only when someone brought some unusual item like a wheel from a baby carriage or a boy scout's belt buckle.

I paid with my precious shrapnel and got inside the yard and stood in line, a few feet away from the potato-sack curtain of the outhouse. When my turn came, I entered the space behind the curtain and came face to face with the yellow fluff of fur that was the freak chicken. Little Beggar appeared beside me, his eyes fixed on his prize possession, propped up on an old suitcase with brass corners on top of an ancient toilet seat. The chick was sitting down. It had one head and I couldn't see its legs. It looked frightened, its head darting up and down like a sub periscope and its eyes blinking, but normal.

"What's freakish about it?" I asked, ready to demand a refund. If Vouss, the cashier, tried to give me any old jagged piece of shrapnel for a refund, instead of the one orange streaked, medium-sized, arrowhead-shaped one I had given him, there would be a fight. I was a foot shorter than him and half his weight, but I could punch and kick and scratch and even bite, if I had to. But, I knew that in the end, I would end up with a black eye, if not a concussion. I didn't look forward to taking on Vouss, but I would do what I had to do to get back that piece of shrapnel. Little

Beggar mumbled something about the legs being tucked under the body of the chick, and the chick being tired from showing its legs by standing up every time a customer appeared. I got the idea that he wanted me to trust him, that the chick was a freak and I had indeed seen a freaky, four-legged chick. But, for better or worse, I wasn't ready to trust him yet.

"I got to see!" I insisted.

Little Beggar tickled the back of the chick with his boney finger and the little yellow bundle stood up on two legs, lifting under its body two other, shorter, stunted legs under its breast like a dwarfish dinosaur.

I was filled with sorrow by the sight and closed my eyes.

"Satisfied?" the Beggar sneered and pushed me back toward the curtain. Before I turned my eyes away, I caught sight of the little freak as it tried to take a step toward me, and stumbled, and fell down flat on top of the suitcase where it was planted.

"Satisfied?" the Beggar challenged me.

I couldn't utter a word. Sadness, so profound and deep came over me that I was numb. I just shook my head and pushed past the hanging potato sacks and out of the yard.

I didn't answer the questions the kids on the line were asking: "Hey, Chinaman, does it have four legs or two heads?" someone asked, and everybody laughed. I didn't feel like fighting with anyone just then. I trudged back home. Gradually, my sadness was turning to anger. I was angry at Kefalas who, as I found out later, had convinced Bourèka to sell the chick to Little Beggar for 10,000 drachmas, while getting the middleman's fee of 10 cigarette box tops, domestic, and two good size ball-bearing steelies; and, I was angry at the impresario and his side-kick, Vouss, who profited from marketing a creature's misery; but most of all, I was angry at myself for supporting the evil enterprise with my payment of admission. It dawned on me, that I was also furious with the chick for being born a freak and parading its impotence among us, now that we were all crippled and impotent. Did we need a reminder for our misery? It took a long time to apologize to Kefalas for laughing at him. I didn't like the person I was becoming; I had no use for it. It didn't occur to me to be angry with God, who creates and oversees all creation. Perhaps I was too afraid of God's wrath and pushed away any thought that came close to blaming God for anything. Later in life, I would learn enough by studying theodicy on my own for more than a dozen years and I would conclude that God is Love and doesn't intend the creation of freaks or disasters. But, the way he made the world makes some terrible things possible. When it comes down to it, if we want a vibrant world with freedom for all, mistakes by free agents are bound to happen – be they persons, molecules of air, particles of rocks, or DNA genes; and we'll have murders and wars and earthquakes and freak chicks as well.

Two days later the little chick died. Beggar and Vouss announced that the enterprise had been profitable and a hungry cat had taken the chick under her protective custody. I listened to everybody laugh, but I couldn't. I felt sad and had no idea what to do with that. I was angry, but I didn't know where to strike. I wanted to be alone at home, hiding inside my closeted space, and there, in the dark, to cry my anger and sadness away. To this very day, I confuse sadness with anger. It is hard for me to let others know that I am sad, because sadness was weakness in the jungle I grew up, whereas anger was strength. It has been hard to ditch that learning when I left the jungle. I'm ready to defend myself with all the cunning and the tricks I learned. I'm ready for anything other than nothing. The street was our playground, our stage, our arena and the proving ground of our character. It was there that we challenged one another and learned when to stand our ground and when to yield and fight another day. The street was also a battleground and some of us were wounded. It was all part of growing up. It was all right.

In those, days many street vendors crisscrossed our street in *Neos Kosmos*, bellowing the freshness of their fruits, fish and vegetables, the healing powers of their herbs, the tight weave of their rugs, the strength of their feather dusters and marvels galore. They offered their services with gusto and self-assurance: they would grind your coffee beans or your roasted garbanzo beans with a dash of coffee beans, if you were short on coffee beans, and the mix would taste like the best brew in Arabia; they would polish your brass and silver, sharpen your knives so sharp you had to sign a release indemnifying the vendor before he could let you use his services; and there were mattress rejuvenators who offered to fluff the cotton in your mattress and your pillows, or throw in an extra fixing of your broken umbrella, if you weren't as happy as a dancing dervish with your fluffed-puffed pillows and mattress.

We often watched them work, sometimes for hours on end, as they selected and weighed their wares, or as they sat on their stools or our stoops and performed the services the women hired them for, using their mysterious tools. Some of the vendors were friendly, but others chased us away. Our job was to learn from them whatever they were good at, whether that was picking and peddling tomatoes or sharpening somebody's scissors, and later to scrutinize them and their work and argue about it and come to some kind of judgment. Some were "sharpies," and shouldn't be trusted, while others were "masters" and couldn't cheat if you put guns to their heads. But I cannot recall anyone who wasn't good at what he was doing. The neighborhood didn't allow slackers to work.

One of these peddlers was Barco, a man with a small head stuck without any evidence of neck to a long lean torso. He wore a blue denim shirt and jeans but didn't look like a factory worker because he always had on a brown apron with a bib and a Greek sailor's hat. His face was pockmarked with features permanently set to convey a mocking frown. He hawked a kind of nickelodeon show for a drachma when the war began or for a thousand drachmas when the occupation was most oppressive and inflation was skyrocketing. His attraction was a hand wheeled box, about five feet long by three feet wide by two feet high, with little oval glass windows on the edges, large enough to fit the face of any young viewer who paid for his or her ticket and couldn't wait to see the show. The box was painted blue with all sorts of figures and decorative designs around the windows, which remained closed with tiny, little curtains until show time. On top of the box stood a stuffed clown under a striped red and white umbrella, which would turn slowly when Barco turned one of his cranks. The master of ceremonies was constantly in motion around his cart, which he liked to park across the street from the local *kafeneion* and in the shade of an old pine tree. He was upset on those occasions that he had to park at some other spot because the *kafeneion's* customers had spread out too far, hogging the shade, and wouldn't move an inch to accommodate his cart. The sun would beat down on his theater-on-wheels and chase customers away. "Have you no feeling for your children and grandchildren?" he would shout at the old men, who were solving the problems of the world over coffee.

We would gather around the box and watch the customers come, discuss the situation, pay the price and wait by one of the windows until Barco was ready to crank the roll of painted paper and start the performance. He had all sorts of different shows to peddle, some with car races, others with trains going over bridges and mountain passes, and others yet with safaris in the jungles of Africa and India. I had resisted the lure of the show because I didn't think that the show was worth most of the money I had in the world. Besides, the reviews I had heard from the viewers were mixed. But one day he set up shop in our neighborhood in the shade of the pine tree by the *kafeneion* and started peddling something that made me more curious than I had ever been with any other of his offerings.

"Come one, and come all . . . See the wonders of the river Nile," Barco shouted. "Let yourself get out of this drab world and see nature at its best and its worst: see the crocodiles swim in the river Nile. They were gods, once, these great monsters of the longest river on earth. They don't swim my friends, they glide, they slide, they dive and thrive in the river. And right there, right by these fearsome creatures, see the little people of Egypt in their white robes peddle their wares from their head-born baskets. See the children of the desert swim so carefree and joyous in the land of the pharaohs, the great kings, who built the pyramids and carved the Sphinx and ruled the oldest kingdom on this earth. Give me your hundred drachmas and I'll give you the thrill of your life. Next!" And, Barco would grab the money from the little fist that offered it to him and steer the child to one of the empty windows. "Keep your snout and your buggers off my clean windows you little creeps . . . Keep coming and keep your nose out of the glass," he would holler. Sometimes, he would grab the shirt of some kid who had his face pressed against the glass and jerk him back.

When he finished a show, he would change the roll of paper with new action and wait as kids made their decisions to continue or leave. When he had enough viewers for him to make a showing worthwhile, usually half a dozen kids, he would issue one final call and, if no one else approached the box, he would start to crank the roll of colored pictures which produced the sensation of traveling down a river as the riverbanks went by, or the train crossing bridges in the mountains as the scenery moved or a boat braving huge waves in a storm at sea.

And there came a day when I could no longer resist the lure of the river Nile and the pyramids and the pharaohs with all the mystery of the tombs and the mummies I had discovered in bits and pieces of the encyclopedic pamphlets my father brought home from time to time. I paid the price of admission and stuck my face up against the oval glass window, which, I saw was curved as a lens to produce some magnification, and pressed the little curtains up against my face with my cupped hands to shut off all light from the sides. The images started moving. I saw a shallow, stringy boat with a native in a white robe steering it from the stern, while three white people dressed in white tropical clothes and wearing cork hats sat in the boat, holding their rifles on their knees as the boat floated down the river Nile. "See the palm trees, watch the hunters headed for the heart of Africa," I heard Barco hawking the narration. "Watch the explorers in the distance looking for mummies in the dungeons of the pyramid of Cheops." Then a few black children waded in the water. They were having fun splashing and chasing each other. They must have been laughing, but Barco didn't give them any sounds. And, I saw a huge crocodile surface from the water and slide ever so slowly, ever so deadly toward the children. "Watch the little black children play . . . see how good they swim, like fish . . . and keep your peepers on the monster rising from the deep . . . the animal that tears flesh and eats and gulps, but his belly never gets filled . . . the croc by the rock," Barco's voice reached a crescendo as the scene unfolded. My fingers squeezed the curtain around my face, as if I wanted no one else to witness what I was watching. The crocodile's mouth opened like a hole parting the waters. The beast rose up from the water, and the deadly jaws snapped shut around the tiny body of a child, the hands flailing, the water painted red, and children running out of the water, running on the riverbank sand. The hunters stood up on the boat, aimed their rifles at the beast, but there was no sound . . . just Barco's raspy voice, wailing in the desert, "the children of the Nile are having fun on the sand . . ." the plea of a peddler making a living by showing a few pictures on a moving roll of paper, oblivious to the crimes taking place inside his box. I thought I saw a couple of wispy strands of smoke rising from the white hunters' guns, three men taking aim and firing as if from the turret of a tank in the direction of the beast that had now vanished in the river Nile, gone, yet forever present. Barco wouldn't give away the plot by clapping his hands, making a racket, booming out the sounds of gunshots, if there were any. He had to earn a living, and kids needed the suspense of not knowing the fate of the hero in the tale he was telling. The guns may have been fired, but the shots never rung out. The real hero was the little African child, but Barco had no time for that. The killing was eerily silent. "The river Nile has many dangers, my little ones, many hazards lurking under the water . . . You have to pay first, and then you've got to be alert. Mind your back. Watch out! You have to know . . ."

I was lost in the horror of the scene, scarred for life, I thought. Had I really seen a child being devoured by a crocodile, or did my imagination run amok? Had the hunters cared enough to try and save the boy, or just sat back and watched the horror? Was that a boy or a girl that vanished?

I found Kefalas, who had watched the show with me that day. He was chewing something as usual. "Did you like it?" I asked him, afraid to come right out and ask him directly the question that was churning my gut.

"Stupid, except for the action in the end."

"What action," I prodded.

"Were you asleep? The croc ate that Blackie. Wasn't that something? One bite and out . . . gone for good. Like you might swallow a peanut!" he laughed. His mouth was stuffed with a fig.

"Could you tell if the hunters fired their guns?" I asked.

"Nah! They just watched the show," Kefalas said.

"I thought I saw puffs of smoke rising up from their guns."

"Yeah, after the croc had checked out and was sunning himself in Timbuktu.

Kefàlas had a point. I let it go. The child was lost.

21 • Sins, Miracles and the God Who Loves Us

It was declared at first by the Lord, and it was attested to us by those who heard him, while God also bore witness by signs and wonders and various miracles and by gifts of the Holy Spirit distributed according to his own will.

The Bible, Heb. 2: 3b-4

Whatever a man prays for, he prays for a miracle. Every prayer reduces itself to this: Great God, grant that twice two be not four.

Ivan Turgenev, *Fathers and Sons*

Our apartment was two blocks away from Saint Mary's Greek Orthodox Church in the *Neos Kosmos* area of Athens. The church was the biggest structure in the neighborhood, had the most traffic of any other public place, and was the assembly hall and center of communications for the entire neighborhood. When something happened in the community, any unusual action, criminal or heroic, threatening like a fire, or joyous like a victory in battle for the Allies before the occupation, the news would spread from the courtyard of the church to the outer reaches of the neighborhood. Before the occupation, ringing the church bells heralded the victories our army scored against Mussolini's Fascists. After the occupation the church bells could only toll for religious occasions. After that, we did all right with whispers. We heard about the war in Africa and El Alamein and Rimini, where Greek soldiers fought again for freedom with the British army of Montgomery. And we heard about people who left their homes to join the guerrillas up in the mountains of northern Greece, about people who were caught at German checkpoints and taken prisoner, people who used mediums and tea leaf readers to find answers to whatever troubled them and their missing kin, or people who were hang at some other part of Athens for gouging their fellow citizens in the black market.

Once, I heard that the owner of the neighborhood clothing store made a public appearance, dressed up as an archbishop on the Greek Mardi Gras, just before Lent, and was rebuked by the clergy and boycotted by God-fearing shoppers for a couple of days. I was horrified, at first, but after a while, I too managed to laugh about it. There were also rumors of excommunicating the daredevil shopkeeper, but the outrage didn't go very far when somebody pointed out that making fun of the archbishop wasn't at all like making fun of God, which would be a blasphemy and a serious sin. Separating the church matters from God was an insight I never had before. It didn't make any difference to me then, but it would fifty years later.

It was at the churchyard of Saint Mary's where we would first hear about any miracle that might be happening anywhere in greater Athens. I spent a lot of time playing table games and chase games at the churchyard – cops and robbers, free the prisoners, hide and seek – with other children in the neighborhood. Sometimes I would help with the production of candles, or count coins from the collection brass boxes.

During the civil war that followed the occupation, or "the fratricides," as Nikos Kazantzakis so aptly called it, I watched in utter disbelief the gravediggers bury bodies behind the church, because nobody dared to risk going to the cemetery with bullets flying about from every direction. After the fratricides ended, I watched them dig up the graves all over again to exhume the bodies and take them away for a proper burial in the cemetery. I didn't want anyone to disturb the dead, but the priest and my mother said that the graves at the church were always intended to be temporary. So, it was to be. The only grave that wasn't disturbed, but is still there to this day was the grave of Father Haralambos, the chief priest of Saint Mary's, who was killed by the Communists during the civil war, a topic that will come up later.

In my early years, I did a lot of living in and around that church and learned a lot of things from priests, deacons, other kids and the parishioners that came to be consoled, find hope and strength to face the challenges of life. But I never stopped being afraid of God. He was there to judge every thought I had, every move I made, every feeling I had and it was hard to love him that way. No matter how often I heard that loving God means fearing him and obeying him, I never quite understood it. The message was always like an equation with a symbol that made a solution incomprehensible.

Later, when I heard for the first time that one could go to hell for calling his brother "a fool," I *did* have a serious problem. The word for calling someone a fool in Greek is μωρε ("*mo-reh,*" which has the same root as moron) and the Bible does say specifically "whoever says, 'You fool!' shall be liable to the hell of fire" (Mat. 5:22). So, why should that make me so upset? All I would have to do is stop calling anyone a fool. But, it's not as simple as that. The problem is that boys and adult men could hardly carry on a conversation without attaching the little Greek word ρε, "*reh,*" in front of the person's name. Now, "*reh*" is an abbreviation for "*mo-reh*" for which the Bible says people go to hell, even though when we said it, we never meant it to be a curse or a slur. If you were angry with Thomas, you would say " *reh* Thomas, take a walk;" but, even if you wanted to be chummy with Thomas and tried to cheer him up, you would say to him "*reh* Thomas, why do you worry about little things like that?" I used that little "*reh*" all the time talking to my friends, and so did all my friends when talking to me. But, when I asked the priest about that and he said that I must not use "*reh*" for anyone because I could burn in hell, I felt hopeless. The word was vulgar – girls and women considered to be more refined or more constrained, never used it – but was it a deadly sin? Were we all going t o hell? I must have been nine or ten years old then, and it was the first time that I questioned the understanding of God I had been taught. I started rejecting some of the things that were said about God's wrath, hellfire and damnation. They just didn't make sense anymore.

I didn't know it then, but I was beginning to realize that God never intends evil, no matter what human beings say that God does.

I wish that I had been given then the single, most powerful message that I found out later in my life, the message that, now I believe, is the essence of my faith, from 1 John 4:8 "God is love," or as my wife with her Lutheran upbringing puts it, describing the message she got from her church, "Jesus loves me." Then it makes sense to love God with all you've got and love your fellowman as you love yourself. It implies that you do the right thing, not because you are scared stiff of God's judgment pincers coming down on you, grabbing you, lifting you up and dumping you in hell's fires or some unseen eternal suffering, but because you love God, because you want to do right by him, who sacrificed himself for us. Why weren't we told a hundred times over that God is love? Did all the adults around us believe that only fear could make us good Christians? Or, did the Church want to keep everyone obedient to its rules and regulations by interpreting the Bible in ways that make us afraid of God? I'm still sorting things out, but "God is love and he doesn't intend evil" is where I draw the line.

As I grew older, my range of action increased, much to the consternation of my mother and the repeated admonitions of my father for breaking the rules he never tired of setting. But, I had to see for myself what was happening by God and men outside our small domain and I tracked down every opportunity that came up. In the process, I sometimes was late for dinner; sometimes I forgot to pick up the shoes from the shoemaker, or mail the letters at the post office, and my mother would lecture me while my father glowered at me for having dropped the ball or because I joined the demonstration of the Liberal Party in downtown Athens, or spent an afternoon in a crowd waiting to scc a miracle.

One time, when I was in the fourth or fifth grade hanging out at the churchyard, I heard that the sign of the cross had appeared on one of the windows of a bank office building, some distance away from our neighborhood. I went there with some of the other guys from our gang, my heart pounding, expecting to see proof of God's presence amid the chaos of the city. There were hundreds of people in the street, in front of the building, looking upward and occasionally pointing up, toward a particular area of the building. "There! There, do you see it?" they would say to those next to them. And sometimes people would nod and shake their heads and agree and other times they would say they saw nothing, nothing at all. I looked and looked for a long time, but I never was sure that I saw anything like a cross. I thought I saw a glimpse of a rainbow as from a film of oil on a glass surface – or was that my imagination, desperately trying to shore up what I thought was my shaky faith?

Besides, I could never swear that there was no cross up there, since I always had trouble seeing far away and hadn't yet discovered that I was nearsighted. That happened when I was in the sixth grade, and I got my first pair of glasses. I was crushed when I was told that I would have to add hardware to my appearance for life. It wasn't that I disliked my appearance, but I resented my dependence on that hardware, and the inefficiency and insufficiency of my body. My father, who had worn glasses all his life, assured me that he had felt that way at first, but got used to glasses and so would I. Somehow, I believed him and never thought much about the subject after that.

I was all set to see a miracle. I had been looking for a miracle more persistently than most, because I remember several occasions concerning miracles. The possibility of things happening in the world in violation of physical laws was and is fascinating to me. But it never occurred to me until I had experienced the world more fully as a young man and as an adult that there are other phenomena that happen against all odds, that go beyond reasonable expectations, things that happen even though they have close to zero probability of happening. I have often thought of some of the things that happened to me in this way more as miracles than coincidences. Someday I'll lay bare my thoughts and write about the dozen or so such providential happenings that may be coincidences and ask the reader to judge whether they were random events or God's doings.

There was once a miracle reported at our church and the rumor spread like wildfire in the neighborhood that one of the icons in the church had tears running down from the face of the person in the icon. I cannot remember whose icon it was – it could have been a saint, Holy Mary or our Lord Jesus Christ. People said these were tears of sorrow, shed for the ills our country suffered during the fratricides in 1945. Others were saying that the tears were for the horrible sins we had committed and for which God had imposed a harsh punishment on us.

I went to the church and waited in line with great anticipation and fear for what I might see. It took awhile before the queue inched forward, and I found myself in front of the icon. I crossed myself and lifted up my head, but in the momentary look I took, I saw no tears, though I could not be sure there were no tears there and I missed them. There were so many things going on around me, people talking, people lighting candles, others crossing themselves and whispering prayers, genuflecting and squeezing past one another, and feet shuffling and children crying, there was so much commotion that I was never able to study the icon carefully. One look and I was past the icon and the chance to see God's supernatural power. It would take decades and intensive study of the Bible to understand that God's miracles are everywhere, if only one knows how to look for them.

In spite of my inability to secure the proof of a miracle, I never ceased to believe in the possibility of miracles, because I never ceased to believe that we were created and befriended by an all powerful and all loving, albeit strict and demanding, God. At first, I believed that God would punish me on the spot, if I didn't obey his commands. He could scramble my speech, if I cursed; he could paralyze my hand, if I shoplifted; he could twist my head so I could see behind me, if I looked at lewd things as some people said that he had done to a young man in Kallithea, another neighborhood of Athens. I couldn't quite drop the idea that God would do something horrible to me, if I went astray. I took all that in and tried my best to obey. God is the only person I have never wanted to rebel against. It seemed to me that it was pointless to rebel against an omnipotent Being. I haven't figured out yet whether any Being can be God without being omnipotent, but I know there are some people who believe that God doesn't have to be omnipotent to govern his Creation. He doesn't overpower it, but woes it to move in ways that are best for all.

When I was thirteen, I gave up my total abstinence from cursing, and started using some of the common variety foul words, like saying damn and hell and bastard. The more offensive curses including the "f" word were reserved for particularly egregious offenses. Yet God didn't scramble my speech as punishment for my sins, and my head wasn't twisted around, either. I thought that cursing anyone was bad, but I didn't believe my God thought that it should lead to eternal damnation, either. One of the things I never did, or ever felt any inclination to do, was blaspheme against God or anything sacred or holy, even though it wasn't rare in the culture I grew up. My parents never blasphemed either, but some of my uncles, to my horror, did so. I cannot remember any female ever blaspheming or using any offensive curses back then. Equality in sin and everything else was decades away.

I remember the times I spent hanging around the church during the festivals, when all sorts of peddlers came to sell their wares. One of the peddlers was a monk who sold incense and crosses and ceramic pots he made himself. We became friends and used to talk about religion a lot. His head was full of strange stories that were as real to him as the ground he stood on. He told me about a monk who was seen in two different places, miles apart, at the same time. He believed that there was a certain tub in one of the monasteries on Mount Athos, which was filled by monks with water on a certain date, and Holy Mary turned the water into olive oil overnight. He told me about a saintly monk's tomb that was opened after a hundred years had passed and a wonderful perfume of roses filled the air. Another monk's tomb was opened after a hundred years and the candle buried with him was still burning bright. He told me that if I ever went to Mount Athos in the northern part of Greece, I would hear stories like these from the monks who live there year round. We talked about ghosts and angels and the second coming, a favorite topic of mine in my formative years. I wanted to believe his stories and his testimonies, but I was held back by the fact that he was so eager to accept everything he was told without asking questions. Sometimes I would watch his stuff when he took a break. Sometimes I managed to do more than keep an eye on his stuff. I sold a few of his things for prices that were higher than he ever got when he was selling them. He sold his stuff for whatever price his customers offered him. He just wouldn't set a price and insist on it, or even bargain. When asked "How much for this?" he would just say, "Whatever your heart wants to offer." I had his lasting gratitude, but I never got a straight answer on why he did what he did. And what does one call this behavior? I can understand charity and I can understand business, but what my monk friend was doing had me baffled. I couldn't even tell whether he was spiritually advanced or psychologically stunted. But, it didn't matter, because I thought he was a humble man and I admired what was difficult for me to be. Later in my life, I visited Mount Athos and heard the same miracle stories from the monks up there.

When I was about fifteen, I started searching for other, more earthly and more loving understandings of God. I left my neighborhood Sunday school and found another one downtown Athens, at Saint Constantine and Helen's church, the Metropolis, near Syntagma Square, where I felt the Word of God wasn't taken literally, but in context and with more emphasis on God's love and reason. It took me awhile, but eventually the love of God was made clear in my life. Later, I would experience some very strange coincidences, or, what I have come to believe were, acts of Providence, which eased my life toward outcomes that I had no right to hope for, or kept me from falling into one of the many pits that one should avoid in life.

Searching for miracles during the years of the occupation was always a hunt for the trapdoor out of our dungeon. If a miracle broke through our bleak reality, there would be no need for fearing the barbarians around us anymore. I never lost hope or tired of that search. Holy monks were seen at the same time in different places; sailors lost at sea surfaced and appeared to their loved ones and foretold the demise of our enemies; the iconographer across the street from our house swore that a saint visited him in the very room where he was painting and immortalized him by painting exactly what he saw. The strange, the extraordinary, the incomprehensible gave me hope. Wasn't that a miracle?

22 • Wheeler-dealers and Free Lunch Seekers

Profit is sweet, even if it comes from deception.

Sophocles

We weren't looking only for miracles. There were other events we flocked to -- accidents, fights, arrests, disturbances at queues for cigarettes, which sometimes stretched out for a couple of blocks in the neighborhood, longer than queues for beans or even meat and bread. And there were places that we had to go to stay alive, such as the soup kitchen of our school district. I must have been in the second or third grade when I started going to the District Commons Meals all by myself. I would go there with my tin cup, stand in line for as long as it took, and get my slice of bread, some bean or lentil soup and half a dozen olives. Sometimes, there was also a little piece of smoked herring or a couple of sardines pickled in brine. You had to be on your toes to keep your place in the queue, and you had to defend your portion after you got it, fighting the bullies, if it came to that. You couldn't allow anyone to get ahead of you because the bread or the olives or even the soup could run out just before your turn came. You had to avoid contact with other kids, most of them dirty, some with open sores or sick looking, if you didn't want to catch lice and infections. You had to be aware of everything happening around you. You had to learn how to read intentions on people's faces, so you could be ready for the actions that might follow and you could never afford to relax and trust that all would turn out the way you hoped. You had to read gestures, signals, sudden perturbations in the air that might precede an outburst. Wars make people suspicious, mistrusting and painfully aware of how fickle reality is and how tenuous life can be. Who would attack and what would he go after? These were details. If you have your cup full and your bread at hand, you are a target, and you need to know that you will be vulnerable. You go on alert because everything can change for the worse in a split second. Reflex defenses become part of your being, your way, your psychic armor. And, once you get that armor on, if the time comes when it is no longer needed, you are stuck with that pile of junk. It takes years to get out of it and trust people again. Survivors must also pay. But, survival is a needed art and everyone tries to master it. Little Beggar was probably the most adept in it among us. But even he could slip up and find himself in peril.

One day we heard that some angry customers trapped Little Beggar in the yard of a shop that sold flagstones, tombstones and other stones and ceramic tiles. We all thought that he got into trouble protecting his stash of cigarettes aggressively as he was known to do. I don't recall why all of us, Rebels and Warriors, rushed to find out what would happen to him. Perhaps, some of us wanted to help him, but didn't declare our intentions. Did we go there to defend the business interests of a shrewd operator, or to watch him get his comeuppance? I think, curiosity got us there: we couldn't afford to miss how this master of trades, tricks and inventions would manage to get away again. The angry customers told anyone who asked that the Beggar was a dirty, little thief. They had found out how Little Beggar was getting all these cigarettes he sold and were seething with anger. The word was out: Little Beggar was making his smokes out of butts he picked up from the streets of Athens. His loyal customers didn't appreciate paying for the singed, spit-spattered butts that other smokers tossed and often stepped on. We knew right away Little Beggar was in trouble.

Apparently, the smokers had never bothered to ask how Little Beggar was able to get generic cigarettes and sell them as cheap as he did. They must have thought of themselves as clever, or lucky and enjoyed their cigarettes until they felt some gravel at the tips of their tongues or crunched some dirt and, horrified, stopped puffing away. But how did these idiots think Little Beggar was coming up with cigarettes so cheap? Could they have believed that he stole cigarettes regularly, or that he grew tobacco in his backyard and processed it in his finished basement using German machinery? They were getting generic cigarettes, not Lucky Strikes or Chesterfields, but even so they should have known that something was wrong with the enterprise. *Caveat emptor*, gents!

Under Little Beggar's direction, Vouss, Goose and who knows who else, had been working day and night gathering butts, extracting the unburned tobacco from them and rolling cigarettes from that messy bulk with fresh paper. A little saliva, perhaps, a trace of singed tobacco, or a speck of dirt from pure Athenian soil should have been expected. But they had faithful users of these cigarettes for a long time, why did they discover the deception now? Those of us who had nothing to do with the making or selling of these cigarettes felt disgust with their enterprise, pity for the besieged Beggar, and, I cannot hide it, some admiration for the entrepreneurial genius of the rascal. Thinking of Little Beggar sandwiched between two granite slabs I might have laughed to tears, if there was time for such amusement. But his customers were enraged and getting closer. We sprang into action, determined to find the little creep and save him from his pursuers. We started with deception, yelling and arguing among ourselves as we backed ourselves inside the stone and mosaics yard and scattered in all directions to find and help the Beggar out of the jam he was in.

He was curled up like a fetus and trembling with fear on the upper level of one of the large flagstone bins in the yard. He looked at us with suspicion, still holding onto his head as if to protect it from blows that might land on it at any moment. We might be the ones who had come to grab him and hand him over to his ex-customers. The Abyssinian grabbed him by the shoulders and yanked him out of his roost. The rest of us bunched up around him, engulfed him in our midst, and like one, huge, hand-flailing, multi-legged blob of humanity run for the back fence-wall of the stone yard, slithered up over it, and poured out toward the woods at the First Cemetery's *terra incognita*. It would be a long time before Little Beggar could show his face among the smokers of the neighborhood. But Athens is a big city with many neighborhoods where people didn't have a clue about the content of the cigarettes Little Beggar sold, and he and his associates could ply their products. We lost no time celebrating the liberation of one of our own, weaving truths and tales to create legends with laughter and jokes as all clans do to commemorate their battles.

We didn't see Little Beggar for a long time after this fiasco. One day Vouss brought us news of his latest survival maneuvers. Little Beggar had always been an entrepreneur, and sometimes a beggar. Then, we heard that he had switched and become a con man playing the role of a starving child just as the newspapers were reporting some kids had to do in the streets of downtown Athens. Vouss said he regularly faked a starving boy and passed out at some intersection in downtown Athens, so that passersby would come to his aid and give him something to eat or some money to feed himself and live. Apparently the con had been going on for some time, when some German soldiers run into him and took pity on him. They picked him up and took him to their barracks, where they brought him back to his senses and fed him. He presented such a grateful face to the soldiers that they wanted to befriend him. In time they gave him a job shining boots, and Little Beggar was delighted.

"The bastard is a regular employee of the damn occupation army," Vouss would repeat on every occasion Little Beggar's name came up. But we couldn't tell if he was angry with his buddy or just a little jealous of him.

When Little Beggar showed up in the neighborhood again, he was beginning to gain weight and was happy with his steady job. To prove that he wasn't turning into some kind of collaborator, however, he bragged about all the things he had stolen from the Germans, like cigarettes and chocolates and uniform metal buttons. He took some cigarettes and some buttons out of his pocket and showed them to us. Then he passed around a fistful of candy and said he knew something important and wanted to pass it around to us. "The end is near," he said, but refused to explain how he knew that. We didn't know what to make of all that, but we were glad that Little Beggar was alive and still thriving. Somehow, his condition was a metaphor for ours

23 • The Alcazar Stalemate

> You have to learn the rules of the game. And then you have to
> play better than anyone else.
>
> **Albert Einstein**

A few days after the demise of Little Beggar's Tobacco Enterprises, we heard that a gang from the hill of Ay-Yannis, north of us, was coming down to our neighborhood "to get even with Vouss and his friends." These were older kids with a reputation for trouble. There were rumors that Vouss and Little Beggar were doing business with the Ay-Yannis gang and something went wrong. We all thought that our two sharpies had taken the Ay-Yannis gang to the cleaners, but no one was sure. Zervas – no relation to the right-wing general Napoleon Zervas, who was fighting the Germans up in the mountains of Epirus, in northwestern Greece – sent three of his toadies to find Vouss and Little Beggar and arrange for a meeting. Our neighborhood gangs were playing at war without real stakes, but this bunch from Ay-Yannis was at war with anyone who didn't serve their real life interests. Vouss, Little Beggar and some of their buddies weren't exactly pious acolytes; they joined us and were sometimes participants in our little games, but they were into other games, shady deals, perhaps, dangerous enterprises that we knew nothing about. We suspected that the Tobacco debacle was just the tip of the iceberg. We had to clarify our position and take a stand before Zervas and his gang descended upon us. We found Vouss and told him to bring Little Beggar with him so we can find out what the deal with Zervas was.

Little Beggar, Vouss and Goose showed up and told us that the Ay-Yannis gang was their partner in the cigarette-making business. They had a whole bunch of their younger kids roaming the streets of Athens, hotels, bust stations and picking up cigarette butts. They turned their butts to our entrepreneurs and received from them a percentage of the cigarettes that were produced. Depending on the quality of the butts collected, the percentage of cigarettes they received for the butts varied. Little Beggar said that this gave the butt collectors an incentive to find bigger and better preserved butts, than they would have received from just giving them so many cigarettes for so many butts. Right away we all knew why Zervas was after them: the exchange rate of cigarettes for butts was left in the hands of Little Beggar, and they didn't trust him.

"So, why did they get so pissed off now?" Andonis asked.

Little Beggar chose his words carefully. "After the troubles we had around here, we decided to upgrade the quality. We made fewer smokes from the butts we got and we gave Zervas and his people fewer smokes." He stopped.

"They didn't like that at all!" Vouss growled.

"Did you discuss this with them?" someone put in.

"They would have none of it. They demanded the same rate of exchange no matter what," Little Beggar went on. "We told them that we would have to stop the whole business, if they insisted."

"And?" asked Andonis.

"And they told us they'd come down here and raise hell, if we changed the old agreement," was Little Beggar's reluctant reply.

We exchanged a few thoughts on our predicament, but the decision was obvious. Even if we chose to do nothing to protect our two troublemakers, something no one had the desire to do, we couldn't stop the Ay-Yannis gang from making us their vassals. The gang of Zervas was in no mood for clarifications and negotiations when it came to protecting their vital interests. And we were in no mood of becoming slaves. Without much discussion we started organizing for battle. When necessity bumps reason aside, the gods of war are dancing like devils.

With remarkable naïveté, we all sat at the stoop of Kortessis and sanded our wooden rifles and bayonets, sharpened our pocket knives, dusted mock helmets and told stories of heroes who won great battles against the Persians and the Turks and against all odds. I prayed for protection and victory, so we could have peace in the end. I went home, donned my Greek army helmet, the best helmet anyone could find, strapped my shiny army bayonet from a makeshift belt and was ready for a real do-or-die battle in the streets. But my mother had got wind of the war preparations and was watching me like a hawk. She caught me as I was heading out fully armed and dragged me back to the house.

"Get rid of the sword," she said. I was weighing the costs of disobeying and dashing out of the house, when she fired her second command, this time for effect, as they say: "If you take that thing out in the streets, you'll have to deal with your father."

That was one of her most effective ultimatums, and she used it with unfailing results when the end of discussion had been reached. Reluctantly, I obeyed.

"And that helmet is too big for your head. It can hurt you, rather than protect you."

She was right about the helmet. I didn't want to wear it at a time when I might have to move stealthily, or run, or duck under something, but I didn't know how to face my friends who knew of my helmet and were envious of me when I had shown it to them. What would I tell them? The helmet is no damn good for battle? I couldn't say that! My mother gave me a good excuse, so I ditched the helmet in a hurry and emerged from the house holding only my wooden rifle with its slingshot, determined to fight just as fiercely as if I was a Greek guerrilla ready to hit Nazis.

I don't know how news spreads in a crisis, but there is no doubt every question asked, somehow, generates several answers, and the best of them are repeated more often than the rest, until they are the only answers given, and reality takes shape slowly out of rumors.

We were told that everyone who wanted to fight should gather outside the Alcazar, our open-air movie theater in the neighborhood. After years of abandonment, the Alcazar was just an empty lot, with a six-foot stone-and-mortar wall fence around it and a couple of boarded doorways. Inside this corral of bygone love scenes, horror pictures, dramas and comedies, thistles and weeds were growing wild, and only the ruin of the projection tower was left to signify its long gone golden era.

Though more than half a century has passed, I remember the approaching confrontation with its anxiety and excitement. I was alert to everything around me and ready to act. Something was going to happen, but no one knew what. The Warriors gathered at the stoop of my house, because it was close to Alcazar, and waited for orders to join the battle. We expected that Vouss would be in command of all those who came to the defense of the leaders of the Tobacco Enterprise and the neighborhood. We heard that Vouss was making decisions and giving orders like a general, but we had heard nothing from him. Wasn't he going to give us an inspiring explanation before sending us to battle? When would he tell us what we were fighting for, besides protecting their interests? He showed no interest in explaining or inspiring or strategizing with us. He showed no interest in us, yet we were there for him and Little Beggar and those close to them. We blew that off, saying that our leader was Andonis and he would be the one to tell us where the Warriors would fight and when. String Bean, Koula and the Abyssinian were present as well as some of the other Rebels, but it wasn't clear that they would follow Andonis' commands. After waiting for some time and hearing nothing, Andonis decided to send the Abyssinian to Alcazar to find out from Vouss himself what was the plan for us. Everyone was relieved when the Abyssinian accepted this key assignment without objection.

We were restless, making suggestions on how to proceed and asking questions that produced answers of uncertain value. When the Abyssinian got back, he reported that some older guys, most of them Vouss' buddies he had never seen before, were inside Alcazar, waiting for Zervas and the Ay-Yannis gang to attack. They wanted us to stay outside and attack the invaders from behind, when they went after them inside Alcazar. "We are the extra hammer," the Abyssinian announced with pride.

Andonis smiled. "Somebody must know about the battle of Marathon," he mumbled to himself. We heard, but didn't understand. We were too young to have studied that historic battle, but the time would come.

At first, no one questioned the orders. They made sense. Armies often have some strategy that is clever, unexpected, and often wins the battle. That's what the Athenian general Miltiades had done at Marathon, when he beat the Persians in 490 BC, and what the Great admiral Themistocles did in Salamis when he beat the Persians at sea in 479 BC, and the great Theban general Epaminondas had done in the battle of Leuctra against the Spartans in 371 BC. And so on.

But then, someone asked why should we fight, at all. The consensus was that, if we don't, the Ay-Yannis gang could intimidate and harass us for having lost the war. Someone said that we couldn't lose a war, if we didn't fight in that war. The rest of us had to straighten him out: you lose wars by not engaging a vicious enemy, we said.

Then it was my turn to object to this war on moral grounds. "But we didn't do anything wrong to anyone," I said, somehow feeling the searing injustice of the situation. Are we responsible for all the stupid things our friends choose to do?"

"Vouss and the Beggar fleece the Ay-Yannis gang, and we end up paying for it," mumbled Beanpole, lending his support to me.

"Sometimes we fight, to protect the future," said Andonis and we started discussing the details of the pending action. We weren't sure how to fight a battle that had as its purpose to hurt other people. Would we have to aim and strike their bodies and their heads, injuring their eyes with our rocks, instead of throwing tin can "bombs" and rocks at the walls of each other's house? Did we want to draw blood and maim other people? And, were we ready to get hit by rocks and bleed or be maimed for the rights of wheeler-dealers to make more profit in their business?

"We should have talked about all that stuff before, " said Kefalas. "There is no time anymore."

Some of us had second thoughts and didn't want to engage in a war without hard evidence of wrongdoing by the Ay-Yannis gang. Why should we believe what Little Beggar and Vouss told us? But Vouss and Goose and Little Beggar were with us, part of the neighborhood, and we owed them our help. We *had* to go and use whatever weapons we were carrying. Suddenly my wooden riffle with the elastic band that required great patience and lots of concentration to prepare the slingshot so it could shoot a pebble fifty feet at a stationary target seemed totally inadequate in the furor of a battle with bodies in frenzied motion. I thought about my bayonet, and was glad I had left it back home. It didn't seem right to take it along and not use it; and it would be wrong to slash people in the heat of battle for no clear reason. Raising the bayonet against another human being at arm's length away could be more deadly to me than to anybody else, if I didn't have the stomach for using it. Perhaps, very few people have that kind of stomach, and that's why guns are used from far away, and bombs are dropped from distant airplanes, and missiles are fired from thousands of miles away. When you are far away, you can't see the fear in the eye of a man or the blood from the cuts you make on children's bodies.

As zero hour approached, Andonis became very agitated. He started pacing near the stoop, as if he had to travel some distance before getting rid of the load he was carrying. We knew he didn't get rattled very easily, so we sat and waited to hear what the result of his thinking would be. Then he told us what he had decided how we might want to act.

"Vouss and his buddies are inside a fortress, but we are out here in the open, and we'll face the Ay-Yannites with our bodies exposed to anything they throw at us." He paused and waited for our response, but there was none. "We'll wait here before we attack anyone," he said with authority. "No one moves from this stoop, unless I say so," he added, looking at everyone around him in succession. "We'll fight to defend ourselves or to protect our friends, if they cannot do so on their own. But we won't fight to beat the Ay-Yannites and win this war for them." He paused. "Does everyone agree?" All of us said yes, and the plan was accepted.

We waited for something to happen. We waited for what seemed to be an hour or half a day. And then, the Ay-Yannis gang appeared two blocks away, marching with a steady clip, toward the Alcazar. We could hear drums signaling their approach. None of our people moved. We waited for Andonis' command. Then, we saw Vouss up on the projection tower of the theater, wielding a brick and threatening to throw it in the direction of the enemy. Vouss and his buddies had taken the high ground up on the tower and behind the fence walls surrounding the Movie Theater and appeared to be invulnerable.

Zervas, wearing a long, khaki army coat was leading the Ay-Yannites with two commanders at his sides. Next to the commanders we could make out two drummers driving the beat of battle through our hesitant warriors, the would-be hammer of the upcoming battle, according to Vouss' plan. Their leaders had helmets on and seemed ready for action. More than a couple of dozen kids followed in triangular formation behind Zervas, his commanders and the drummers. They were older, a menacing crowd, waiving sticks and clubs, shouting and coming ever closer toward the Alcazar and us. They were close enough to the theater when Zervas raised his hand. They all stopped and the street was silent.

"Come down Little Beggar, and we'll settle things, right now!" Zervas shouted, cupping his hands, and pointing toward the projection tower.

Andonis raised his hand. "Stay put," he ordered.

Vouss raised his arm and lobbed a brick like a discus thrower at Zervas and his gang. Others got ready to throw their rocks and bricks and strike the invaders, and drive them back to where they came from. The brick landed on the ground ahead of Zervas doing no damage.

Then something no one had expected took place: Zervas- opened his long coat took out a gun from his holster and brandished it once and fired straight at Vouss. At the burst of gunfire, all of us at the stoop fell to the ground.

"Stay down!" cried Andonis.

We saw Vouss and his gang changing position and throwing bricks at the Ay-Yannis gang. More gunshots were fired, but I couldn't tell where they came from. Vouss abandoned his post, ran down the stairs and disappeared from view. Someone fired a gun from the Alcazar. Little Beggar, Goose and others inside the theater climbed down from the projection tower, abandoned the wall fence and run. We couldn't see what was happening inside the theater, but we saw them coming out a back door and running for their lives. We watched the Ay-Yannis gang turn back. We couldn't understand why they didn't rush the Alcazar. We also turned and ran back toward the stoop of Kortessis.

Some of us thought that Zervas felt he had won and decided to withdraw. When we had all calmed down a bit, we discussed in detail the battle that never took place. Everybody had a point of view and wanted to be heard and get the approval of the group for his brilliant insight. No one dared to say that we had just been part of a sound rout. No one wanted to be tagged as a coward, but we were all agreed that going up against a real gun with our wooden swords and clothespin slingshots was madness, and we weren't crazy.

Later that day we found out that one of the Ay-Yannis kids was hurt and one of his ears was bleeding. Zervas had taken him to the clinic in somebody's truck.

"Maybe the Ay-Yannites didn't win, after all," Kefalas said with glee.

"Nobody should mess with Little Beggar!" piped Beanpole. Everyone agreed that Little Beggar was a very cunning character and Vouss was his weapon.

Andonis was quiet for a long time. Then he got up and said he had some homework to do. "I hope that Zervas believes that he won," he said and walked away.

We were somber after that and the gathering broke up.

Someone named this encounter the "Alcazar Stalemate," and we were all happy to have been eyewitnesses to it. We became convinced that we had a just cause to fight and would have defended bravely our neighborhood, if we had to. We were proud of our leader, Andonis, and praised his wise decision to hold back and avoid unnecessary harm. Our heroic stance, we thought, was similar to the struggle of the Greek army when it encountered the panzers and the mechanized might of the Third Reich up in the freezing cold of Macedonia's mountains. We had bonded with each other as soldiers do in battle, and had a story to tell to anyone who wanted to hear it. The outcome of that stalemate made little difference to our life in the streets, which was always treacherous and challenging, but not as dangerous as it would have been, if Zervas and his gang had ever come to believe that they lost that battle.

We never knew what was going to happen next. Uncertainty in the real world made our days feel like random snapshots from dreams. We could have a quiet afternoon playing marbles with skill, or feel the thrill of gambling for bottle-caps or cigarette box-tops, or the street could be invaded by a herd of hungry youths from other neighborhoods looking for food, or fall under the boots of a squad of Nazi goons, looking for contraband, or rounding up suspected communist guerrillas for some atrocities that they or some of their comrades committed somewhere else in the city. Whatever happened, the anxiety of coping with the ever-changing rules set by people with power stuck in my mind like a bloodsucker on a milk-white leg. We had no external resources, and no way of making things go our way, so we grew antennae to sense the smallest change in the shape of reality around us and respond to it instantly to avoid harm. Being careful, deliberate, planned, thoughtful or considerate was dangerous because people with such qualities were slowed down, became vulnerable and got hurt. It just didn't pay to make plans of action in the streets, because anything could happen to upend them, and often did, and any plans, to be useful, have to be updated, a hard thing to do when change is rapid and unpredictable.

By the time the war ended, most of us had been terrified by unexpected explosions somewhere near our homes; we had heard the rattle of machine guns, seen them spew white streaks of fire in the night; and, when the fratricides started after the occupation, we would be there to see the government fighter planes hunt down the communists, strafing the streets of our neighborhood and dropping brass bullet shells on our rooftops and terraces by the thousands; we would feel our hearts explode when mortars landed in the streets with a deafening noise and dug holes and shattered glass from a hundred windows at once, and we had to run or crawl under something to escape from the madness, looking for someone we knew or were close to for shelter. It was time for a prayer, time to let go and let God help us with living.

And when one horseman of the Apocalypse passed, another one would gallop toward us to taunt and harass us in a new way. Many of us had seen slender figures of skin and bones stumbling and falling down and dying on the streets. I saw people hanging out of street car doors like bunches of grapes, and one was pushed out and fell down on the street; I saw sick beggars in public squares display their bare legs with boils and open sores and buzzing flies to collect a few alms and live another day. There were crimes and misdemeanors and accidents that spread cruelty and callousness and took a toll upon everyone. Our peaceful streets turned into battlefields when tanks roared a block away from our homes, their turrets slewing and their guns pointing menacingly, searching for moving flesh. And, there were illnesses, rare for the Athens area, that plagued us in tandem with the colds and stomachaches: Andonis' mother was near death with Typhoid fever for a month, and my mother was at her bedside most of that time, while my father argued with her and shouted at her to stay away, or risk getting sick, also; shortly after that my mother suffered from Melitensis Fever and almost died. Hepatitis of some kind that turns the skin yellow like gold (the Greeks call it "the Golden") ravaged the kids in the neighborhood, especially kids in the shacks that were never included in our gangs because they were dirty and had red eyes and boils and stunk.

When I fell sick with the Golden, my father accused me of not being careful of the company I kept. I was too sick to feel bad for any additional evils I might have committed, and my mother agreed. When I wasn't sick, the round-the-clock alertness made me edgy, anxious and wore me out. The toll wasn't apparent just then; it took years to realize that the world isn't always a battlefield, or a jungle, and there are people around who didn't want to take advantage of my weaknesses, my errors and my trust. Years later, I learned that there are more war casualties than there are dead and wounded in battle. They are the non-combatants, who get touched by war and end up twisted or broken by it. It took me over a decade to get used to sudden noises around me and not be startled, and half a lifetime to trust anyone other than my immediate family.

Some years after the war ended, I heard that one of the guys in the neighborhood was serving as a lieutenant in the army. I never found out why, but I learned that a soldier with a grudge against him threw a grenade in his barracks room and blew him up. Such a world has no joy, and it's a sad, gray world to inhabit. Zervas never learned how to live in a peaceful world and the last time someone pointed him out to me, he was drifting aimless like a parasite looking for a host in downtown Athens. I often wonder what happened to Stellian, the kid that no one wanted to have in his team because he was slow in everything he did, but we ended up including him in our games because we felt guilty as if we were the cause of his problem. I never heard how Goose fared with his disabilities after the war. Beanpole took over his father's printing press, and was busy printing forms and pamphlets for businesses. He was sipping coffee at a small sidewalk café in Lamentations Square, downtown Athens when I met him many years later, and looked quite content with the routines of his life. He seemed to come to life as we remembered the battles we fought in the neighborhood and the fun we had learning how to survive. I thought he was ready to go back there and start living again those long gone days. He told me that he was getting ready for the annual pilgrimage to the island of Tenos, to worship there and bow down at the icon of the Holy Mary, the Miracle Worker, known throughout Greece.

In spite of the hard times we had and the scars we were left with, I don't think that our world was as cruel, as vicious and as deadly as the world described in the papers and the TV nightly news, today. We, at least, knew that the dire need for sustenance was the cause of most violence. Evil seemed to have some rational explanation, and reality was more understandable than it is now. Perhaps, the evils we never experienced but want to avoid at all costs anyway by isolating ourselves from those who endure them, are more threatening than the evils we experienced bonded with others.

24 • My Mother and the Arvanites

My mother, Marina Laskos, was born in Eleusis, a coastal city like Aigion, but only ten miles from Athens. Eleusis was home of the Eleusinian Mysteries, the sacred rite for the celebration of spiritual insight that served the needs for transcendence of the Ancient Greeks for almost a millennium. Though many people tried to find out exactly what took place during the ceremonies of the Mysteries no one ever succeeded. We do know that it involved a ceremony of purification in honor of goddess Demeter and her daughter Persephone and some kind of participation in a ritual. To become initiated, one had to speak Greek and not be a murderer. People who didn't speak the language made *bar-bar* noises in the mind of the Greeks, so they called them barbarians. They wanted to state in no uncertain terms that the initiated people or *mystae* should be law-abiding, civilized people. My mother had no interest in the history of the institution but talked instead about the rape of Persephone by Pluto and the grief of her mother, Demeter, which provided the underpinnings of the Mysteries. The initiates had to sacrifice a pig and cleanse themselves in the blue waters of the Mediterranean. Unlike my father, my mother loved the sea.

My mother was a free spirit, living in the moment and open to the joys and sorrows life brings to all of us. She could be fuming with anger at one moment and laugh like a child the next. I don't ever remember her holding a grudge for anyone all the years I knew her. She was content with what she had, while hoping for the best for everyone. "As long as I have some bread and a little feta, I'm happy," she would say to me. She should have added that she also needed her two children and her husband around her and, in later years, a cigarette now and then. She was a dreamer, forever surprised by the real world, but never intimidated by it. Every day came with hope in my mother's mind, and no one could cast a heavy shadow upon it. My mother was a grasshopper!

Perhaps, I can capture my mother's way of dealing with the world by mentioning some specific examples. My mother's way of playing the lottery was totally different from my father's way. Every year, my mother, bought all the "Editors' Lottery" tickets she could afford. The prizes for this lottery were about a dozen buildings, among them houses, luxury apartments and a grand apartment building in a posh location of Athens. From the moment my mother bought her lottery tickets, she dreamed of the mansion she was going to win and live in for the rest of her life. She spent several months living the dream of the winner, and never thought about losing, until the lottery had ended and the winners' photographs had appeared in the newspaper. Then she rejoiced vicariously with the people who won.

She was an optimist, never giving a second thought to the problems that many actions bring along, hoping that solutions would be found, somehow. And she was willing to take some risks to get where she wanted to go. She is, for example, the only close family member from Greece who visited my family and me, here in America. She took the risk of a transoceanic voyage, even though she spoke no English, had very little money for the trip and had no idea what surprises America held for her. She was irrepressible and never gave in to adversity, a trait that helped keep my father functioning until he got a stable job, until the war ended without us starving to death, until he could build another house and wipe out the guilt he felt from losing their first house . . .

When she was close to death from leukemia, I asked my mother, if she was afraid of dying. She looked at me calmly with a faint smile, her eyes still shining with optimism through the pain that ravaged her face: "I've got my little satchel ready for the trip," she said. "There is nothing to be afraid of. My 'dearest Jesus' will be there to welcome me."

She was an affectionate person and enjoyed people's company without regard to their social standing. She enjoyed talking to the poor gypsy woman who stopped by our house a couple times a month for alms, as much as she did talking with the grocer, the butcher and the pharmacist. She could crack a joke with soldiers, doctors and priests and never hesitated expressing her opinions in any circle she happened to find herself, including the group of intellectuals that gathered at the house after my sister came back from her studies in France and started writing poetry. When I visited my parents at home, after living in America for many years, all I had to do to get the best possible service from anyone in the new neighborhood where they lived, was to tell them that I was Kyra-Marina's son. She was everyone's friend, and no one's enemy.

Mother was very smart, but not very sophisticated. She was a voracious reader of romance novels, probably because they were readily available, and no one took the time to guide her into more enduring literature. She was a superb artist in embroidery, needlepoint, knitting and other arts and crafts. I know that she also liked sewing and would have enjoyed making some of our clothes as well, but that required a sewing machine, and we couldn't afford one. I brought some of her beautiful tablecloths, table runners and other artwork to America to remember her by.

More than anything else however, my mother wanted to study French with the Catholic nuns in the island of Paros, after she finished eighth grade. Unfortunately, her father refused to allow any of his three daughters to go to any school beyond the eighth grade. His stubborn refusal broke her heart. She talked many times with sadness about the dream that didn't come true, but I never heard her blame anyone for it.

She was the last daughter left at home with her parents when her father fell sick for a long time and she took care of him like a nurse. Sometimes she recalled lovingly and with sadness the days when she was his caretaker, as he was dying. I wish I had been able to feel her disappointment and sadness, but I was too young to know. It took many years of experiencing life's injustices and sorrows to get a taste of my mother's grief and leave the chauvinism of that stunted culture behind.

My mother was inquisitive and would always ask me to explain some of the things I was learning in my high school classes. She was eager to learn new things and ready to tackle problems that she had never encountered before. If I ever had a puzzle that everybody in my class was trying to solve, my mother would get right into it as if that was a job needing immediate attention.

Over the years, she became my resident tutor, helping my friends and me with the preparations for our final exams. She would hold the history textbook, or the religion textbook or the geography textbook, and ask us questions to make sure we knew all that was required to excel. She was a stickler for details and more patient than she was with her normal work. She would dictate to us Homer and Lysias and other Ancient Greek texts to make sure we could spell and translate the text in accordance with the translations we managed to find. She also had a chance to dictate to us from our French textbooks, and I could tell that she was dreaming of being far away in that Aegean island where dreams come true and people converse with the French nuns. She had a great sense of pronouncing the language and could even understand some of it. I would tease her at times, telling her that she was ahead of the rest of us when it came to languages. Wasn't she bilingual after all, since she could speak fluent Arvanitika, a form of Albanian, spoken by the Arvanites in Greece? She would laugh, shove me away from her and tell me to go take a walk in Siberia.

My mother was an *Arvanitissa* (a woman with *Arvanites* in her family roots; *Arvanitis*, being the word for the male gender, singular, and *Arvanites* for the general group of male and female persons, in the plural). So, I ought to say a few words about the Greek *Arvanites*, who may be more Greek than many Greeks with no ethnic designation, yet they are not always recognized as such by uneducated Greeks. The Arvanites of Greece are very different from the Albanians, i.e. the citizens of Albania today. The Arvanites have been citizens of Greece for hundreds or, as some say, thousands of years. According to Aristides Kollias, who wrote a history of the *Arvanites*, they are the original Pelagians who populated Greece and the surrounding terrain, as far as Central Italy, Sicily, Asia Minor and the northern coast of Africa in pre-historic times. Others identify *Arvanites* with the ancient Illyrians, one of the many ethnic groups inhabiting Greece, who came to Greece in ancient times. The Illyrians were a mountain-dwelling people, in the north of the Greek province of Epirus and in the area of present-day, southern Albania.

They came south to central Greece, where they displaced the Vlaques (probably of Rumania) who occupied Thessaly, and were an agricultural, peasant people. These *Arvanites* were a tough, unruly and warlike ethnic group that gave priority to the perpetuity of their ethnic group and its dominance among the other ethnic groups they encountered. They also preserved their own language, *Arvanitika*, a variant of modern Albanian, without any written records, and spoke it whenever they were among themselves.

The influx of Arvanites grew in the 14th century A.D., when they were welcomed to Greece as guardians of forts and cities by the Venetians, Franks and other Western hegemons of various parts of Greece who needed soldiers for their protection. They settled mostly in Attica, where Eleusis is, in the island of Euboea, the islands on the Saronic Gulf, south of Athens, and in the Peloponnese. In time, they developed a Greek national consciousness and became the fiercest warriors in the War of Independence that liberated Greece from the Ottoman Turks, after 400 years of occupation, in 1821.

The *Arvanites* became famous for their heroic deeds on land and at sea against the Turks. Many military leaders of the Revolution were *Arvanites,* including Kolokotronis, Karaiskakis, Botsaris, Androutsos, Diakos and Kanaris, to mention just a few of them. We heard their names when we celebrated our National holidays, and we read their names in our history books, though I cannot remember a single word about their being anything other than just Greeks. One can also find their names to this day on the streets and squares that were named after them, all over Athens. There are statues for many of these Arvanites in the main squares of Athens. Moreover, eleven of the first fifteen prime ministers of liberated Greece, after 1821, were *Arvanites*!

The Arvanites seemed to thrive on risk-taking and competition in any field they pursued. Besides being great warriors, like my uncle Vassos, or barba Vassos, they distinguished themselves in the arts, like my uncle Orestes, and were shrewd businessmen like my uncle Yannis, my grandmother Marigo and my grandfather Epaminondas, who died before I was born. Many Arvanites were known for their passionate, devil-may-care character that often drove them to leadership positions, and by the mid-eighteen hundreds they comprised the wealthiest socio-economic class of the free city of Athens, as one reads in William Miller's book *The Latins in the Levant*.

I mention these historical details about the Arvanites because the words and deeds of several of my mother's kin, all Arvanites and Arvanitisses, like barba Vassos, uncle Orestes and grandma-Marigo, influenced my development even though I had no idea of the history and character of the *Arvanites* at that time.

I grew up respecting my father's organized and well-reasoned thinking and learned from him the value and dignity of living a stable life as a family man without seeking fame, wealth or glory. At the same time, I felt the attraction of my mother's expansive mind and her zest for life, and admired the guts, the achievements and the adventurous mind of my mother's relatives and the *Arvanites* in general. If it hadn't been for my father's example, I might have had a much harder time settling down to raise a family and enjoy the life of a productive and fulfilled citizen. But, if it hadn't been for my mother's relatives' examples, I might have never aspired to reach as high as I could or take the many risks that satisfied my restless nature. I might have never left Greece for America with eighty dollars in my pocket, or abandoned my engineering career that had become a drain of emotional energy, or launched a new career in working with people and organizations without any credentials, or write books in a language that wasn't my native tongue, or teach management courses at the graduate level without a degree in the discipline and embark upon many other ventures. I inherited enough of my mother's daring-do and, perhaps my paternal grandfather's wildness, to take the many chances I took, and push myself to the limit of my abilities in the careers I pursued. There are many battles to be fought within the self and for a better society in all fields of human endeavor, and warriors are needed to fight them and sometimes win them.

So, my mother was an Arvanitissa, proud of her heritage and her family. When she was with people from her hometown, she spoke *Arvanitika*. All members of her family understood Arvanitika, but not all chose or knew how to speak the language when they were together. I remember trying to learn the language because, it seemed to me, people were less inhibited when they dealt with one another in *Arvanitika* than when they spoke Greek. I never got the hang of it.

25 • Mourning for a Hero

Dirges don't become a hero like our Vassos.
Bring out the clarinet, the lute and the violin
. . . .
Orestes Laskos, Captain Laskos' brother

Finding out what was happening outside Greece during the years of the occupation was very difficult. The Nazis required us to register all our radios, and they "sealed" them, so we couldn't get any shortwave bands outside Greece, which included the BBC broadcasts, that everyone wanted to hear. Failure to register a radio was a serious offense, punishable with jailtime. Of course, there were always people like my grandfather and uncle Paul, who took the risk and found ways to hide their radios so they could listen to BBC broadcasts. In Athens we didn't have a radio at all. My uncle Andonis, the doctor in Eleusis, had a radio that wasn't sealed, because half his house was taken up by German officers, and they wanted to hear the news from every part of the world they could reach via shortawave radio. Now and then there would be some good news, but often there were news we didn't want to hear. Most of what we heard from the German controlled radio stations however was a mishmash of propaganda and boosterism, and there was no way to know the truth.

One day, we heard rumors that barba Vassos and his submarine *Lambros Katsonis*, based in Alexandria, Egypt, were doing great things to win the war. The Greek newspapers reported that there was an accident at the port of Gytheion in the Peloponese, but the rumor was that the submarine *Lambros Katsonis* had sneaked deep behind the Nazi defenses and inflicted serious damage to the German port instalations. That kind of dare-do was pure Vassilios Laskos and, as it turned out after the war, we had guessed right. My parents decided to celebrate the joyous occasion and opened a can of beef and okra for dinner. We had hoped that this was a prelude to liberation.

For my mother liberation had already come, but for my father, it was not yet to be. A few months after the news of the Gytheion strike, possibly by the submarine *Katsonis*, in September 1943, we heard rumors of a Greek submarine missing near the island of Skiathos, and, some said, it was the *Katsonis*, others said it was another sub, the *Papanicolis*, and others yet had it from a good source that it was a destroyer, not a submarine at all. No one in the family knew anything about that vessel for sure, but everyone was worried.

Everyone in the family was worried and they launched a number of frantic searches to find out what happened near Skiathos and what happened to barba Vassos. My mother, her sisters Katina and Noula, her brothers Orestes and Yannis, Nondas' father, and other members of the family would try to glean information from official sources, and when these were exhausted without results, they sought help from agents of the supernatural. They prayed, but they also started hitting the mediums, the card readers and the readers of coffee cup leftovers, the astrologers and anyone else with a pipeline to the real world, through the occult, or the metaphysical and spiritual realms of the universe. For several months, my aunt Sophia's house became the headquarters of the search because of its central location, her managemnt skills and her welcoming attitude. Aunt Sophia knew how to make her house a home for everybody in those long, bleak days.

My mother would drop me off at aunt Sophia's house to play with my cousin Nondas, and, sometimes, another cousin, also named Nondas, Noula's son. Sometimes we would hang around the older cousins, Nondas' sisters Maria and Vivi, and Katina' children, Rena and Omiros, some of whom were University students and had their friends hanging around the house as well. I remember that Maria, a law student at the time, had her own study off the huge spiral stairway that went up to the main part of their house. She had her library there and a desk and chairs and she and her friends would gather there and argue endlessly about Marx and Capitalism and Fascism. I envied my cousin Nondas for the intellectual environment his sister and her friends provided him with and vowed that, if I grew up and had a house, I would try and, at least, build a study like that for myself. Nondas, "the other" Nondas and I would play, and fight and snoop around to overhear what the adults were saying about the submarine and barba Vassos.

In the evening, my mother and the other relatives, who had been looking for news from any source they could get it, would return, and the discussions would begin in earnest: Mrs Sandra was the best medium according to aunt Noula's trusted friend Eleni, and she said that the submarine that sunk was *Katsonis*, indeed, but barba Vassos had fallen into the sea, and though wounded, he swam far enough to be picked up by a fishing boat and escape to the island of Skopelos, where he was sheltered by fishermen. All was well, and he was waiting for naval rescue. This would be contradicted by the most reliable prognosticator, Mr. Aslanian, who was supposed to give very reliable information because aunt Katina's friend, Mrs. Nikolaedes, said that he had helped her find her son who disppeared near Kalavrita in the Peloponese. Her son's body was found among the victims of a massacre in a nearby

village. Mr Aslanian. gave a grim account of what happened. He said
"Commander Laskos fought bravely and was captured by the Nazis. He
is doing poorly as a war prisoner in Germany." Everybody took the
news well: "at least, he is alive," somebody would say in the end, sighing
with relief, and the others would cross themselves and thank God for
that.

It was about that time of maximum effort and worry that my father,
who hadn't participated in the search for supernatural information, had
one of the most significant dreams of his life, as he told us later. The
dream was about a letter that he received, which disturbed him greatly.
The letter wasn't addressed to him. Rather, it was addressed to:

Captain Vassilios Laskos
Eleusis, Greece

But, the name was overwritten with branches of golden, laurel
leaves.

My father was very disturbed by the dream and didn't reveal it to
anyone for several days. He had come to believe that it meant barba
Vassos had fallen heroically on the field of battle. When he finally told
my mother and me, he said that it probably didn't mean anything other
than the fact that he had such a high regard for Vassos that he always
imagined he would die as a hero. He tried to minimize the importance of
his dream and give us hope by emphasizing that there was no date on the
letter, so it could have merely presaged some other time, far into the
future, when Vassos would indeed die as a hero.

The relatives took note of "Petros' strange dream" and his
commentary, but kept their search going at full speed. Vassos was the
pride and joy of the entire family because he was the hope of passion and
freedom others dreamed about. Hope was, once again, needed to keep
going, and they produced it by going to seers and psychics for a fee. But,
they didn't trust anyone's authority to tell them what had happened. They
just wanted news, the good news and the bad news, mixed with the
reputations of the seers and the psychics and with their optimism or
pessimism to shape a message for getting through the day. My mother,
true to her nature, took the most hopeful news and held it in her heart and
wouldn't let it go.

The German occupation of Greece ended in October 1944. A few weeks
later, the Greek armed forces stationed in Alexandria, Cairo, Beirut and
other cities in the Middle East started returning home. On the day that the
naval forces were scheduled to disembark and parade down the Syngrou

Boulevard, one of the grand avenues of Athens, my mother and I were on the sidelines waiting for them to appear. She was several months pregnant at the time and was getting a little slow in moving around, but we arrived at the parade route so fast she was out of breath. Officially, the submarine Katsonis was lost in battle and my uncle was missing in action. That meant little to my mother. She was still hoping to see her brother marching proudly with his crew, or on a wheelchair, being wheeled by his comrades at arms. By that time we had also been looking for him in many places where the POWs were being returned, including those returning from German concentration camps, but we hadn't found any trace of him. No one had heard of a captain Laskos among any group of prisoners. So now we were finally going to see him again, or find out what happened to him from his comrades in the navy. My mother's anticipation was contagious. I was ready to welcome my uncle, waving a little Greek, paper flag on a stick I had made from bamboo for the occasion. I was excited and proud and ready for a celebration.

It was a festive day; the crowds were enthused to see their proud defenders return after more than three years' absence. Greek sailors sunk German boats and ferried troops, and soldiers who fought in Rimini and El Alamein, in Africa. Some died, many were wounded, and the rest were now coming home. People were clapping, screaming, waving Greek flags and shouting the names of their loved ones, who happened to go by. The sailors and officers wearing their ceremonial white uniforms waived and greeted people they recognized. And all these peripheral communications were taking place without any sailor missing a step, or disturbing the tight formations in which they marched.

Suddenly, my mother tensed up and slid under the rope that held back the crowd on the parade route. With me in tow, she made a beeline for the officer who was leading a large formation of junior officers and sailors, his sword held up against his shoulder. I followed my mother as we entered the parade route. The officer raised his arm with the sword up in the air, and the entire procession behind him stopped dead on their tracks and stood at attention.

"Captain Londos," my mother called out to the officer, "Captain Londos, I'm Vassilis Laskos' sister, Marina," she called out, standing now in front of him, barring his progress. She didn't wait for a response. "Can you tell me where is my brother?"

Captain Londos brought the sword back to his shoulder, and greeted my mother with his free hand. "Marina, our Vassilis is not coming with us," he said with gravity. "Captain Laskos died a hero in a naval battle against the Nazis last September. You must be very proud to be a hero's sister, and I salute you!" He bowed slightly and gazed at my mother with affection.

I heard my mother choke an anguished cry with the palm of her hand. "Oh, my God, why?" she managed to utter as she was about to drop and the captain held her, embraced her and steadied her. She drew back, and managed to thank the officer, recovering her composure. She grabbed my hand, turned around, and we sped toward the sidelines, out into the streets that led back to our home.

She was breathing hard as we trudged uphill, but she was in a hurry to get home and I could hardly keep up with her. When we got there, she collapsed on her bed and cried uncontrollably. She cried for a long time. I was afraid that she would never be her old self again, that she would remain sad and sink deep into her grief, forever.

She cried for three straight days, and then she stopped, and never cried for her brother again. She was a Laskos at heart, an *Arvanitissa*, and that's how these proud, passionate people deal with their strong emotions. They let them out, pour them out, until the bile of sorrow and the hatred of death are wrung out, and hope can take root again in their hearts.

Her brother Orestes wrote one of his best poems, "Captain Laskos" after barba Vassos' death. He tells his story to his mother who has lost another son, and consoles her by reminding her that Vassos is now in the company of the other Arvanites heroes of Greece, Miaoulis, Tombazis and Sahtouris. In the excerpt from this poem below, he orders the women who wail at funerals to stop their sad songs, and urges the musicians of Eleusis to raise the roof with joy. Finally he tells his mother the desire of his heart:

> Dirges don't become a hero like our Vassos.
> Bring out the clarinet, the lute and the violin
> My kinsmen from our Eleusis
> And, let's begin the dance of joyful rebels
> This night without end
> Just as it was done when he lived, just as then.
>
> My mother, peasant-woman,
> Kyra Pameinontaina,
> Kyra Marigo,
> I wish I could die like Vassos too.

26 • Barba Vassos in History and in My Mind

A hero is someone who has given his or her life to something bigger than oneself.

Joseph Campbell

Don't be afraid of death so much as an inadequate life.

Bertolt Brecht, *Pelagea Vlasova*

Uncle Vassos, or barba Vassos, as all of us youngsters called him, was my mother's beloved, older brother. (I believe that "barba" means "uncle" in the language of the Arvanites, though I never heard anyone call uncle Orestes barba Orestes). He eventually became a national hero of Greece for his daring, his success in sinking enemy vessels and his heroic death while leading his submarine crew in a pitched battle against a German antisubmarine corvette in WWII. He was a man of great talents and serious flaws, and his life was made up of deeds found in sagas and in tragedies. It is hard to understand how a man who loved life with passion could make so many self-defeating decisions and waste so much of his vitality in fighting for lost causes. But, as the wise Athenian legislator Solon said two and a half millennia before our time, we should "judge no one before his end comes." And uncle Vassos' end was a sacrifice for his country, beyond the call of duty that will live on, redeeming his mistakes.

His name made newspaper headlines on many occasions and my uncle Orestes, the poet, my mother's youngest brother, was often heard reciting his poem on the heroic death of Captain Laskos at the national radio station. At least two books were written about Captain Laskos' daring exploits and his heroic death. City streets and a navy ship were named after him. His portrait hangs in the Greek War Museum in Athens and in the city hall of Eleusis, and his statue stands at the port of Eleusis, his birthplace. He is in full uniform gazing beyond the fray of war at his beloved sea. The reason for dwelling briefly on his life and the history of the times is that his fearless pursuit of goals of great moment, though sometimes misconceived or hastily executed, was heroic and influenced my thinking. What I knew of his life became exemplary for me during my childhood years and my adolescence through the stories my mother told me. I wanted to be like him, rather than anybody else. I never met barba Vassos, but I vaguely remember being held by him once, when I was but a tot and the family had gathered at the family home in Eleusis. He was carrying me in his arms on the main outdoor staircase while everybody was gathered in the flagstone yard, by the old pine tree, looking at us and waving. He stopped, and I looked at the people gathered below us. He looked at me and gently bumped his forehead against mine several times, saying "toff-toff . . . toff-toff . . . toff-toff . . ." Years later, my mother told me that this was the loving way he greeted all the children in our family.

Ever since I was a child I was told that he was a fearless man, who took big risks and accepted responsibility for his actions when he was wrong. I gathered that he craved for independence from rules and regulations of any kind, and I followed his example to risk ridicule and punishment, challenging teachers and fellow students in class on things that mattered to me. Even my father, who was almost the polar opposite of him in style and disposition, liked him and admired him, I thought, more than he admired anyone else in either family or the country.

Relatives used to say that barba Vassos believed he was destined to play a role in the history of Greece and did just that. Later, I learned that my heroic uncle was at times given wholeheartedly to drinking and gambling and promiscuous sex. He was a goodhearted, generous, fearless but flawed man, restless in fulfilling his destiny, as I would find out later, reading about his life. Sometimes I think that there was only one thing that he was afraid of: the life of the common man, who has the courage to built lasting relationships and live with dignity and in peace doing useful work for a lifetime. I believe that uncle Vassos was a lonely man, who found solace either in ephemeral pleasures or in extraordinary undertakings. I hope that he has found peace at last, among extraordinary souls who did ordinary things. Because some of the specific events of his life became guideposts in my early years, I'll give here a brief account of some of these as my mother related them to me, or as they were discussed by relatives in family gatherings or as they were reported in books and newspapers.

My mother would sometimes iron her brother's white naval uniforms, bent over her ironing board, and tell me stories of my uncle when he was a cadet at the Naval Academy of Greece. Once, barba Vassos rebelled against wearing the antiquated long-john underwear that naval cadets had to wear by regulation. He decided to protest by cutting short the long legs and recruited several other cadets to follow his lead. When the head of the Academy realized the organized nature of the rebellious prank, he called a general assembly of the entire class and demanded to know, who was the leader of such a defiant act. According to my mother, "Laskos stood up and admitted that he was responsible for organizing the violation of the rules." When I asked why he cut short the legs, my mother said with defiance matching that which she imagined her brother must have felt, "He just didn't like long underwear!"

Another time, also as a cadet, barba Vassos was supposed to be learning how to use the radio for communications, when he got the fantastic idea to test the effectiveness of the naval defenses of Greece by sounding an invasion alarm for the Greek Naval forces. The entire fleet went on alert, and he admitted that he was the perpetrator of the false alert, so he could be properly punished.

Barba Vassos had shown that he had guts mixed with recklessness and uncompromising honesty long before he went to the Naval Academy. Even in his early years, in grade school, there are stories of his explosive anger and fearless behavior coupled with leadership skills that got him in trouble with other kids and his teachers. In the navy he was known as a considerate leader and an officer who would do anything for the welfare of the people under his command. Unfortunately, as I found out later, my uncle was also a restless and impulsive man. He participated in some ill-conceived political actions that all but derailed his career. He served as the *aide de camp* to the dictator Pangalos in 1925, perhaps, because he was a fellow Arvanitis and couldn't refuse. After the fall of the dictator, he managed to escape prosecution since he was just a military officer following orders, but his career was blemished.

When a right-wing government was elected in 1933 and continued the tradition of partisan politics that divided Greece, some irresponsible right-wing party stalwarts attempted to assassinate Venizelos, the leader of the democrats. In retaliation, the democrats decided to carry out a *coup d'état*. It was 1935 and my uncle had enough of rebellions and dictatorships, and refused to participate in the group of conspirators who were organizing the coup. But, they needed Laskos to succeed. A close friend of his was sent to see him. There was no way to threaten Laskos and he knew it. But, he also knew the way to get to him. "Vassilis Laskos is a brave warrior, not a desk-bound coward," his friend challenged him. I believe that my uncle wasn't sure enough of himself to withstand the scorn and the possible shunning of his peers. So, he joined the rebellious democrats and performed his assigned role, which was to take over, single-handedly, the submarine base of the Greek Navy in Piraeus. He went alone to the base and succeeded in placing it under his command, helped by people who knew and trusted him.

But, as he might say, Lady Luck wasn't on his side that time either, and the coup failed. He did consider standing up once again and taking his punishment as he had done in the past, but an old seadog petty officer in his crew that he consulted, urged him to leave the country. "If all the other mutineers leave the country and the government was left with you only in jail," the old seadog reasoned, "the men in power will take their wrath out on you and execute you."

He took the sailor's advice and decided to leave by ship and ended up in Italy with all the other rebels. As expected, a Navy court martial found him and the other coup leaders guilty of treason *in absentia* and sentenced him to death *twice*. He lived penniless and forgotten for a few months in Italy, until the government pardoned all the instigators of the coup, and he, along with all the other co-conspirators, returned to Greece. His career was finished, and he was left to ponder the rest of his life from his paternal home in Eleusis.

That was the time when he fell in love with Artemis, a young woman from Eleusis he had known for a long time. He wanted to marry her. But grandma Marigo and most other relatives except for my mother, I believe, had serious doubts. Though women held a strong position in the traditional Arvanitic society, and had a say in public issues of the community and even bore arms and inherited the status and privileges of their husbands, thus playing a leading roles in public, my grandmother didn't like Artemis, but no one was sure why.

Artemis was liberated decades before women's lib became a fact of modern life. She had some mannerisms that the old matriarch probably couldn't stomach: she sat with legs spread out and feet planted down on the ground, and smoked cigarettes without letup; she was loud and laughed with a belly laugh that made you turn your head to make sure you weren't responsible for any of that noise. I remember these things because, when I was a teenager, she was one of my mother's friends and she would visit my grandmother's house to chat and play cards with other friends there. I was embarrassed to be around her, but I didn't know why. In time, however, I got used to her style and found out that she was a very kind and friendly person.

My uncle, as I've read in the quasi-biographical book *Vassilis Laskos* by the Greek writer M. Karagatsis, made every effort to overcome his mother's objections, but he couldn't. Grandma Marigo knew what she wanted and could control situations and events to make it happen, even if her son's happiness was at risk. She was a very stubborn and willful woman and nothing could budge her. M. Karagatsis thinks that grandmother wanted her son to marry into a family of some distinction, not a penniless girl from Eleusis like Artemis, not now that they had stripped the gold from his sleeves, and, perhaps, not a girl who was as fearless and brash as she was.

While in Eleusis, barba Vassos worked for Bodosakis, the same wealthy manufacturer that my father worked for. He built a plant for processing rice, and then became the director of that plant. He did a great job in both roles, but he wasn't happy on land. The sea was in his blood and was calling him. He was a sea-faring Arvanitis warrior, like so many other Arvanitic warriors, out of his element in the world of business and family life. He quit his job and looked for a job with a merchant ship. The love affair with Artemis lasted for a few years, but in the end my uncle was unable to overcome the obstacles he encountered, and they split up.

Ever since I learned about this love story, I have been puzzled by my uncle's response to the obstinacy of his mother. How could this great rebel obey his mother's wishes like a compliant schoolboy? Why didn't he just take the risk of doing what he felt was crucial to his life in the hope that his mother would understand in good time and accept his decision? Viewed from the perspective of the Greek culture and, in particular, the culture of the Arvanites, this kind of obedience may have been the rule. After all, my uncle Agesilaos wanted to become a philosopher but was driven by his father's dreams to become a naval officer, which he was, when he was killed in a naval accident soon after he graduated from the naval academy. They tried to force Orestes to become an army officer and sent him to the military academy, but Orestes jumped over the walls and escaped. And wasn't my grandfather the person who refused to allow his daughters to study beyond the eighth grade and all of them obeyed? We look back and find these actions bizarre: how could a man who has the moxie to take over a naval base all by himself as part of a *coup d'état* be such a pushover when his mother doesn't approve of the woman he loves? But some cultures have a hold on people's hearts and minds and we cannot understand what is happening, looking from afar. But, perhaps, barba Vassos didn't want to give up the life of adventure and become a family man and used his mother's opposition as a convenient excuse. The other explanation that has occurred to me is that M. Karagatsis, the author of my uncle's quasi-biography, got it wrong. Perhaps barba Vassos and Artemis had their own problems and the only way they could solve them was to go their own separate ways and my grandmother's displeasure was irrelevant. Who can ever know the secrets of relationships between lovers?

Barba Vassos left Eleusis and hired as a captain of a merchantman around 1939. The war in Europe had started, and he was hired to transport 700 Jews fleeing from Eastern Europe to the Holy Land. He was happy to be back in command of a ship and performed his mission without a hitch. Later he was hired as captain of a merchantman carrying onions from Italy to England. This time they had problems with water leaking into the ship and causing it to list. They pumped water with all the pumps they had, but couldn't stop the leakage. The convoy to which they were attached left their ship behind, and a German submarine spotted it. The German captain allowed the crew to escape into their two lifeboats, and then proceeded to sink their ship. It was after four days of rowing at sea that uncle Vassos and the onion ship's sailors reached land and were rescued. Gradually they found their way back to Greece, which by that time was entering the war against Mussolini's fascist regime.

Barba Vassos wanted to be useful in the war effort, but the royalists were still in control of the government, and he was still not welcome into the ranks of the navy. When the Germans were entering Greece, barba Vassos was still in Athens, trying to get a commission in the Greek Navy. In time, he managed to leave for Cairo where he convinced the navy bureaucrats to restore his commission. They offered him the command of a destroyer, an appropriate assignment for a man of his age and experience. The trouble was that barba Vassos wanted to be a submariner and nothing else. The family legend is that he went straight to the head of the navy, admiral Konstas, who also happened to be an *Arvanitis* from a town near Eleusis, and presented his case. Admiral Konstas tried to persuade him that the assignment he was given was best for his career, that he was too old to be a submariner and that the country needed him to lead a destroyer into battle. The story that the family tells about that fateful meeting between the two *Arvanites* sea-wolves is that "Vassos took out his 45 and threatened to shoot the admiral right there and then, if he refused to assign him to submarines." The family lamented that if he had obeyed and left "that rickety, deathtrap of a submarine" he was finally given he might not have perished with it. But, he didn't obey and got the admiral to agree with him.

Barba Vassos found a rust bucket sitting in the harbor, the submarine *Lambros Katsonis*, assembled a crew, and asked to be given the necessary help in repairing it and taking it out on patrols. The Navy told him that the submarine was unsafe, too unsafe for modern warfare and too expensive to repair; but, he, like his mother, was persistent. He kept pestering the brass until they agreed to help him, just to get him off their hair. The British agreed to give him the technical aid he was asking for, and he and the crew he had selected went to work. After almost a year of hard work under the tropical sun of Egypt, Captain Laskos and his submariners were ready to fight for Greece. But, it wasn't time yet. Someone forgot to secure the submarine when the crew was away, and water flooded it. The submarine they had worked for a year to rebuilt, sunk to the bottom of the harbor. Lady Luck was against him, again. Everyone lost all hope of overcoming that disaster. Everyone, that is, but barba Vassos. He must have blamed himself something awful and wasn't going to rest until he set things right again. Undaunted, he pleaded and begged and got the British who were astounded by his commitment and fervor to assign a crane ship to bring up the submarine from the bottom of the harbor. He threw himself with his loyal crew to the job of restoring the submarine, and in a few months they were ready again.

Captain Laskos took his beloved crew and his submarine, the *Lambros Katsonis*, for their first patrol in 1943. In no time at all they were sinking enemy vessels and terrorizing the enemy troops that occupied the coastal cities of the Peloponnese. That was the fulfillment of his dream. Years later, people who knew him said that they had never seen him happier than when he took command of that submarine and started out on his first patrol. He would ride that submarine, *Lambros Katsonis*, into history and glory and death.

In an interview, in 1995, Captain Elias Tsoukalas, who was the executive officer of the submarine commanded by my uncle, survived and wrote a book about the submarine and its people, titled, *Submarine Y 1: Katsonis*. He said this to the reporter about of my uncle's character and leadership: "Laskos was a brave man. Katsonis men literally adored him and carried out his orders blindly." Then, the reporter asked Captain Tsoukalas to describe the last battle of the submarine Katsonis. The Captain said this:

"Well, while we were patrolling the Skiathos straights, we received a signal saying that a large German troop transporter was about to reach us. The sub was very old and we couldn't stay submerged for long. So, we had to stay on the surface for a long time. This had the result of us being spotted by a German observation station at Trikeri Island. Suddenly we spotted over the periscope a large ship coming on us. We thought it was the troop ship. Instead of the transport ship, however, it was a German sub chaser [a corvette I think], which started immediately launching depth charges. As I said, our ship was old and couldn't last submerged for long. Laskos did not hesitate, never crossed his mind the possibility of surrender: 'To the surface...Prepare for surface battle,' he ordered. Soon, Katsonis was on the surface. The German ship, started firing on us with her guns. A gun shell cut off the gunner's foot. Laskos immediately took his place on the gun. There, uncovered, was trying to give us courage, when suddenly, an enemy shell killed him, granting him a long wished and proud death." (*Source: Hellenicnavy.gr*)

The same source (*Hellenicnavy.gr*) makes the following remark about barba Vassos:

> "The most heroic figure of the Royal Hellenic Navy, during WWII, Commander Vassilios Laskos, Royal Hellenic Navy, was the [last] Commanding Officer of the submarine [Lambros Katsonis]."

The British government archivist William Spencer sent me the following message along with a copy of the lengthy official award citation, when I inquired about my uncle's award from the British government:

> "The decoration your uncle was awarded, was the Distinguished Service Order award from the British Government, which was the second highest award for gallantry during the Second World War, and as such was the highest award which could be bestowed upon a member of the Royal Hellenic Navy." (The highest award is the Victoria Cross, but it can only be given to British citizens.)

The submarine was sunk and my uncle died on September 14, 1943. Though my uncle was a flawed man, I believe that a loving God won't forget that Vassilis Laskos fought on the side of the angels against the Nazis.

27 • Civil War in Athens: Chronicle of a Nightmare

I came to the cities in a time of disorder
When hunger ruled.
I came among men in a time of uprising
And I revolted with them.
So the time passed away
Which on earth was given me.

I ate my food between massacres.
The shadow of murder lay upon my sleep.

Bertolt Brecht, *To Posterity*

The Axis was in shambles, and everyone was relieved to see the war end. The people wanted the celebrations to last forever, but their leaders' greed for power wouldn't let them enjoy their hard won freedom for long. On December 3, 1944, there was a demonstration in downtown Athens, organized by leftists, which got out of hand. More than 28 people were killed and more than a hundred were injured. Historians differ as to who fired the first shot. The right-wingers along with the police and some British forces over-reacted, and the violence began. By December 12, Athens was in the throes of a vicious civil war, waged between leftists (mostly Communists and Socialists), and the British who supported the government. The British, unable to gather enough troops of their own, formed the "Athens Battalions" which included "rowdies, criminals and collaborators, even former security battalions members," reports D. M. Condit in a Department of the Army publication, "Case Study in Guerrilla War: Greece During World War II."

The Communists in the Southern suburbs, where *Neos Kosmos* is located, were asserting their power by knocking on doors to arrest people and constituting "Peoples Courts," which brought anyone with a trace of anti-communist behavior to trial, quick verdict and execution. At one point, they had arrested 14,000 people and made them march for miles on end in the freezing cold of that winter. Many atrocities were committed. Survivors reported that anyone who couldn't walk and fell down was shot to death on the spot. By January, the bodies of 4000 of those who had been arrested were discovered and some historians put the number killed to more than 10,000. It is said that this death march, destroyed whatever goodwill had existed for the Communists up to that time. People refer to this atrocity as "the tin-can-lid slicing of innocents' necks" to signify the brutality of these Communists. Death was in control now, not a mere shadow stalking us, as he had been during the Nazi occupation. The fighters were our neighbors, and the fighting wasn't a block away but right in front of our houses. I have never been as afraid for my life as I was on that December 1944 and January 1945.

One of the people taken hostage by the communists was Father Haralambos, the owner of my grade school, the United Pedagogical Grade School. He was taken from his home and after a few days he was killed and his body abandoned in the countryside. We cried for Father Haralambos' death, and the community made a special grave in the churchyard and buried his body there, as I have already mentioned. In the back of the church were the graves of many others who died during the 37 days of this "December War," as it was called. These graves were temporary and the bodies were removed later and buried in a cemetery.

My mother was fighting for her family's survival with her public relations skills from our balcony. Yoryies, who used to be a machinist during the war, the son of Kyra-Chrysoula, the fat widow lady next door, was now a two star general in the ELAS, the Communist guerilla army. He paid a visit to his mother with his motorcade, and my mother was on the balcony cheering for him. Two motorcycles, abandoned by the retreating German army were now in the service of the ELAS army, and preceded the cars. An open convertible with four guerillas came next. The guerillas were armed to the teeth with bandoliers, pistols, machine guns, and grenades dangling from their belts. Then came a sedan, black and shiny. Yoryies came, out only when his bodyguards had made sure that all was clear. My mother was the first to greet them all.

"Hello guys! Yoryie, my boy, how are we doing?"

Yoryies looked up at her smiling. "We are doing great, Kyra-Marina," he shouted, holding his left fist up in the air. "We are going to win," he added, and walked briskly to the door of his mother's house.

My mother waved so that the guerillas could see her, mark her as a sympathizer, remember her as a friend and bypass our house, If evil ever hovered around us. "Bravo, Yoryie; I wish you the best!" She called out and re-entered our apartment. "The monsters! They'll pay for their sins," she mumbled to herself, as she picked up her broom and attacked the parquet floor that had been worn out from cleaning.

After the Communists left, we enjoyed a few hours of peace. Then a fascist guerrilla appeared with a funnel-shaped, hardboard megaphone on the street corner across from our house and delivered his message for "a meeting of all patriots," as he put it. "Everyone who cares for a free Greece must attend," he called out and gave the time and the place. Then, he added with as much volume as his lungs could hold: "Anyone who doesn't attend is a traitor, a collaborator of the godless Communists, who slice throats with tin-can lids."

Next day the big shot of the Fascists stopped in our street on his way to the meeting at the empty lot of the Alcazar. This leader, a stocky man in a dark suit and a coat thrown over his shoulders like a cape, came out of the biggest sedan in the motorcade and looked around at the neighbors waiting at doorways, balconies, and windows for whatever message he had to deliver.

My mother was at the balcony ready for a warm welcome. "We've been waiting for you guys," she called out in her cheerful manner. The heavy in the dark suit raised up his head and tapped his finger on his hat.

"We are here, madam. We haven't forgotten our brothers and sisters in *Neos Kosmos*."

My mother appeared delighted. The eyes of the neighbors were upon her. She knew that Yoryies' mother, the widow next door, was gone with her son, and everyone around wanted good relations with everyone else. "We're all hungry for freedom, Sir," she said. "May God's will be done!" And she waved at the man and his minions.

"We hope that all of you will be at our gathering in one hour. You must attend, because your freedom depends on what you'll hear," he insisted, and quickly got back in his car. The motorcade moved on.

My mother came back inside. "The creeps have grown fat sucking the blood of little people with their Nazi buddies," she growled and picked up the bamboo duster and started beating the rug hanging from the balcony railing. I listened to her and tried to understand the dangerous game she felt she had to play. She and most of the people in the neighborhood didn't give a damn about Communists and Fascists. All they wanted was to have some peace. But, that was precisely what these fanatics of the left and the right wouldn't let them have. They were determined to draw everyone out and make them their subjects. They gave speeches and asked for subscriptions, little favors for their party, some demonstration of loyalty; later they would discuss terms of subjugation.

My mother knew that they had already visited some families at night and asked for loyalty to the party. No one could refuse without risking punishment. Her information was that both sides were taking hostages. The trick was to avoid a visit from these monsters. So, she tried to maintain friendly relations with both sides, but despised both. My mother would lie and cheat and do anything she could to protect my father and her children. I sensed her fear and understood vaguely what she was trying to do. She prayed to God every night in whispers, burning a candle in front of the icons. She was asking for help and had no doubt that what she was doing was what God wanted her to do. Life is sacred, and she would protect it. So, her campaign would go on, as long as killers prowled the streets, as long as the evil of fanatical partisanship slithered in our midst. She believed that her strategy had worked thus far and, with God's help, would continue to work. She was an Arvanitissa and getting involved with the public issues of her community must have been in ger blood. Who can really say that God's plan doesn't include some cunning Christians put on earth to outfox Satan and his followers?

At first my father wanted no part of these interactions, but when he saw how effective she was, he went along, muttering his cautionary remarks every time my mother reported the comings and goings of significant visitors in our neck of the woods.

When the hostilities broke out, more than a dozen neighbors left their homes and sought shelter on the first floor of the building where we were renting because it was one of three concrete structures in the neighborhood. My parents and I also spent the better part of December on the first floor, in the apartment of Kyra-Katina, the old lady who liked to look young and put on lipstick and rouge and crèmes and perfumes, and never said a cross word to anyone who invaded her humble abode, God may bless her soul. She was innocent like a child and might have even been a saint, but for that little vanity problem she had. Her daughter was a gracious host also and hosted all of us with a welcoming attitude. Children and some grownups hang around for hours, telling stories and jokes to each other, playing cards and various table and word games, and waiting for the fighting to end or, at least for the gunfire to subside. Some of the older men argued about "the situation," as Greek old timers have done from time immemorial at the *kafeneion* or coffee shop, swinging their komboloys' beads deftly. After a few days, food became scarce, and we shared whatever we could find.

Many young men had joined either the right-wingers or the Communists and were fighting in the streets. From time to time one or two of them would come to our shelter and bring whatever they could spare for their families, who often shared it with everybody. They brought news of fighting and casualties; they described atrocities we could hardly believe; the right-wingers announced that the body of Father Haralambos was identified and told us he was killed by the Communists. The Communists insisted that the thugs of the Security Battalions, used by the Germans to spread terror, had been abducting innocent civilians and slicing their throats. Some of the young visitors were hungry and were looking for food. All of us kids couldn't take our eyes off their guns and their bandoliers full of bullets. Something magical kept our eyes fixed on the yellow shiny bullets. We forgot the words, but not the sights.

My father preferred to stay at our apartment upstairs, alone in the cold, grinding barley, rye, wheat and other grains into flour. He had bought a sack with these grains just before the hostilities broke out and was bent on using every bit of it to feed his family, at least. My mother thought that most of the grains in that sack were unfit for human consumption, "grains left on the stalks, used for making brooms," she would mumble under her breath, as she kneaded the dough made from that flour. Making flour from grains is comforting to me. Sometimes I touch the little pile of flour my father has accumulated in a little bowl he keeps on the table beside him. It feels good to the tips of my fingers. It feels good inside. But, eating the product of his labor takes as much work as he puts into grinding it.

When the sound of guns would quiet down for awhile, I would run upstairs, find my toy soldiers and my books and spend some time playing or reading. Since we couldn't get out of the house to go to school, I felt some obligation to read something that made the day productive. After several hours with the same two dozen people crowded in the two-bedroom apartment of Kyra-Katina, downstairs, I wanted to be alone, so I could make sense out of what others had been saying and doing. I never knew for sure who was with the Communists and who was with the Fascists. They had an alphabet soup of organizations – EAM, ELAS, OPLA, EDES, X and others – that no one could possibly know who belonged to which. Kyra-Katina's apartment was a neutral zone and people who entered it never tried to claim it as their own.

I still see my father now, some sixty years later. He is still there. He sits for hours on the frayed straw chair, in the cold, dark kitchen, wearing his black overcoat and a moth-eaten blue beret, and grinds his grains in the brass coffee-grinder my mother had bought from a gypsy peddler. A cup of flour every hour is the product of my father's labor. He turns the handle evenly, looking out the back window at the gray sky, his face totally without expression. Mortars explode with thuds in the distance, machine guns chatter and shells whistle by, but his hand turns steadily the handle of the coffee grinder and never stops. My father is in a trance, oblivious to the turmoil of the world.

My mother will crank life into this rundown state of existence, when she'll make pitas with the powder we call flour. We'll spread a drop of olive oil on each pita, and open a can of sardines and a can of beans, or peas and have our dinner. If there is a glass of wine, we'll all have a sip to warm ourselves up and find the spirit to say something cheerful about "the situation." If some hen in the neighborhood happened to lay an extra egg and my mother was quick enough to hear of it that morning, she'll have gotten it and she'll serve it to me fried, sunny-side-up, as a special treat. She cares about me and doesn't want me to be stunted in my growth, or go blind for lack of vitamins, or get sick with rheumatism again. The egg is insurance against all thse potential ills that may strike me. When it comes to her little boy, her imagination races to a tie with her love.

One evening, things were unusually quiet, but I couldn't let myself believe that we could ever be safe again. Sometime had gone by without a single burst from a machine gun, or a *turtura*, as we called that infernal weapon. The little gasoline burner my mother used to fry the pitas and the eggs and warm the canned food was already lit and its puny, blue flame gave a hint of light and a welcome glow to the room. Lights had been off for days – somebody said the gas storage plant had been bombed. Silence was sweet music as I watched the wisps of my own and my father's breaths appear and then fade away in the chilly air.

Hope is dying out around me, but I'm working hard to keep it alive. I don't exactly know how hope connects with life, but I have heard that living without it is horrible. My mother uses the word when talking to my father, but I don't think he knows what it means, either. All I know is survival against the unexpected. The winners of the game we have been forced to play are the survivors. The dead must have been inept, slow, lost, incapable, losers, you name it. Sometimes I have a problem with the brave who die, like barba Vassos. They are not inept, just selfless or crazy. So, some losers may be winners in some other game that is also going on. And, there is the game of giving your life for others, who are just unable to fend for themselves, as Christ taught us to do. But why should I throw it all away for some slow and stubborn Krokas, or a retarded Stellian or a compliant pushover like Kalamata? My mother would kill me before I could offer myself for such sacrifice! Where is the logic of this game? Deep down I know that these people play a different game, and in that game they are winners. I vow to stop reading history, the Bible and the lives of the saints, and concentrate on surviving in the flesh-and-blood game I understand best. There will be time to sort things out later. Fear makes me alert, and danger is a familiar visitor. I am even afraid for my father when I see him so calm, so remote, so far away from reality. He looks old and defeated, cut off from the raging death outside. My father has found something worthwhile to do with his time. There is nothing he can do about the war around us, but there is something he can do to feed his family. He sees me waiting at the doorway, smiles, but says nothing. I try to argue myself out of my feeling pity for my father, but it is hard to do. Perhaps, I tell myself, he's also playing in that different game.

My mother is eight months pregnant and is lying down in the bedroom. What will we do, if she has to give birth now? I don't know all the details of childbirth, but I know that there has to be a doctor or a midwife around, or bad things can happen. She is unusually sad tonight because she just found out Kyr-Argyris' teenage son was missing and he was worried he might have taken by the Communists. The jagged tin can tops I've heard that Communists use to slash the throats of their victims hover in the back of my mind and, probably, in the back of hers.

Soon, I will offer to relieve my father at the grinder. I've done this before, but for a few minutes only. I don't know how he can grind that stuff for hours on end. I admire his patience, his persistence and his fearlessness. He stops, shakes the grinder, unscrews the bottom part, and empties the few spoonfuls of flour into the brass bowl by his side. He spreads it with a spoon, satisfied.

"How much more?" I ask.

"A little more," he says.

"You want me to do some?"

"How's your mother?"

Before I can answer, there is an explosion, a deafening noise. All hell breaks loose with echoes of shrieks, thudding, glass breaking, crashing, closing in from everywhere. We dash out of the kitchen, toward the bedroom and bump into my mother in the hallway headed toward us, and all three of us in one hug-bundle fall down to the floor.

Stillness. It was moments later but it seemed like hours, when we realized that we were not hurt. We hugged each other some more, patted eachother and laughed with joy, because all we had lost was every window in the front of the house. And, we thanked God for our survival, and laughed and hugged each other again, because it was a surprise to be so utterly alive. Oh, how good it was to see my father laughing again! I thought I recognized the young man I had seen in some old picture album in the closet.

"Must have been close," my mother said. She was already up and going toward the window to reconoiter the situation in the street below.

"Get down," my father shouted at her. "Watch out for the glass." But she was already there, peering out.

"People running . . . somebody must be hurt," she said.

"Are you sure you're all right?" my father asks her.

She shusses him. "It'll take a direct hit to finish me up!" she whispers without moving her eyes away from the street.

"And you? Are you all right?" he asks me.

I look at him as if he had asked a question about something everyone knew the answer to. If I was hurt, I thought that I would be screeching, and there would be blood all over. Didn't he know that? He felt my arms and legs. "We spilled the flour," I said.

"The flour?" he said and gave me a hug.

"I'm going downstairs," my mother announced. "They'll need some help."

"Are you crazy?" my father admonished her. But, when it came to interactions with neighbors, my mother didn't pay attention to his advice. She seemed to know that her time wasn't right yet.

"I'll be right back." She grabbed an old bed sheet and rushed out.

My father and I spent some time salvaging as much flour as we could from the tile floor in the kitchen. He gave me a strainer and showed me how to pass the flour through, just in case it had picked up any dirt from the floor. I repeated to him the words he often said himself about mother's floors being clean enough to lick, and I could tell, he felt a little guilty. While I was sifting the flour, he started grinding again. Once in a while, he would stop and listen for my mother's footsteps. We had almost enough for a meal by the time she came back. She looked tired and disheartened. She lay down on the chest that doubled as my bed in the kitchen and sighed. I knew my father was relieved to see her back.

"We tried, but we couldn't do it," she mumbled. "Soula, from across the street was hit. She was climbing up the basement steps from Manolis' *taverna* when the mortar exploded. Her husband was right behind her. A piece of shrapnel found her. The baby too . . . Two steps lower . . . if she had been just two steps lower, they would both be alive."

"She would have been struck in the head," my father said without stopping the grinding.

"Dimitris – you know her husband, don't you? He has the paint store. He went crazy. They took him to the church to calm him down."

She buried her head in the pillow and started to cry. My father bent over her, kissed her and stroked her hair. And, when I went by her, she hugged me tight and held me for a long while. I kept still, knowing that this also would end as the mourning for her brother had ended. I knew now and didn't panic.

Time passed.

Then, she wiped the tears from her eyes and got up.

She took the bowl with the flour and lifted it up high. "You guys have been working very hard, haven't you?" she said. "I'm going to make you the best pitas you ever ate in your lives! And I'm going to throw in plenty of olive oil and something extra special," she said. My eyes were fixed on her free hand, watching her every move. She got the bowl down on the counter. "Look at this," she said, pulling out of her apron pocket a large chunk of cheese.

"Manolis' way of making everybody there feel a little better. He feels bad about what happened," she said pensively. Manolis' *taverna* was at the corner of our block and most neighbors knew him well. He was a nice man as far as I was concerned; but, now Manolis was on top of my list, and I could hardly keep myself from grabbing the cheese and devouring it right there and then. Mother guessed my heart's desire. She cut a piece with a knife and offered it to me. She was about to cut a piece for my father too, but he stopped her.

"I'll wait," he said and got up.

We said a prayer for Soula and her unborn child and for Dimitris and for Kyr-Argyris' son, and then ate the hot pita with the cheese and some pork and beans from a can, still left over from our nearly depleted stash. I have had dinners at some very fancy restaurants since that time, but no filet mignon or cordon bleu or broiled lobster has ever tasted as delicious as the meal I had that cold December evening, in 1944. As I was chewing my pita, I felt a little speck of something hard on my teeth, but I didn't do what I had always done impulsively before. I held back my protest and found it and removed it without ever telling my mother.

Death came close to us, touched us but didn't kill us. We were alive, and we broke bread together, and thanked God Almighty for his blessings. That night I slept the sleep of the blessed, wrapped in the best *velentza* blanket from my mother's dowry, hand-woven by aunt Assimo, in her own loom. Hopeful dreams were always spun when it was over me.

Next day we were back, working hard on the needs of the day. Three weeks had gone by, and food was getting scarcer by the day. We had been inside the house all this time, to escape the dangers in the streets. Now and then my mother or some other neighbor would bring a couple of cans of beans or sardines, or some spaghetti in a package, but it wasn't enough to feed everybody, and we were almost out of everything. No one had seen bread for days, and without bread people were feeling hopeless. Kyr-Manolis swore that he had given all the cheese he had in the *taverna*, and Kyr-Philippas, the grocer, did likewise. There was a need to do something about food. There were about a dozen kids in that apartment playing all sorts of games, but no one I can remember talked about food. It was always present in our thoughts but we kept it out of our speech.

A rumor reached us that Votsis' bakery, about half a mile away, was going to get a shipment of flour from the Red Cross. Four men got together and talked about going to the bakery to get some bread. The women didn't want them to risk the trip because there was gunfire all around us. But, people had to eat. The men huddled together and talked quietly among themselves. We were all uneasy. My father didn't think it was wise to risk lives for the mere chance at finding bread. They had to cross Frantzes street, the main avenue that run through *Neos Kosmos*, and we all knew the combatants disputed it. We could hear the firefights – it was suicide, somebody said – but these four men were undeterred by the pleas of their wives and decided to go. From the moment they left the apartment, time started weighing heavy on everyone's mind. How many of them would come back? Would they find an abundance of goods and come back loaded with sacks of it, or would it all be for nothing? We started singing hymns and prayed for their safe return. We talked about the most deadly bullets and the size of shrapnel that would maim or kill a person. We heard gunfire again and again in the distance, but people said there was nothing to worry about because it came from the opposite direction than the direction the men had taken. I thought the echoes came from every direction there was.

I was in another room when the men returned a couple of hours later. Everybody wanted to see them and believe that they were still alive and hear their story. They came back with a single loaf of bread the British soldiers gave them, because there was nothing left at Votsis' bakery. They told us how they had to duck bullets, and hide behind British armored vehicles, and run from wall to wall, and pray all the way. The women took the bread and distributed it among the families. We got a small piece of bread, in recognition of the tin cans my mother had offered from time to time to the group.

Next day, I remember that I was sitting on a chair watching some other kids play a table game. We were hungry again and we now knew that there was nothing out there to be had. What would happen? How long could we manage to survive? And then, the door burst open and Kyra-Nota, our neighbor lady who had lost a son in the Big War and rarely visited our shelter, came flying in with the biggest loaf of the whitest bread I have ever seen. She broke chunks of bread with her hands and passed them around to all the children gathered in the room and said only "here," and then with such joy, another chunk, and "here, you too." She shoved a huge piece of that fresh, white, crusty bread on my hands and told me to share it with my mother, because she needed it, and moved on, passing bread to the young and then the old, never stopping, never waiting for thanks or any acknowledgment. No one ever asked how she found the bread, or who gave her the bread. It just wasn't important. I ate part of my portion right there and then, without waiting, thinking only that whatever was before me at that moment could be gone in an instant, if I didn't eat it. Having finished half of it, I thought I could last forever. I hadn't felt so satisfied in a long time. I left enough for my mother because I knew she needed it for the baby. "That Kyra-Nota is a jewel," my mother said, eating some of her portion. "She has offered to help when the baby comes," she said, but I had no idea why we would ever need her.

My father was upstairs grinding that awful flour and my mother was making pitas, which were hard to swallow without getting some of the chaff stuck on the back of your palate. There were both horrible and hopeful stories told by people who came to our shelter from the outside. They said that he collaborators were chasing the Communists out of the city; or, the English were coming slowly toward us; or, the Communists are threatening to starve the population of Athens, if they are not given more portfolios in the new government. Or, a ship loaded with foodstuffs from Sweden was unloading at the port of Piraeus.

A few days later, when my mother and I came down to the apartment in the morning, we found everyone gloomy and silent. Early that morning a bullet had struck and killed one of the men from the neighborhood, right across the street from our house. He was one of the Communist guerrillas on guard duty at that corner of the neighborhood. Someone said that he lived in the tenement house half a block away from us. Several kids were staring out the window at the street. I joined them and saw a young woman bent down on her knees.

I couldn't see what she was doing, but someone with a better vision said she was his sister, marking a little square space with rocks, something like a grave. They said that you could see the blood on the dirt inside the square, but I couldn't tell. Someone else said that they took the body of the man away, earlier that morning. I heard the word "killed," but I kept thinking "wounded," because I couldn't take in another killing just then. It took some time to think, "killed," and know that he could never come back.

When we were able to go outside and play freely again, I inspected the rocks and the dirt inside the square that the dead man's sister had marked with rocks. The rocks had not been disturbed. I cannot say that I saw blood, but the rocks had a couple of brown spots on them that could have been dried blood. No one would dare move them. They belonged to a sacred space and were left there a long time.

28 • My Sister, Vasso, Is Born in the Rebellion

> I learned that courage was not the absence of fear, but the triumph over it. The brave man is not he who does not feel afraid, but he who conquers that fear.
>
> **Nelson Mandela**

On December 25, Christmas Day, Winston Churchill flew into Athens and called a conference of all Greek parties, including the Communists. They all met at the end of December, but after two days of deliberations the conference came to a deadlock. Churchill decided that Greece was too important a country to concede to the Communists and launched an all out attack against the armed forces of the Communist Party in the Athens area. By December 30 1944, the British, with reinforcements from their forces in Italy, had cleared from Communists the southern half of Athens and north of the port of Piraeus. *Neos Kosmos* was again more or less peaceful. We had spent almost a month inside the apartment of the wonderful coquette Kyra-Katina and we were only too glad to move on. On January 4, a New Greek government took office. By mid January all the Communist forces were out of Athens and were suing for an armistice. Hostilities in Athens and the surrounding areas finally ended on January 15, 1945. The civil war in the rest of Greece went on for another three years.

My mother was very upset by the violence she saw all around us. She was big now and worried about fighting breaking out suddenly and having to run for cover. She moved slowly and deliberately outside the house to avoid tripping on ruts as she had done a few months earlier. She worried about the baby's health because the things we ate to survive were not very nutritious. She didn't want anything to happen to her baby. She was ready to give birth, but the world showed no interest in receiving a baby.

On January 6, a cold dark night, she started to have pains and lay down in bed. My father sat by her side and stroked her forehead. They talked for a few minutes and then he told me to stay with her, no matter what happened, because he was going out to find the midwife that they had contacted previously. He said that he would try to phone the lady, but he wasn't sure that phone service was restored yet and, besides, he didn't know where he could find a working public phone at such a late hour. To reach the midwife's house, he had to walk in the freezing night, through *Neos Kosmos*, which was now controlled by the British, or the police or rowdies, no one knew by whom. Then he had to get to

Koukaki, at least a mile away, which, he hoped, was controlled by British troops, supported by Greek policemen. He said very little, but I knew that the chances of his getting through and coming back in time with a midwife were not very good. And, given the atrocities committed around us, there was a chance, I thought, that he wouldn't come back at all. "If you need help, go and get Kyra-Nota," my father said. "And don't worry about me. I'll be back in no time at all," he said. He gave me a hug and went out. I tried to concentrate on the job I was given – to take care of my mother's needs.

My mother told me to go in the kitchen and check the municipal gas stove we had for cooking. Sometimes, unpredictably, there would be gas, and other times there was no pressure and she would have to use the portable kerosene burner. "If there is gas," she said, "light the stove and boil some water in the large kettle under the sink." Fortunately, there was gas. I found the pot, ladled some water in it from the ceramic urn where we stored it – faucet water was never on at night – and set it on the burner I had lit. I went back to her side to keep my vigil. She asked me to mark the time between pains, explaining that, if the pains got closer than five minutes, I should go and get Kyra-Nota, our neighbor from across the street, who had offered to help. The landlady who lived with her family next door to us wasn't our friend. She was always nagging us to pay a rent above the controlled rate, and expected my mother to do most of the work in keeping clean the common space we used. Mother rarely had anything to do with her. To my relief and hers, I found that the interval between pains was closer to ten minutes. She smiled. "Maybe your dad will be back before we have to wake up Kyra-Nota and her family," she said, as if the main issue of the night was the maintenance of peace and tranquility for Kyra-Nota's family.

"What happens when the pains are two minutes apart?" I asked, as I tried to understand what pain, time, boiling water, neighbors and a midwife had to do with a baby being born. As far as I was concerned, the bellybutton opens magically and the baby comes out.

"At two minutes we scream and whatever happens, happens," she said with clenched teeth. I could tell she was in pain. I held her hand and squeezed, as I always did when I had my earaches, and my infected toe, and measles, and mumps. Time passed slowly. As I sat there I kept thinking of what needed to be done to end up with a baby. Perhaps, I should be ready to grab it and lift it up? I told her that I was going to be a great big brother. I reminded her that she had told me she was not sick, so she would be just fine. I would have done anything to see her smile again. Instead the pains got worse and more frequent – seven minutes, six minutes . . .

"How's the water doing?"

"Not boiling, yet."

"Turn it down a bit, and then go and get Kyra-Nota." I could see the sweat on her forehead. "When you get to the street, stay close to the house. Don't go walking in the middle of the street. Cross fast. Hear me?"

I wanted to protest that these were instructions for little children, not persons boiling water on large pots and measuring time intervals for a baby's birth but I said nothing.

"Go!" she cried out as pain gripped her.

I ran to the hallway to put on my coat when I heard the key at the door, and my father walked in with an Amazon of a woman in tow. She carried a big black bag like our regular lady doctor carried every time she made a call at our home. He introduced me and asked how mother was. The Amazon midwife heard the moaning from the bedroom and took off in that direction with my father trailing behind her.

A minute later she came back out and started issuing orders to my father and me. She wanted the kitchen dinning table cleared and moved in the middle of the living room. She wanted an old blanket and clean sheets to spread on it and some to tear up, "just in case," she said, and she wanted more boiling water in another kettle, "a pan if you don't have another kettle . . ." She spread the bed sheets on the table, and with my father's help, she moved my mother onto it. Her final order to me was to go in the bedroom and try to sleep. "I'll call you if I need you," she said. I did as she ordered. I was glad to see that my father had made it back and with a midwife in tow. I was proud of my father's brave deed. They moved mother on to the table. I heard her moaning and screams and prayed for a quick delivery. I also prayed for a healthy baby. I had heard so many horrible stories about women giving birth to all sorts of monstrous creatures that the possibility of any abnormality terrified me.

An hour or so later, I heard a baby's cry, and the midwife said "It's a beautiful girl," and I laughed with joy to myself because from that time on I would have a sister. The midwife, whose name I cannot recall, appeared at the bedroom door. "Your sister, buddy boy," she said proudly, holding the baby for display in front of me. I saw the little creature and caressed her cheek and loved her instantly. She was a beautiful baby, a wonderful little girl, and I never tired taking care of her, feeding her, rocking her to sleep, teasing her and playing with her. I was ten years older than she was, but she was fun to be around, because she was uniquely connected to me. My parents named her Vassiliki, in honor of my mother's fallen brother, Captain Vassilios Laskos. For a while, we called her "the pea-soup-baby," because of the poor diet my mother had to endure during her pregnancy, but that was soon forgotten, and she became "Vasso," which is the nickname for Vassiliki. To me, however, she will always be, lovingly "Vassaki," which is Little Vasso, in Greek.

Vasso was born on January 6, 1945, right at the end of the hostilities in Athens. She was always the top student in her class at the United Pedagogical Grade School and later, when she attended Arsakeion, the top high school for girls, in Greece. I always wanted to ask Papa-Kostas, if she was as good a student as I was, but I never remembered to do it. Vasso was and is a sharp thinker. She became an architect and, later, a city planner, with a long career in the field. At the apex of her career, she was the project manager for several large public projects. She is a poet and has published several books of poetry, written from the heart and with mastery of the Greek language. She and have a loving relationship with each other, but we have very different worldviews and lifestyles. She is married to Makis Kavouriaris, a Greek economist, who taught at the University of Paris before his retirement. Vasso and Makis have two children, Stathis and Marina, both educated, living and working in Paris France.

We knew that the British troops were nearby, but we didn't know when they would enter our neighborhood and liberate us officially. And no one was sure that all the rebels were gone from our neighborhood. One morning there was a knock on the front door. We all got up, trembling with fear. The knocks got louder. Could it be that we would become the last hostages to be taken by the communists? Could we be mistaken for communists and be rounded up for execution by the fascist collaborators or the police? They'll break down the door. My father went to the door and asked who was there.

"Open, please," we heard in English! My father all but fell on the door and opened it before the visitors changed their minds and left. A giant Indian soldier with a black beard filled the doorway. I recognized his *Sten* machine gun now pointed straight at us. He wore a khaki safari jacket with bandoliers around his shoulders, and a British army helmet. With a handgun hanging from his belt on one side and a canteen on the other, he could hardly squeeze through the doorway. I saw the three chevrons on his arm, and I figured he was some kind of sergeant.

"Back," he ordered my father, and motioned him with his weapon to move back. Two other Indian soldiers stood guard at the door of our apartment as he moved inside and looked around. We were up against the wall in no time at all. But, we were all happy, thrilled to see real evidence of the British army's presence in our midst. My father explained to the sergeant our feeling, putting his English to good use, and slowly the sergeant lowered his gun. My father reached for a bottle of *Metaxas* seven star cognac from the cabinet nearby and, constantly asking with his eyes for permission, poured the sergeant a drink and offered it to him.

"You first," the sergeant ordered my father. My father was taken aback. He was offering his guest the best liquor he had in the house and he didn't like to be turned down. He couldn't quite grasp the meaning of the social transaction. "Drink!" The sergeant's command was urgent. Clearly, the man didn't have all day for these amenities.

"You drink first! He doesn't trust you not to poison him," my mother called out in Greek, standing up against the wall and holding Vasso. The sergeant became uneasy with another person, this one pretty quick and frisky in the mix.

My father snapped out of being the offended party and became a solicitous host again. He smiled and drank the cognac in a hurry. The sergeant smiled in return, and we breathed easily again. My father took another glass and poured another drink of cognac for him, and more for the other soldiers, and they all drunk cheerfully. The sergeant kept glancing at my father as he searched the house. I wanted to shout, "We are not Communists, man! We are not Fascists or collaborators or X-party fanatics, or Security Battalion irregulars . . . We are just people who want to be free of all the damned struggles that plague this world." I wanted him to know that he had brought us freedom, but I didn't say a thing. It was enough that they were here.

My father was delighted to welcome these liberators. One of the soldiers gave me a chocolate bar, and the other gave my mother a little package of tea. The sergeant gave my father a round tin can with fifty Canadian Sailor brand cigarettes inside, the most precious small gift one could give to anyone back then. I knew my cigarette-box brands very well, and I even knew about these cans, because the Beggar had shown us a couple, taken from British soldiers who became POWs when the Nazis took over. The soldiers told us there was nothing to worry about anymore. Their troop would patrol the neighborhood for at least a week. The communists were leaving Athens. The war was over for us.

Though the civil war in Greece lasted till 1948, after this visit of the British soldiers to our home, life in Athens returned gradually to normal. Archbishop Damaskenos was appointed Regent and the new government established the rule of law again. The days of fear and atrocities were over. Feeling free made me think that all things are possible with no limits of time, distance or ability.

29 • A Summer in Eleusis with Grandmother Marigo

When I completed the fifth grade, in the summer of 1946, at the end of the hostilities in greater Athens, I visited my maternal grandmother, Marigo, in the Laskos family home, in Eleusis, where she lived alone for a two-week vacation. Everyone except her sons, daughters and grandchildren called grandma "Kyra-Marigo," "Kyra" meaning Mistress or Missus in the language of common folk, and *Marigo* being an *Arvanitissa*'s nickname for Mary. She was a tough old bird, aware of everything in her domain, quick to spot any misbehavior on my part, and able, not to mention willing, to let me know how I should conduct myself, if I wanted to have her approval and derive the benefits of her authority. I knew from the moment I saw her in her own habitat that she could run anything she set her mind to run, and could talk back to anyone who displeased her. Many years later, I would remember my days with grandma and understand better how barba Vassos must have felt under her watchful and disapproving eye when he was in love with a woman she didn't approve of.

I remember her coming in my room in Athens when I was sick and immediately filling it with her commanding presence. Grandma's coming meant that all was going to be fine. At least, my mother and I were sure of that. I think, my father knew that she was a very formidable lady, having heard how she ran the family business and some aspects of her sons' lives, and was always respectful but cautious. Before I visited her in Eleusis, he instructed me to obey her direction and be helpful to her, if I wanted to have a good vacation at her home.

Soon after I arrived at grandma's house I discovered that the property included not only the house with its flagstone-paved yard with a glorious, old pine tree at its center but also a vineyard and a small peach and apple tree orchard. And more importantly, as I will explain, it included a huge warehouse, where in olden days the workers used to store the olives harvested from the olive groves the family owned and make olive oil in the warehouse presses. That use of the warehouse was abandoned and of no great interest to me; what was of great interest to me, however, was the fact that, according to neighbors and relatives in the area, the Germans had used that warehouse to store a variety of equipment from bicycles to guns and bombs, tools, electronic devices, and all sorts of materials for repairing their machines, such as wires, cables, connectors and so on. From the first description I heard to the latest detail I could gather by persistent questioning, I imagined the inside of that warehouse as a treasure trove beyond my wildest dreams: brand new red and green bicycles with bells and lights for night riding, German helmets and bayonets, pistols, including Luger pistols in leather holsters and other finds a boy would risk a lot to get. So, one day, soon after my arrival, I asked my grandmother if I could go inside the warehouse and look around. She looked at me as if I had grown an extra head and said without the slightest hesitation that the warehouse was dangerous and would be locked up until the junkmen came and took out of there whatever the Nazis had left behind. It was the worst possible scenario for the realization of my dreams.

My desire to get into that warehouse grew even stronger when I discovered that several neighbors had broken into my grandmother's yard and into the warehouse soon after the Germans left town and taken most, if not all the bicycles they could find. I could recognize some of them as they rode them in town and felt a strong urge to confront them and demand the return of the stolen property to my grandmother. The reason that I held back was that my grandmother would have probably packed my bags and sent me home, no questions asked; or, she would have died of embarrassment. On retrospect, she would have never died of embarrassment, but I didn't know her well, yet. Thieves aside, I was sure that there were valuable things left inside the warehouse, items which, as I argued the case to my grandmother, were a proper and just compensation for all that she had to put up with when half a dozen German officers took over her house and lived there as masters of the manor with her as their servant, confined in one room and her tiny kitchen. Why on earth would anyone want to give away to strangers in "the authorities" any number of perfectly working bicycles, or sets of tools, or other valuable items?

"It isn't safe to go in there," grandma said and felt with the slightest of touches the bundle of keys hanging from a steel ring on the side of her apron's belt. Right there and then, I decided that I would have to get into the warehouse by stealth. It was wrong, but I couldn't overcome the lure of exploration, the dream of getting a bike, and, as I tried to tell myself, the sense of injustice that was done to us. I studied grandma's habits – when she laid down her apron, where she kept her keys, when she took naps, what the warehouse lock looked like, what keys were on that key ring and how difficult it was to take a key out of the ring. I was afraid of getting caught in the act and being branded a thief in her eyes as well as having to live the rest of my life without having ever seen the inside of that warehouse.

After considerable thought and reflection on the problem, I decided that it would be best if I had collaborators in the dirty deed. I waited until my cousin Nondas, who was the same age as me, came for a visit, and confided in him the discovery I had made. He suggested that we needed a local person, who knew the situation better than we did, so we approached Mitsos, a second cousin, who lived with his family across the street from grandma's house. He was a year or two older than we were, but since he wasn't a city slicker, we thought we could trust him with a secret and a fair deal. Mitsos was delighted to join the caper, because he was sure that there was a lot more stuff there, especially guns, which, he confessed, were his passion and fantasized of using in hunting. Because of his passion for guns, we called him "the Sheriff," which made him feel proud and bold enough to take on the riskiest task of every adventure we dreamed up. That was the lineup we had for the liberation of the Nazi loot.

One afternoon, while grandma was snoozing peacefully in her chaise lounge under the pine tree in the yard, we noticed that she had hung her apron in the kitchen. Mitsos went straight for the bundle of keys and removed the key, which we knew fit the lock on the warehouse door. We ran to the warehouse and, with hearts pounding with excitement and fear, we opened the door. The darkness began to recede as faint sunlight trickled in through the huge wooden door. Immediately I was taken aback by the overwhelming odor that I had smelled before from electrical equipment, the electric iron my mother had used, electric plugs, wires and the like. We watched in silence. No bicycles. All around us contraptions we had never seen before took shape. I picked up a piece of metal with enameled wire wrapped around it and shoved it in my pocket.

Before I could think through all the consequences of my actions, I was inside a capsule that looked like a bullet-shaped coffin with a bump like a seat inside and a hood that opened up. I looked around and saw my two buddies rummaging through tangled wires and mechanical parts at the other end of the warehouse. This was my chance to try this baby first. I slipped into the seat, found an instrument panel before me and started to push buttons and turn knobs as if I had practiced the routine countless times before. The only thing similar to what I had before me now was cockpit images from the few movies with aircraft I had seen. Must be some kind of underwater vehicle, I thought, and imagined dragging this thing to the shore and exploring the bottom of Eleusis' harbor. One of the knobs had graduated markings around it and looked like my aunt Katina's stove timer knob. Impulsively, I turned it and pushed it in. And the counter, started to click rhythmically back: sssssssss-tick . . . sssssssss-tick . . . sssssssss-tick . . . and move ever closer to zero. I froze. "Bomb!" I thought in terror. This thing looked like a bomb, had a timer like bombs can be imagined to have – could it be a bomb? I don't know how long it took me to put two and two together, but it couldn't have been more than a few seconds. "It isn't safe to go in there," grandma's words flashed by in my brain. I imagined the warehouse going up in a huge explosion, in a blaze of fire, blown up into pieces of metal and limbs.

"It's a bomb!" I cried out as jumped out of the capsule.

Nondas and Mitsos dropped things they were holding and ran after me, out of the warehouse, into the fruit trees, behind the fence wall that separated the warehouse from the house.

We waited in silence for the explosion to come. Seconds passed . . . a minute . . . Mitsos raised his head over the fence. "There's no smoke, " he announced. " No fire, I can see."

"Give it a couple of minutes," I said. My cousin Nondas stared at me. I didn't like his look. "It was a timer for something," I protested.

"Probably a dud," Mitsos volunteered.

We waited for a few minutes, but heard nothing. We waited for the burst of an explosion, the flames and the smoke, but nothing happened. And we started worrying about going back to the warehouse to at least lock the door, so no one would know what we had done. But, how could we be sure that the device wouldn't go off just as we got there? We had to approach with caution, in total quiet, listening for the deadly hissing timer ticks I had described in detail to give credence to my alarm. The objective now was to lock the door and walk away alive. For some reason we huddled together on the way to the door, as if we wanted to make sure no one stayed behind and walked away from the explosion, while the others were blown up.

All was quiet. I pulled back the ancient wood door and locked it. Nothing happened. We turned and ran. I sung praises to the Almighty God for sparing our lives from our stupidity. It was a hot summer afternoon and the cicadas were singing away like there would be no end to joy in the world.

Grandma was up and about, watering her flowers at the edge of the flagstone yard with a water canister. Immediately, I noticed that she wasn't wearing her apron. Grandma was slim and bony, but she had a potbelly that was not as prominently outlined without her apron. "Where have you boys been?" she asked, but didn't wait for an answer. "Here, take this can and the other one under the stairs, and start giving some life to these God-forsaken flowers. They'll die without a little of your sweat."

I slipped the key to Mitsos, rushed to her side and grabbed the can from her hand, while Nondas scrambled to find the other can, fill it with water and get busy watering the flowers. Mitsos said that he wanted a drink of water from the tank with a faucet and ran into the little kitchen to insert the key back into grandma's key ring.

A few minutes later she inspected the job we were doing with unusual fervor. "That's enough now, boys," she said, which meant that we had done a good job. "You better get upstairs and catch a little sleep."

The cicadas hadn't missed a beat. They had a ball on hot days like this. They never thought that the party would end. I lay down for a siesta, and thought that life was good. I also knew that it could end in a second. It was a joy to be alive. Good to sleep in the cool upstairs room of grandma's house with revelers outside raising the roof.

Grandma never found out about our break in. We often debated among ourselves the issues that came up from our brief incursion into the warehouse: Had anyone seen any bicycles there? There weren't any, because the neighbors had taken them all. Mitsos was a local and was sure of that. Was the device I had started up a ticking bomb or what? We decided it was the casing of a torpedo and contained no explosives, or we would all be dead or maimed. There were many rifle shells on the dirt floor of the warehouse among the remnants of hay, but where were the rifles? We didn't know, but we were sure that the neighbors had cleaned them out and planned to use them for hunting, if any animals bigger than rabbits could ever be found in the fields around Eleusis.

30 • Short Circuit for Goodness Sake

A few months later, when winter came to Athens and the cold made us shiver inside the house, I decided to build an electric heater for our bedroom with some of the enameled wire from grandma's warehouse as its element, as I had planned all along. To test the ability of the wire to get hot, I stretched out some of it from the spool, cut it and stuck the ends into the electric outlet in our kitchen. I had expected that the wire would get warm, perhaps, glow a little and feel warm. But that's not what happened. A huge spark leaped out of the electric socket, and darkness engulfed me. Normally, the house fuse would have burned out and the damage would have been contained to our house. But, I had been repairing the house fuse whenever the fuse was blown and the wire I used, the only wire I could find around, was too heavy and didn't burn out and break the circuit as it was supposed to do. Because of this second error, the misbegotten connection short-circuited not only our house but also the electric distribution system for the entire neighborhood. In that near-deadly experiment, I had blown the main fuse for the entire neighborhood, and more than a hundred people had to go without power for several days. But, it could have been worse. I could have been electrocuted as I held the wires, and nobody would have been able to help me because I was alone in the house at the time. The reason that this didn't happen, I think, was that the heavy enamel coating on the wire provided adequate insulation and protected me. I've had enormous respect for the quality of German products since that time! But, I didn't thank the Germans for their thoughtful design; rather, I thanked God, who wanted me to go on living.

Scared out of my wits, I confessed my transgression to my mother. For reasons that I cannot quite fathom, my mother – perhaps, she wanted to brag about my technological risk-taking ability, or my noble motives for helping the family with some warmth in the cold winter that was coming –told my father when he demanded to know, if the disaster was my doing. She failed to recognize that my father wasn't looking for information that would push the frontier of his scientific knowledge, or for the Good Samaritan he was blessed to have as a son, but was after the perpetrator of a communal catastrophe. He knew I was capable of some mischief and he wasn't going to allow it to blossom into outright criminality. Immediately, he started looking for me, trying to track me down and teach me a lesson about gross disregard of safety and common sense – what kind of a maniac goes around plugging wires into electric outlets? I overheard his anger and slipped out into the street. He heard the door close and came after me.

My father came after me thinking, I suppose, that he would catch me after a few steps, but I was running as fast as I could and he was chasing me with his belt in his hand and wasn't catching up. All along I felt ashamed that we had sunk so low as to become theater for the neighbors. I thought of stopping, but I couldn't take the additional humiliation of being beaten in public by my father who had run amok. I turned my head and caught a glimpse of him as he was straining to breathe, and I felt more sorry for him than for myself. There had been a couple of times when my father lost his temper and came after me with his belt, only to be blocked by mother, who took some of the belt strikes intended for me and pleaded for the madness to stop, but this was the only time when the uglier part of our private life was made public in such an unseemly way. I could imagine the neighbors laughing at him for his ineptitude, as we passed by all the familiar places in our street and beyond, and people we knew came out of their stores and their houses to watch the spectacle. I could hear the neighbors gloating that the family in the two-story building up the street wasn't as dignified and proper as they had thought. They must be very troubled people – sad, isn't it? Pity! They seemed to be so nice.

When I got back into the house, I was ready to stop and take whatever I had coming, but my mother was afraid that my father was too angry to restrain himself, so she hid me inside the kitchen wardrobe, under a pile of blankets that weighed a ton. The trick was to make myself invisible and inaudible without suffocating. I could hear him three feet away from the other side of the wardrobe door. The giant came back and asked where Jack was, and my mother told him that he had run out the back door. I spent the night under the wool *velentza* blankets from her trousseau, breathing the mothball-reeking air of the closet and giving thanks to the Almighty for having shielded me once again from early death and my father's belt. My father never found me that night. He went to bed early, exhausted from the chase, but also, I think, trying to avoid me when his anger subsided. We met at dinner next day and made jokes about my escape. He also praised my good intension to make a heater for us and said that this was another indication of my desire to become an engineer. I think he was very happy that he didn't catch me. He didn't like himself when he lost his cool. Many years later, I would understand my father better. Life had not been kind to him, and he carried the scars of his childhood with him. Without wanting, he was passing them to me and that distressed him. Somehow, I caught on to that destructive process, and tried to do better.

When I became a father and happened to lose my temper on occasion and struck my sons by hand on their rear end and threatened but never used "the belt," I was always distraught. This was failure writ large. I wanted so much to be better, and I would resolve to fight against my demons all over again. But it was never easy. How long does it take to shape a father who loves his children and has all his emotions under control and never strikes his children, or shouts angrily at them, or terrorizes them with his look, or shows a throbbing vein under the skin of his temple that threatens an angry outburst? Knowing what I know today, it wouldn't have been the first time that an innocent human being had been electrocuted, but it might have been the first time that an electrocution survivor had been walloped.

I think that one of the reasons I decided to become an engineer was to learn how to build devices like heaters that help people stay alive and be comfortable. I felt that doing something that contributed to a better life would be important in whatever line of work I ended up doing.

31 • Summertime Dangers and Adventures

Summer afternoon, summer afternoon: to me those have always been the two most beautiful words in the English language.

Henry James

I was a fighter and very determined. There was no way I was going to back out without winning.

Christine Lahti

Summers in Eleusis were infused with magic. Many exciting things happened that filled the days with vibrant memories. The salty breeze of the sea caressed us after a swim and the perfume of the pine trees filled our hearts as we ate out in the yard under the old pine tree. For many years, whenever I was down, I would think of the hot summer afternoons with the cicadas singing outside in the merciless sun and myself lying down for a siesta in one of the cool, shady bedrooms of my grandmother's house, reading "Gone with the Wind" or the short stories of Karkavitsas' sailors, or some other story of adventure, love or mystery I would borrow from my uncle Andonis' library. I would sleep for a couple of hours and wake up refreshed and ready for athletic games or for mischievous adventures with my cousin Nondas, with Mitsos the "Sheriff," "The Other Nondas," our cousin, who was almost two years older than we were, and anyone else who cared to join us in our improvised madness.

We wasted time pleasantly like the cicadas, with swimming, sports, reading books before siestas and making up games no one had ever played before or would ever play again. We took trips to the farms of relatives and local friends on the back of donkeys, sometimes riding horses and acting like cowboys after that. And every evening, dressed in our summer whites, we strolled in the town square to watch the girls go by and talk about the day's happenings. Most evenings we'd end up going to the outdoor movies to see Alan Ladd rounding cattle and fighting Indians in the West or gawk at Esther Williams diving into blue waters of some exotic island of the Pacific. Sometimes we paid the full price of admission, now and then we mooched off an uncle or an older cousin. Like Omiros or "The Other Nondas." More often than not, we climbed up on trees overlooking the wall fence of the theater and watched the movie hanging from the branches like great apes, or made friends who lived next to the movie theater and watched movies hugging the wall fences between the movie theater and the friend's yard. But, none of these alternatives were certain, so we had a final option that was more of an adventure than a means of watching a movie on the cheap: we would sneak into the theater by deception.

One way was to sneak in with a rush of paying customers, hoping that the doorman would be so preoccupied with the collection of tickets that he wouldn't notice us. That approach worked some of the time, but now and then one of us would get caught by the doorman, grabbed by the ear and dragged out of the group of paying customers, where he could be seen by people and shamed as a cheap, sneaky scoundrel. It was a high-risk maneuver and I attempted it only once, out of desperation to see a good movie.

The final but most exciting approach to joining the comfortably seated customers in the theater as they enjoyed the moments before the movie started chewing *passatempo* or peanuts, required planning, cunning and agility. It could work only for one of the two movie theaters, the *Rex*, because it was located next to a peach orchard. A wall fence separated the peach orchard, from the movie theater and it could be scaled. First, you had to scale a wall fence to get into the orchard from the street; then you had to find your way among the trees to the spot on the wall separating the orchard from the movie theater grounds and climb over that. Scaling this separating wall was tricky, because on top of it rested a barbed wire coil, which had to be stretched out enough to allow a boy's torso to twist through it without the barbs gouging his flesh. If one succeeded doing that, he landed on the waiting area in front of the toilets stalls. We had done this often enough to know all the moves, but there was always a chance that the fat doorman who guarded the main entrance to the theater would start nosing around the toilet area and find us slithering through the fence.

One night, a clear starry warm night, I was the first to make it through the fence and quickly run into the first open toilet stall to pass as a paying customer doing his business; Nondas was next, but his pants got stuck on a barb of the fence and Mitsos was trying to free him. I watched and waited, unable to reach him and help him from my side. It took a couple of minutes, but he finally made it and jumped down and took the stall next to mine. Last to drop down the wall was Mitsos who was built like a cat and slid through and landed in the anteroom. The three of us now straightened our clothes and got ready to leave the toilet area and proceed to blend with the rest of the theatergoers. Mitsos opened the door and stepped out with a cowboy swagger headed for a gunfight. Nondas and I followed close by. We hadn't taken more than ten steps when the fat doorman fell upon Mitsos and Nondas and grabbed them by their shirts. "I got you," I heard the fat man call out and flew to the side, away form the scuffle. I had no time to look. I run bobbing and weaving through the crowd until I managed to slow down and blend with the people entering the seating areas. Nondas and Mitsos were stunned by the booming command of the doorman but they struggled to get out of the man's grip. Nondas escaped first and found a seat near me. Mitsos tore his shirt but he slipped away. Because he was last to get loose, the doorman took after him and chased him around and around the seats of the theater. We watched the shadows of the fat doorman chasing the spindly Mitsos on the screen as the *Fox Movietone News* was playing. Later Mitsos told us that he had to run all the way out of the theater to escape his pursuer. He cussed and shouted and was furious that the fat man deprived him of the pleasure to watch Gary Cooper in *Sergeant York*. Nondas and I tried to console him, telling him that it wasn't one of Cooper's best movies, anyway. Of course, by the time the movie was shown at *Rex* in Eleusis, Gary Cooper had already received his first Oscar for Best Actor, as Sergeant York, though none of us knew it yet. That was the last time we dropped into the *Rex* toilets like parachutists from the Garden of Peaches. No one wanted to risk another attempt that might end up with a public humiliation. I was worried for a while that the fat man might have seen and remembered my face, but when you pay for a ticket and show it with bravado, nobody remembers any previous transgressions. But money wasn't easy to come by. There had to be other things to do besides going to the movies every night. We would have to find them.

I still had no wheels, but I was doing my best to have a good time without a bike. The girls were wonderful to look at and yearn for their company as they sat around the benches at the square and talked and laughed at things we could only dream about, but they were beyond reach to blathering idiots on foot. I wonder whether my fortunes would have been any different if I had managed to get my hands on a bike. I suspect that I might have felt like a blathering idiot on wheels.

The incursion into the abandoned German depot was partly motivated by a desire to own a bike. The distance from my grandmother's house to the sea was about a mile, but getting back from it in the middle of a hot summer afternoon, after three or four hours of swimming, playing and baking in the sun wasn't an easy walk. It would help a lot if I had a bike to get there and back. Besides, any notion of meeting and befriending girls required a bicycle, because they were spread all over town, and I couldn't very well show up promenading a mile away in some residential area without a good reason. I had to have a bike to bump casually into the girl I liked and make the meeting look accidental. You had to have a bike to say, "I happened to be in the neighborhood and thought . . ."

I used to save the meager allowance I had and spend it on bike rentals. I would get the oldest and most beat up bike in the store for half an hour or an hour at the most, and go as far as I could go in the allotted time. The desire for a bike had become an obsession. Sometimes, I would hang around the bicycle store and do some chores, so the owner, who was my grandmother's neighbor, could give me a freebie for an hour or so. I would have done hard labor to get the money and buy a used bike, but no one had that kind of work.

One day I happened to go down the basement of my aunt Katina's house and saw for the first time that there was an almost new bike, hanging from a hook on the wall. It was red and silver and was missing the front wheel. I found out that the bicycle belonged to my cousin Rena who was three or four years older than me. I had never seen Rena with a bike. She was a beautiful girl, interested in music and nursing, but never in athletics. Immediately I went to work on her, explaining to her that I could fix the bike at the bike shop of our neighbor and use it for a couple of months in the summer while she could use it the rest of the year. I thought it was a win-win proposition and there was no reason to turn it down. She said that she had intended to fix it herself; that she planned to do so at the earliest possible time; that she needed the bike to get around town now that it was safe, and that she wasn't sure she could spare it for two whole months in the summer. Seeing, I suppose, my glum face, she added that she'd think about letting me have it sometimes, after the bike was fixed.

A few weeks passed and there was no effort on her part to fix the bike. I wrote her a letter, making a heart-rending plea to let me fix the bike and use it, but I never sent it to her. I had been asking her every week, if there was any progress with the repairs, or if she had changed her mind, but that was as far as I was willing to beg. I suspected that her bike was one of the bikes abandoned by the German officers who had occupied her house. It was in lieu of war reparations that she came to own it, I supposed. Many years later, when I told Rena how I had pined for that bike, she couldn't even remember that she had a bike, let alone that I had wanted it so much.

The desire for a bike kept me alert for any opportunities that might come my way. One day, I had been swimming with the entire gang at one of the piers of the main harbor of Eleusis and, as I climbed out after a dive, I saw a beautiful red bike leaning up against one of the nearby bushes. I was dripping seawater as I approached and stared with admiration at that bike. A man appeared from behind the bush and stared at me.

"You like my bike?" he asked with a friendly smile.

"It's a great looking bike," I said, my eyes fixed on it. "Is it English?" I asked, recognizing the shield of a Raleigh bicycle.

"Sure is. You want to take a ride?"

"My swimsuit is still wet," I said.

"It's fine. Go ahead and go around the harbor."

I climbed up and pedaled away. I felt the wind on my face and the thrill of freedom. I was elated. If I could only get a damn bike, I kept thinking as I passed by all the stores I knew so well around the harbor.

I returned to the place I had started from and rested the bike back on the bush where I had found it. I told the man that he had a terrific bike, thanked him for letting me use it, and turned to leave.

"I can lend you the bike sometimes, if you want it," the man said.

I stopped dead on my tracks. "You could?"

"Sure! Come to the place I work some afternoon, and I'll let you use it until I leave at midnight. I don't need it when I'm working."

I said that I might take him up on that and thanked him.

The man worked at the local soap factory, a chemical plant near the harbor, which stunk the whole area with its odors. The father of one of my friends was the chief technologist there and their whole family lived in housing provided by the plant for key executives. The man asked if I knew that boy and I said that, indeed, I did. He told me that I could arrange to get into the factory through him. I thanked him and left. I was delighted that I had finally found someone willing to share his bike with me. It wasn't every day one comes across people like that, but they are out there, I thought thankfully.

A few days later, I went to the factory, got in with the help of my friend and headed for the warehouse where the man stored his bike. There was no one around. The place seemed deserted. The sun was burning and I needed shade. The warehouse was dark and much cooler than the burning ground outside. I got in and called out, "Hello," as loud as I could.

"Over here," I heard a voice respond from the depths of the dark space of the warehouse.

I walked cautiously toward the source of the sound. "Where are you?" I called out.

A few moments later I found myself staring at one of the building's walls and stopped.

"How are you, my friend?" the man said and came from behind and hugged me. "The bike is right over there."

I knew I was in trouble. I felt his arms tighten around my body and panicked. I kicked with my elbows and heels and pushed down to slide under his hold. I don't know if I screamed or not, but I turned around and pushed back. Somehow, I jumped out free and ran away toward the light.

I remember running up the hill that starts at the edge of the city of Eleusis, where the "Eleusinian Mysteries" were held for more than a thousand years. I had been there before, looking for shards from ancient vessels and small marble chunks with something sculpted on them, but I had never sought sanctuary there before. All along, I kept scouring the landscape behind me to make sure my attacker wasn't following me. I hadn't gone out through the factory gate. I had jumped over a low fence surrounding the back of the factory and found myself at the foot of the hill. I climbed to the top, by the small chapel where uncle Orestes, the poet, had married a year before, and sat down on the stoop to catch my breath. The clock up on the tower, a few yards away from the chapel, tolled the hours.

I thanked God for having given me the strength to fight and escape the pervert I had run into. I was angry with myself. I had allowed my obsession for a bicycle to blunt my judgment of people and circumstances and put myself in danger. I reflected on coming close to ruining my life. Sitting down on the marble step outside the chapel of the Holy Mary, I asked Christ to forgive me for my greed and my foolishness and I thanked him for saving me from a horrible ordeal. I learned first hand that there is no free lunch. Years later, I heard with sorrow, that my friend, whose father in that factory, had become a drifter with a messed up life. I always suspected that his friendship with that creep who attacked me was the cause of his ruin. I've always wondered whether somebody else might have been saved, if I had reported that criminal to the police, back then. I don't know, but I do know that it wasn't possible for me to talk about what could have happened in that warehouse from hell. I was too ashamed and too enraged to admit that a man had come after me and I hadn't been able to kill him. It took many years to talk about the incident. And, even though I escaped, I think I understand how the children who are molested by priests and other such pedophiles must feel. They feel like they are looking at a mirror, and the mirror is cracked, and will never show their image whole again.

It felt good to have fought and escaped disaster. I was enabled to overcome and survive other crises. I felt more confident. I thought that I could take on more challenges. I could be the person I wanted to be, because I could survive and prevail. I felt as if I had been resurrected.

32 • Grandma's Strong Presence

It will not be summer always; build barns.

Hesiod

In the summer of 1948, I remember running around grandma's flagstone yard and down the dirt paths that led to her orchard because the Olympics were on again, the fever of sports was at its peak, and Emil Zatopek was running the long distances and Fanny Blankers Cohen was sprinting and winning races on record times. I was desperately trying to change my high jump style from the scissors to the straddle and having no luck at all. Nondas and I with the help of "the Other Nondas" and Mitsos, the Sheriff, set up poles to jump over, dug up pits and filled them with sand to fall onto, measured distances to run, and marked the shot put arc to throw from. We proclaimed our competitions the Eleusinian Games and went at them with every bit of energy and determination we had. We never tired of arguing and contesting the results, blaming each other for unfair treatment, bias, bad intentions, errors, interference, ignorance of the rules and crimes against the spirit of the Games, perhaps, even against humanity.

After a couple of days or so the others would usually return to their homes, and I would be left alone with grandma. Some evenings I would water grandma's fruit trees and her vineyards by channeling the water into the ditches that led to the pools around the trees. I had to open dirt gates here and close them there and go from watering one tree to watering another tree. I liked to pluck a fruit from a tree and sit down on the dirt beside the flowing water to enjoy it. How many dreams did I start, listening to the water lap the red earth by the pomegranate and the peach trees? Because the grapes on the vines were green most of the summer, the only thing to taste were the tiny, sour, curling, green shoots that grow near the bunches of grapes. I had to pay attention to the height of the water and keep the gates open long enough for the tree to get some benefit from it, but not too long, because, according to grandma, too much water would "drown" the tree. Dusk would come and my work would be done, but I would linger and receive every drop of magical peace I could. I felt safe and free in grandma's house and her garden. My mind let go of all cares, and I joined the crickets chirping joyfully around me and sung with them a silent song of thanksgiving. Grandma would saunter down the path and look around her domain. She would inspect the quality of the watering and would look at me and ask me to get back soon for dinner. Though she never showed it, and never expressed her judgment with words, I knew when she was pleased and when I had come short of her expectations. I don't know if she ever tailored the dinner according to my performance, but I thought I got better dinner when the watering was done right. I was already trained to expect my just desserts.

Grandma Marigo – I just called her *Yaya*, in Greek – was a very sharp lady with a very sharp tongue and an iron will. You couldn't get anything past her. I wasn't afraid of her, but I had a lot of respect for her. I knew that she liked me, because she put up with all sorts of deviations from her rules without castigating me. When her ways of doing things clashed with mine in the open, I had no chance. I wanted to dip my bread into any sauce I could find, but she would have none of it, unless I used my fork to carry the bite of bread into the sauce. After the second or third violation, enforcement of the rule would turn from words to deeds in the form of a gentle tap on the wrist. You learn faster that way. There was one time when a serious issue came up and her patience seemed to run out.

I had been with her for a week or so, when I received a letter in the mail from my father containing, as usual, a variety of instructions on health, moral and spiritual procedure to follow and other advice. But, this time, in addition to his admonitions to behave properly, obey grandma, remember to pray and study topics relevant to my education, he sent me some money, the equivalent of today's $10 or so, for special foods, my weekly allowance and any special needs I might have. "Please, use the funds to make sure you supplement your breakfast with orange juice, eat a cup of yogurt before going to sleep, fruits after lunch and dinner." Then he concluded by saying that he knew that "fresh eggs are hard to find, but an effort should be made to secure a couple of 'little fresh eggs' at least a couple of times a week, since the vitamins and nutrients they contain are essential for proper growth." Finally, my father added his standard admonition: "If you have any money left, it is always wise to save it for future needs."

I was happy that my father had sent me any money at all, and I was going to pocket the money and forget the rest of his instructions, but grandma saw me receiving a letter with money and reading it with concentration, so she asked casually what was my father up to these days. I thought that it might be a good idea if grandma had the same information as I now had so that she would know what was good for me, and I went ahead with a word for word reading of the letter. I finished reading and waited. Silence held sway for a long time.

"So, your father thinks that you are starving here and wants me to feed you in a royal way because you are a special boy – is that it?" I was stunned by her tone of voice. The old lady was furious. "So, orange juice, yogurt, eggs – no, '*little fresh eggs*' for our boy, and then movies and candy, and let me see – did I cover the whole list? Yeah, he wants you to put some money in the bank for a rainy day. Right?" She looked at me, as if I had orchestrated a *coup d'état* against her rule. I said nothing. "Is that father of yours crazy?" I knew that this wasn't the time to open my mouth. "Speak, my boy; speak!" She wasn't fooling.

"I only asked for some allowance," I said, which was the truth.

She looked at me with her penetrating gaze weighing my guilt in this matter. A moment later she stood up. "Tell your father that fresh eggs are expensive and you need more money."

Some weeks later, I heard grandma tell my mother how she felt about that letter of my father. "He told the boy to eat all these things, eggs, yogurt, fruits and take his allowance from out of that measly sum . . . a few lousy drachmas . . . and then . . . then, if you can believe it, he told him to save some for 'future needs!' Can you believe that? He wanted that boy to invest for the future. Where? Does he want him to start and account at the bank? Is that man for real? Is he *that* tight?"

My mother chuckled. "Oh, he's tight all right," she said. "He still feels bad about losing the house."

"The house is gone. A lot of people got burned. Tell him to get over it," grandma said impatiently.

"He wants to build a new house for us. He won't quit."

Grandma reached into her pocket, where she kept a wad of large denomination bills, peeled out some and stuffed them in my mother's dress pocket. "Until I come to Athens and collect my pensions," she said. Every month she would come to Athens to collect the pensions from the government for her two fallen sons, Vassos and Agesilaos. (Agesilaos was killed in a ship explosion when he was a young naval officer, many years before I was born.) Sometimes she would stop by our house to visit with us. We were always glad to see her. My father also had a lot of respect and admiration for her. I had seen her push some money into my mother's pocket before, but I hadn't paid attention to it. No matter what might be happening, her presence was always a joyous occasion. Her strength mattered to me, especially when I was sick; it was a sure sign that I would get well and be out in the streets in no time at all having fun as always.

My father was tight with his money because of the deprivations he experienced in his formative years, as I have already mentioned. He found a measure of security when he was able to accumulate some savings. Many years later he told me how good he felt selling his shoemaker string spools for a few pennies profit and saving it. When he was a boy he saved every penny he made wrapping up customers' shoes as well. As he grew older, he lost sight of the fact that money is nothing in itself, but becomes something when used. He had money, but because he didn't use it, he never really had it. When he had accumulated enough, he spent it to build a big house in Athens. He felt honor bound, I think, to restore to my mother the house she had been given in her dowry and he had lost in the Great Depression.

But, he couldn't stop saving. He said that he didn't spend money because he wanted it for his children, but I think, he had also come to like just having it, or he was afraid to be without it. Grandmother Marigo liked him because he was smart, honest, worked hard and cared greatly for his family; but she had no use for the burden his obsession with saving money put on his family. Grandma Marigo didn't understand any better how complicated my father was than she had understood the complicated nature of her son, Vassos, when he was in love.

In spite of his tight ways, my father and mother took good care of my sister and me and supported me with as much money as Greece allowed students to take out of the country for college studies and helped me with the travel expenses when I needed his help. Perhaps, he could have done more, but he did spend enough to make it possible for me to come to America and, later, for my sister, who studied in Greece and in France. In the end, we all benefited from his saving habits – all except himself and mother. The world would be better if our parents had no flaws, but they do, and it is right for us to struggle from generation to generation, trying to make things better.

My mother, Vasso and I had started going to Eleusis regularly for summer vacations, when I was through with grade school. My father would send a truck to load our stuff and take us to the city we all loved so much. Mother was generally upbeat and took life without many expectations, but she became especially cheerful returning to her hometown, where she knew everyone, I thought, from the times of her youth. She was always friendly and, though she was a great one for information gathering and dissemination, she never used such information to her advantage. She just enjoyed the banter between friends. She was an avid moviegoer and, like me, she would go to as many movies as she could. She might have gone to the movies every night of the week were it not for having to take care of us and especially my little sister, who was quite a curious child and got into trouble exploring the strange environment.

I remember watching over my sister, Vasso, and being very proud of her ever-widening range of interests. I was always worried that something would distract me, and she would go tumbling down the stone steps from the second story of the house to the yard below, or that she would find some sharp tool, or stick, and fall and pluck an eye out. This was very real to me because it almost happened when we were playing at our home in Athens.

I was holding a sharp tent stake I had found somewhere, as we were playing on my parents' bed, and she fell on it and the stake dug into her little cheek. Blood came gushing out and I rushed for help. We took her to the doctor to stop the bleeding. The doctor said that she was lucky because the stake missed her eye by less than an inch. Anyway, I was always on pins and needles when I was in charge of her. Many years later, one of our cousins asked me whether I might not have driven that stake into the baby's cheek because I was jealous of the attention she was getting from my parents, edging me out of their love after ten years of exclusive attention. I thought she was crazy and told her so. I loved Vasso very much. Vasso was the most precious person in my life back in those days and, if anything, I was overprotective of her.

We were in Eleusis for the summer and Vasso was four years old, when she slipped away. I was distracted playing chess with Nondas, and she found her way to the yard door, which was left open. When I realized that she wasn't where I had left her, I looked around and saw her just outside the door, talking to a gypsy woman.

Most gypsies were poor people, consigned by society to be outcasts. They were trying to stay alive, but society demonized them and shunned them. Most of them walked barefoot all day long in the sun, hungry, thirsty and friendless, begging food to stay alive. Most Greeks shunned gypsies. No one would think of having any give-and-take with a gypsy. Unlike most people, my mother saw them as poor wretches who needed help and gave them alms regularly. But, people not only avoided them, they also feared them, because they could give you "the evil eye" and do other terrible things to you, if they managed to get close enough to you. I can't say that I despised gypsies, but I was afraid of them, felt sorry for them and didn't want any close contact with them.

It is not easy to admit, but we were all prejudiced against Gypsies, Jews, Armenians and others. They were "different" in some undesirable way. Even if you never felt that these minorities were inferior, you couldn't escape the disease of prejudice and discrimination. I cannot forget the time when I was riding my scooter in Eleusis, and two of my buddies started telling the story of how Jews kidnap children, stuff then in a barrel with nails on its sides, and roll the barrels downhill to draw out all the blood, which they then use to make their special bread. I heard a Jewish survivor of the holocaust tell this story fifty years later in America, describing the hatred some people harbor against Jews, and I wasn't surprised. I had heard it with my own ears, barely four or five years after the holocaust. What I wanted to convey with this lengthy digression, is that the sight of my baby sister being alone with a gypsy woman, for I don't know exactly how long, made me afraid, and I run toward her to protect her. The poor gypsy woman, thin, bent, barefoot and covered with rags jumped.

"I'm hungry, little Mister," she said, raising her shawl higher up on her face with her arm to cover it.

I stared at her but said nothing. Somehow, I knew that I was supposed to shout something at her and chase her away with some harsh words, but she was so bereft that I felt ashamed to utter any word. I gathered my sister and got back inside.

One of the women saw me and asked what was wrong. I said nothing, at first, but eventually I had to tell her and the others that Vasso had stepped outside and I had found her talking to a gypsy. All hell broke loose, and I was rebuked for letting my sister come under a gypsy's spell. What spell? I kept thinking. That poor gypsy was exhausted, hungry, tired – what would she be doing casting spells on a baby girl she just saw for two minutes at the most? My mother blamed me for taking my eyes off the baby, but said nothing against the gypsy woman.

Later that evening, my sister's face turned white and she passed out. "She's got the "evil eye," an old friend of my grandmother said. My mother was convinced that she could give the evil eye to others without willing any of it, if she admired their health or beauty or happiness, so she had no problem believing that somebody gave Vasso the evil eye; but she was very reluctant to blame the poor gypsy. She lost no time, however, taking her to aunt Assimo, across the street. Mitsos' mother, aunt Assimo, wasn't only the most renowned velentza blanket weaver for miles around but also the best exorcist in town. She took Vasso on her lap and examined her, getting ready to cast out the spell that the gypsy had allegedly cast upon her. We waited patiently for aunt Assimo to concentrate and do her job with prayer and various ritualistic moves like spitting in the air in front of the baby, ordering evil powers to depart and crossing herself and the baby. Then she yawned several times, taking whatever was lurking in the baby upon herself.

"She will be fine," she said when she had finished praying, and handed Vasso back to my mother.

"The demons are gone," someone announced as my mother carried Vasso upstairs to her bedroom. I was relieved that my baby sister was cured, even though I never believed that her sickness had anything to do with the gypsy she met. I didn't quite believe my mother either, when she said that once, she was watching a beautiful horse trot by and admired it so much that the evil eye got into the horse and it dropped right in front of my mother to everyone's astonishment. But, the culture presses down upon everyone and stuffs its prejudices into most psyches, and many don't have the critical ability to separate tales from facts, and they believe such hunches as if they were facts. Why didn't we ever ask what my baby sister ate that day? We had no refrigerators and many times food would spoil and cause stomachaches and nausea. No one cared about breaking the poor gypsy woman's heart with our fear and hatred. She was alone, somewhere out there, thirsty, dirty and starving under the sun that poured it scorching heat upon us all.

My mother was a good friend of Artemis, the woman my uncle had loved so passionately in the past. Now that Vassos was gone, Artemis reconciled with my grandmother, and hang around her house discussing the current happenings around town and politics as most Greek do. As far as I know, grandma and Artemis never talked about the old days, when Vassos was around. As I have described, Artemis was an eccentric and I'm convinced that her peculiar ways were partly the reason my grandmother disliked her. The old matriarch with her narrow limits of propriety couldn't stand a liberated daughter-in-law. But, I know, that if her son somehow appeared before her and told her that he wanted to marry Artemis, she would have said "yes" and danced a jig to celebrate.

For a time, I couldn't understand how my uncle could have been attracted to her, but after I got to know her a little better, I understood: she was a straight arrow, quick to catch on to everything around her; she was funny and oblivious to the gossip that followed her around town. She fit the stereotype of the manly woman, but she was a caring and upbeat person. She wanted to know what games we were playing and who was winning and how he was doing it so she could encourage and analyze. And she was a good friend with my mother, Mrs. Mara, the English woman who was renting part of grandma's house, and several other locals who knew my mother's and Artemis's families and started gathering in grandma's yard.

Mrs. Mara, as everyone knew her, was incorporated into the group, broken Greek, weird tastes and all. I had never met a person who liked to eat tomato salad with sugar and watermelon with salt. She said that where she came from, farting was OK but belching was definitely rude. She was responsible for expanding diversity in that little community, especially when they found out that she had been a lady sailor during the war, and her husband was a Greek naval officer. My certainty in the order of the world was shaken but I got over it. Why shouldn't women be sailors? But, the education she provided us was more extensive than that. Mrs. Mara liked to wear shorts and she had great legs to show. One hot summer afternoon, Nondas discovered that she liked to take cold showers out in the open, behind the house, using grandma's garden hose. He called me to see, but as usual, my myopia messed up the images and all I saw was a fuzzy white shape undulating like an apparition in the distance. I never saw the details of Mrs. Mara's naked body but I had her covered in my imagination even before the shower.

When grandma was still around, there weren't many cultural innovations in the community. She was always making sure that "the girls" were doing the right things and had a good life with her sons in law. She also kept her eye on the sons-in-law because they had a lot to do with the peace and prosperity of her daughters. I think that grandma didn't think that any of her sons in law measured up to her own sons, but she never quite disclosed her feelings about that. But, she had a few criticisms for every one of them. Uncle Kostas, who was married to aunt Athena, who went by the nickname Noula, for sure wasn't grandma's favorite. Perhaps, in the old lady's mind, being a mechanic and later an auto repair ship-owner, who worked with his hands, carried grease smells around and had a stevedore's mannerisms wasn't commendable enough. Perhaps, these are my own prejudices, not grandma's, in which case, I have no idea why she didn't like uncle Kostas very much. In any case, she didn't look forward to any of his visits, no matter how deferential he was. The family knew that, and her attitude toward uncle Kostas became a source of whispered jokes.

Uncle Kostas would stop by after driving his Jeep from Athens in a hot summer afternoon, and would open the yard door at grandma's house and look inside.

Grandma would see him and say, with a voice devoid of enthusiasm, but short of being rude, "Hello, Kostas; come in; you don't care for a cup of coffee, do you?"

Uncle Kostas would gulp, approach the old lady, and pining for a fresh cup of coffee even as he accepted his fate, would say, "No, Kyra-Marigo; I wouldn't think of coffee this time of day."

Grandma, perhaps out of feeling a conscience pang, would force out a meek, "Maybe some water, then?"

And, uncle Kostas would sit down and drink his hard won glass of water, talk a little about Noula, his wife, the children, Eleftheria and Nondas, give a snapshot of progress with his business and then get back in his Jeep and go about his business in Eleusis or one of the towns around it. Aunt Noula was, a chunk of pure gold, as they say in Greece about a very warm and kindly person, and I would always stop whatever I was doing and listen to news of her with interest. I spent a few days now and then at my aunt Noula's house and always felt at home. Noula was a master of sewing and good home cooking, but most of all I felt very relaxed when I was with her and loved her for her friendliness and patience.

Before I move on, I need to say that her other two sons-in-laws, that is my uncle Andonis and my father Petros, were a bit higher up in her esteem ladder because of their education or their career, but she had problems with them as well. Uncle Antonis was too remote, a cold fish, running his family with an iron fist, but a very good doctor, and my father – well, I have said enough already about her view of my father's problems and his gifts.

Sometimes, when I was alone in the house with grandma, I would skip the siesta, sneak down to the basement and start rummaging through the lockers where she kept all the memorabilia the family had accumulated over the years from the feats and the travels of her sons. I would sit at the edge of a locker and reach behind me at the pile of letters, postcards, manuscripts, receipts, certificates, theater programs, photographs, bulletins of various kinds, notes and booklets, pick one up, dust it and wipe it, unfold it carefully along its creases and start reading as I breathed in the musty air and the adventures of my uncles and their friends. I was in the desert with my uncle Orestes, a poet at work on a love poem to the woman of his dreams or his heart; I was at the port of Beirut, Lebanon, with barba Vassos in his naval officer's uniform, sending greetings to his mother and telling her he missed her homemade *jolia*-pasta and would be home soon to eat at her table again; I was watching the performance of *Daphnis and Chloe*, the best movie my uncle Orestes ever made and enjoying his moment of elation at its premier. And there were the difficult times when the walls of the room closed in on me and became the jail where barba Vassos, Commander Vassilios Laskos of the Greek Royal Navy, was detained while his fate was being decided, after his participation in the rebellion against the government; then, I had in my hands the letter from the Secretary of the Navy, expressing his profound sorrow to my grandmother at the time when my uncle Agesilaos was killed in the explosion of the *Leon*, the ship that he was in, and a man with a brilliant mind and a generous heart was lost. Sometimes I would catch a waft of the olive oil essence from the nearby wooden tanks with galvanized steel linings, where grandma used to store the oil produced in the olive groves the family owned. This olive-oil-flavored air, the moldy papers, the images of people and places I met or conjured down there in the wispy basement light and the words I read or imagined on those blessed afternoons flavored many events of my life.

Grandmother Marigo died after the Olympics of 1948. I remember the emptiness I felt on the day of her funeral, as I chewed on the traditional cookies and sipped coffee, which I had never done before. The old women who sung at wakes in Eleusis had been up at her room the night before and had wailed and cried and mourned all night long. Orestes was in awe of her strength, especially her stubborn countrywoman's courage to stare at death without despair.

The night before she died, she turned to the two women friends who kept her company and asked calmly. "Did you get wine?" The women looked at each other and thought that she was just babbling incoherently. They weren't planning any celebrations, so who needed wine? After she died, these same women friends performed the ritual washing of the dead body and as they poured the wine over it, they remembered grandma's words, "Did you get wine?" They told her three daughters, Noula, Katina and Marina, who couldn't contain their grief and they spread the word to those who knew and respected her. They all recognized grandma in the last, cool reminder she offered. They knew she was taking care of business and meant, "Get wine for my corpse." I heard something about the wine and grandma's death, but didn't catch the drift until Orestes, the only one out of her four sons still alive, mourning his beloved mother, wrote a poem that turned out to be one of his best. I quote the last stanza of his poem "*Mother's Death*" with my own translation:

> Our mother died tonight.
> We said our goodbyes with tears
> The few of us, her loved ones
> And they took her and left
> With laughter and joy, her husband
> And her three brave sons . . .

Grandmother Marigo was the most imposing woman I got to know in my youth, and a model of tough love and integrity. But, as I have already discussed, she had her dark side, like the rest of us. She was too strong-willed at times.

33 • My Impressions from Orestes' Words and Ways

Poets and heroes are of the same race; the latter do what the former conceive.

Alphonse de Lamartine

Uncle Orestes, my mother's youngest brother, was a free spirit whose talent and adventures mixed with my dreams and spiced my imagination and creative bent. He was the black sheep of the family but my father got along with him, not because he was a gifted poet or a dreamer, but because he was generous and needy of some order in his business. My father believed that he could give Orestes' life and business some common sense and a much needed stability. In spite of the fact that my father despised his bohemian lifestyle, he worked part-time in several of his theatrical enterprises as a bookkeeper, during and shortly after the war, and appeared to be content. Perhaps, he felt that using his considerable accounting skills to help a totally inept businessman-artist, who was a close relative, was an act of mercy, providing him with profitable part-time work. Orestes didn't have any special affinity for my father, but he trusted his expertise and respected his judgment so much that he was willing to put up with his conformist ways. More than that, however, Orestes wanted my father to handle all his business affairs because my father was known to be blunt and very honest, apparently a rare quality at that time. I always thought it strange that these two totally different people with very different temperaments and sensibilities, worldviews and lines of work, could find so much common ground. I think my father felt that Orestes needed a protector because of his naïveté and his incompetence in organizing his business and accepted the challenge of working for him. My father never had much respect for any of the Laskos' business savvy, except for my grandmother's, but in spite of that he was fond of them for the things he didn't have.

Orestes was as restless as his brother Vassos, but his venue was poetry and theater, not war and politics. I think he lived to experience life to the fullest and write poetry about it. He had traveled to Europe, the Middle East and Africa and had been a guest of Haile Selassie, the Lion of Judah, Emperor of Ethiopia, before the Fascists of Mussolini dropped their poisonous hyperite powder on the people and conquered the country. Orestes wrote a hugely successful poem ridiculing Mussolini in which the frogs of Lake Tsana in Ethiopia are extolling the mighty deeds of Mussolini against the defenseless, and impoverished people of Africa, like dropping hyperite powder to burn people alive. For his well-crafted and loving response to Ethiopia's plight, the Emperor was indebted to him and received him always with open arms in his court.

Orestes was a rebellious non-conformist; refusing to obey rules, no matter who set them or for what purpose. He was sent to the Greek Army Academy for a short time, but couldn't take the discipline and jumped over the walls of the institution to be free. He tried Medical School also, and there was photograph of him I found holding a human skull and pondering the big questions of life *a la* Hamlet, but he got out of there also, having no head for the study of facts. Before the Big War started, he made one of the most imaginative movies of the early Greek Cinema, *Daphnis and Chloe,* which is still considered a pioneering work of art. On and off he run a number of Variety Shows, as I have mentioned, to make ends meet during the hard times of occupation and shortly thereafter. Later in life, after he got married and had a child to support, he also made a bunch of B movies that he never talked much about.

His poetry was always daring and exuberant, always celebrating the courage of the poor and the helpless, the black people and the immigrants. He was a romantic, in love with people, places and dreams of a better world, but he had no head for planning, as his mother had, and his old age wasn't as carefree and exciting as his youth. He was a grasshopper and there was no ant around to gather provisions for the lean times. I always regarded him with a mixture of admiration for his zest of life and his flare, his adventurous life and his art, and with sadness for needing the adulation of others and the resulting waste of his talent. I could never quite decide whether he was someone to admire and imitate or feel sorry for. The best way to explain how I felt about Orestes is to describe how I got to know his mind, probably, better than most of my relatives.

I read his poems when I was a boy and a teenager and found most of them to be travels through the minds and hearts of people searching for their dreams, beyond the confines of geography. He had a sense of the absurd and understood well the power of metaphor, which made his poems intriguing and memorable.

One of his famous metaphorical poems, "Paris," is about a man who has been obsessed all his life by the thought of going to Paris, sometime in the future. Everything he does is motivated by the thought of going to Paris someday. He is one of those people that talk only about one thing every time you meet them, and for him that one thing was going to Paris. As the years pass, he makes definite plans to visit Paris, and one day, now an older man, he buys a railroad ticket and is off to fulfill his lifelong dream. He is filled with excitement as the train speeds toward Paris, and a feeling of elation grows in him, as he approaches the place that has given him reason to go on. He can't contain himself as he thinks of his dream becoming a reality.

Then, something unexpected and bizarre happens. In the parting fog of dawn he sees the outline of the Eiffel Tower approaching, and a terrifying thought rushes in his mind: "And then what? What would happen afterward? How could he possibly go on, without this yearning to go to Paris?" As the train approaches Paris' suburb of Saint Denise he arrives at a momentous decision. When the train stops, he gets off the train. With no qualms about his decision, he takes the next train going in the opposite direction, back to where he had just come from.

"And now," my uncle, the poet Orestes Laskos, writes, "as in the past, before he left, the man talks with yearning, and tells everyone he knows that the only purpose of his life, is to go to Paris, some day."

I often think of the many yearnings I have left unfulfilled, and resolve to wipe the slate clean. But, that too is a yearning and a purpose, so I cannot escape the trap of things I yearn for. Must we always have something that drives us forward, even if it's working toward having nothing that drives us forward?

Besides studying his poetry, I got to know uncle Orestes from gaining access to some of his other papers and from watching him in action, as he performed on stage for a living. On summer afternoons in Eleusis, when it was unbearably hot outside and the cicadas raised the roof with their monotone songs, I sat alone in the dark musty basement of my grandmother's house, where it was cool and quiet, and browsed through hundreds of postcards sent by uncle Orestes to his mother from Africa, the Middle East and Europe, and read many letters and captions of photographs and scraps of paper with scribbled fragments of notes and drafts of poems, all written by uncle Orestes over many years, or received by him from friends and relatives, and kept unsorted and unprotected from mildew and the occasional mouse that fancied feasting on Egyptian paper or doing its dirt on European *carte postal* pictures of great fountains. I felt that I was privy to the life of a restless soul seeking redemption from ordinary life and was encouraged to write, but not to follow in his steps. These explorations into the life of Orestes fueled my imagination with adventures to be desired and risks to be taken. If my uncles had seen and done so many things in the world, perhaps I could also.

I also got to know about uncle Orestes from his days as the MC at the Alcazar Theater in another neighborhood of Athens and when he became the owner and MC of the Zephyr Theater and, as I said, my father worked for him as a bookkeeper and business manager. Zephyr was an open air, variety theater under the bright stars that studded the summer sky, featuring bawdy songs, dancing girls in bright costumes on stage, skits with lots of jokes with double entendres and other entertaining bits dreamed up by Orestes and his fellow artists. I went there occasionally and watched the actors play their parts and tell jokes, and the women dance the cancan and show their long legs and their attractive bodies. Sometimes, I would sneak with my cousins behind the stage to gawk for a while longer at the women getting ready to perform, until someone with more rigid moral sensibility than most around there, would come by and chase us away for the night. We often talked about the possibility that one of these women would take pity on us and be our guide into the landscapes of our teenage imagination, but none ever did.

Orestes knew how to work a crowd and was quick to respond with the right joke to any wisecracks that wise guys in the audience often make in the *varieté*. One of his favorite games was to ask for words, any words that anyone in the audience cared to shout at him, write them down in a little notebook, go behind the stage for a few minutes and emerge with a meaningful, often hilarious poem, with rhymes for all the words the audience gave him and with fully fledged meter.

I remember one night, in particular, when someone shouted at him a seven-syllable word that doesn't exist in the Greek dictionary but sounds unbelievably funny and makes perfect sense anyway, being a combination of meaningful words.

"Lasko, Lasko, *Pagotopipilestra*," the man shouted his well-crafted word, and the whole theater burst out with a roaring laughter." (*Pagotopipilestra* "ice-cream-suckeroo," was the word, roughly translated into English). How on earth will he rhyme that? I thought with some concern. I should have known better. Orestes left the stage for a few minutes and returned with a poem that drove the audience berserk with laughter and adulation. I think he rhymed the word with Clytemnestra, the legendary wife of Agamemnon, king of Mycenae and leader of the Achaean army and navy in the Trojan War, as told by the great Greek poet, Homer. I admired Orestes' quick wit and tried to imitate him a couple of times with my friends, but it wasn't easy.

So, I got to know many sides of uncle Orestes. He was a dreamer with a gift for making words fly; in his lust for life he knocked down many boundaries but made a prison out of freedom; he was unselfish to the point of irresponsibility. Like his brother Vassos, he was a man of extremes, but people weren't as forgiving of him as they were of his heroic brother. He never saw limits coming; he just bumped into them. He married a wonderful woman when he was in his thirties and had a happy life with her, but he just wouldn't settle down and raise a family, as she desperately wanted to do. She was a famous singer in Greece and all the relatives loved her, but she couldn't make Orestes understand that the family life required some limits. Finally, they divorced. She left Greece for America and married a Greek ship-owner in New York.

Orestes married again, later in his life, and settled down, ironically, with a woman that didn't really want to invest much in raising a family. She had a career as an actress and her duties as a mother were delegated mostly to her mother, who didn't do a good job of raising the only son they had. The boy must have heard the stories told about his heroic uncle and the adventures of his father, but must have been unable to sort out the good lessons from the bad, so he ended up being a man without a college education, without any skills or trade, without a career or a job, without a definite plan for his life, without limits and with a lot of debts. The family has no praise for the son of Orestes, but no one should judge before a person's end comes. The last I heard of him is that he had a child with medical problems and was acting responsibly and lovingly in caring for his son. There is always time to change and do things right.

The ambivalence I felt about Orestes, and Vassos for that matter, came from my being rooted to the middle ground, from living in the gray areas of choice. When I encounter a new situation, I can do no less that see both sides of any picture, any argument, any proposition, and dream any goal and idea and choose sometimes this and sometimes that, but never skip the anxiety of choice and the twists and turns that reasoning imposes upon the straight path of impulse. But, there is a downside to this way of looking at the world: sometimes I get stuck in the midst of indecision and I have to suffer more than I want until the answer comes out of nowhere and breaks through the cloud of alternatives I often stuck up around me.

Many years later, while in America and working as an engineer, I wrote a book about my college years, to escape the stifling atmosphere of working in the defense industry. The protagonist compares many events of his life to the adventures of Jason, a character that parallels the life and times of uncle Orestes. I translated portions of the unpublished novel into Greek and showed them to Orestes. He was depressed at the time, relegated to spending most of his days at his wife's little hole-in-the-wall of a store where she sold antiques. She was an actress, the *ingénue* in his

B movies, and wanted Orestes around, I think, as a draw for their business. He liked the novel and urged me repeatedly to go ahead and publish it. I asked him if he was still writing poetry. I remember that his face clouded, and his eyes lost all their intensity as if their focus was far away, in a world out of reach to anyone but him.

"No more," he said. "The muse has no more gifts for me."

I felt profoundly sad and wished that there were something I could say or do for him, riveted as he was in a wooden chair confined in triviality and commerce. The adventurer of life and word was depleted. We went out a couple of times for dinner and he joked a little about my having left Greece for the "icebergs" of Minnesota. He wanted to know everything about the cold and the ice and the frozen lakes and the people.

"What are you doing out there in those bear-lands, nephew?" he asked. "You should come back here. Look up at the sky and the stars – do you have anything like that in Minnesota?"

I humored him and joked about the good life in the polluted city of Athens. Before I left him, he confided in me.

"I like Jason, in your book," he said. "Thanks for remembering me. Not many do."

34 • City, Marsh and Sea Adventures

After grandma's death, part of her house in Eleusis was rented to Mrs. Mara, the English lady I have already mentioned above and her family, and partly used by all the relatives as a summer vacation place. My mother and I continued to be regular summer visitors. My father would come Fridays from work and stay for the weekend. Nondas had lost his father and mother and would come to stay in Eleusis with one of his sisters. We were good friends and we lived in a state of constant competition. "The Other Nondas" was an occasional visitor, and Mitsos, Takis and other local boys would come and go as it suited them. "The Other Nondas" would sometimes come with his father, uncle Kostas, and join the gang in its adventures.

Nondas and I were scavengers. We rummaged through grandma's basement nooks and crannies regularly unearthing old photographs, flower vases, Japanese teacups, embroidered drop cloths, blankets from Australia, knives, letters, a leftover German magneto and other stuff. We used whatever was of interest to us for the games we played. The most precious find was barba Vassos' ceremonial sword with his name engraved on the steel blade that was inside a gold-sculpted scabbard and kept inside a black leather case. We would take the sword out, hold it from its golden handle and take turns parading with it rested on our shoulder. There were arguments about who found it and who should have it some day and whether we should even disclose its existence to anyone else, but overall we managed to resolve all of these issues by never having to decide. It was generally accepted among all the surviving sisters and uncle Orestes that all memorabilia would go to the authorities some day, to be displayed in a place of honor for the public. The Navy, I think, got the sword for the naval museum. In time, the city of Eleusis bolted a marble plaque at the front of the house with my uncle's name, designating it as the house where Captain Vassilios Laskos, our barba Vassos, was born and raised. A braid of laurel leaves embossed in the marble with gold surrounded the inscription. One of my aunts found a painting of Captain Laskos in ceremonial uniform, which was later given to the city of Eleusis and hung in his memory at the City Hall where it still is as far as I know. Uncle Orestes inherited the family home, and later, against the protests of everyone in the family, sold it to a realtor to provide living expenses for his family. The realtor tore down the historic house and built a multistory office building. Everybody disapproved of Orestes' decision, and talked about it behind his back, but everybody knew that they would have done the same thing, if they had inherited the house. There is no market for memories, but real estate can always be sold and put food on the table.

One afternoon, rummaging deep into grandma's basement, Nondas and I came across a WWI rusted rifle that we called "the Mauser" because that was the only name of any old rifle we knew. The wood of the butt had rotted away and the moving parts were stuck together by rust. But we had been looking for a gun for a long time and this was a find that could not be dismissed out of hand. We decided to bring it back to life at all costs. It took us days to clean the rotten wood away, scrape and sand the rust as much as we could, oil and grease every surface we could reach and end up with a rifle that had a sluggishly moving bolt, and a metal outline of a butt but no wooden butt at all.

After all the work we put into it, we realized that the rifle couldn't be fired because we had no way of holding it. We were disheartened. When we started the cleanup, no one had actually thought that the rifle could be fired, but the more rust we cleaned, and the more easily the parts moved, the more we thought about firing it. Mitsos got a bullet from his father's stash of bullets and loaded the rifle. We now had solved all the problems involved in shooting the rifle except the problem of holding the thing and pulling the trigger.

One morning, we were sitting on the sidewalk, outside grandma's house, when the horse drawn water cart came by. Eleusis had no central drinking water supply at the time, so everyone had to buy water from the waterman. The neighbors flocked to the stopped cart and the waterman started filling their jugs and five-gallon jars and canisters and collecting his money. The barrel, out of which water was dispensed, was held tight up against the frame of the horse-drawn cart with ropes. "That's it! Ropes!" Mitsos cried out triumphantly and proceeded to explain how we could solve the rifle problem that had stumped us.

We tied the rifle with rope around a concrete block and placed the assembly on top of the wall fence that separated grandma's house from the warehouse. Mitsos was ready to pull the trigger, but Nondas and I stopped him. We insisted on tying the trigger to a string and pulling it from far away as if it was a lanyard for a canon. We loaded the gun, and gave Mitsos the string. We hid some twenty feet away, sitting down low and behind the wall fence. We had no idea whether the gun would fire the bullet or explode and spread shrapnel all around us, maiming anyone who hadn't sought cover. Something seemed to be out of whack. It seemed to me that what we were doing at the time wasn't real. The three people ready to endanger themselves were familiar figures related to us, but not us. Nondas started counting, and when he called out "three,"

Mitsos pulled the lanyard. The gun moved and fired the bullet in a direction no one could fix until we went closer and saw that the door of the infernal warehouse had a hole now. We congratulated each other for the feat we had accomplished like the NASA team at Houston did when the Lunar Lander touched the moon surface. But when the celebration was over, we vowed that we would never fire the rifle again. The gun was too unpredictable even for us. Mitsos took it, promising to fit it with a wooden butt and bring it back sometime. He never did, and no one ever asked to know anything more about it.

Besides the inner circle of friends I have already discussed, I had some other, occasional friends I met swimming or in the square of Eleusis or the bike rental store. One of them was Nassos, whose family had a farm a couple of miles out of town. Sometimes he would ask me to go with him and help him with the chores. We would saddle up a donkey and head for the farm, riding on dirt roads, barren fields and other not so friendly terrain. We gathered figs and pistachios, picked tomatoes and watched the oxen draw water from the well as they went around and around their post. We ate wheat bread fresh from the stone oven of his grandmother and feta from their goats with tomatoes that never saw a chemical in their lives. We would find a thriving plane tree lie under its heavy shade and take a siesta on the grass with a stone for pillow. Later in the afternoon, we and other kids from nearby farms would dive into the holding tank used for irrigation, filled chest-high with well water and, shaking from the cold, we would scream and flap our arms as hard as we could in the small space to keep ourselves from freezing.

When the chores and the fun and games were done we would climb back on the donkey and head home the same way. That's what we always did, except for that one time when, either out of curiosity or on a dare, or a bet of some kind, or just out of that urge for adventure that somehow kicks in at times in adolescent minds, we decided to go through Kalimbaki, which was a huge swamp on the outskirts of town. We weren't sure we could make it, but Nassos put a lot of stock on his trusty burrow and I had no reason to be afraid.

We made our way to the edge of the swamp, where the reeds were growing thicker, and planned our crossing with care. The donkey balked at first, as if it knew that we were up to no good, but Nassos reassured it that all would be well and dug his heels into its ribs, commanding instant obedience. We started slogging it through the muddy water, which became thicker and gradually deeper as we moved out. Thirty yards out into the dark morass below the reeds, we jumped down from the saddle to help the poor beast float. At fifty yards into the swamp, the donkey was no longer floating; it got stuck in the muddy bottom and had trouble keeping its head above water. We could barely move and the donkey was going nowhere; standing was becoming a problem; breathing for the beast was about to become not only a problem but also the end of all problems. Both of us put our shoulders on the donkey's underside, trying to lift it up enough so it could get its legs out of whatever hole they were in.

I remember thinking rationally, that what we were doing couldn't possibly solve the problem: the donkey's legs had to stand on something, and standing six inches out from where they were now couldn't possibly help, since the mud was as treacherous there as it was where the legs were planted now. But, there was no other apparent action I could think of, so instead of protesting or giving up, I pushed up and up with all my strength, thinking of Atlas as he took Heaven and Earth upon his shoulders. I could feel the donkey flexing its leg muscles and shifting its weight in a desperate effort to get out. And then, Nassos and I happened to look at each other and burst out laughing.

At the brink of disaster we were laughing uncontrollably. But the donkey kept fighting to move and instead sunk deeper into the mud. We cut out the laughter and came to our senses. The sight of the poor beast swallowing water as it went under and drowned in the muddy waters of Kalimbaki horrified me. Terror swept over me. We had made a bad mistake. I was thinking of death when I felt that my foothold was a tad firmer than it had been a moment ago.

I took a step on what felt like a more solid ground and we pushed with all we had. The donkey lifted one leg, then the other. Its jaw was no longer in the muck. We pushed and dragged the animal to a firmer ground. Against all odds, we made it to the field, where reeds left off and the grass took over. Nassos said that we had "hit a soft spot in an otherwise rock-hard bottom." I told him to get back on the road and forget the swamp forever. We got back to the city and stopped at one of the street fountains with brackish water that Eleusis had been left with due to some plumbing foul-up, years ago, and cleaned the mud from our bodies and the donkey. The only thing that stuck on me was the memory of dread at the donkey's plight, coupled to an uncontrollable urge to laugh at the donkey as it struggled to stay alive. Tragicomedy made no sense until the donkey fought to stay alive, as if it had unalienable rights and would fight to protect them.

It should be clear by now that my summers in Eleusis were filled with adventures that were often dangerous. Every morning, half a dozen of us would gather outside grandma's house and head for the harbor of Eleusis on foot, about a mile away. We wore our swimsuits and walked, usually barefoot, which was almost unbearably hard to do when coming back home from the harbor in high noon, when the sun was beating down on the asphalt and made it soft in places and burning. Sometimes the water peddler would stop his horse-drawn cart and let us hitch a ride back to the house.

We swam in the harbor or in the waters around it, which were sometimes polluted by leakage from the ships or the effluent from the factories that were near the harbor. We had no cheap transportation to get to the clean, sandy beaches west of Eleusis. After the navy yards and the steel mills were built the entire coastline around Eleusis was polluted and no one would dream of swimming there anymore.

Sometimes, my cousin Omiros and his friends would also go swimming in the harbor and my friends and I would hang around them. They were several years older than us and liked to play polo and dive from every high place they could find. One of Omiros' friends was the best diver around Eleusis and had taken a dive from one of the cranes that were used to unload ships, sixty feet up in the air. Another friend tried to match that dive and hit the water at an angle less than ninety degrees and got badly hurt. They said that doctors had to take out his spleen, which wasn't so bad, but sounded ominous at the time. I liked my cousin Omiros because he also had been a top student in school and now he was at the University studying to become a doctor. He was a very good chess player, and I learned a lot from watching him and his friends play. He also was quite adept with girls, and I was always trying to find out how he went about making contact with them. It took me a while, but I found out how: he wasn't interested in making friends with girls; he was interested in sex. That was a different problem and I didn't have to solve it at the time.

I learned how to swim when my cousin Omiros, out of the blue, threw me into the harbor of Eleusis. The water was about twenty feet deep, and I went down in a daze. I felt the terror of sinking and beat the water in a panic. Somehow in the few moments I felt so utterly helpless and doomed, I became aware that my flailing produced results. My head was out of the water and I breathed and spewed water out, and blew air and water and shook my head around to prove to myself that I was indeed up like a cork out of the depths. I beat the water some more and got to the edge of the harbor, a few feet from where I had plumbed the depths of the sea.

Omiros gave me a hand and congratulated me. I was furious with him, but also thankful for having made a swimmer out of me by brute force. Before this incident, when I was learning how to swim by going a few inches deeper every day, I never believed those who bragged about having learned the art of swimming in the sink-or-swim manner. Now I was one of them and I was elated. I was ready to learn all the styles of swimming and diving. In no time at all, I learned how to swim every which way, but never correctly, never without all the flaws that beginners invent.

Diving was another matter, however. There was no margin to stretch and make up for errors. I would dive head first from the concrete docks that were only three or four feet high, from the fishermen's boats that were anchored nearby and from anything we could stand on or climb upon. Sometimes we would sneak into the merchant ships that came from all over the world and docked in the harbor, and we would dive from their decks. I never mastered the art of diving head first from a board or from a solid platform. I would climb up twenty or thirty feet high on the decks of the ships and jump holding my legs and my seat together, landing on my bottom. I was clumsy, had nothing to brag about in front of any girls, but I had a lot of fun, anyway.

That summer, all of us wanted to swim like Furuhashi of Japan, who had broken some world records and swam like a fish. Since I always had looked a bit Oriental, I laid the most potent claim on Furuhashi and had my picture taken swimming the crawl to prove the similarities in style.

Teenagers can be incredibly deluded, but the phase passes with time. If one has grown up, and likes the child he once was, the childish delusions become warm memories of past awkwardness.

After I had mastered swimming and a few crude forms of diving I began to think of finding a boat to get around with. The German torpedo-like object we had discovered at grandma's warehouse would come to mind often, and I would start regretting the missed opportunity to make something out of it. With a few appropriate modifications, it would become a kind of speedboat in my overactive imagination. To my great disappointment, by the time I developed the urge for a naval operations, the warehouse had been emptied. Grandma had sold everything in it to a junk dealer before she left us. Trucks had come and hauled away all the wonders that had been inside that technological Mecca. The torpedo-like vessel was gone, but the urge to be in one persisted.

I decided to build a boat. I had another friend, Spyros, who lived near the seashore and his father was in construction. I sold Spyros on my plan to build a boat. Spyros was looking for some adventure, and building and sailing a boat turned him on. Immediately he wanted to know how, and how big, and out of what, and all the things that go into making a boat happen, as if I had been building boats all my life and knew all about them.

We converted a corner of his father's workshop into a shipbuilding dock. We needed some two by twos, a lot of sheet metal, some nails and a bucket of tar, all of which we found in the workshop and the yard outside. We ended up with a ten-foot long by a foot and half wide and a foot deep boat. It wasn't a very wide or a very deep boat, but we could both fit inside it. We pasted tar generously on all the joints to seal the hull and stared at our work for long intervals as if that would correct any mistakes we made. I wasn't entirely happy with the way we were holding the metal sheets together, but I agreed that we should take the boat for a spin the next day and make changes, if needed. The boat was much heavier than I had imagined, but I thought it would keep us afloat, anyway. Spyros' house wasn't far from the waterfront and with a little effort and few stops we carried the boat to the sea and lowered it down from the pier to the water with ropes.

We let go and watched as the boat floated. "The vessel is seaworthy. It floats and seems to be stable," I lectured Spyros. He placed a lot of trust on me and was willing to follow me without asking many questions.

"We did it," he shouted and jumped and applauded.

"Not yet," I cautioned. "We've got to get inside and go some distance out to see if it holds." Spyros got in after me, and I pushed us away. We started rowing with our hands. I couldn't believe that all our mistakes had been overcome. "We are moving," I screamed in disbelief.

"We're sailing away," hollered Spyros, even more surprised than me.

When we had covered about twenty five yards or so, Spyros, sitting up front turned his head and with eyes glazed by terror announced, "We are taking water," and pointed to the bow of the boat, where metal was joined to the two by twos and the seams were leaking. I looked at the back of the boat, where I sat, and water was trickling into the boat. We were going down. We tried to stop the leaks by applying pressure on the joints but it was no use. We started to row as fast as we could toward the shore.

In trying to seal the leaks and row, we moved our bodies around and before we knew what happened the boat capsized and we were in the water. We found the boat at the bottom of the sea and lifted it up enough so we could hold it under the water. "We can hold onto the boat and swim," I cried out after diving and looking at the boat. "We can drag the boat out and fix it," I said.

"Are you crazy?" Spyros shouted, struggling to keep his head above water.

"We can do it. Just fifteen yards or so, and we'll be in the shallows and walk out."

And so began one of the most gruesome ordeals I have ever stumbled into. I had no idea how heavy a boatful of water could be, when you try to move it underwater. It was hard work. Heavy! Sluggish! After ten yards or so of swimming with the boat, we could stand on the tips of our toes and walk with it. When we reached the pier, we fell down exhausted. We knew that we had to lift the boat up about four feet, to the top of the pier, but we were worn out and just stared up at that final ordeal and did nothing for a long while.

"Damn junk!" Spyros cursed the boat.

"We didn't seal the seams right," I said. "Let's get it out of the water now and be done."

"What for?" Spyros protested.

"I don't know. We can't leave it here."

We lifted up the boat with whatever remaining strength we had left, and carried it back to the workshop on our backs.

"We'll have to do it right next time," I said as I was leaving.

"Sorry it didn't work out," Spyros said.

"I'm sorry too. I wanted to show you the boat I had in mind."

I left and never saw that boat or Spyros again. We never quarreled, or broke up our friendship; it was just that our joint enterprise was such a failure that we both must have wanted to forget all about it.

I wish I knew what happened to Spyros. As for me, I went to study Engineering, though I never really was enamored with the actual making of things. My work was done when I had finished imagining the thing I wanted to make. But the process of building the boat, solving the problems that cropped up and the thrill of those first twenty yards of rowing the boat we made was worth all the disappointment of failure. I've always managed to gain something from every failure I've had. You just don't lose it all.

35 • Pointers for Life and Love from an Old Tar

Why, I'd like nothing better than to achieve some bold
adventure, worthy of our trip.

Aristophanes

Not all my activities were mischievous in the summertime at Eleusis. As
I have already mentioned, I read a lot of books, worked on many puzzles,
wrote a few poems and had some fruitful conversations with my friends
and some of the older people who gathered at grandma's house every
day. Sometimes, after a healthy afternoon siesta, I would go to Kitsos'
workshop and watch him make furniture. My grandmother gave him the
old garage at the back of the house to use as a workshop, and he went
about making furniture from scratch with the most primitive hand tools
around.

Kitsos (the name for Dimitris in Arvanitika) had been a sailor, my
uncle's steward, his "Man Friday" always with him at sea, in whatever
ship, on whatever adventures my uncle had undertaken. Kitsos survived
the disaster that befell my uncle, and came back to his hometown in
Eleusis after the war to earn a living as a carpenter. The man was a
natural in carpentry, judging from the furniture he made and a kind of
philosopher or "Dear Abby" adviser. I remember discussing all sorts of
subjects with him, when he worked on making my uncle-doctor
Andonis's desk and his wall-to-wall bookcase. He was one of those
people who like to talk to kids as if they could handle grown up work
and conversation, and I liked that. Sometimes he needed an extra hand to
hold a board, and he let me help him set the clamps that held together the
longer pieces of the furniture he was working on; he let me plane a few
boards when they were still pretty rough, and he let me make holes with
his hand drills on discarded boards to get the hang of the tools. Once, he
showed me how to make glue from scratch, though I could never get too
close to that brown, gooey stuff because its fishy smell was too much for
me to bear. I did like the smell of the varnish, however, and the smell of
olive oil that he used to finish the furniture, after he stained it. It would
have never occurred to me that there was so much labor, so many steps
and patience and care in making a piece of furniture. Kitsos was a
perfectionist and every detail was important to the work he had in mind.
When one of the neighbors stopped by one time and suggested a way for
making the bookcase more versatile, Kitsos all but laughed at him. He
said in no uncertain terms that the bookcase he had in mind was finished

before he started making it. "I've always known what I want to make," he said; "I don't do trying very well, even if sometimes I botch it up."

When he took a break to smoke a cigarette, we talked about the sea, the places he and my uncle Vassos had visited, and the people around the world they had met. He said my uncle would do anything for his friends and his crew, and that's why people loved him. But, he added, that's also what caused most of his troubles. He told me that being my uncle's trusted aide was the best thing he could have done with his life. In spite of all the disasters he had been in, including being with my uncle when their cargo ship, carrying onions to England was blown out of the water by a German submarine in the Mediterranean, in spite of having followed my uncle in rebellion, in spite of having been robbed and mugged in strange harbors keeping my uncle company in his adventures, even in spite of having lost many a friend including my uncle in the final battle of the submarine *Katsonis*, he wouldn't want to live any other way. "That's what I wanted, and that's what I did with my life. Take the risk and deal with the results," he said.

"What about carpentry?"

He stared at me with a smile. "There's adventure here too . . . as long as you do it right: fix on something in your mind and build it without second thoughts and compromises. Sometimes it works and it's the best you can make it."

My mother had told him about my dream of going to America to study engineering. He told me how much he had wanted to travel there, but never made it. He would have loved to see the Empire State in New York, the tallest building in the world. He told me about the Grand Canyon and Hollywood. He said that those who dream must always know that some of their dreams may turn to nightmares. "That's how it's been, and that's how it will be."

Many years later, when I taught a course on *"Technology and the Humanities"* at the University of Minnesota, I came across a very relevant metaphor. It was an epitaph left by the shipmates of a Greek sailor on his grave, after he was lost at sea. It reminded me of a conversation I had with Kitsos, centered on the fact that worthy enterprises require us to take a risk. Here is what the shipmates of that ancient mariner wrote on his tombstone, as quoted by Gordon W. Allport, in *"Psychological Models for Guidance"* and published in *Science and Literature* by Edward M. Jennings, 1970:

A shipwrecked sailor buried on this coast
Bids you set sail.

Full many a bark, when we were lost,
Weathered the gale.

Gordon Allport explains: "The dead sailor urges us to make the wager, take the risk, although we cannot be sure of coming through to our destination."

Sometimes I went to see Kitsos to talk to him about my heartaches with the girls I got to meet in Eleusis, hoping that he would give me some hints on how to relate like a human being with the opposite sex, rather than turn to a porcupine with its needles turned inside and getting gouged. I was about fifteen or sixteen by then, and I had already separated all girls into two categories: those I could befriend and be polite with, and one or two select others, who made me feel tongue-tied, clumsy, small and helpless. Kitsos told me to stay away from the "little mothers," because they could and, at my age, for sure would make my life miserable. "Better have friends now and learn how to think before you jump," is the way he put it. When I asked who were these "little mothers," he said "all those girls that you cannot get out of your mind, because you want to feel their warmth and snuggle with, but you must not, because you'll get burnt."

That was precious little advice to venture into the world of relationships with girls at my age. And, every summer, there were a couple of "little mothers," around, who made my head spin. One of them fit very nicely the image of a cherub that I had seen in art books. I hardly knew this girl; I met her through one of my buddies in Eleusis and talked to her for a minute or two. But, that's all it took for me to be hooked. I met her in groups once or twice after that, but I couldn't find the words to impress a cat, let alone get the attention of the most sought after girl around. But, I was persistent, and tried to get my friends to find excuses so I could meet with her. I rented bikes and took rides around her house, but I never managed to be with her. I came close to ringing the door bell to her house a couple of times, but I couldn't cook up a good enough excuse to give, if one of her parents answered the door. "Hello. I'm your daughter's friend and I came to hug her and kiss her and take her away and fly blissfully to Hawaii," I would say, and they'd lock me up at the insane asylum in nearby Daphni. I went swimming to a dozen different beaches looking for her, but I cannot recall a single occasion when I met up with her.

One of my buddies had a sister, a nice approachable girl without a boyfriend or other suitors, who, I thought, liked my company. The problem was that I was fixated on the "little mother" and couldn't stand the girl who cared for me. When I found out that she knew the cherub, I schemed on how to get to her good side and use her to reach my ethereal beloved. But, my schemes stunk, and I usually knew that they did, and I had enough sense to never carry them out. Well, never is, perhaps, a bit too strong. The reality is that I did some stupid things from time to time, but I always knew that I was doing them. I don't think that I ever had the luxury of ignorance or lack of awareness when doing the wrong thing. This way, in my own mind, I was always the guilty perpetrator, but never the innocent victim. I often wondered if others knew when they were doing wrong.

Sometimes, I felt guilty even when I didn't do anything wrong. That, I think, I owe to my mother, who tried her best to teach me right from wrong, but bundled some right things along with some wrong ones, and helped me construct a big bruiser conscience. She wanted to know everything I had done, or planned to do, or was thinking about doing, or wanted to do but hadn't had the opportunity to do yet, and managed to gain joint custody of my private thoughts. So, when I attempted to keep anything to myself, I thought I did something wrong, and felt guilty. I grew up sitting right on the old horns of a dilemma: I could hold on to a secret and suffer as if I had done something wrong, or feel the bliss of having no guilt to carry around but have no secrets at all from my mother. Telling Kitsos about my troubles with girls was a relief. It was a way out of the dilemma, since I could have secrets from my mother, but felt no guilt because I had disclosed my thoughts to Kitsos. So, Kitsos, the old tar with a knack for carpentry and philosophy, became my surrogate mother for a couple of summers. And for Kitsos, a boy having feelings about girls, wanting love, passion, delirium, whatever, wasn't a problem at all. He had no family of his own, and he must have felt useful passing his life's experience to a boy who could make something out of them.

I got free of my fixation on the cherub only when I saw her a year later with a face marred by full-blown acne. My face probably was a mess also at the time, but since she had no desire for me I don't think my sorry face made any difference to her.

I was always exaggerating what I felt for a girl I liked, like an amplifier of romantic feelings, which made me totally inept at protecting myself from these feelings! My cousin Nondas used to call me an "ethereal lover." I think he got sick of listening to me tell him all about my feelings for the angel I had created out of brown braids and silky skin, or green eyes and a blond pony tail and branded me to shame me into silence. It didn't work. The two of us would stretch a couple of heavy blankets out in grandma's flagstone yard, under the old pine tree, and staring at the star-studded Attic sky on August nights we would talk about our goals and our dreams and our loves before falling under the spell of Morpheus.

Nondas wasn't poetic in his expression, but he was a good buddy and gave me good advice. He was pragmatic, a born trader, and, in time, he found a way to use his gifts for business as a corporate executive. But at the time, he also succumbed to the lure that engineering had for the brightest kids around. I know that he had a passion for trading, because he was always looking for opportunities to make a profit. He used to go around town and collect things people didn't need or had discarded, which he could later sell for a nice profit. He had a grasp of trade, and became the best salesman at his uncle's grocery store, after both his parents died and he had to find a job to survive. We were competing all the time, on anything that could possibly be conceived to be a scarce resource and remained lifelong friends. The competition between us for top honors in high school became perennial and lasted through the six years we were together at Varvakeion high school. His time to find the love of his life came a couple of years later. Myrto was a wonderful woman, and he was the happiest of men when they got married.

The other "little mother" I was struck by in the summer after my non-adventure with the cherub, wasn't a cherub at all. I don't even think that she was a "little mother," either. Rather, she was an Amazon. She was a desirable young woman, radiating health, vigor and energy. How on earth could I have ever thought that I could get close and personal with that fireball, having come out of my previous adventure (or virtual adventure) with a robust complex of inadequacy and incompetence, is not easy for me to understand. But that's what I attempted to do, only I spent another miserable summer chasing after her and worrying now about the suitors who might get to her before I could. After many stargazing and strategizing nights, after countless schemes on attempts to get her to talk about herself, us, our plans after high school, the beauty of nature or anything else more serious than who met whom swimming where and when, I began to have doubts about my feelings for her. By that time, I was the top student in my high school class, and I had higher expectations. Still, her appearance was so striking that I was perfectly willing to overlook her mind and her character. I was perfectly willing to trade my brainpower for her sex appeal. But, the trade of resources wasn't working out. Without the advanced marketing techniques developed by Americans many years later, you couldn't sell what people didn't need. And this Amazon had no interest in brains, either hers or mine, whereas I was perfectly willing to close the deal, any deal. To complicate matters, she liked me, but, as they say, "not in that way." She had a twin sister, however, who liked me precisely "in that way," even though, as it usually happens, I had no eyes for her. My insecurities wouldn't allow me to be interested in anyone whom I perceived to be a consolation prize. And my object of affection was bent on directing me toward her twin sister like a traffic cop ordering traffic to another lane.

I was furious at the turn of events. I felt that a superior power was demoting me to a lesser class than the one in which I rightfully belonged. I could imagine the two sisters talking about me like Nondas and I talked, and having fun at my expense for my inexperience. I don't know why it is so, but there were several occasions in my young life when I would go after one girl who had no interest in me, and at the same time there would be another girl – her sister, her friend, a fellow student – who would hit on me. I would strike out with the object of my affection, and the girl chasing me would strike out with me. The pieces just didn't fit, but I had no idea why. Was this one of Mother Nature's jokes? Perhaps, this is nature's way of making sure that young adults don't go berserk, falling in love prematurely only to drop out just as fast. My cynical self wants to say that these days, some sixty years after the events I'm describing, nature has been twisted enough so anyone is to everyone's liking, but, I hope, that it is not so. Anyway, my desire to be with the Amazon of those summer fantasies began to abate when I realized that every time I saw her, her twin sister was with her. I started dreading those meetings. I got the message. This crisscross triangle (with a potential to turn to a square at any moment) was getting me down. Besides, by that time, the main attraction, my Amazon, just wasn't meeting all my standards, anyway.

Many years later, when my sons were looking for their soul mates, they concluded that there were four main criteria to check: looks, brains, heart and character. This girl came up a little short on a couple of these, or, more likely, I was doing a masterfully disguised "sour grapes" job on myself to cope with the pain of rejection – I don't really know. The truth is that I was free and ready for more adventures and heartaches. The lesson I learned from these misadventures was that they don't knock you out. Everything changes, and life is a struggle to adapt and reduce the pain of the next change and increase the fun of living. Nothing has to hurt forever unless you make it do so; everything becomes new and, often, worth exploring. I was sure there was a girl out there, waiting to meet a more mature existence of myself.

36 • My Father and the Bohemians

> I used to think then that I was Bohemian, but I know now that I
> am not. I prefer order and precision to untidiness and looseness.
>
> **Conrad Veidt**

Sometimes, Kitsos would join the women after finishing his workday, and all of them would chat for hours, smoke and drink lemonade. Some of them were avid bridge players and played or discussed bridge nonstop. Others examined every aspect of the world's politics arguing the redemption of the past and the salvation of the future. I had no idea why any of that mattered. Sometimes they analyzed the previous night's movie in one of the two theaters in Eleusis and feathers would fly, if Humphrey Bogart wasn't in his best form in someone's opinion, or Joan Crawford had been bitchier than she usually was.

Miltos was another frequent visitor to the yard gatherings. He would stop to chat with my mother and the others gathered under the pine tree in grandma's yard. I am surprised by the impression Miltos made on me, even though I knew almost nothing about him. He was memorable because he was very different from everybody else. He was the oldest, healthiest, weirdest and most mysteriously private man I knew. He was in his seventies, or eighties, sported a twisted moustache, and always wore khaki shorts and sandals with bare feet around town. No one had ever seen Miltos in anything but shorts and sandals, in summer or winter. On hot days, he would move around town without a shirt, and I realized that chest hairs as well as all other body hairs must turn gray and then white with old age. (Why should that be memorable?) Miltos swam every day at sea, come hail or shine, by his own account, and, rumor had it, that he ate octopus and yogurt for breakfast every single day. He spoke softly and deliberately, as if words were expensive and he wanted to save money, except when he got into an argument on health issues, nutrition matters or bridge plays. He walked with his hands always crossed behind his back as if he was in a never-ending stroll in some garden of wonders. He was known around town as an eccentric, which, of course, meant that most townies thought he was out of kilter, and he was still loose only because he was harmless. Actually, he got all this attention because he did what he wanted, regardless of the social norms. The others in the group made a little good-natured fun of him, but overall they respected him for his "devil may care" attitude and his accomplishments. He was an educated and wealthy man, having a diploma from the University of Athens and having been a very successful businessman in town as the owner of the city's largest liquor store. He never showed off either his knowledge or his wealth. We thought that Miltos would live to be a hundred, and for all I know, he was or did.

When the cards were brought out, a fierce game of bridge would break out, outside the kitchen in the yard, under one of the big branches of the old pine tree. Miltos was some kind of a bridge master, so there would be lengthy commentaries after some plays, which Mara and Artemis appreciated, but the rest of the gang couldn't stand. It was a circus, and they all had fun one way or another. My mother didn't play bridge, but she would get in the discussion with a variety of questions, observations and comments that drove Miltos up the wall, but delighted the ladies. Kitsos observed the card games from afar, as if he had already played all the games and knew the moves and the outcomes. I was often puzzled by the emotions adults expressed with such fervor for such trivial matters.

Artemis had introduced Hepatia to the group and the possibilities of having enough people to play bridge increased. Hepatia was a very forthcoming lady, but she smoked incessantly and had such a booming baritone voice that I had trouble concentrating on what she was talking about. When she spoke, she made a lot of sense, but the noise she made with coughing and her throaty crackling, booming words delivered with machine gun rapidity made understanding her a challenge. I remember that she made a point of stating without hesitation or equivocation that she would never shave her legs. Her legs were kind of dark, with curly long hairs that I had trouble fitting in my young brain's compartment of female legs that required females to have smooth legs, or the world would stop turning and we'd all fall off. She was friendly with everybody and, I sensed that Miltos was sweet on her, occasionally stopping at the bakery and getting fresh *tiropitas* for everybody, but stating emphatically that they were Hepatia's favorite snack. I saw no response from Hepatia toward him. I empathized with Miltos, because I thought he had some of the same problems with the opposite sex as I had. A romance between an octogenarian, bare-chested eccentric and a rebellious, hairy feminist with an awfully low and loud voice gave my buddies and me plenty of food for discussion with many lurid metaphors and giggles to go around.

This collection of bohemians and fun loving people was a bit too much for my father, so when he came to town on weekends, there wasn't much schmoozing as we say these days. He wanted to relax, spend some time with my mother and his children, eat well and talk about the problems he encountered at work and beyond. Problems related to work, finances, the landlord's extravagant demands for rent and other such everyday issues were not my mother's favorite topics, but like a good companion in life, she listened to his problems and tried to instill in him some sense of the absurd, the ephemeral and the hopeful elements that make for a better outlook in life. He wasn't a fast learner. He was always thinking of tomorrow and let many moments of fun slip by unnoticed. Artemis would tease him for his seriousness, and he would tease her about her waste of time playing card games. But there were times when he would loosen up after a glass of wine and tell jokes making fun of his own ways. Whatever else he was, unlike me, my father never thought that he was special. It wasn't hard for him to laugh at himself.

"But, it is bridge, Petros, a game for thinkers. You'd be good at it. Let me teach you and, I bet, it'll change your life," Artemis would say and pick up a deck of cards to lure him into a lesson.

"I have no time for card games, Artemis. I'm a workingman. If I forgot that and started playing games, the cops would come and arrest me. Laborers have no right to gamble and carouse."

"Piss on the cops! And, it's not about money, Petros; it's about staying young and active," she would reply forcefully.

My father knew that Artemis had been my uncle Vassos' sweetheart, and understood her heartache well. He knew, from what my mother had told him, that the break in their relationship had cost her dearly and didn't want to say anything that would add to her pain. "You're right, Artemis, but I just can't do more than I'm doing now. Perhaps, someday I'll have the time and the frame of mind to play cards."

I felt sad that my father had to slog it all alone in the city under the relentless pressure at work, while we were having a great old time in the countryside. My father had never really been happy at work and staying alone in Athens was weighing on him, even though, as far as I know, he never complained. I remember that his right hand would break out with eczema in the summer, and I know now that stress can be the cause of it. I was sure that he thought work had to be unpleasant, or it wouldn't be work. I think that he really liked what he was doing, both as a supervisor and as an accountant, but he hated the conflicts created by his adherence to a strict work ethic and honest dealing with everyone. He hated opportunism and cutting corners and he couldn't stand incompetence. He just didn't know how to be diplomatic, how to maneuver and get his way, how to butter up a boss, or let down gently a wayward subordinate. He was too serious at work, uncompromising in protecting the interests of his employees and the property of the owners, and had a hell of a time getting things done without confronting wrongdoers. I think that if anyone had ever told my father that it was possible to have fun at work, he would have told that person to get lost and stop lying to himself and other hardworking people.

Many years later, when I got one of my first work appraisals as a young engineer, my boss told me that my performance was exceptional with one reservation: I wasn't diplomatic enough with other people. I told him that in my book, being diplomatic wasn't a virtue to aspire to. Diplomatic people, I said, are people who, for various reasons, choose to hide their true feelings and the truth. He tried to explain, that 'being diplomatic" wasn't lying, that it was good because it didn't alienate people, didn't create resistance in others, didn't offer a chance for escalation of disagreements into arguments and so on. I tried to understand, but our minds never really met. I never wanted to become diplomatic, but I did discover that one could be frank and cordial rather than confront others every time; I also learned that I could have a lot of fun at work –not only satisfaction, but fun and joy – though it took me awhile before I felt that it was not a sin to enjoy work and let others know. The key, as I said before, was to do things that one likes to do and becomes good at doing them when others need to get them done. I felt happy when I became an ombudsman, and later an organization development consultant and learned the elements of effective communication and other interpersonal skills and could solve problems that troubled the people who came to see me. I enjoyed helping people by solving problems that troubled them; I didn't really seek other people just to be with them and schmooze.

While my mother and the group of loiterers analyzed the past and planned the future, my friends and I would play cops and robbers, or compete on the high jump, or the shot-put, or water the trees and vines, and then clean up and get ready to go to town. I usually made my rounds about town in white shorts, white shirt and white tennis shoes. And, there was a time, in my early teens, when I would promenade in the town square, sporting a cane with a silver handle that I happened to find in one of grandma's basement closets. I wanted a cane that was also the sheath for a dagger, as I had seen in the movies, but no such cane could be found, so I imagined it and talked to my friends about having one some day. I would hang around the benches at the main square of Eleusis, near the statue of the general who had saved the city from catastrophe in the past and whose name I never knew, waiting with my friends for our dream girls to show up, around the corner, or rise up from the fountain scantily clad in their bikinis.

I say "bikini" because I remember that it was somehow around that time that the world waited for the nuclear explosion at the synonymous atoll to start a self-sustaining conflagration of the atmosphere that would obliterate us all. "Bikini" was the dark side of "Nylon," which, for a time, symbolized everything that was magical, plentiful and hopeful about America and the future. The nylon craze subsided, and fortunately, the atmosphere didn't catch fire, so Bikini remained just a sexy swimsuit. The nuclear age and the cold war were born, but so were many technical innovations that made life more comfortable and, some would say, more enjoyable.

Part Two

High School Years in Athens

37 • Life at Varvakeion Model High School

Change is the end result of all true learning.

Leo Buscaglia

When I was in the sixth grade, I found myself preparing for the entrance exams of the elite high school of Varvakeion Model High School, or Varvakeion, for short. I don't know whether this was my idea, or it came from my mother or father, but no matter how it came to me, I made it my goal. Varvakeion was the best high school for boys in Greece at the time, and therefore it was proper to test myself by attending it. I believe that one finds out what is the best that one can do, by competing for worthy goals. Since my goal was academic excellence, it made sense to try to attend Varvakeion. Besides, my uncles, Vassos and Agesilaos as well as my cousin Omiros had attended the school before me, and all of them were known to be the "brains" in the family. Nondas and I were going to find out whether we were able to follow on their steps.

Everybody in Greece, upon completion of the sixth grade, was required to attend a public or a private high school. There were no examinations for entry into these high schools, but Varvakeion was the exception. To attend Varvakeion, one had to pass very stringent written and oral entrance examinations in math and language.

Varvakeion Model High School, which translates to Varvakeion Model High School, was a public school for boys founded by Ioannis Varvakis around 1860, one of the great benefactors of Greece, who made his money doing business in Russia. The school employed the top teachers in the country, and was used to educate not only top students for the professions needed for the country's progress, but also to train teachers, who came to observe various classes as they were being taught, or practiced teaching the students of Varvakeion on rare occasions.

Some 500 students were competing for the 80 available positions, and most of the 500 were at the top of their school classes. It was a competition for excellence, if there ever was one. Three of my classmates from my grade school class and I participated in the exams, Kefalas, Yannis and Sotos. Three of us, as I have already explained, were neck and neck in class. Kefalas was not a top student, but he was determined to follow the rest of us and compete in the exams. I think he got the motivation to try for Varvakeion from my mother, who used to coach him and me together, sometimes. The four of us were kids from middle class families and we were there to match wits with the children of the rich and famous. We knew that many of the country's leaders had graduated form Varvakeion, and if we were admitted, we had a chance to reach as high as we could. I was ready for the competition. I believed then, as I believe now, that everyone who wants should have a chance to get to the top, if he or she has what it takes.

My cousin, Nondas, was also preparing for the exams, under his sister Maria's guidance. She was a law student and was considered the intellectual in the family. Everyone in my mother's family was lining up behind us. I can't vouch for that, but I wouldn't be surprised to learn that they were betting on one or the other of us, in secret.

I remember the anxiety I felt, but also the excitement. Varvakeion was located in downtown Athens and, if I were to attend school there, I would be spending a lot of time traveling every day by bus and on foot around the big city. This would be a big change for a kid used to having a three-block-long radius of operation in one of the second rate neighborhoods of Athens. When things were closing in on me I prayed to God to guide me.

I took the exams believing that I would succeed. I kept thinking that one of those eighty spots was mine. In the Modern Greek examination, I wrote an essay about my career plans that was a far out fiction, paralleling the successful careers of Greek benefactors, like Ioannis Varvakis, the founder of the school, whose example I wanted to follow. It was a far out fantasy, full of daring-do and lofty goals cast in a dreamlike narrative that showed in no uncertain terms what an ambitious little rascal I was, and how determined I was to work hard and succeed in the world. When I handed the essay to the teacher, I remember, I had second thoughts. Had I taken this matter seriously enough, or had I just written a story for fun at the most critical time of my young life? I felt embarrassed by what I had written. What on earth was I doing, dreaming of mythical success out in the open? Well, what was done was done. I consoled myself with the hope of excelling in the coming oral exams. If I couldn't ace the orals, nobody could, I told myself. After all, what had I been doing all these years in grade school, but competing in hit and run oral exams? Wasn't standing up and expressing myself my forte? I was scared, but also ready for the competition.

A couple of days later the oral exams were upon us. I did well in Math and then I had to cope with the essay I had written. I entered the examination room and faced half a dozen senior teacher-examiners sitting around a large desk. I wasn't relaxed, but I was confident that my nature would see me through the ordeal.

They had read my essay and wanted to know more about my plans for the future. Was I really interested in hunting wild animals in the jungles of Africa while searching for gold and diamonds? How was this beneficial to society? And why would I give all the profits from gold mining to Greece, rather than have a rich and pleasurable life? Was there something wrong with money? What if I didn't find gold, but instead was gored by a rhinoceros while searching for gold? I could see that they wanted to have some fun with me, and I was ready to oblige.

Well, I answered with some defensiveness, but also with chutzpah, the hunt is the search, and the gold is the lofty objective everyone ought to have for his life's work. The wild animals are the obstacles we encounter in our search for the objective; killing animals is overcoming obstacles. What one does when he achieves his objective varies among people, but I admire our founder and the other benefactors and philanthropists of Greece, and I want to be like them and give most of my money, as they did, to create institutions of excellence. It would satisfy me to do that, and perhaps to be remembered by future generations for my contributions to our society. I didn't give a very good response when they asked me why I saw myself sitting on an ivory throne in some jungle palace, but I muddled through by saying that the magnificent seat was a sign of authority gained by the power of wisdom. I thought fast and I gave these unusual answers, which called for more questions, which I answered with even more extravagant answers. I know that I believed what I said, and I must have convinced them that I was serious about making something worthwhile out of my life. I took chances, coming across a little more defiant, perhaps, than I should have. I needed their approval so bad, that I didn't give a darn for their approval. With a chance for success close to one in ten, I thought, that I had to take chances. Somehow, I felt that I had to stand out as a thinker and go-getter, even at the risk of being taken for a deluded child.

I felt good after I got out of the oral examination room. I figured that what I wrote made more sense with the oral commentary I provided. I did well in math also, and finished with a feeling of having done a good job – not great, but also not poor. A lot would depend on how well my competitors had done. Nondas also reported that he had done well. Kefalas wasn't sure, and I didn't find out what the other two guys from our grade school class thought of their performance.

The summer of 1947 was almost over when the newspapers announced that the results were out. When I got to the schoolyard, the crowd around the rosters pinned on a wall was huge. I remember pushing through the crowd to get close enough, so I could read the names. I found my name: Apostolos Kizilos #44; and then, Epaminondas Laskos #26. Kefalas was also within the eighty who made it, and so was Sotos from my grade school. Yannis didn't make it. He was always cautious, an example of propriety and correctness, and never broke any rules, never got into a fight and, probably, never dreamed that he would ever be a big game hunter in the jungles of Africa. It would have been too much if four of us had made it to Varvakeion from that little grade school in the backwoods of Athens. But, Nondas had entered ahead of me and the competition between us, I knew, would heat up.

The winners of the competition began the school year with a spirit of confidence. It never crossed our minds that we were lucky as well as smart and diligent, but it should have. I was delighted to be in one of the two sections of forty students each, and vowed to do my best. I became a model of good conduct and studied hard to excel. I asked questions when I didn't understand something, or when I was curious about something, and was quiet when I had nothing to say. Sometimes, when one of the teachers asked a question and I didn't know the answer, I made myself inconspicuous and tried to avoid being asked to respond. Flubbing a question with a bad answer was like making a mistake in a written exam. Everything counted in class.

I always sat on the first row, because I couldn't see very well, but also to avoid the distractions, sometimes taking place at the back of the class. The desks were made for two students, and often, the two boys who sat together for six years remained friends for life. I sat next to Takis, a quiet, very steady boy, with strong Christian values and a prodigious memory, who became a very noteworthy medical doctor in Greece. Nondas sat next to Andreas Manoussos, a sharp kid with a great sense of humor, who became an M.D. and a general in the Medical corps of the Greek Army. We were an exceptionally motivated class, and just about everyone participated in the discussions and gave his best.

There wasn't a girl to be seen for miles around the school, and we often talked about finding out where the girls were, as if they were a rare, precious resource, like palladium or platinum. Of course, girls were everywhere and nowhere. The best place to find beautiful girls was in each boy's imagination. Some public high schools were separated by gender but others, like the high school in Eleusis, were not. We were always envious of the lucky dogs that didn't have to look further than the desk next to them to talk to a girl or get an uplifting smile. We were bereft of girls like some city monks. Some of the guys could meet girls through family acquaintances, through siblings, in clubs and organizations that they or their families belonged to, but I had none of these ways available to me. So, I found myself without any kind of relationship with a girl. Since I had to spend most of my day out of the neighborhood, I even lost track of the few neighborhood girls that I might have had some relationship with since they spent most of their time in the local school and met the boys who were students there.

In the first two or three years this deprivation of female friendship didn't matter a lot, but later the need for relationships with girls grew and, as usual, I had to improvise and find places for meeting girls, like The Young People's Center associated with *The Young Hellene,* a young people's magazine with a lively literary life for various groups, or the *Alliance Française* school, which was an Institute for learning French for boys and girls, or an Academy for learning English in mixed classes, and so on. But for the first few years I was focused on doing well in school and enjoying the big city with my school friends.

All the guys I had spent the first twelve years of my life in daily contact on and around the stoop of Kortessis, Vouss, Beanpole, Koula the Tomboy, the Little Beggar and Katie out meticulous nurse, or the Abyssinian and Stellian and Kalamata and all the rest of them except for Kefalas, faded in the background. Only the memories we shared together in the harsh years of war and occupation remained with me. We grew apart and weeks would go by without meeting any of them. Once in a while I would see the Devil hustling newspapers in Plateia Klathmonos (which means Square of Lamentations) and I would say hello to him. I think that most of the other guys continued getting together because they attended the same school, but the world had changed for me and I had to cope with different circumstances than they did. Sometimes, I wonder how my friends remember the same events that shaped our young lives. What memories did they retain? What did they learn from our common experiences? I'm sure that all of us built different worlds in our minds using the same facts, and all these worlds are real and true for us even though they are different. The memory of facts changes, but the feelings upon which they stand are common and unite us.

Varvakeion high school had to hold classes in the afternoon and evening at the Koleti Grade School building, near Kanigos Square because the Nazis had burned down the original Varvakeion building that the founder of the school had built, and no funds had been made available for reconstruction, yet. That meant that I spent six years going to school from about one in the afternoon to about six or seven in the evening. I had to take two busses and walk about half a mile, or take one bus and walk more than a mile. I often went to school with Kefalas because we lived close to each other. We were often joined by other guys on the way back and made up quite a raucous teenage gang that carried on in the streets, the arcades and the squares of Athens with shouts, laughter and all sorts of fun and games. Sometimes, we would stop at one of the specialty stores for *tiropitas* and a glass of beer, or a *bougatsa*, or *loukoumades* and engage in long, loud discussions about the political parties running in the coming elections – there were over 150 parties in the first election held after the liberation – or the standings and the chances of the three or four great soccer teams in the country, or the weird personality of a new teacher, or the clumsiness of one of the geography teachers being trained last week in our class, or the antics of the class clown, or the next day's physics problem that no one had figured out yet. There were of course many discussions on Hollywood movies and life in America and stories of movies that were not for teenagers that one of us had managed to sneak in and see and was very enthusiastic about reporting. There was always a medley of risqué jokes and an occasional account of a budding relationship that one of the guys had with the girl of his dreams and wanted to tell us.

Theodore, one of the guys, who later came to America for graduate studies, knew dozens of jokes and told them so well that no one else could top him. He became the official joke teller of the group while the rest of us listened and laughed with abandon. Theodore remembered all his jokes and identified each joke with a number, which he announced every time before telling the joke. After several repetitions, instead of wasting time and energy telling the joke of the shoemaker and his fat wife who beat him up when he glanced at another woman, he would say, "Remember Thirty Four?" and everyone would burst out laughing at the joke of the shoemaker and his fat wife. "Do you guys remember Number Forty Three?" Someone else would counter, and everyone would laugh, "Wow! I remember – the albino monkey with his redheaded lover!" someone else would add, proving to everybody that he knew the code and was, therefore, a bona fide member of the gang. Joke number "Sixteen" was my favorite, but I cannot remember it!

Sometimes on the way home we'd encounter street peddlers, usually selling "super" razor blades, or "extra nylon" stockings or "Chinese silk" ties, all of them with phony shoppers buying what they sold to prime the pump of commerce. These boosters would crowd around them and create the impression that these were indeed very hot items on a fire sale. Our pastime was to stand back, watch the phony shoppers circle around and identify them as fast as we could. And, when the police would break up the operation, often to the dismay of the country bumpkins who were disappointed that they missed buying the whole year's supply of Gillette blades or Zippo lighters, we would move on to the windows of *Lambropoulos*, the best department store in the capital and find out which one of the dummies modeling the latest dress or suit was a real human being, posing as a dummy. There would be arguments and debates about who how, and for how long and how much would one want to bet on him or her to stand still. Once we reached a consensus on the real human, we did everything we could to distract him or her, and make the "dummy" come to life by yelling, laughing, making faces and acting in bizarre ways in front of the window. Most of us never made a dent on any "dummy's" poise, pose or posture. The only one who managed to get one manikin to smile and change pose with gusto, was Basoukos, one of the students from the Classics Section who started the Brotherhood of Disturbed Juveniles and came close to being expelled.

Basoukos did it by having frosting and lemonade coming out of his nose and saliva dripping down his chin, while reciting "Andra me enepe mousa polytropon os mala pola plangthin epi Troies ieron ptoliethron," which is the first line of Homer's Odyssey in ancient Greek ("Tell me, O Muse, of that ingenious man, who travelled far and wide after he sacked the great city of Troy.") We held our breaths while Basoukos howled, scrutinizing every inch of that model's figure. The beautiful blond woman in the green dress, green pumps and green handbag held her pose as long as she could. She clenched her fists and tried to stifle the rising laughter inside her, but she finally succumbed to the puffy, dripping, round clown face that Basoukos had conjured, and her entire body relaxed. When Basoukos managed to animate the doll in the window, we broke out with howls too and laughed ourselves silly. She smiled at us and resumed a slightly different pose but as ethereal as ever. "Perhaps, the green lady took pity on him and saved him from ridicule," someone mused later, when the green lady entered one of our many conversations. Basoukos went to the military academy and became an officer in the armed forces, a colonel, someone told me. I bet the green lady still poses in the memories of the young students who made her laugh and change position.

When these nomadic evening tours were finished, there would be time for me and a couple of others guys to visit one or two Travel Bureaus and pick up some travel folders of places to dream of going someday, or time to stop by at the American Information Center, the USIA agency had established, and browse some of the many magazines they had. There were countless places to visit and learn from, or just enjoy the sweet waste of time. We were glad to be students at the top school in the country; to be in the city that gave birth to Western Civilization; to be alive after the Nazis were wiped out by our great friends, led by the United States of America; to live at this time, and be among friends. We knew that we had found the best platform for launching our dreams into reality and enjoyed every moment on it.

38 • My Father and I

As I grew older, getting home in time for dinner every evening became a problem. I wanted freedom to go places and meet people, but my father wanted a family life and my mother didn't want me to go astray by staying out late. I could always get around my mother but my father was firm on what he wanted. My strategy was to keep my mother informed on my whereabouts so she could calm my father down when I was late. My relationship with my father when I was growing up was characterized by mutual respect, but we didn't get to be friends until many years later, when I was in my forties and fifties.

I remember the times before high school, when we had wood to burn and all of us would sit around the stove on winter nights toasting bread on the stovetop plate and talked about the happenings around us and in the world. Before bedtime my father and I would say our prayers and thank God for our lives. Afterward, my father and I would have a race about who would put on his pajamas fastest and when I won I would crawl in bed between my parents and pretend that I was inside an igloo and getting warm under the blankets with a flashlight as my fire. Sometimes, my father and I would sing religious and folk songs together, because both of us thought we could carry a tune, which was an opinion that few people with a sense of music have shared in later years. My father would tickle me and we would laugh and play until it was time for me to go to my bed, and sleep happily for the rest of the night.

When I was a little older, I wanted to read in bed before I went to sleep, but my father wanted the lights off so he could sleep. I solved the problem by reading with a flashlight under the covers, but only for a few minutes because batteries were expensive.

Our bedroom was the only room in the apartment that we could afford to keep warm, and visiting other rooms at night required a coat and courage. During Christmas and New Years, we would play cards and gamble for pennies. My father was more playful in my early years, but his playfulness seemed to wane as I grew older and we found no common pastimes or things to do together.

I loved and respected my father because he worked as hard as he could to provide for us in times of extreme deprivation and give us a chance to use the skills and talents we had. He labored to give us a better life, a good education and give my mother a house of her own – a better house than the one he had lost after he mortgaged it and took a risk in the market.

In turn, he was proud of me and took care of me when I was sick and supported me in any way needed on the critical issues I faced. He attended all my school events and conferences, becoming familiar with every teacher's expectations of me and advising me on how to proceed. I remember how proud he was when he saw me receive the first prize of the Ministry of Education for my academic performance. He was there every year to see me win the top honors and recite poems flawlessly before the entire school assembly. I know that he appreciated very much the honor I paid to the Kizilos name through my work. I know he was proud that he had contributed to my success. It happened that he understood grading and numbers, so we talked about these, but he rarely engaged me on any topics other than grades. He knew nothing about sports; he had no hobbies or other pastimes; he had seen only one movie in fifteen years and got all his news from the paper. And, he never talked to me about girls or sex issues at any time, relying, perhaps, on my mother's social skills to handle such topics. Sometimes we discussed politics, but only in general terms because he didn't believe that it was prudent to disclose his voting preferences to anyone, though I knew he was at the center of the political spectrum. He was often preoccupied by problems at work and he talked to my mother about them, expressing his feelings of disappointment and frustration with mediocre performers, slackers, retired military officers who acted dictatorially and people's disregard of ethical standards. From some discussions I overheard, I think he also felt mistreated by some of his superiors because they valued sycophants and smooth talkers more than people who delivered results. He was determined to prove to the bosses above him, including Bodosakis, the owner, that he deserved recognition and should be trusted with greater responsibilities. He never achieved the goal of becoming a director at the company. Years later, I found out that my father had been an organization wizard who had restructured departments, improved efficiency, developed new processes and saved a lot of money for the companies he served. After he retired from the munitions plant, he worked for an independent contractor and helped to organize and control the finances for the construction of the largest steel mill in Greece. He was very sharp in accounting and knew tax law so well that in later years, after he retired from the contractor's company and had some free time, people from miles around would seek him out at his favorite *kafeneion* and ask for his advice with their taxes, which he was glad to offer freely.

Before the Nazis took over the company, my father buried all the industrial diamonds and other expensive tools he was in charge of, as Section Chief of Materials, in underground caskets to prevent their use by the enemy. After the war, he presented everything he had saved to Bodosakis, the owner of the company, and was given a pat on the back, a small bonus and some other perks like a car and a driver for getting to work and back, but no promotion. He came home the day he had seen the owner and received the bonus and showed us the packet of new bills he had received. It was a day drenched in sunlight and the bills were in mint condition with the striking reddish colors of higher denomination drachma bills. My mother and I hugged him and congratulated him hoping that a promotion would follow. He gave us a generous bonus that day and we spent some time talking of bigger and better things to come.

Every year my father would pay a visit to Bodosakis at the headquarters of the company, wish him a Happy New Year, report to him the progress he had made, receive a bonus in cash, sometimes enhanced by bundles of very expensive cloth for a coat or a suit, because Bodosakis owned textile mills as well, and leave with promises of better things to come, which never did. One time a colonel got the promotion he had hoped for and another time, a metallurgist. I couldn't understand the depths of his disappointments until I went to work for a company that played similar games with me. Fortunately, their games were never important enough to me and made no serious dent in my life. My goal was to feel useful by solving problems that helped others. But, my father didn't have a college education, or any other outlets for his skills and talents as I did and receiving recognition with a promotion was very important to him. He didn't feel free to quit, as, I know, he would have wanted to do. He suffered and cried inside, but like many working people, he stood at his post and took the pounding of the sly, the slickers and the slackers, the well connected and the toadies. And the pounding took its toll and shrunk his emotional world, as it does for many working people everywhere. He finally had a heart attack at 53, due to stress, and left that rat race, quit smoking and lived another 33 years, many of them working productively, in good health and relative peace.

I know my father loved me, but he expressed his love with controlled warmth when I was growing up. As I became more independent and there was less need for his support, he gradually withdrew. He had a sense of humor, but we didn't see it very often. On the other hand he was easily angered and could hold his anger for days. When my parents fought and distanced themselves from each other, I was often fearful and depressed. My mother would sometimes make an effort to break the pall, but it wasn't always guaranteed that he would drop his utter aloneness and rejoin the family. As a last resort, my mother would ask me to approach him in his solitary gloom and try to get him to reconcile. Sometimes, he would find a graceful way to break the isolation, and we'd all be back together again laughing at any stupid thing that happened around us. Seeing my parents talking to each other again felt like Easter.

The sadness I felt for my father was one of the heaviest loads I had to carry when I was a child. And that dark emotion was followed by fear. If I transgressed the limits of his tolerance, he would lash out at me and on occasion hit me with his open palm or, on rare occasions, try to strike me with his belt, if he could get past my mother's protection. He hated himself when he lost control, and so did I, many years later, on those occasions that I lost my temper and spanked my sons. When I understood better who my father was and why he behaved so irrationally at times, I forgave him. Life had not been kind to him, and he carried the scars of his upbringing and his work life ordeals. When I understood, I tried to do better, but it has never been easy for me to stay calm.

When I traveled to Greece and spent some time with him in his old age, I saw how frail and tender he was inside, and I could forget the anger and isolation with which he tried to cope in his earlier years. We became friends and talked about some of the things I had always wanted to discuss with him – politics, economics, women, ethics, religion, work, writing, careers, life and death, the whole spectrum of the interests we shared but never discussed. I knew what had happened between us and I think he did, also. But, by then, he was more my friend than my father. We told jokes and laughed together. Then I would engage him in all sorts of discussions and sometimes he would disclose some feeling he had kept inside him a long time, but didn't dare express.

One time he confided in me that he was disappointed because I had not been promoted from Director to Vice President at Honeywell, the company where I worked. I assured him the reason was that I had decided I didn't want further advancement in the corporate hierarchy because I didn't value the corporate goals of profit and perpetuity over family life, writing and advancing employee wellbeing, which was my job for twenty years. I wanted time to solve problems that helped people and to be free to think, write and teach. And I wanted to enjoy life with my children before they grew up and left home. He looked at me mournfully, but I don't think he ever believed me. He was sure that I wanted to advance but wasn't able, as he had not been able. He was still sure that nobody would stop trying to get more money and recognition from those above him, if, with greater effort, he could do so. Freedom to act at work, building a dynamic and caring workplace and time to think and search for meaning were not his priorities. He didn't know that family life required more than providing for its needs and didn't continue to spend time with my sister and me as we were growing up. I think he had lived some of his dreams of success through me and wasn't very happy stopping his trip and dream my dreams for a while. Perhaps, it was too much to ask that he could even conceive of such roles as those of a conflict resolver, a team builder, an organization developer, a writer and a teacher of participative management. He was limited by a culture that fixed people to a spot on the socioeconomic scale and wouldn't allow them to rise to the level of their abilities. I, somehow, sensed that and didn't want to find myself in the same position when I grew up. I wanted freedom to choose my work. When America won the war and gave us the gift of freedom, I knew that things could be different in society. I gathered thoughts from reading and the movies and started thinking of life in America. The power of the American Dream to motivate action should never be underestimated.

Sometimes, I would give him problems to ponder and cause him to think through his past and present beliefs. One time, discussing his preoccupation with money and his disinterest for things intellectual and spiritual, I asked him to tell me the person he would choose to be, if, by magic, he could be either Aristotle Onassis or Saint Paul. He was up against the horns of a dilemma because he was both very religious and believed money was proof of success. He tried to wiggle out of it, claiming that he didn't do "hypothetical problem solving," but I insisted. He finally begged me to stop because his head was spinning. He never came out with a definitive response, but we teased each other and had a good time, anyway.

On many of these occasions my heart went out to him, and I would feel the love I had been so afraid to show him as a child, the love he pushed away, as if it would thaw his heart and make him vulnerable to the pain he had to put up with in the world he knew. My sister, a grown woman by then and quite an intellectual, couldn't figure out how I could spend so many hours with a man who, in her opinion, had no interest in others. She had her own difficulties with my father when she was growing up, and I wasn't there to explore how she dealt with my father's ways. She was an ideological leftist, a bohemian of sorts, a poet and a career woman, and my father was from another era long past its time. He was very proud of her academic excellence and her work achievements but he could never understand her lifestyle and her values. She identified with mother and couldn't get past his harsh behavior to see his soft side. She couldn't convert pity or sadness into love, because she couldn't quite forgive his anger and the hard life he imposed on her and on mother with his "economical ways."

Like most Greek Orthodox believers in Greece at that time, my father followed many of the traditions of the Greek Orthodox Church, although he also had a streak of independence from the clergy and their rituals that often turned to superstitions. Unlike many of his contemporaries, he never cursed the "sacred" objects or persons; going against many of the business practices at the time, he had unusually strict principles of ethical conduct and believed in serving the church and the community in various ways, particularly with his service as a deacon of the church, as a treasurer and as a builder and renovator of the physical structure.

He helped many people, who sought him out for a job, by finding jobs for them at the plant, and stood by them when their jobs were threatened. He was tight with his money, but he did help a few people with severe handicaps and visited them sometimes. I also know that he gave money to some charities related to the church. When I was in high school, my father took it upon himself to build a chapel right inside the company grounds, the church of Saint Barbara, protector of soldiers in artillery. He scraped some funding from his bosses and fellow employees, encouraged contributions from subcontractors to the company and used leftover materials from building projects inside the company to do it. He felt a tremendous sense of accomplishment when the chapel was built and dedicated. And I remember how happy he was when he took me there for a visit, as well as when, in his old age, he recalled the days of scraping up the materials and begging for favors to get it done.

After the war, when Saint Mary's congregation in our neighborhood grew and the leaders decided to expand and renovate the old building of the church, he agreed to help as treasurer of the church and treasurer of St. Mary's Rebuilding Project, which proved to be an enormous undertaking. He completed everything he started and was proud of his work, but never bragged about what he did. The bigger and better, new St. Mary's church he helped build still stands today. Papa-Kostas, the old priest of the congregation who had been my teacher, never forgot his work and always remembered him with fondness.

Papa-Kostas, a couple of other deacons of the expanding congregation and a couple of British officers my father had met at the factory after the liberation were the only people that I remember being invited to have dinner at our house. These were memorable occasions because my father's good sense of humor would kick in and he would make fun of himself, telling jokes in Greek and in Pidgin English.

When I was a little child, I was never afraid of him when he was laughing. Unfortunately he didn't let go very often. As I think of him, I cannot help but feel sorry that he didn't find the time and the energy to enjoy life more fully. I hope that people won't say this about me, because I've had the same tendencies, but I fought as hard as I could against them and I did have a lot of fun at work and in family life. I wish that my father had trusted his own capabilities more and felt the power that was possible for him to have, rather than depend so much upon the approval of the bureaucrats in the military-industrial complex of Greece.

I believe that in his later years, without the concerns that had preoccupied him when he was younger, he did find a measure of peace and contentment. His sense of humor was returning and he was more open with me about his feelings and concerns. I was always happy to see him laugh. Once, many years after my mother's death, I was visiting with him and found out that he was seeing a lady in the neighborhood and had a good time with her. He was in his late seventies then, and I thought it prudent to advise him to be careful that the lady doesn't find a way to get hold of his savings, if he was thinking of marriage. He looked at me as if I had sprouted a second head. He smiled. "If I ever get married," he said with confidence, "I intend to get a dowry from her!" We looked at each other and burst out laughing. It wasn't easy to separate my father from his money and both of us knew it. The money was for his family, period.

39 • Mother and I

My mother was often interested in many of the same things as I was and made it her business to become involved in my life, and, as I have already mentioned, her involvement was sometimes overwhelming. Mother and I were avid radio listeners and, later, movie fans. She had a good sense of politics and would often ask me what I thought of various people and events. We would listen to political speeches and then analyze them to death. We were both liberals, who never saw a royalist or a staunch conservative that we liked.

When the first post-war Miss Universe competition was announced, my mother and I followed the candidates' progression in the newspapers examining pictures and biographical statements. We'd argue who had the better body, or the most appealing face; who looked refined, who was better educated and who was sexy; why the winner should be a blond or a brunette; who was a little chubby, and who had legs like toothpicks, or had the smallest waist. Then we would get to the talent qualifications and all hell would break loose as we covered the gamut of our likes and dislikes. You don't want to send to an international competition a gal whose only talent is dancing the *syrtaki*, or do you? But, playing the piano? Everybody and her aunt could play the piano – is that the way to impress the world with our culture? And, so it was. We cheered when our candidates advanced and became more enthusiastic. Toward the end, both of us backed the same young woman to win, and we danced when she was crowned Miss Greece. We berated the radio announcer when he announced that Miss Greece wasn't picked as Miss Universe and gave up the Miss Universe pageant and its stupidity altogether at the same time. But, I remember all the lively discussions and heated arguments with my mother. I even remember the name of that first post-war Miss Greece: Daisy Mavraki! I forgot the names of some prime ministers of Greece, but not the name of the first Miss Greece. With my mother, not everything had to be serious to become important. We went through the same type of data gathering and judging candidates for the parliamentary elections. On election night, I would make forms and tally the results late into the night, as the radio announced them. Mother and I would cheer for the liberal democrats, the party my mother usually voted for in elections. My father couldn't resist the process and would get involved in our counting and prognostications while we tried to figure out which candidate he supported when he voted that day.

My mother's involvement in my education increased as I progressed in high school. I think that I had become her life's work, and she devoted much of her time to my development. She helped me prepare for exams by dictating the ancient Greek texts, or the French textbook passages we had covered, while I copied down what she read. Afterward we would correct the spelling and study the errors, so I wouldn't repeat them during the exams. Then, she would get my history textbook, or the textbooks of geography, or religion, and she would ask me questions, which I would answer with the appropriate narrative, names and dates, and she would approve or correct them, guided by the textbook. There was a time when I could recite the succession of the Byzantine emperors for the 1100 years that the empire lasted. These tutorial sessions took place whenever an exam was immanent or during the week before the final examinations, at the end of every semester. She was patient, interested to learn new things, and competitive. She tried to ask tough questions because she wanted to prepare me well, but also, I think, because she got a kick out of catching me off guard and having some fun straightening me out. When I gave the right answer, she was thrilled and would let me know how she admired that. I think that she also loved doing these preparations because she had a chance to study the books she couldn't even get close to when she was growing up. What a waste of talent and vitality. She was helping me do what she wasn't allowed to do. She was patient, competitive and empowering. She was a great tutor, and would have inspired a lot of children to become the best they could be. Later, my friend Kefalas joined us sometimes and got the benefit of her tutoring efforts. I heard that after I left for America and Kefalas went somewhere in Europe for further studies, my mother started preparing Spirto, Kefalas' little brother, for greater things. I'm sure he couldn't have found a better coach than my mother.

My mother believed that I wasn't getting into any trouble because she had a pipeline into my head and got me to tell her everything I was doing or planning to do. She was such a good listener, and I was so full of enthusiasm that I wanted to share my ups and downs with someone I trusted. And that someone was my mother. In time, however, this trust relationship became a habit that manifested itself as a need to tell her what I had in mind. And if I ever tried to hold back anything, I felt guilty of hiding from what she had a right to know.

When I was, perhaps, fourteen or fifteen and told her that I would like to go out on a date, she said, "Not yet; wait till you are a little older." When I was sixteen or seventeen I brought up the subject again. "I know that you eventually have to date some girls, but not yet. Wait until you are a senior and have most of your high school work behind you, before thinking about relationships," she said. So, I became a senior, and raised the subject one more time. She had another reason why I should avoid dates. "Well, you have managed fine thus far, and I know you can handle things, but it's less than a year before you are no longer a high school student. Give yourself a chance, and there will be plenty of time when you are in college for such things." She had a stalling strategy for handling my requests but I didn't catch on for a long time. Before I left home for America, I found out that, had I asked the same questions after high school, she would have tried to postpone my dating desires until I was finished with college. And then? "I would have suggested that you wait until you are finished with your military draft obligations," she admitted unabashedly, and we both burst out laughing at her extravagant maternal machinations. The fact that I was asking her permission to date had little to do with going out on a date, if I had found a girl to date. The request and her response became my gauge of her willingness to admit that I had grown up and could think for myself. Of course, she wouldn't admit such a thing. I had to go away before she knew that I was my own man.

As I reached my late teens, the close relationship I had with my mother was too limiting and became a problem that I had to solve. I started to both resent her intrusions and found myself unable to do without them. We quarreled often, but I wasn't afraid of her and we made up without difficulty. A couple of times however she made the mistake of switching from the "buddy" role to the role of the "controller", and that made me angry and painfully aware of the fix that I had got myself in.

The first time we had a serious break in our relationship, I was a junior in high school. After a lot of discussions, she agreed that it was OK for me to go to a dance, where, I knew, a particular girl I liked would be present. I asked my cousin Vivi, one of Nondas' older sisters, to go with me, because the girl I was after had her own date. Vivi was a talented, good looking, fun loving person, and I was looking forward to enjoying her company. The logic of my decision to go to a dance with a relative so I could hook up with the girl I liked, even though she had her own date, made no sense and I knew it. But, it lodged itself in my mind and wouldn't go away. Vivi told me I was nuts to do it, but would keep me company, anyway. I was a mush of emotions with little trace of reason. It was an act of desperation and sheer stupidity, and I knew it but couldn't quite act on it. I was going to that dance, no matter what.

My mother consented, if I promised not to get drunk and come back at a reasonable time. I accepted the conditions and I went to the dance, filled with uncertainty, anxiety and yearning. Nothing went my way at the dance. The girl was there with her boyfriend, and I was relegated to dancing with my cousin and keeping an eye on that girl. She saw Vivi and me, greeted us politely and went on dancing. Fortunately, my cousin was older, a good dancer and very understanding, so we managed to get through the night with me in one piece. I never cared much for drinking, but I had one or two glasses of wine during the course of the evening and felt quite fine. By the time I got my cousin back to her house and found a taxi home, it was very late. I went up to the front door and took my key out of my pocket. Before I had a chance to insert it into the lock, the door opened and my mother stood like the guard in front of a castle's gate.

"Do you know what time it is?" she asked in a stern tone.

"It's late. I had some trouble finding a taxi," I said, and made a vague motion to get closer to the door so I could enter. She didn't budge.

"Say, haah," she ordered and stared at me coldly.

"I'm not drunk!" I protested, taken aback. Drinking was the thing furthest away from my mind that night.

"Let me smell your breath," she insisted.

I felt diminished and angry, as I had never felt before. After all the disclosures I had made to her, after so many good experiences together, after such a great friendship between us, I realized that she just didn't trust me. The thought hit me hard like a slap on the face, and I refused to obey. I just edged her to the side of the door and squeezed inside the house. What was she going to do, if I had been drunk? My mind was racing toward ugly places. Was she going to kick me out of the house? Was she going to wake up my father and have him eject me from our home? I felt the sting of betrayal grip my gut.

I kept pondering that exchange between us for days, but I couldn't come up with a way to change my snarled emotions. I stopped talking to her. I demanded an apology for her demonstration of such mistrust. Who did she take me for? Could she really believe that I was some kind of a secret lush? Did she think I was some kind of a rake partying in dives with dopers? I went like a ghost from room to room, sullen and moody, like my father had done on so many occasions in the past. I hated it, but I wanted to punish my mother for having no faith in me.

There were some good things that came out of that incident, however: I never had to tell her what happened that night, or before or after any other night; it was hard, but I let go of her hand and I felt some open space around me. After a couple of days, she signaled in her own way with kindnesses and smiles that she might have been a bit too hard on me. I felt that I had gained the right to be a separate person and let go of my anger. But I wasn't free yet. I had to fight a few more battles to gain my independence.

The second break in the relationship I had with my parents came a few months later and involved both of them. I came back from school early one evening. My father was still out working and shopping as he often did. My mother was waiting for me. I could tell right away that she was troubled and had something to say to me. I had just laid down on my table the briefcase full of schoolbooks I was carrying when she confronted me.

"What's all that drivel you've been writing about in this notebook?" she said and waived at me the notebook I usually kept among my schoolbooks, on top of my desk because the table I used for a desk had no drawers.

"What?" I screamed with indignation and tore the notebook out of her hands. "This is *my* notebook. I write whatever the hell I want to write, and it's nobody's business but mine," I exploded like a bomb.

"Your father was very disappointed to see all the things you write about girls. How far have you been going with girls without our knowing anything about it?"

I couldn't talk. My anger made me dumb. My head was buzzing with fragments of thoughts that made no sense. If I did anything, it would be wrong, and I had the good sense even at that critical moment to hold back so I wouldn't regret it.

"You had no business reading any of it!" I protested after she backed off. "Did dad read this?"

"We read some from it and saw all the other papers you have stashed away in there with your books. Is that what you've been doing when you pretended to be studying?"

"I pretended nothing! What I write is my business. You have no right to any of it!" I screamed at her. She backed away with horror in her eyes, as if she couldn't believe what she saw and heard. "If that's what you feel about my poems and my thoughts, you won't have to put up with it anymore: You've done me harm, and I won't do a damn thing more to displease you." And with that, I picked up the diary and a bunch of papers with various notes, dumped them into the kitchen sink and set them on fire.

"What are you doing? You'll set the house on fire!" my mother protested, and came running, ready to put out the flames.

"You better let me be!" I warned, staring straight at her. She stopped dead on her tracks. She got it. What I said wasn't debatable, or negotiable, or otherwise reversible. The diary had to be burned, as if it was contaminated now. I wished that there was some reality to back up what I had written, but it was all imagination, fantasy, desire, fiction, the yearning of a boy for the warmth of a girl. It hurt a lot more to be judged for alleged wrongs that never happened.

She moved away in sadness, as she began to realize how important my privacy was to me. She must have known then that our friendly *tête-à-têtes* had ended forever. I had let her come too close to me for my own good. I knew that I had to move back and be alone now. I had to choose what to do on my own, or I would be choked by her encircling love. I had to learn how to love her and others without sacrificing chunks of my freedom and without encircling them. It hasn't been easy.

40 • Striving for Excellence in High School

> The claim of excellence is recognized [in Athens]; and when a
> citizen is in any way distinguished, he is preferred to the public
> service, not as a matter of privilege, but as the reward of merit.
>
> **Thucydides, Pericles' "Funeral Oration" in the**
> ***Peloponnesian War***

Every year we had to study ten to twelve different subjects, four to six
hours per day, seven days a week in school and three to four hours of
homework. In Ancient Greek, we studied parts of Homer's Iliad and
Odyssey, which, along with Thucydides' Peloponnesian War and
Pindar's Odes, were the most complex texts in syntax and grammar that I
have come across, except for a book by Korzybski on Semantics that I
tried to read at MIT. We had lively debates as we argued the beliefs of
Socrates in several of Plato's Dialogues, and learned a lot about the
origins of history and political oratory, reading Herodotus, Xenophon
and the speeches of Lysias and others, the latter two being among the
easier texts. In Modern Greek, we got a good look at Modern Greek
Poets, like Solomos, the Greek poet laureate and author of the Greek
national anthem among other significant poems, Palamas, Sikelianos and
Drosinis, and went deep into the writers of essays and fiction, including
some of my favorite story writers, Karkavitsas and Papadiamantis, whom
I had enjoyed reading before my siestas in the summers at grandma's
house in Eleusis. Seferis, Elytis, Hatzes, Samarakis and other Modern
Greek writers weren't known at that time, or like Kazantzakis, weren't
accepted as great writers yet, but I read many of them later and found
them to be profound. We didn't only read and discuss these writers; we
also wrote compositions trying to express ourselves with style, accuracy
and depth, influenced by them, or provided analysis of their works.

For me, some of the poets took additional meaning because I was
chosen to deliver a poem on the Greek Independence Day, March 25,
standing before the entire high school student body for all six years I was
in high school. I was one of the smaller students in stature, but I did have
a powerful voice and, with practice before several professors and my
mother, of course, I never failed to deliver an accurate and properly
dramatic recitation. I was always on pins and needles before every
presentation. I worried about forgetting a line or fumbling a verse, or
using the wrong tone of voice at some critical point in the recitation, or
pausing where I shouldn't, but I never thought of walking away from the
task. It was never easy, but things that elicit the respect of other people,

are never easy to achieve. One must accept the risk of failing, if he is to accomplish something worthwhile. Fortunately, I never missed a beat and was always applauded by my fellow students and my teachers. Once, the words of the poem I was assigned to recite could be easily twisted to make a joke with some sexual implications in the minds of teenage boys, and during my recitation a few of the rowdies did start laughing and mumbling the distortions. But, I was ready for them, so I ignored them and plowed through without missing a beat. I wouldn't let them mar the occasion for others.

In addition to Math, Physics, Chemistry and Literature, every week we had classes in History, Religion, Psychology, Geography, French, Latin, Music, Drawing that included the dreaded problems in perspective, and Gymnastics. I learned a lot of useful things in these classes that have served me well through my adult life, but the history we were taught, was often aligned to the misconceived national interests of Greece and the triumphalism of the postwar reality. I cannot correct these errors here, but I will say that the history of the Greek people spans three millennia, not just the hundred years of the Golden Age of Greece, and shows an amazing spirit of independence that helped us defend against many an enemy and prevail in a very tough neighborhood. The Athens of Pericles, Socrates and Plato, the Sparta of Leonidas, the Greece of Aristotle and Alexander and to some extent, Byzantium, are certainly high points of Greek history, but there are many other times of history that we ought to have studied, when ordinary Greeks rose to excellence and fought for freedom and independence, as they did in the mainland of Greece during the dark Middle Ages, and later, in the war of independence from the Ottoman Turks and finally against the Axis forces of the master race of Hither and Mussolini. And we should have been less chauvinistic and paid more attention to the history of Europe, China, America and the world, rather than ignore it. A nation is not well served if its youth is taught next to nothing about the history of other peoples.

The Science Section at Varvakeion was oversubscribed and only the top 40 students with the highest grades after the fourth year were admitted in the class. Kefalas wanted to be an engineer like Sotos and me, but his grades were not good enough, so he had to attend the Classics Section for the last two years in high school. I wonder how poor Kefalas fared, immersing himself in the study of Plato and Pindar with a thirst for physics and math burning inside him. Algebra, Geometry, Trigonometry, Drawing, Geography, Physics, Chemistry and Cosmology, as well as shorter courses in language and the humanities constituted the Science

Section's curriculum. We had to follow the prescribed curriculum without any electives whatsoever. You didn't tell the teachers what you wanted to study; they told you. Every year, two or three students, who couldn't pass all their classes, were sent to attend other public high schools with less rigorous classes, and new students were admitted, so that each of the two sections of every grade consisted always of forty students, who could do the work. There were no labs of any kind and no lab instruments other than a static electricity generator, a few geography maps and two globes one of the earth and the other of the cosmos. There were no teams to belong to or compete with; no musical instruments or bands to play or march with; no plays to act in – only the yearly celebration I mentioned above and a parade in the streets of Athens, on the day of the Great "No" we told Mussolini in October 1940. What we had, however, was the best education in fundamentals a teenager could possibly have.

Every day we had four or five classes lasting fifty-five minutes each, in the same classroom, by different teachers, whom we always called "professors." A class usually started with the professor calling one of the students at his discretion to come to the board and summarize the day's lesson, answering any questions that the professor asked, usually related to the material of that day. The student received a grade for his oral performance, which constituted part of his record in that class. Two, three, or more students would be subjected to this ordeal at random, every day, before the professor stopped the examinations and chose to move on with a lecture on the topic he had chosen for us to learn.

When the professor entered the classroom, sat down and started turning the pages of his roster with our names and grades in it, there was silence, suspense and anxiety gripping every boy in the room. Someone would be called, and he would have no choice but to step forward, stand up at the front of the class and respond to whatever the teacher asked him. Who would be grilled today? Would he be prepared? Would the teacher be nice or nasty today? Standing up for examination was as threatening to one's well being as we could imagine. We knew where our names were located in every professor's roster by the page he flipped, but it wasn't certain, because sometimes he held his roster up and we couldn't see where he started or how many pages were stuck together when he turned them. Those who had stood up in the previous class or a class before that and had come unprepared, thinking that they wouldn't be called up again so soon, were sometimes caught like deer in the headlights of a car, stunned by the dirty trick the professor played on them when he called their name to catch them unprepared. Sometimes the student would stand up mute or mumble nonsense while the class watched in horror and the professor made his point that free rides were unacceptable.

When the ordeals of oral examinations were finished the professor would lecture by involving the entire class in a Socratic dialogue, a third degree interrogation and an oration, all rolled into one. Professors would ask questions, requiring critical thinking and general knowledge as well as preparation and a good memory. You had to think fast and stand your ground, if the professor attacked your position, or tried to intimidate you. You had to hold yourself stubbornly together, and come up with a better answer next time. If you felt humiliated and crawled into your shell, vowing never to stick your neck out anymore, you would be in trouble. The implication was that, if you don't want to be in this game, or if you could not, you might consider attending another, less demanding high school. More often than not, we were vying for the professor's attention and were bent on scoring points in class participation that would somehow count toward the final grade, along with the oral and the written examinations. If the answer was wrong, some professors would just forget it and move on, but others responded with humor or sarcasm and even put downs and ridicule, as it happened to me once, when I was out of line.

One day, professor Mazis, the most demanding and famous Physics professor in the school, called upon Hadjis, one of the tallest students in the class, with a middle range performance record for his oral presentation. Hadjis walked with great effort from the back of the room to the front, next to the professor's desk, by the blackboard. He had a huge head of hair that made him look wild and he stared at the ceiling like a creature gripped by terror. Professor Mazis fired a question at him, and Hadjis' head rotated like a turret of a tank, as if the answer could be found somewhere in the upper part of the classroom.

"What are you? Some kind of Robinson Crusoe lost in a desert island?" Mazis delivered his first volley.

At this very intense moment for the class, my old habit of mouthing a smart remark to get the approval of the teacher or the class, no matter what else was going on, took hold of me and I jumped like a dog at a bone, and heard myself utter the words before I could shut my mouth: "He's the Neanderthal Man, lost in his cave!" I blurted out.

Mazis' head snapped and I saw two black fiery eyes under a baldhead staring at me. "Get out!" came Mazis' command.

I raised my two-ton-heavy body and stumbled out of the classroom, there to take my punishment and learn how to hold my fire, how to respect others and how to repent and go on without breaking up. I like to think that I apologized to Hadjis after the class, and I probably did, but I cannot remember. I wish that my fellow students hadn't thought that my joke was clever, but many did. The approval of the many should never govern one's behavior, but we all want it and sell ourselves short for it. It took time to learn that.

Every professor had his style, and we tried to accommodate ourselves to him or her as best we could. I felt totally at ease during the give-and-take discussions and participated with vigor, taking risks and trying to win by giving the right answer, or make a clever remark, or stump the teacher, or dispute what another student just said, but never again did I make fun of another student, especially one who was struggling to keep his head above water in this demanding school. Some of our professors were the authors of textbooks used by many high school students in Greece because they were the best books on the subject. We considered ourselves privileged when we were taught by one of these "famous" professors, no matter how demanding he or she was. I say "he or she" because we did have one female teacher, who taught drawing, and she was a very tough teacher, stingy like hell with grades and with a smile.

41 • Guideposts for Life from a Physics Teacher

The true teacher defends his pupils against his own personal influence. He inspires self-distrust. He guides their eyes from himself to the spirit that quickens him. He will have no disciple.

Amos Bronson Alcott

Probably, the most knowledgeable, most famous, most demanding and feared teacher we had in high school was Alkinoos Mazis, the physics professor, who threw me out of the class once. When he entered the classroom, silence would roll like a heavy tarp over us. His after-shave lotion was always strong and pleasant and we would know he was with us, even if our eyes were stuck shut. He was a short man, bald, with a short well-trimmed moustache, exactly the length of his upper lip. He was always impeccably dressed and walked with deliberate movements like a diver slogging underwater. He would sit on a chair in front of his desk, cross his legs, and survey the class, as if trying to detect which one of us was least prepared that day, so he could call on him to come up to the board and test him, teach him, ridicule him, encourage him, enlighten him, empower him, humiliate him or, somehow, wake him up to the fascination of science and the struggle in life. We would sneak looks at him, never making eye contact with him for fear of calling attention to ourselves that might land us up on the board in retaliation for disrespect, bravado, challenge or any other unfortunate interpretation of our uninhibited behavior. Some of us thought that he had a slight limp, and it was rumored that he had a wooden leg, but none of us was sure of that. I sat in the front row, no more than ten feet away from him, when he chose to sit with crossed legs in front of his desk. I had his disputed leg in my field of vision for the better part of the duration of every class. I would often fantasize that I got up, stood before him, smiled politely and started tapping on his sock-covered leg with my knuckles, expecting to feel unyielding wood and hear its telltale hollow sound. But, we were all cowards, more or less, and none of us thought that we would ever verify the rumor, even though all of us were on the lookout and cast countless probing glances at that covered leg.

Every teacher taught us something beyond learning the subject matter, but Mazis gave us, probably, the most valuable lessons for life. We were juniors and then seniors, taking physics in the Science Section of the best high school in the country, taught by the top teacher in the country, and we were all highly motivated, because physics was a crucial subject in the entrance exams we would have to pass before qualifying for admission to the Polytechnic, the top technical college for engineers, or the University of Greece, in Athens, which was the top school for scientists. All of Mazis' classes were electric in one way or another, because someone would do something and excel beyond all expectations or fail miserably against all hopes. But on one particular occasion something extraordinary happened, and I remember it with exceptional clarity.

We were seniors, taking the first semester's written examination in physics and all of us were apprehensive because the material had been difficult and essential to our future career success. As always we had to answer two out of three theory questions and then solve one out of two problems. The grade depended equally on the quality of answering the theory questions, and on solving one of the problems correctly. I answered well the theory questions and then I read the first problem. It was an easy problem, but I wasn't sure I understood it well enough, so I read the second problem. It was a tough problem, and required a lot of detailed calculations with plenty of chances for error in the limited time remaining in the exam. I went back to the first problem and read it very carefully. I understood it well now and thought it wouldn't take a lot of time to solve it, so I started working on the first problem. I froze when I realized that there was a mistake in the information given. The problem couldn't be solved the way it was stated. Yet, the problem was stated the way it was stated by professor Alkinoos Mazis, the teacher who had told us that he reserves the top grade for God, the next grade for himself and the third grade for the student who turns in a flawless exam. I felt cold sweat running down my sides. I abandoned the first problem and immediately shifted gears and started to work on the second problem. I had just enough time to arrive at a solution but here was no time left for review or correction of any possible errors. It would have been so easy to do the first problem, if it had only been stated correctly . . . Or, was it stated correctly, but I hadn't been able to see how to read it? I handed in my exam and got out in the schoolyard. Every student I asked had solved problem number two, because, as most of us put it, "there was something wrong with problem number one."

When professor Mazis came to class with the examination papers the first week of the second semester, we were all anxious as always, to see how well we had done, but more than that we wanted to find out how he, Mazis the Magician, had created such a conundrum for us. This time, Mazis didn't pass out the exams to the students right away. He just pulled out the bundle of exam papers from his leather briefcase and set it on his desk. "You can pick up your papers at the end of the class," he said. Standing before the class, he asked what we thought of the exam. Several of us spoke, saying that it was difficult, but fair for the time allotted.

"Which problem did you solve?" he asked pointing to someone in the back of the room.

"Problem Number Two, Sir," came the weak voice of Karakostas, a six foot two giant with an Adonis face, at the last desk, who always shook like a leaf when he was up for oral presentations.

"And you?" he asked Vathis, the restless joker of the class.

"Problem Number Two, Sir," Vathis responded.

"And you, Kizilos?" he asked, and I heard the accusation and the hurt in his voice. I was after all the top student in the class on overall grades for five consecutive years.

"Problem Number Two, Sir." I just couldn't keep from adding, "There was something odd with Problem Number One."

"Were there any others who thought that there was 'something odd' with Problem Number One, as our distinguished Mr. Kizilos puts it?" he asked caricaturing my words to show his disdain for them.

We all raised our hands. Mazis stared at us without showing any sign of recognition. We might as well have been withered flowers in an arid field.

He was silent as he strolled like a caged lion before the class. He brought his chair in front of his desk, sat down and crossed his legs. "There *was* something wrong, but only one of you dared to write that in his exam paper." He let his words sink in, deep into our hearts and minds.

Many heads turned around searching for that one student who dared confront the mighty Mazis with his error.

"There are forty of you, who took the exam, and thirty nine did Problem Number Two. Yet, most of you – all of you – figured out that the other problem was stated incorrectly. You didn't have the guts to write that down on your paper. You played it safe . . ." He stopped as if he wanted to leave the rest of his thought unsaid, but his emotions won out. "You played it safe like all cowards do," he said and handed the bundle of exam papers to one of the students to distribute to the class.

He had worked hard; he had given everything he had to make this a class of star performers; he couldn't accept that our ability to take risks and confront authority was so low. He had no stomach for people who couldn't speak the truth that they were smart enough to discover. We had insulted Science and him by playing it safe. His granite face seemed scratched, and his eyes were dark, tired, it seemed, of staying open.

Silence was the best we could hope for now, but Mazis hadn't finished teaching.

"Solving problems somebody gives you isn't the most important thing in life; you'll need courage to *find* the problems that matter before you can accomplish anything worthwhile. You'll come across many things that are wrong, unfair, second rate, and you'll have to fix them, improve them end them. And for that, you need the courage to take a risk. Courage was what counted in your exam." We felt the weight of his accusation and took note of his words. "Only Kouremenos dared to tell me that Problem Number One was stated wrongly," he said and cast a thankful smile toward him. "He corrected the error by restating the problem correctly, and solved it. One out of forty of you is not a good enough record for any class, and certainly not for my class. You must stand up and be counted!" He replaced his chair behind his desk and then, turning slowly as if he carried a load on his back said to the class, "I am disappointed in you, gentlemen." Then, he dismissed the class early and slogged toward the exit.

It took a few minutes to recover from the blow Mazis had delivered to us, and when we were back in action, the question all of us discussed in the schoolyard that day was this: "Did Mazis make a mistake in Problem Number One, or did he purposely introduce the mistake to teach us a lesson?" In most students' minds Mazis was incapable of making such a stupid mistake and quite capable of resorting to unusual methods to teach us something important.

I believe that Mazis made a mistake. When he realized his mistake, he took advantage of the situation to teach us a lesson like the great teacher he was. I never believed that he introduced a mistake purposely into the exam. But why would he not do so, if he felt that this was the only way he could teach us a very important principle?

We were all proud of our fellow student, Dimitris Kouremenos, who on this occasion represented the best of the class. I was delighted to hear, many years later, that he had become a full professor at the Polytechnic, the most coveted academic position an engineer could attain in Greece. He was an average student overall, but starting a year or two before this incident he had apparently been quietly scoring big in math and physics. I was the first to acknowledge his excellence in these subjects and have praised his performance and his courage ever since.

I followed Kouremenos' example and Mazis' advice to take a risk and stand up to be counted on many occasions throughout my professional and social life. When others sat back and kept their thoughts to themselves, I ventured into the public arena and spoke my piece. Even though I worked for a company that was part of the military industrial complex of America, I protested publically and professionally against many of the technologically harebrained ideas that came to the forefront, among them against the Vietnam War, the use of anti-personnel mines dropped from aircraft, pilotless submarines with nuclear weapons and the idiotic Starwars Program of Ronald Reagan, which could have produced a nuclear confrontation, if it had ever worked as planned or went astray. Sometimes, speaking out changed the course of the discussion and other times it produced an embarrassing silence. Sometimes people laughed with me and other times at me; a few times I split the group, and other times I united it; a few times people approached me and told me how much they appreciated what I had said or done, and a few times people whispered their disapproval by calling me names – radical, weird, Marxist, leftist, Protestantizer, undiplomatic and worse. But, I stood up and was counted. I followed Mazis' appeal to us and was engaged by word and deed on the issues that mattered.

I would move on with the rest of my story, except for the fact that Mazis was involved in a few more "lessons" that influenced my thinking and conduct for years to come. These lessons were also beyond the realm of physics, but had a lot to do with decisions we all have to make in life. As I recall these events I cannot help but think that this man had a vision of the disciplined, creative and courageous human being and tried to pass it to his students in every way he could. But the vision Mazis had for us, though attractive, had a flaw, as it will become apparent later on.

In the earlier years at Varvakeion, professor Saros was our Latin teacher. He was one of the most famous Greek scholars in the Classics. But, he was a mild-mannered, older man, who had some trouble with his hearing and a lot more trouble controlling a herd of forty wild teenagers, chomping at the bit for success in the sciences and, many of them, totally disinterested in Latin.

One day, in the middle of the class lecture that he was delivering, I heard the sound of an electric bell ringing behind me. Everyone must have heard the ringing bell because we were glancing back and snickering at each other. Professor Saros showed no visible sign of having heard the bell. The class went on and then the ringing started again, now more persistent and louder. The professor began to wonder what all the commotion was about and paid closer attention. The class ended without a revelation of the source of the ringing. But it is hard to keep such things secret for long. A day later some of us knew that Sotos, my grade school fellow student, in the back of the room, was the culprit. He had rigged a bell with batteries and a foot-operated switch and concealed the device under his desk. He was well on his way toward the engineering profession and received the approval, if not the admiration, of most of his classmates. I, as usually, had mixed feelings about the prank: on one hand, Sotos was inventive and knowledgeable and I was a bit envious of his creativity and skill; on the other hand, I felt sorry for the old, great teacher, who gave us the best he had, standing before us slim and trim and vulnerable, well groomed and wearing his bowtie for us, who made him the butt end of a joke. I had a gut feeling that what was going on was disrespectful to a good teacher, and didn't laugh or joke about the prank. But, I did not intend to stop the ringing by turning the bell-ringer in. I wondered what Mazis would do in this case.

The approval of so many students emboldened Sotos, and he started ringing the bell when some of the other teachers were conducting their classes. He was careful to synchronize the ringing with a teacher's or a students talking, so it was always a background noise but the new move was bold. One of the teachers suspected that something was going on and took a walk to the back of the room, listening attentively while the class remained totally still. He heard nothing, but seemed to know that something was amiss.

But, a bell that was ringing in class after class in a high school dedicated to academic excellence could not remain undetected forever. The entire student body had found out that we had a bell in our classroom and everyone was talking about it. Those of us who knew the perpetrator did not intend to reveal his name, but we all knew that the wall of secrecy would, somehow, be breached.

Apparently, some of our teachers had also heard more than they let out, because a few days later, when professor Mazis came to teach his Physics class, he started with a statement that made our blood freeze.

"It has come to my attention," he said solemnly, "that someone is making a mockery of his teachers by ringing a bell right here in this classroom." He took a few steps toward the back of the class in one of the corridors formed by the students' desks.

No one in his right mind would have dropped a pin on the floor, let alone ring a bell, when Mazis was in class, and no one ever did. But, respect was due to all teachers, not only to Mazis the Terrible.

"This behavior is unacceptable to me, to your teachers, to the faculty, and to the institution of Varvakeion," he said and every word he uttered seemed to weigh a ton. "We are not here to educate thugs and deceivers. All of you should be incensed and make the perpetrator of this grave indecency an undesirable, a pariah, a bum." He paused, as if waiting for someone to stand up and bellow the name of the hideous bell-ringer. But no one did; no one would have dared to break the code of silence. "I want you to think about what I just told you and report the culprit to me, personally, as soon as possible. Don't be cowards!"

We were stunned. How could we squeal on one of our own? Whoever gave up Sotos' name would be expelling Sotos out of Varvakeion. No one wanted to be responsible for ruining someone's life. Doesn't Mazis realize that human beings bond together and care for one another and have ethics to uphold because of that? He should have demanded that the prank be stopped right there and then. That would have been the end of it all. But Mazis wanted the perpetrator to pay for a prank with his future. We spent a couple of days with heavy hearts. We were afraid that Mazis would cause something hurtful to happen, but we didn't know what. On the third day, Mazis called Vathis to the Principal's office. Vathis was at the brink of failing physics and was already failing trigonometry so he could be kicked out of Varvakeion and be held back a year at some other high school, if he failed to pass the two subjects a second time. Afterward, we found out from one of the guys to whom Vathis had confided, what happened at the principal's office between Mazis and Vathis. It wasn't pretty.

Mazis gave Vathis a choice, to either reveal the prankster's name, or fail Physics, which meant that he would be kicked out of Varvakeion.

"That's blackmail!" someone protested, when we heard the news.

"I was sure Mazis was going to do something nasty to us," I said.

"Report him to the police!" Hadjis suggested.

"Mazis broke the weakest link in the chain!" Karakostas said.

"He's trying to teach us Ethics."

"Ethics, my ass," someone else said in disgust.

"And what happened after that?" we wanted to know.

"Vathis had to tell him. He couldn't afford to be kicked out for somebody else's prank. Mazis took him to the principal's office and he spilled the beans."

And so, Sotos, one of the three students to enter Varvakeion from my grade school class, one of the four boys who excelled in their years there, according to Pappa-Kostas, was identified as the "thug," who tried to ridicule his teachers and was kicked out of Varvakeion. This time Mazis tried to show us the long way we had to travel to discern right from wrong in real life. Our ethics weren't based on the values he wanted us to have: covering up wrongdoing was despicable and should never be tolerated. But, should blackmail be part of our ethics, also? Did the means justify the ends? Is torture ever justified? Was it right to pick the weakest student in class and put him through such a gut wrenching ordeal? After all, Vathis was innocent of any wrongdoing. Was such harsh punishment right for a first offense?

Was Mazis trying to teach us that we had behaved like cowards once again by remaining silent and forcing him to resort to extreme measures, like blackmail, to get at the truth? Do you suppose that he wanted me, or Kouremenos, or my cousin Nondas, as leaders in the class, to stand up and reveal who was the culprit? What would have happened if the weakest link didn't break and instead one of the strongest links gave up the culprit? Did it occur to him to lecture us on the ethics of the various positions one might take and have faith that one of us would see that opting for honesty and respect for others was preferable to betraying a wrongdoer from his affinity group? What Ethics should we use?

Mazis prevailed and Sotos was expelled from Varvakeion. But, Sotos wasn't broken; he went on to become a very successful architect, whereas Vathis, the blackmailed "traitor," had a rough time after he graduated, entangling himself in all sorts of ill-fated schemes. Luckily, he managed to right himself after some ordeals and made a good life for himself and his family. Many years later, I found out that he had retired after a long career in public service and lived happily with his family in Greece. It was one of the happiest messages I had received because I had always felt he had been victimized.

I don't think that Mazis was happy with his resolution of the bell-ringing incident, but who knows – his moral sensibility may have been less vulnerable than we could imagine. Wasting an innocent person to punish a wrongdoer isn't justice, after all.

The third time professor Mazis made a mark on the collective consciousness of our class beyond the field of physics, was also hard to take and hard to forget.

Varvakeion was a school where the boys of some families had been students for three generations or more, just as girls had been students of the equally prestigious high school of Arsakeion in Athens. My cousin Nondas and I, as I have mentioned, were only two of five Varvakeion students related to the Laskos family. Graduates of Varvakeion were among the leaders of the country for several generations. Excellence was celebrated by a yearly parade of the graduating class, a tradition that had been established years before our time. Ever since we entered the school we had dreamed that some day, just before graduation, we would don tuxedos with white silk scarves and gloves, top hats and canes and participate in the traditional horse drawn carriage parade from our schoolyard through the main avenues of downtown Athens, place a wreath at the statue of our school's founder, Ioannis Varvakis, and end up at the Royal Gardens for photographs and merriment. The whole city would take note of the event and our pictures would make the front page of all the newspapers in Athens next day. Our excitement grew as we prepared for the big day. On that afternoon we would cut classes and all eighty of us, seniors of Varvakeion, would show our fellow citizens that we are present and ready to work for the country's good as we build our careers. Some students would hold placards identifying our school and showing to the people who happened to notice us who we were and how hopefully we faced the future. There might be some humor, some frivolity and playful shouting, but overall we were planning a festive, peaceful rite of passage with our traditional Parade. I had seen the articles and the pictures of previous years' classes and I was looking forward to our debut. I was sure my father would give me enough money to pay for the tuxedo rental and the other expenses. He was proud of my performance and wouldn't miss out on the glory. It was a show of achievement and pride, but also a desire to be collectively recognized for our labors and our good intentions. We countered any adverse criticisms for elitism, by telling critics that any other school proud of its accomplishments could parade as well, if the students felt like it. We were all set.

But, something happened before we could make the Parade happen. There was a meeting of the entire school population called at the main yard. We had no idea why we were there. The principal, with Mazis and another professor standing beside him appeared on the dais. There was silence in the yard and the principal read a statement.

"The Parade that has been planned by the seniors will no longer be allowed for safety reasons." He paused, and then added, "Besides, parading is unbecoming to the dignity of Varvakeion and its students."

A pall fell on the gathered students in the schoolyard. The Principal stepped back and Mazis took a step forward. "Anyone who is caught violating this prohibition by organizing, promoting or otherwise participating in it, will not be allowed to graduate with his class," he said staring down at the shocked students.

We all knew that Mazis was behind this prohibition and hated him for it. He had always made fun of any silly display of juvenile immaturity and now wanted to snuff out the tradition of the Parade we all had counted on. He was taking away the punch bowl and everyone hated it. No one knows why he thought that a group of students parading downtown Athens in formalwear aboard horse drawn carriages was disrespectful of the school, unbecoming to serious students and a bad idea altogether. Perhaps, we might have accepted the rule if they had bothered to give us reasons for their worry on safety. We wanted a reason for fearing a disgraceful conduct during the parade, but they didn't give us any. The arbitrariness of the decision was devastating.

Could the Administration stop our graduation, if we all chose to carry out our plan? We were angry and determined to defy the principal. They couldn't flunk the entire class; they couldn't find out the organizers, if we stuck together and refused to yield to all pressures that would be applied on us. Then, somebody thought of Mazis' blackmail of the weakest student in the class and the expulsion of the bell-ringer and the actions that a ruthless Mazis might be able to take. Could the Administration find out who hired the horse drawn carriages and go after him? Could a sizeable portion of the class chicken out and let only some of us be exposed to the rule breaking and the punishments that would follow? Once doubts started arising, and we started considering the things that could go wrong, the enterprise was doomed.

I was prepared to participate in the event, but I had no idea how to organize it. That was the specialty of Basoukos and his friends, but he had already been intimidated a month before graduation because the administration had found out of his efforts to organize "The Brotherhood of Disturbed Juveniles" in school. Alas, genius takes many forms that don't always carry the authorities' stamp of approval. They didn't like his joke.

"We are cowards, like Mazis said," Andreas, one of the more vocal proponents of the Parade shouted when a few of us held a meeting to decide what to do.

I wanted everyone to commit to his fellow students to attend the Parade and stick to that commitment, but I could not get the entire group to agree.

"Perhaps, Mazis wants us to unite and then take the risk and disobey," said Pepas. "If he is the great teacher we all think he is, it's possible."

The discussion had reached a critical juncture. I didn't want to leave the decision on who Mazis was or wasn't, or what he would or would not do. "If we stick together, no one can do anything to us," I said with conviction. "There is no way they'll flunk the entire class! If I hear a public commitment, I'm ready to go."

"Public commitments and proofs of loyalty and oaths and potatoes with oregano," someone said impatiently. "You either come or not."

"O.K. I come," I said without hesitation. And then, "What about you?"

"You bet, I'll come," my fellow student responded. And then Pepas agreed, and Andreas and Nondas and somebody else . . . Before we broke up all of us debating the issue had committed to show up. The only thing that remained was to get those who had not been at the meeting to commit and participate in the act of defiance to preserve the tradition of the Parade. We gathered as many of them as we could and explained to them what we were thinking of doing. "The Administration could do nothing to us, if we stick together," was our message.

One of the students from the Classics section stood up and said that we were crazy to believe that Mazis would accept defeat. "Mazis will convince the Administration to pick five students with discipline or attendance or academic problems and flunk them. The Parade tradition will go on this time at a cost of having five of our fellow students fail to graduate, but it will never take place again. And that is the bottom line. Mazis wins!"

"He's going into politics!" someone whispered to my ear.

"I'm glad it isn't philosophy," I whispered back.

When the students at the gathering had digested the meaning of that argument, they wanted no part of the Parade. The Parade was forever abandoned.

A small group of us who were committed to participate in the Parade, frustrated and wanting to rebel against the unfair rule of Mazis the Terrible, decided to, at least, break the attendance rules and skip classes on the day we had planned to have the Parade. We took off and gathered at a nearby park, huddled around the statue of Ioannis Varvakis, the founder and benefactor of our school, and smiling, but bitter under the happy faces, had our picture taken. It is still a picture I keep in one of my photo albums to remind me of our failed rebellion. Mazis won that round, also.

Perhaps, the school administration had discontinued the Parade because there had been objections to the elitism of our school. Perhaps, they were worried about our safety, riding so many horse drawn carriages in busy streets. Perhaps Mazis had wanted to test us, and find out whether we had learned the importance of standing up and doing what we thought was right, regardless of the risks. Perhaps, Mazis had nothing to do with the prohibition of the parade and he was asked to enter the dispute because of his previous strict enforcement of the rules. I will never know, but I will always wonder what would have happened if we had disobeyed the order and held our parade. But, we'll never know. That's how most of life is. We often know who wins and who loses, but we rarely know the causes of these outcomes.

So, Mazis, one way or another taught us another lesson with his harsh authoritarianism and insistence on the responsibility one has toward his own self. But, it wasn't the last lesson he had to teach me. There was one more lesson coming, and it was a lesson worth learning just when I was about to enter college.

Several years after my class graduated, Varvakeion became just another public high school, without entrance exams to select the most capable students in academics. Elitism was by then politically incorrect. The "democrats" of the times were afraid of rewarding people on their merit and opted instead for the easy road of equal opportunity by lottery. The excellence of Varvakeion that was available by merit to people from all the classes of society was now transferred to the private schools, like the Athens College, only for the wealthy and the powerful. So, the "democrats" debased one of the rare resources Greece had for accomplishing some things that require long and expert training of the most talented and motivated students in the most demanding fields of science and the liberal arts.

42 • The Heartaches of Adolescence

I was about half in love with her by the time we sat down. That's
the thing about girls. Every time they do something pretty... you
fall half in love with them, and then you never know where the
hell you are.

J. D. Salinger

I was focused on mathematics and science not only because I thought
that I wanted to become an engineer, but also because I took a lot of
satisfaction out of solving problems that had an objective solution. But
ever since I was a child, I also liked to draw faces and nature scenes,
especially mountains, and construct elaborate maps with many colors,
and draw old buildings with India ink on vellum paper. When I entered
adolescence I began writing short prose pieces and some poems to give
shape to my impressions and express my feelings. I always liked reading
aloud, singing in the school choir and reciting poems. I never thought it
necessary to restrict my diverse interests, and I expected to do well in all
subjects. It didn't take long to figure out that I derived greater
satisfaction from creating or inventing new things than from analyzing,
organizing or running things.

One day in my junior year in high school, I was asked to read a poem
in class, and did so, being aware that the philosopher Georgoulis, who
was the Director General of Greece's Higher Educational System at the
time, was observing the class and studying our teacher in Modern Greek,
professor Xifaras. I recited the poem for dramatic effect, with proper
pauses, color and intonation. By that time I had a lot of experience in
reciting poems, having been coached by various teachers and having
delivered several recitations. I did a good job improvising for the proper
tone for the occasion, and was pleased that my teacher would benefit
from my performance. Professor Xifaras was one my favorite teachers in
Classical and Modern Greek, and I wanted to be as helpful as I could.

This class in Modern Greek was at the end of the day, so after
chatting with my friends for a few minutes, I was walking across the
schoolyard toward the gate to head for home, when the Director General
approached me and congratulated me for "a spirited recitation." Then, he
asked, "Do you like literature?"

I stared at him with surprise. It took me a moment to collect my
thoughts. No one had ever asked me before how I felt about literature.
"It's a great poem," I managed to say.

"Do you like poetry and literature in general?" he probed further.

"Ever since I was a child . . . I like poems and stories." I noticed a couple of my buddies watching the Director and me. They think I'm being a brownnose, I guessed with discomfort.

The Director looked at me curiously, as if he wanted to really know what I thought. "Then, why did you choose the Science curriculum?" he asked.

It occurred to me that my answer mattered to him. "I like math, too," I said without hesitation.

For a moment he was thoughtful. "Are you aware that mathematics and literature, especially poetry, which is coupled to music, are related?"

I wasn't. I had wondered about my diverse interests in art, literature, science and mathematics, but I had never bothered to find an answer. Actually, I thought they were opposites, but I said nothing.

"Math, music and poetry are concerned with time and the way it is divided and used. Mathematicians are often musically gifted people, and vice a versa," he said and paused to study my blank expression. "Does it make sense to you?"

"I thought that mathematics and literature were as far apart from each other as they can be," I said, emerging from my confusion.

"Just because you don't see the numbers, it doesn't mean that they are not involved in many human processes. It was Pythagoras, the great mathematician, who discovered the system of musical tuning in which the frequency relationships of all intervals are based on the ratio 3:2 . . ." and he went on to talk about perfect fifths and octaves and the chromatic scale while my head was spinning and I felt like an idiot. "And Pythagoras is credited with the discovery of the golden ratio, a mathematical formula, which guides architecture, painting . . ." He paused again. "Do you see?"

"It makes sense," I said, having caught a fragment of his thinking, especially the role of Mathematics with the golden ratio in the aesthetics of architecture, which we had studied in connection with the building of the Parthenon.

"Good," he said pleased. "You should know that and never hold back loving both the arts, science and mathematics." He hesitated for a moment. "Remember that. It will be easier on you," he added.

"I won't forget."

"I wish you success in whatever field you choose to follow," he said and walked away toward the Administration Building. I stood there like a pillar of salt pondering profound thoughts. I felt like somebody had given me a present. No, better than that; I felt that someone had given me a license to express myself in any responsible way I wanted. As I approached the end of my high school years, my parents weren't as enthusiastic about my newfound talents in art and poetry as I was. They were threatened by any interests I might acquire toward the arts, anything that might lead me to pursue a career of frustration, insecurity and adventure, like Orestes had done. I understood that and didn't insist that they agree with me. Now, however, I had the support of the Director, and that was enough.

As my radius of exploration increased to a large part of downtown Athens, I became acquainted with new places and made friends with people who had similar interests. I became active in *The Young Hellene,* one of the magazines for teenagers, which I mentioned before. It published excerpts from classic works of Literature and some original pieces from its young readers. But its main attraction was that it also devoted a couple of pages to messages among its young readers, who paid a fee for the right to correspond with friends using user names. The function of these messages was to connect people and therefore similar to what we see these days with chat rooms, emails and blogs and Tweeter in the Internet. Various small clubs were formed and flourished as friends banded together and competed for a variety of distinctions and prominence in the magazine pages. The club my cousin Nondas and I joined was called the *Pioneers* and we had meetings and wrote short messages to other participants for publication in the magazine. My user name translated in English was "Scholar" and Nondas' was "Periscope." Other fellow students joined other clubs or operated as independent agents. The messages we sent to each other because were very short because we had to pay for each word in them. Since my allowance was very spotty and very meager, my messages were very short. But I participated because I valued the discussions and gatherings with other kids. I became the vice president of the *Pioneers* and after a while, the other members wanted me to run for president, but I declined. I had already realized that I had no desire to run things, but I did want to have a say in everything that was happening. So, I never became president of anything, but I believe that I influenced decisions of many organizations, and there were occasions, when I agreed to be a vice president or a board member.

As a member of the *Pioneers*, Nondas, a couple of other guys and I became obsessed with the idea of publishing a newsletter with the club's name. Nondas had also started writing poems and short pieces and we had a lot more to talk about in those days. We wrote stories, articles and poems, spread some relevant drawings around the pages and published several copies of *The Pioneer* in some kind of lithographic process that has been extinct for a long time. We set a goal and accomplished it after overcoming many obstacles. We were elated at the accomplishment and celebrated with tyropita and a glass of beer at the *Tsitas* restaurant in downtown Athens. The printed word was always fascinating to me. When you write something and print it you bring a new thing into the world. If people read it they may benefit from what you gave them; and if they don't, you expressed yourself, and that benefited you.

As I tried to expand my contacts with other people with similar interests, I discovered the YMCA. They had a building in downtown Athens and one could go there to read current newspapers and magazines and play a variety of games free, including chess and ping-pong. One could also watch people learning fencing, playing basketball and other sports. I started going there to play ping-pong, chess and just hang out. When I became interested in learning English, I found people at the Y who were also interested in learning the language by practicing, and I began studying English for the first time.

When going to America became my top priority, I took English lessons from a young English tutor for a few months, then for another few months, from the wife of an ex-Ambassador of Greece to Washington, Mrs. Tsamados, who looked imperial and kindly at the same time and I called her and all other ladies who had that same demeanor that I associated with "a noble lady." Finally, I attended regular classes, once a week for about a year, at the English Institute, as a beginner.

I remember that my English tutor and I would take walks in downtown Athens and he would point at various things around us and encourage me to name things like busses, trolleys, sidewalks, flags, policemen, stores and so on. One time, when he ran out of cigarettes, we stopped at a kiosk and he asked for a pack of a Canadian brand. The proprietor didn't have them, but offered him one of the best Greek brands by the name of *Ah-ssos,* which means "Ace," in Greek. It was then that, my usually serious teacher burst into uncontrollable laughter, repeating in disbelief "*Ah-ssos*? Did you say *Ah-ssos*?" I had no idea what was so funny – none at all. When he was about to stop his delirium, he would ask the proprietor again what the brand name was, the proprietor would repeat *Ah-ssos,* and my teacher would start laughing and hold his belly all over again. I asked him what was so funny about that, but he refused to tell me. "In good time, you'll learn," he said and went on puffing on his *Ah-ssos*. Clearly, I had a long ways to go in learning English.

The Ambassador's wife, who was my English teacher for a while, taught me a few things about the culture in America and gave me a few pointers about living in the States.

"If you are ever hungry and want to get something quick to eat, go to any little store or a vendor's stand in the street, and ask for a hotdog." Another thing she taught me was that Americans don't like to pronounce words and names that end in the common Greek endings "-is," or "-os" and so on. "Of course, you cannot change your formal first or last name," she lamented, "but your nickname is another story. Instead of calling yourself 'Tolis,' as you do now," the noble lady said, "why don't you start calling yourself 'Tolly'? It would sound better to American ears, and with two ells, it would also look better," she said with such conviction that I took her seriously and started calling myself "Tolly" after I got to America. I should add that since every noun is conjugated in the Greek language, when somebody would call me in Greece, he would say "Toli," not "Tolis," which is the same as "Tolly," not "Tolis." This means that my newly acquired nickname wasn't too far from my Greek name, most of the time, anyway. All this name business shows that I was subjected to my own Ellis Island name-manipulator, like so many immigrants were subjected to, back in the heyday of massive legal immigration, before 1920. Not until I became friends with Stavros, a Greek scholar in Comparative Literature and a Linguist of note, many years later, when I was getting an MFA in Creative Writing from the University of Iowa and writing a book, did I learn that "Tolly" might present some publishers with a problem when it came to publishing a book. "It sounds like 'toll,' and may bring unpleasant associations in people, like 'a bell tolling' or 'a highway toll'," he said. And we concluded that it might be a sad thing, or a costly thing to have a name like that because . . . it could limit book sales! But it was too late by then to change my nickname, so I stuck with it, or was stuck with "Tolly." I don't jump up and down with joy, but it could have been "Apo" or worse. My formal first name is still Apostolos, which means "Apostle."

When I had decided to apply to American colleges for admission, I needed to understand something about the culture of American colleges and the language difficulties I would encounter in my classes. What I knew about American colleges was what I had seen in a couple of movies, so I was ready to soak up information wherever I could find it. The United States Information Service (USIA) was the best source for this kind of information, and I was thrilled with the welcoming attitude its employees showed to all visitors. Everything the library contained was free to read. There were no fees, no need for a Library card and no one checked your age or told you what you could read and what you couldn't. I was excited to find such an abundant source of information. I spent many hours reading in that library on Stadiou Street, and I was angry when I compared it to all the Greek libraries, where I was *persona non grata* because I wasn't a college student, yet. But, reading in English was very hard: it took me an hour to read a page of a magazine, so pictures and numbers were my main way of absorbing information at first. Reading technical information was a different matter because I had a feel for the content. I would go there after classes and spend hours reading physics and math books and solving problems to make sure that I wouldn't be lost, if I ever found myself at an American University. What struck me right away was that college books in math and science were emphasizing the applications of physical laws, not the underlying theory and the mathematics. Instead of diagrams of abstract forces, for example, pushing and pulling on two-dimensional geometrical shapes, ladders were shown, leaning up against walls, or houses withstanding wind forces; instead of starting by deriving the solution to the quadratic equation, they gave you a practical problem in words, which required the use of the quadratic equation for the solution. It seemed to me that it was easier doing math and physics that way, and as it turned out, that was true for the first couple of years wrestling with these subjects. But, studying applications might lead to missing a chance to grasp the fundamentals.

The second thing I learned from this process was that I could figure out what the problem was, even though I had trouble understanding all the words of a problem. I had a sense of what was given and what was asked for, so I was confident that I would do well in math. It would be different, when it came to understanding Shakespeare's *King Lear*.

My knowledge of French was much broader and deeper than that of English, and in some ways Latin and French were helpful to learning English. I had some French in high school because it was the required foreign language at that time, and I had attended the *Ecole d' Alliance Française* for three years, advancing to the Intermediate level. I wished that I had spent those three years at the English Institute instead, but that wasn't possible because it wasn't easy getting to it. Also, most girls from the high schools around my neighborhood were learning French, not English and I went there not only to learn the language but also to meet some girls as my mother had suspected, but was never told.

I don't think I learned anything useful from my timid encounters with girls in Eleusis, since I never formed a relationship with those I liked. So, when I met a girl I liked at the French school, in Athens, I wasn't any more adept at building a relationship than I had been in my summer forays. I would get smitten and could do nothing but brood about it. There were several girls at the *Ecole*, who liked me and one or two that were coming on to me, but as it usually happens, I had no time for their silliness – only for mine! My dream girl wasn't a "little mother," as Kitsos would have put it, or any other kind of mother. She was the top student in her high school class with a lot of poise and a good sense of humor. I suspected that she was more mature than I was, and she knew how I felt and how shy I was, but wanted me to take the risk and tell her outright how I felt, anyway. And that was the rub, because I simply couldn't take that risk. I didn't even know why I couldn't. I was too proud to be turned down, I think, and I would have to learn the hard way the advantages of a more humble ego.

We were the same age, but she was one year ahead of me in French classes, so I met her only now and then at intermissions and tried to utter half a dozen well rehearsed words, expressing in some convoluted way my affection for her. Every one of these precious utterances was received with an undecipherable smile. A buddy of mine overheard one of these utterances and told me later not to communicate with girls using . . . "enigmas." I think that the girl was mostly amused by my clumsy attempts at romance, but didn't ridicule me as I imagined that she would. Her girlfriends hinted that they understood my plight and either tried to help me or teased me.

Only once I mustered enough courage to give her a poem I had written with a pen, using multicolored India inks on vellum paper. I had rolled it up like it was some kind of a sacred scroll with a declaration of eternal truths to be preserved for the sake of history. For days, I sought a response of some kind from her, even some comment about the nice penmanship, but none was offered. After a week or so had gone by, I asked her whether she had liked my poem.

"Yes; very nice poem," she said and dug in her briefcase, found the little roll and handed it to me.

I made no move to take it from her. "What is it about, anyway?" she asked, staring at me with her large green eyes.

"Just some feelings I had and thought you might find interesting," I said sheepishly.

'"Here!" she said and tapped the paper on my hand. "I didn't know you were a poet . . . What else do you do?"

"I wrote it for you," I managed to get the words out in a hurry.

"Thank you," she said, as if I had just opened a door for her. "Sorry, I have to go and brush up on the lesson. We have a test today," she said and moved away.

I took the roll of paper from her and as I shoved it into my briefcase, I crumpled it. Later I tore it up and flushed the pieces down the toilet. I never made a copy of that poem. It was a bad way to get to that girl's heart. I learned that poems must be offered after one's feelings have been reciprocated, never in lieu of expressing them in person.

I was Don Quixote, and she was my Dulcinea! Instead of slaying windmills, I tackled complex algebraic equations, puzzled over geometry problems from a famous book the Jesuits compiled in the Middle Ages, calculated speeds and times of objects going down inclined planes or fired by cannons in parabolic trajectories and wrote love poems that I tore up and tossed into remote areas of the planet. One of Dulcinea's girl friends that liked me a lot, had the face of Gwyneth Paltrow and the body of Rosanne Barr, and must have been struck by the same kind of disease that afflicted me, because she was following me as I had followed her girl friend. Euclidian geometry could explain that triangle, but I couldn't. Another of the girls at the French school offered to let me borrow books from her father's library, one volume per week. It didn't occur to me that she might have wanted a closer relationship than that of a librarian to a bookworm. And, come to think of it, she was probably the best looking girl in the group, but not the brainiest. And so, I learned that I wasn't as sharp in forming relationships as I was in algebra. I had a lot to learn by trial and torment.

When my friends would talk about the girls in their lives, I would be silent, having nothing to contribute. I didn't think they knew any more about relationships with the opposite sex than I did, but my ineptitude was more real to me than theirs.

I was a junior when I started hanging out with one of the guys in the neighborhood who hadn't been part of the gang that met at the stoop of Kortessis. He was a couple of years older than me and seemed to understand girls much better than any of my other friends. So, I decided to confide in him and ask him for advice on how to get a foothold on the heart of my dream girl.

He listened carefully, as I explained to him how substantial this Dulcinea was and, when I was finished, he looked at me as if I had turned to a stray dog looking for pity, and said, "You'll never get a girl to pay attention to you, if you put her up on a pedestal like that! Who the hell cares how smart she is, or what grades she has, or what her career plans are? You are on the wrong track, buddy!" He had contempt for the respect I had for my Dulcinea.

"This is a special person!" I protested.

"All girls are the same kind of special," he said dismissively. "They want to be wooed, to be told they are great and then they want to take a little trip to heaven, if you know what I mean."

"You are dead wrong about this girl."

"Who the hell is this girl we are talking about, anyway?" he asked with a sudden interest.

I described the girl's house in a nearby street and then the girl herself. "Hell, I know that girl: she's built like a church bell," he said, laughing.

"I think she is a very good looking girl, and a very good person," I said stubbornly.

"She is playing with you and wants to have fun."

"I don't think so," I insisted. "I bet she has no use for anyone who thinks like that!"

"Are you serious?" He just didn't believe what I was telling him.

I was furious with him, his dirty mind and his lousy attitude. "I'm absolutely sure," I said stubbornly. "I would bet on it."

"You're on, buddy! Let me work on this and I'll tell you how it goes."

"I won't believe a thing. She'll tell you to go to hell."

"OK, I won't tell you. I'll do better than that: I'll show you!"

And so we parted company. I really didn't want to have anything to do with him anymore. I was sure the girl of my dreams would have nothing to do with him either. I felt some vague malaise from that exchange, perhaps guilt. Had I set that girl up with my stupid challenge? This guy had been around, after all, and could ensnare an innocent girl before she knew what was happening to her. I felt bad thinking there was a chance that she might not meet the challenge, but, on the other hand, nothing could happen to her, if she didn't want it to happen. Everyone must decide on one's own.

I saw this Don Juan again a couple of weeks later, and he told me that everything was going well in his relationship with Dulcinea. I didn't believe him, so he said that I could see him with her on a date, if I showed up at some sponsored evening function at the main office of the *Ecole d' Alliance Française* where she had invited him to go with her. He gave me the appointed time. "We'll stay outside for awhile, so you can see us," he said. I already felt that whatever was happening between these two people had nothing to do with me. But, I had to see. I had to know. I didn't want to just believe the worst.

So, I showed up outside the French school building and waited some distance away, behind some hedges marking the front garden of the building. I saw him waiting for a few minutes, and then Dulcinea got off the bus and ran into his arms. And they hugged and kissed and spread their joy around them. I turned my back and moved away, feeling a hundred years old and weighing a ton. I knew close to nothing about relations between the sexes. Don Juan was handsome and had been around the block a few times, so he knew the calculus of relations between the sexes, and spoke the pantomime of love, something you can't learn even at the *Ecole d' Alliance Française*. And the girl I had liked and respected so much didn't see any of the things I was hoping she would see. She would have to learn even more than me, or I was an idiot. I was willing to rest in peace with that thought.

I found out that even a messy and costly end of a relationship is not without some benefits. A new beginning is possible, and the word "now" is loaded with hope again. The future is no longer squeezed into shapes formed in the mind by desire, but becomes an endless array of "nows" and extends to all dimensions of time, space and dreams. I felt I could go anywhere and do anything in the pursuit of excellence. I didn't become a cynic, but I was disappointed and realized that people are not always, or ever, what one wishes them to be. I was hurt and disillusioned for a while, but I wasn't even knocked down. I was tempted to turn off the world, but I loved too many things in it and had no desire to be alone. I tried to see the world as a cesspool without clean and noble people, but I couldn't do that either, because there were many decent people I knew. So, I had no choice but to do my best, as always in the world that is, hoping that it will become better.

Now I pushed hard to achieve my goal of getting the best education I could. I wanted no more complications. I was surprised that I was able to bounce back as quickly as I did. And, having no real or imagined romantic ties, with anyone anymore, I felt freer and more motivated to expand my horizon beyond Greece than I had been before. I was ready to go to America, but I still had no money for tuition or for the fare, and no guarantee for funds to live on, once I got to where I was going.

43 • Class Consciousness and College Lore

"In order to stand well in the eyes of the community, it is necessary to come up to a certain, somewhat indefinite, conventional standard of wealth."

Thorstein Veblen in *Theory of the Leisure Class*

Great dreams... never even get out of the box. It takes an uncommon amount of guts to put your dreams on the line, to hold them up and say, "How good or how bad am I?" That's where courage comes in.

Erma Bombeck

I started the search for a scholarship at an American University, without thinking about the odds of success, by visiting after class, as frequently as I could, the USIA library in downtown Athens and trying to make sense out of the catalogues and the college books I found there. I had no idea of the application process, the criteria for admission or how to evaluate different schools. I struggled long and hard with these unknowns, familiarizing myself with the language and the steps of the process. There were no guidebooks for college admissions back then, but I could find clues of what each college wanted as I browsed college catalogues. I went on alert as I searched and tried to connect everything and everyone I saw or heard of with studies in American colleges. People who had relatives in America; people who had travelled by ship on long voyages; what Americans value as a people; the history of the United States of America; how American soldiers lived in Greece; what kind of people studied in America and what professions they practiced in America or in Greece. I learned about the climate of New York, California, Syracuse and Louisiana; the process of getting a passport; the types of scholarships one can get and everything else that could be of use in achieving my objective.

I heard on the radio that the Massachusetts Institute of Technology, MIT, was the top school in the world for a technical education and the California Institute of Technology was second, so I started composing a letter, one word at a time, requesting admission and a scholarship there. One night I had an inspiration: Why not apply to a school, which had a name I could at least recognize? After a couple of evenings of research, I zeroed in on Syracuse University, because Syracuse was a colony of Athens in the Golden Era of Athens, in the fifth century BC, and the people who named their city after that famed ancient colony couldn't be anything other than generous and welcoming to Athenians, as the Syracusans of old surely must have been, before the Athenians under the leadership of the brilliant but corrupt general, Alcibiades, sacked their city. There was a chance that the New York branch of Syracusans forgave Athens and forgot that event.

I sent the letter and had a ball imagining the admissions officers reading my letter in pidgin English and deciding what to do with me. It felt good to have "irons in the fire," which, as my English book pointed out, was an "English Expression" I needed to learn along with "don't poke your nose into other people's business," which took me a long time to understand and accept because, in Greece, interfering with other people's business shows that you care for them, and keeping your nose out of their business means that you are insensitive and you don't give a damn about them.

Another evening, at the same Library and Center of Culture reading room, I came upon a catalogue from Louisiana State University. I kept pronouncing the word, Lou-i-si-ana, fascinated by the beautiful sound it made and the romantic connotations I could conjure, looking at pictures of the bayous and the nightlife and the Mardi Gras parades. So, I applied to the University of Louisiana. The more applications I filled and sent, the more hopeful I became.

In my junior and senior years, I made some new friends from other high schools, when I attended a preparatory school to get ready for the exams at the Greek Polytechnic, which was my back up college, if I couldn't attend an American college. We were learning how to solve problems in Math, Physics and Chemistry that were way beyond what we had learned in high school classes. At the time, the Algebra of Absolute Values was fashionable, and we learned how to solve problems involving inequalities as well as equations in a system of several unknowns. The topic was maddening to a degree that made us feel discouraged. We had been trained to solve problems that had definite answers. When you solve for x, you know what x is. But with inequalities in the mix, the best you can do after half an hour's work at times, is to say something like x is bigger than the absolute value of 14 but less or equal to 39. Where is the satisfaction in that? The competition for the Engineering departments at the Polytechnic was fierce, and the odds of success were about one in ten for a top student from the average high school. To select the best students, the questions asked in the exams had become increasingly difficult over the years, hence Absolute Values and inequalities. High school grades were not taken into account at all. Nobody cared what school you had attended or what your record was. Performance on the day of the exam was the only thing that counted. Having the name of the participant in every exam covered securely by a glued flap of opaque paper provided anonymity in grading and guarded against favoritism and other types of cheating. If one was sick on one or two days of the exams and could not perform at the top of his form, he could fail and have to wait a whole year to take the exams again because no excuses were accepted for any reason, including sickness. Many of the people succeeded in the entrance exams of the Polytechnic only on their second or third try. Some high school students from the countryside, where schools were not as strong in Math and Science as those in Athens, didn't even bother taking the Polytechnic exams right after graduation, choosing instead to come to Athens and devote a whole year studying for the Polytechnic exams in one of the many private preparatory schools.

One of my new friends at the preparatory school was Kostis, who attended the American College, the most prestigious private high school of Greece. We were both trying as hard as we could to be admitted to the Polytechnic and both had an interest in going to America. We started studying together a couple of times a week, sometimes in my house under my mother's guidance and loving care, and sometimes at his house. I never saw or met his parents because they were not there and never found out anything about them because Kostis didn't like to talk about them. I would help him with a Math problem now and then, and he would help me with my English. On our way out after classes, walking to the bus station, we would talk about art, music, engineering and his architecture, the profession he thought brought together arts, science and mathematics, especially as it was practiced by Phidias, Kallikratis and others masters in Pericles' ancient Athens. I told him about the lecturette the philosopher Georgoulis gave me once, and he was delighted that someone else recognized the connection. I had found somebody who was a kindred spirit, interested in similar things as I was, so we could talk intelligently about them.

Kostis was fluent in English and, when we were with a bunch of other guys, noisily cavorting in the streets of Athens, we all took advantage of his presence and practiced whatever English we knew. We would often come upon an English word that we hadn't heard or seen before, and we would save it and ask Kostis to tell us what it meant, while threatening to take away his Master of the English Language certificate, if he didn't give the right answer. Good-natured Kostis smiled and never failed to come through. We would then tease him and call him The Monster of Britannia, and speak in bar-bar, nonsense language and laugh our heads off. He was soft spoken, introverted and unflappable to the point of appearing to be a bit of a cold fish, which is to say that he and I got along together very well. He helped me edit some of my letters to colleges, though neither one of us knew how to appeal to directors of admissions in American colleges. Kostis wasn't very good at arguing and, when we disagreed, it was easy to corner him with Socratic jujitsu and win the argument. It was my way of showing him that I too was good at something, though I'm sure he never cared about who won and who lost anything. He didn't have to. He came from a well to do family and didn't have to assert himself to anyone before he could be heard, or before he could get what he wanted in the wild streets of *Neos Kosmos*.

Sometimes, when I was at his home, I wished that I had come from a family that didn't have to struggle for survival as mine had. I wished that I would derive self-confidence from some other source, as Kostis apparently did, rather than solely from excelling in school. I was sure his father didn't have to hoard beans and tin cans form Argentina behind a wardrobe, and his mother didn't have to travel on top of loaded trucks to barter for olive oil and cheese with shoes, all over the countryside. That desire to rise up higher than where I had come from motivated me to do better. I wanted to rise up as much as I could. I didn't know how, or how far up, or where I would do that, but I had to reach further than my parents had done, so my children and grandchildren would be more secure than I was. The answer of the equation I was trying to solve in my mind when I got into a fix kept coming out again and again as "college in America."

Kostis had many years of instruction in playing the piano and taught me some basic elements of music appreciation. I got to hear for the first time some classical music played in a high fidelity system at his home and understood a little more about the structure of some compositions. I listened to Bach's *Toccata and Fugue in D Minor* and *The Well Tempered Clavier* and felt as if a door had been opened and a new vista lay before me. I regret that I didn't get the time and the energy to learn more about music, but my world was very different from Kostis' and didn't make allowances for music appreciation until it was too late to start; or, not!

44 • Foray into the Fulbright

Concern yourself not with what you tried and failed in, but with what it is still possible for you to do.

Pope John XXIII

As I became serious about going to America, the search for funds, any kind of funds, that I could somehow win and use to study abroad became an obsession. One of the widely known fund sources was the "Fulbright." I heard about the Fulbright Scholarships, and immediately started exploring how I could win one. If I were awarded one of these scholarships, it would pay for my trip to America and that would help me get closer to my goal. I was also hoping that there might be additional funds for college expenses. The problem was that one had to pass a written exam in English proficiency and then do well in an oral interview with a Fulbright representative about the educational plans one had made. At that time, I had very little knowledge of English, but there was no fee for entering the competition, so I was thinking seriously of participating on a "why not?" basis. As I think back now, I cannot believe my chutzpah! As the Greeks say, I was going to the wedding with bare feet because my knowledge of English was rudimentary. In talking this matter over with Kostis, he decided that he would also like to try and win a Fulbright scholarship for the prestige of the award. His chances of winning were very good and mine were very bleak, but we both felt good about having a common goal.

So, we registered for the Fulbright exam and, at the appointed time, we appeared at the exam room in the designated hall of the American College, Kostis' high school, in a suburb of Athens. In the dictation part of the exam, I could catch, perhaps, one out of three words, but I struggled valiantly to make sense out of what the instructor was saying, putting together lots of "ands" and "buts" "go's" and "get's" and all the Greek and French and Latin and Greek word words that one can find in the English language. I wasn't having much success. I felt frustrated, as if I was trying to fill a bucket with water, using a sieve. It seemed like the reader wasn't going to wait for the words to gain a foothold in my brain, let alone for my hand to produce them on paper. And since many of the words were alien to me, the spelling I invented for these words was bizarre. The lady dictating was on the move, with long sentences assaulting my ears and snaking through my head long after they were released.

Then, there was an essay on what I planned to do in America, which I completed, probably the language proficiency of a second grader. And, finally, there was a multiple-choice test, in which most of the words made no sense whatsoever to me. My choice on the multiple-choice test was to rely on luck. Kostis, on a nearby desk, was breezing through the exam, while I stared at the ceiling for inspiration and picked answers out of thin air. I must add here that Kostis tried to devise a method of communicating to me the number of the item to check in the multiple-choice test and then give me the correct choice by flicking his fingers, but I was so confused that I couldn't overcome both my conscience and my confusion and make any sense out of his signals. I walked out of the examination hall punch-drunk.

When the results were announced a couple of weeks later, we found out that Kostis had creamed the exam, finishing among the top five participants, and I, with my meager English and a bunch of quasi-random answers, had scored well enough to be second runner-up below those who had passed the exam and entitled to have an interview, just in case a couple of the winners dropped out and an extra place or two became available. I was delighted with my good luck and encouraged that my knowledge of English might be better than I had believed it to be. Sometimes, I think, we don't really know how much we know; and sometimes we don't really know, but we delude ourselves until we learn.

At the appointed day, I went for the interview with a Greek representative of the Fulbright Scholarships in an office building, downtown Athens. He was a pleasant and welcoming man, probably an executive, doing his part to help young people, as a volunteer. He asked a variety of questions and told me that, to qualify for a Fulbright scholarship, I would have to want to study in a field that didn't exist in Greece. Then he asked me what field I wanted to study. The Polytechnic offered a degree in combined Mechanical and Electrical Engineering, which included courses from both fields, but no separate degree for Electrical Engineering. That's what I planned to study, if I couldn't go to an American college. I knew very little at that time about these fields so, after just a moment's hesitation, I said that I wanted to study pure, unadulterated Electrical Engineering and nothing else. I decided this on the spur of the moment because I got a hint from the interviewer that, if I wanted to study something that was available in Greece, I would not be eligible for the Fulbright. Why not create my career right there and then? What did I know from Electrical or Mechanical engineering, anyway? I would have said that I wanted to study Sanitary Technology if that was the only specialty they gave scholarships for. If I didn't like it at some future time, I would change it! The interview in Greek went very well, and I left feeling satisfied with my performance.

Kostis and several other participants were waiting to be interviewed when I came out of the office. They didn't know that the Fulbright scholarships were available only for fields that didn't exist in Greece, so I told them. Kostis listened attentively. "It's got to be Architecture!" he said stubbornly. The interviewer told him how sorry he was to refuse him an award, since he was one of the top participants after the written exam, but architecture was certainly one of the areas where Greece excelled and was very qualified to offer a degree, as in fact it did, at the Polytechnic. Kostis told me that he agreed wholeheartedly and left the room, thanking the interviewer for the experience of participation. I saw him outside and, I thought, "He is walking on a cloud." He was happy because he had chosen correctly. He was happy because the interviewer had told him he respected his decision and wished him success in his studies.

"I would have said that I wanted to study Mathematical Architecture, Landscape Architecture, Paleo-Architecture, Primitive Architecture, Pyramid Construction, Architecture of Tunnel Burrowing, any damn thing, anything architectural but absent from the Greek educational menu of disciplines," I protested. "Did you think of that?" I persisted. He said that he would have never thought of betraying his love for Architecture by playing games.

He stared at me puzzled, as if to say, "Are you crazy, or what?" I had to calm down and say that I didn't know what I would have done. I wondered what would he have done, if he had no pot to piss in. I decided that from that time on and until some other event changed my mind, I would study Electrical Engineering, period.

The results of the Fulbright were still pending when I visited the American Embassy to learn about the necessary arrangements for an interview with a consulate official and fill some papers for the required visa. I became friends with Mrs. Metaxas, the lady, who was the assistant of the special counsel for Educational Affairs. I told her about my trying to win a Fulbright scholarship, and she immediately informed me that, were I to win it, it would cover my expenses for the trip and back, but I would be obligated to travel with a Visitor's Visa, and I wouldn't be allowed to work in the United States. "What you need to have, if you plan to work as a student in America, is a Student Visa," she said in a very emphatic voice. The way I had planned my finances, working in America was my primary means of support. I thought of all the agony I had put myself through, the hours I had invested brushing up my pitiful English and I felt exhausted. I thought that I was chasing phantoms and capturing air. But, without hesitation and even with some relief for putting an end to the chancy waiting for two people to drop out so I could be included among the Fulbright winners, I informed the Fulbright people that I would not be a candidate anymore, and gave them my reasons. They understood. I wanted to tell them that it would be more fair to the participants, if the conditions for the scholarship were explained well in advance, but I didn't. Probably, they were in the application form, but I hadn't been able to read and understand them. And fixing the Fulbright Fellowship Program wasn't my top priority just then.

45 • Coincidence or Providence?

"The heart is a beggar . . .There is no asking without receiving
and no receiving without asking."
James P. Carse, *The Silence of God: Meditations on a Prayer.*

Every perfect gift is from above, coming down from the Father
of lights.

Jas. 1:17a

I was just coming out of my disappointment with the Fulbright fiasco
when I started getting back some responses to my college applications
for admission. The University of Louisiana offered me admission and a
full tuition scholarship of $200. I got a shot of self-confidence from that
admission: I had understood the application process, competed in an
alien environment and achieved the objective. It proved that I was on the
right track. I was happy that at least one American institution of higher
learning had recognized my ability and granted me admission with a
scholarship. I went about telling my friends that I had already been
admitted to an American college with a scholarship. There was no need
for shouting all the details. The school wasn't exactly touted in any kind
of media as a model of higher education, and the tuition was a bit on the
cheap side, but it was an American college and that was good enough for
me to go on exploring. And, the more I found out about the school, the
more doubts I began to have about the value of its education.

Next, I received a response from MIT. The letter contained some
encouraging words about my excellent performance and concluded with
this statement: *"I regret to inform you that foreign students are not
eligible for scholarship aid until they have completed one year of work at
the Institute."* I stared at the letter as if I was in front of the Great Wall of
China and had to get on the other side of it.

The frustration lasted until I got a letter admitting me to Cal Tech
with a $600 full tuition scholarship. I got the letter as I was headed for
the bus stop on my way to school and read it in the bus, going downtown
Athens. I got off at my usual stop, and started walking to school. I felt
that I had torn down the wall that stood between me and my dreams of
being a college student in America, an engineer, an inventor, a
benefactor, an explorer of any field of knowledge that I wanted. But the
living expenses for Cal Tech were steep. I had always counted on some
help from my parents, but there was no way they could handle all of it.
Perhaps, I could work and make up the difference. Somehow I should be

able to make it. Ship fare, scholarship, living expenses, parents' contribution, help from relatives, work during school year, work in the summers – I found myself calculating and exploring every avenue I could imagine for any revenue I could possibly get. I would compete for it; I would work for it; I would ask for it; and, if need be, I would beg for it.

Syracuse University offered me admission, but no scholarship. So much for the ancient ties of a colony to the motherland, I thought. I wasn't interested. There must be other schools to apply to, but which ones? The lady I knew at the American Embassy told me that it was an honor to be admitted with a scholarship at Cal Tech. I forgot about Louisiana. Everybody seemed to think that Cal Tech was a top school in the country. If one wanted to get the best education possible, that was the school to attend. California, here I come.

With thoughts of connections and calculations bouncing in my head, I was crossing the schoolyard one late afternoon in the spring of my last year. To my left, standing at the entrance of the administration building that housed the principal's office and the offices of a couple of other senior professors, my eye caught a young man, a little older than me. I had seen him before in the schoolyard.

"How's it going?" he asked smiling.

I recognized him as Kalegos' cousin. He had visited the school with Kalegos the previous year, and, after that, Kalegos mentioned that his cousin was studying abroad. "You must be Kalegos' cousin, studying abroad," I said, a little embarrassed that I couldn't recall his name.

"Tony, that's right, Tony Condaratos," he said in a welcoming tone. "I've seen *you* around."

He was short, powerfully built, with wavy black hair and a well-trimmed moustache. He seemed to enjoy being there. He said he had stopped by to say hello to some of his old professors. I was so intent on trying to explain my situation that I forgot to introduce myself.

"I'm trying to find a way to go to College in America," I said.

He smiled. "It isn't easy," he said. For a moment I thought he was sharing my predicament.

"It is; if you got the money," I snapped back. Why did I have to be so quick with an argument? I hated it when my impulses slid past my controls and produced the opposite result from what I intended. I didn't want to entertain even for a moment the idea that it was difficult, perhaps, impossible for me to study in America. "I'll need help to make it there," I admitted.

"Have you applied for scholarships? Americans are very generous people," he said. "But you have to have good grades."

He still doesn't remember me, I thought. Everyone knew that I had the grades. "I have a scholarship from Cal Tech, but it's not enough," I blurted out, anxious to show him that I was working on the goals I had set and even getting some results.

"Yeah," he said laughing, as if he just found the answer to a puzzle. "Sure. You do have the grades! I remember you getting the prize from the Ministry: Kizilos, right?"

"Tolly Kizilos," I said. "I got the grades, but not the dough." I took a step closer, and we shook hands.

"Cal Tech is good." Then, after a moment's hesitation, he asked, "Have you applied to MIT?" He was staring at me eagerly, still sporting that half silly, half mocking, yet welcoming smile.

"I did, but they turned me down," I said, tired of thinking about applications again. "I asked if they could give me a scholarship, and they said foreign students have to be there for a year before they are eligible."

He looked at me for a long moment as if I wasn't there; his eyes were staring at some faraway vision. Then, something happened for which I have no explanation.

"If you send me your grades and your prizes from the Ministry of Education, all of these, officially translated, along with a letter asking for admission to MIT with a scholarship, I'll take them personally to the Advisor of Foreign Students." He stopped, as if to weigh a thought. "Professor Chalmers is always looking for good students. And, I'll put in a good word for you," he said and now looked me in the eye waiting for my response as if we were in a dare.

I stared at him, unable to believe what he had just said. Without voicing my cry for help or casting spells on him, Tony Condaratos, a total stranger before our chance meeting, had offered to champion my cause. He heard my asking for help and had offered some. Why? People don't just take on another person's burdens and carry them for the distance without some benefit to themselves. Do they? What could he be up to?

"I appreciate any help I can get, and I certainly will get all my papers to you," I said as sincerely as I could. I still couldn't believe that anything would come out of his noble gesture. "Cal Tech gave me $600 for tuition, but it's not enough to cover books and living expenses," I added plaintively, as if he was the man who personally limited the amount of that scholarship.

"MIT is a great school and they may do better."

"You think they can make an exception in my case?" I persisted in my doubts.

"Write a good letter and have all your papers in order. Paul Chalmers is a man who can move mountains to help foreign students, especially top students; but he wants to have all the facts and papers properly done." He took out a little notepad from his back pocket and jotted something down. He took his eyes off the writing and stared at me. "Chalmers has a heart of gold. He's a very caring person. Don't forget: everything officially done." He finished writing, tore the page and handed it to me. "Send your stuff to me on this address."

I reached out and took the little scrap of paper with the key to my future on it. I shook his hand and thanked him for his goodwill and all that he was willing to do for me.

"I'll be back in America in a couple of weeks, so I'll get your package in person. It'll take you more than a month to get everything translated officially and validated. The bureaucracy is killing this country."

"It took me a month to get my passport, and I had to pull some strings to get it that fast," I said, agreeing with him completely.

I hated the waiting and the sleazy ways government clerks forced you to deal with them, if you needed approval for any kind of papers. Every clerk of the bureaucracy became a plenipotentiary of the realm when he held his seal in his hand and decided if he would convert your paper to an official document of the government or let you dangle in limbo for days or weeks or forever.

"The American government is more efficient. People have a job to do and they do it well without money under the table."

"Are there many Greek students at MIT?" I asked, having regained my emotional balance.

He named several students from Varvakeion who were studying there, most of them in graduate school, and a couple of the stars, who had become professors. "We have a good community," he said, and then, laughing, "The Greek Americans are always trying to get us to marry their daughters. They believe that MIT graduates are good catches." He glanced at his watch. "I better check and see if any of the wise men of yore are available now. I knew that there was a meeting, but it was supposed to be over almost half an hour ago."

"Was Mazis one of the teachers you wanted to see?" I asked, thinking that if the teachers' meeting hadn't run over, I wouldn't have met Tony.

"Yeah. We all have been touched by his quirks, his tricks and his brilliance, haven't we?" He had already turned to get back into the building, but he stopped abruptly. "It would also help, if you could get a couple of professors to write letters of recommendation. Some guys say that that they help."

"I can do that. I'll have them translated, also."

"Good," he said, waving goodbye. "I hope we'll see each other in Cambridge next fall," he said, as if everything between now and that day was only a matter of time.

"From your mouth to God's ear," I called out to him, the way Greeks say "I hope so."

I walked toward the bus stop on Lamentation Square taking in the cool air of that spring evening filled with hope. It was drizzling, tiny drops suspended in space and memory. Riding the bus I slipped into a reverie and felt the passage of the colored lights from all the marquis wash over the store windows and statues and sparkling cars flowing like a river up ahead of us. I wanted the people hurrying in the wet streets to have something in mind that gave them hope for tomorrow. I was still in my head when we reached *Neos Kosmos*, now a neighborhood bustling with construction work and life. This abode of outsiders with the tantalizing smells of souvlaki and shish kabob from the tavernas out on the streets had been my home for a long time; but it wouldn't be forever. The air was electric, charged with hints of adventure and the joy of discovery. Nothing had smelled that good for a very long, long time, and I would have to leave it all behind, perhaps forever.

"Hey, young man," Kyr-Philippas, the grocer, greeted me as I went by. "Tell your mother we just got the tomatoes she was asking for."

"Thanks; I'll tell her," I said and moved on. I passed by the gardenia plant being reborn in Koula's garden. The chef in white work clothes at "The Taverna Nostimos," standing beside the pit of his revolving gyros smiled and tapped his toque with a couple of fingers toward me. The neighborhood was trying to lure me back, and it was good to know it.

I couldn't help but feel buoyed by Tony's optimism. But how could this stranger be at the spot where I found him, at the time that I happened to walk by, because a meeting he had happened to be delayed? And why did we start talking about scholarships rather than gossip about his cousin who happened to be in my class, or his pending meeting with Mazis and the other old professors he had come by to see? Coincidence, I thought, the remarkable alignment of two or more events or circumstances without obvious causal connection. Two people headed toward different destinations meet, without any intention to do so, at a given place and time and produce a greatly desired outcome. Meeting Tony was unpredictable, improbable and potentially life altering. I didn't dare believe that God almighty would bother to throw such a good pass my way, even though I had been asking for his help for some time. That would mean that I was good and had God's favor, and no one is good enough in the eyes of God to get freebies like that. Yet, any other explanation just didn't seem logical. What can we say about all these providential acts that happen with wondrous randomness, so often in this world? For whom do they happen, and why?

That night I told my parents the good news. My mother acted as if she had been expecting something like that. Why not? She believed that these things were a child's play for the Creator of the universe and his saints. I had to work a little harder to convince my father that something good would come out of this encounter with Tony Condaratos.

I worked very hard to write the best letter I was able to write for MIT. Kostis had already left for a trip to Europe with his parents, so I had no one to help me with the English. I remember a paraphrase of the gist of my argument as follows:

> If you help me with scholarship, I promise you that I will put myself to work very hardly and attain excellently my record in your school. The only matter I ask is you provide for me some food and a room with your University. I believe that you have a bed and a plate food in your great country for me too who works very hardly and succeeded much of time.

I asked professor Xifaras, my teacher of Modern Greek, and professor Passas my Algebra teacher, to write letters of recommendation for me. Professor Passas signed the letter I translated as soon as I presented it to him, but professor Xifaras wanted me to read him the translated letter before he could sign it.

"How do I know that the letter says what I wrote?" he asked me. He had a point, and for a moment we stared at each other like strangers struggling to place each other's face. I couldn't believe that I hadn't thought about that and brought his letter in Greek with me.

"You could take the letter with you, Sir, and have somebody else translate what I wrote," I replied a little hurt.

"Start reading slowly," professor Xifaras suggested.

"Can you understand English, Sir?"

"How far from Latin, Greek and French can it be?" he said with resolve. "Read slowly and I'll stop you and ask you to translate a specific word, if I can't understand it, or if it is not the word I remember writing."

I read the entire letter to him while he stared intently at the ceiling. I had to stop and translate only half a dozen words. "It's not that I don't trust you to translate accurately," he said gently, "or that I don't trust you to be honest when you translate, but it is irresponsible for me to sign something that I don't understand. You must remember that. It could save you a lot of grief later in life."

"Thank you for the advice, Sir," I mumbled. "And for your very kind letter."

"Mr. Kizilos, you earned every word I wrote for you," he said thoughtfully. "When you go to America, don't forget your heritage." And the great Xifaras who had given 40 years of his life to instill the right Greek ideas and values to the most promising high school students of the country shook my hand and left.

It did occur to me to ask professor Mazis for a letter of recommendation, but I decided not to risk it.

I went through the pain of having all my documents officially translated at the appropriate office at the Ministry of Education, got photocopies of my prizes, included the translated letters of recommendation signed by my professors, wrote a "thank you" letter to Tony Condaratos, bundled everything together in a brown manila envelope and mailed it to him. "Regardless of the outcome of your effort," I wrote to Tony Condaratos, "your willingness to help me, a person you hardly knew, is heartwarming and has moved me profoundly. I won't let you down and, I pray, that God will help you in all your goals as you have helped me."

Now, a word about Tony Condaratos, because good people must never be forgotten: he returned to Greece after his education at MIT and left disappointed with the treatment he received from his colleagues at his job as an electrical engineer at a power plant. But he didn't give up his dream to return to Greece and help any way he could. He worked for the space program of the U.S.A., developed management systems and had management responsibilities for various government agencies in Washington DC for many years. Eventually, he returned to Greece and assumed a prominent administrative post in the healthcare field. Our paths crossed a few times in later years, and I found that he was always a congenial person, dedicated to the goals he set for himself. When my father was hurt and close to death and needed help with his hospital care, I tried to get in touch with him and mentioned his name to the hospital staff. Somehow, I never found out how, my father's hospital problem was resolved and he had a few more peaceful days before he died.

Tony was from Santorini, the island that was home for many of our neighbors in *Neos Kosmos*, and one of his goals was to prove that the Atlantis of Plato and Herodotus was once located in between Santorini and Crete and disappeared under the sea when the Santorini volcano erupted. Atlantis would then be the precursor of the Greek world! He did extensive research and wrote a book on that topic. Sometimes, I wonder if he feels that he is done with that pursuit. But, Atlantis remains a mystery to this day and, I bet, the Tony Condaratos I know hasn't given up the search for a definitive proof, yet.

Though my heart and mind were focused on leaving for America, I was still attending the preparatory school and getting ready for the entrance exams at the Polytechnic, as my back up alternative. In addition, I never let up on my performance in high school, refusing to believe that no one cared about grades after the junior year. I researched Columbia University and tried to find some connection with it because there are a lot of Greeks in the New York area, but I found none and never applied. So, a lot was riding on MIT and Cal Tech. By that time I had become an expert in estimating the costs of different colleges, and I give below the results of my research, as written on the back of an envelope more than half a century ago:

	MIT	Cal Tech	Louisiana	Columbia
Tuition	700	500	200	450
Room	260	250	100	250
Board	360	280	230	430
Books, etc	100	100	100	230
TOTAL	1420	1130	630	1360

I kept going over these and other figures in my head, trying to find the answer to my problem. Asking people and reading more about Colleges, I knew now that MIT and Cal Tech were a cut above Louisiana and Dakota Wesleyan University in Mitchell, South Dakota (total cost $635), which was another one of those schools that I was looking at in my early enthusiastic searches. Cal Tech was certainly the best buy for the money, but without a better scholarship and extra costs for transportation, it was still beyond my reach. As I look back upon my efforts, I believe I was way ahead of my time in my methodology of searching for a solution to my problem: though I had no name for what I was doing, I had developed the techniques of networking thirty years before it became known as such. I talked about my plans to anyone willing to listen and asked anyone I knew, if they knew any way I might be able to earn the money for the ship fare, or how to earn money as a student in America, what summer jobs could a student find, or if they had a relative or friend in whose house I could stay, if I found myself in the Boston area, or in Pasadena. My mother, always a supporter of my efforts, was doing the same thing and so was my father, who had some connections through his workplace.

I had been busy studying at my table when the doorbell drilled through the noon quietness. My mother rushed out to answer the door downstairs. I heard her chatting, but paid no attention. "The mailman came!" she shouted even before she had come in and shut the door. "Letter for you, Tolly. From America!"

Professor Paul Chalmers, the Advisor of Foreign Students at MIT had responded with congratulations and an offer of admission with a package of $900.00 for a full tuition scholarship plus books and miscellaneous expenses. My hope of going to MIT to study had just come closer to becoming a reality. I felt that I had just been freed from bondage. "I'm in! I'm in!" I shouted at my mother and grabbed her and hugged her and we danced in the little hallway and the kitchen of our home. "MIT has given me a good scholarship."

First chance my mother had to get free, she turned east and crossed herself, saying, "Thank you dearest Jesus for giving my son the help we asked for." I also thanked God for his help. And then, looking at me severely and shaking a finger, my mother said, "I hope you don't let this go to your head, young man." She gave me a smile. "I knew you were ready to fly . . . " she stopped and tears flooded her face.

"Now, now, mom," I tried to console her, "I'll always be around." But she knew that I was gone and would never be as close to her as I had been all these years.

I thought of Tony Condaratos' promise and the result and kept him in my mind with a thankful prayer all that day. I couldn't believe that he was able to reverse the policy of the mighty school regarding scholarships to foreign students. It was an uplifting event.

My father was moved by the success of my effort. He congratulated me and contrasted the Greek narrow-mindedness that would have never reversed its official pronouncement with the Americans' open minds and their willingness to change. I could tell that he wished he had lived his life in the American culture. He just couldn't stand the convoluted system of human interactions that prevailed in Greece. He liked everything about America, but he never came to visit us in America. He was one of those people who wanted to be where he was and didn't want to risk the unpredictable effects of change.

Somehow, my mother heard from one of her sisters that the daughter of one of their aunts was married to the influential director of the electric power generation station for greater Athens, a man whose name in English, literally translated, means Dragon! My aunt said that her aunt thought it would be a good idea to get in touch with the Dragon's wife and find out if her husband knew anyone who might be able to help me. My mother contacted the Dragon lady, and got a promise from her that she would indeed talk to the Dragon. The Dragon lady called back and asked that I call her husband in a couple of days. She gave my mother a telephone number where he could be reached.

When I called two days later, Mr. Dragon told me that he had discussed my situation with a ship-owner friend of his, who was willing to see me and discuss my transportation problem. He gave me his name and a phone number to call. The ship owner's name was Pateras, which literally means Father, in Greek. So, a connection was established from me to my mother to my aunt to her aunt to the Dragon's wife, to Mr. Dragon and finally to Mr. Father. Nothing was the result of planning; everything happening was improbable. Were these coincidences of unrelated events, or another set of providential acts? I was beginning to think that God was working some of the levers that made my life run.

A week later, I found myself in Mr. Father's office. He listened to my story and told me that he might be able to help me with the travel expenses, if I was willing to work for them. He told me that he had several ships that go all over the world, including America, and he would arrange for me to travel in one of them as a sailor, if I could get a sailor's work license and passport, in addition to my regular passport, so he could hire me for the duration of the trip. I accepted his generous offer and thanked him. The next day I started working on ways and means on how to get the documents I needed.

Uncle Gerassimos, was a lieutenant in the Greek Coast Guard at that time, and immediately offered to help me get my papers in order. To get the process rolling I had to pass a physical exam by the Piraeus Harbor Authorities. I remember standing half-naked in a large hall with a couple of dozen sailors and stevedores and comparing my puny body's musculature to the powerfully built bodies of seasoned sailors and dock workers, who had spend years doing hard physical labor. I was healthy, but I wasn't sure that they would find me fit for duty on a merchantman. I tried to look tough and cool and even spat on the floor a couple of times as they were doing to show everybody what a crude character I was. I passed the exam, and uncle Gerassimos helped me with all the papers I needed to have issued at the Ministry of Commercial Shipping. I got my naval passport and admired it because it would give me the opportunity to do "real" work for the first time in my life.

Then, I spent three weeks in the maze of the Greek bureaucracy, going from government office to government office, filling applications, signing affidavits, licking and affixing dozens of service stamps on them and swearing in front of various cogs of the machinery, to get documents for taking foreign exchange out of the country, and documents for postponing my military service where I was supposed to serve as a naval officer, if I wasn't a college student in good standing at the time I became twenty one years old.

The more I dealt with the government bureaucrats, the less contact I wanted to have with them. Every official wielding his stamp of approval made me feel powerless, and I hated having to beg for my rights. Dealing with the little bossy bureaucrats behind battered desks when barking their directions at my face was painful. I bore the brunt of their gruff ways because a part of me felt sorry for these lifers, occupying their little miserable cubbyholes without any prospect of change. I was so frustrated with the government bureaucracy that I counted it as one of the reasons I wanted to get out of Greece and be rid of it. I remember the elation I felt many years later, when I received my passport ten days after spending ten minutes at the County Government Center in Minnesota filling up an application form for it! What a country!

I met Tony Hambouris at the American Embassy when he was applying for his visa. He had been admitted to MIT and was getting ready to leave for America. We became friends and agreed to stick together when we found ourselves in Cambridge and, perhaps, get rooms in the same dormitory. Tony had already bought his tickets on an ocean liner, and had passed with flying colors the interview with the consular official. His English was near perfect, having studied at the American College of Athens, probably, I thought, with some kind of scholarship, because he wasn't rich.

Living with uncertainty had never been a big problem for me, because I could focus my energies on any issue at hand and usually come up with a solution that was helpful; but, the situation I found myself in required living with many uncertainties for weeks on end and without anything I could do to end the uncertainty. I wasn't sure whether the government would approve any of my applications, whether I could pass the consular exam, whether Mr. Pateras would find a ship to send me to America in time, whether my father could scrape up enough money to support me at MIT for the first year at least, whether I could find enough work at school to supplement my expenses, whether I could find a summer job, whether my visa would permit me to work at any job I found outside the school, whether I could find somebody to stay with for the few days or weeks before the dormitories were open and the school started . . .

When time for my interview with a consular official came, I was very nervous. Mrs. Metaxas told me that all would go just fine because I had worked hard, but I couldn't believe in myself enough to relax. I walked in the official's room like a lamb ready for slaughter. How on earth could I impress this American bureaucrat with my "Hello" and "How are you" English? I wanted to burry my emotions deep inside myself beneath my soul, where they could never be detected. This however is something I'll ever be able to do in this lifetime. So, I looked scared and lost and embarrassed at my inadequate ability to express myself, and everyone could see it.

The official who received me was probably working for the ambassador, but I thought of him as "the Ambassador," and treated him like one. He asked me to sit down, pointing to a chair in front of his desk, and he took his seat behind his desk and started reading my file. He said something, which I understood to be approval of my record in high school performance and something about my interest in poetry and math, the American culture, and in playing chess and belonging to clubs. He chuckled at my enthusiasm when he read my comments about the USIA books. He asked me a question about America and MIT that I didn't understand, but I gave him the answer I had rehearsed with Kostis and Tony: "America is tops in technology."

At some point in the Pidgin English conversation I was using, guessing and taking chances, he handed me a magazine, which I had seen at the racks of the USIA library and recognized it as the *Readers' Digest*. Somehow, recognizing the magazine had a calming effect on me. "Can you read the first paragraph, please?" he asked as politely as one could possibly do, pointing to the article where he had opened the magazine.

He has decided to put me out of my misery, I thought, as I picked up the magazine and held it like a sharp blade one could use to slash his throat. The first paragraph of the first column was about five lines long. It contained no more than three short sentences. I started reading. I wasn't too bad at reading simple sentences, and my words were recognizable, if there weren't too many curves thrown at me by w's and s-h's and other unsavory letters like u's and various a combinations like those one finds in "enough" or "aunt." I thought I did all right in reading, and the Ambassador smiled. "And, what does this paragraph say, Mr. Kizilos?" he asked.

I had no idea what I had just read. All my attention had been channeled in the reading, not the understanding of the paragraph. Even I was surprised at my ignorance, but I must have looked sick. He was getting ready to ask me to relax for a bit, or lie down on the couch behind me and rest, but I glanced again at my paragraph of doom and desolation and the word "soap" jumped up before my eyes, my consciousness, my very soul. "It says something about "soap," I said grasping at "soap" as if it were a lifeline.

"That's right," he said helpfully. "Anything else?"

"Soap fabrication facts," I said throwing the dice on the French word "*fabrique*," and the Italian word "*fabrica*" and the Latin "de facto," all of which had something to do, I supposed, with "factory" in the paragraph.

"That's exactly right!" the Ambassador cheered, as if he had won the lottery.

"I am poor with my no English, but will make better," I mumbled, exhausted by the effort. It sounded worse than anything I had said thus far, and I knew it. I was ashamed and shut up.

He kept talking, and I picked up a few words here and there to piece together his message, more or less. He said that the important thing was that I had demonstrated remarkable "motivation for learning," and my "English would improve" rapidly once I was "in America." He said that they wanted students who had shown their willingness to "work hard and perform with excellence." He was sure that I would "do well in America," gave me the student Visa I wanted and wished me "smooth sailing." This bureaucrat is a pleasure to deal with, I thought, and looked forward to a good stay in America. All I had to do is get there, somehow. And find some more money to live by.

Mr. Pateras called my father on the phone and asked that I get in touch with him. I went to his office sometime after my interview at the Embassy, and he told me that the ship he was planning to place me in was going first to Antwerp, Belgium, where it was scheduled to stay for a couple of weeks before heading for America. He advised me to go to the Belgian Embassy and obtain a visitor's Visa from them, so I could get out of the ship during my stay there. The Belgians had some difficulty grasping the complications of my roundabout scheme to get from point A to point B, but they accepted my story nevertheless and gave me a Visitor's Visa for two weeks. So the second entry in my Greek passport was a Visa from the Belgian Embassy! I kept looking at it in disbelief. What other unpredictable things were in store for me? Immediately, my father found a trusted friend he had worked with at the plant, who had a friend that lived in Belgium and gave us a letter of recommendation. The letter was addressed to a Mr. Finkelstein and was asking him to assist me, if I needed help while in Belgium. I have no idea what catastrophe my father imagined might befall me, but he was covering all the bases he could, and I had learned not to object to any help that was given to me, even help that I didn't need to use. I reported to Mr. Pateras with some pride that I had executed the orders he gave me, trying to demonstrate to him that obstacles would not discourage me. The time of departure was near.

46 • More Gifts from Above

I sensed that my parents had been worried for months about the entire enterprise of my study abroad, but they were very careful to be supportive of my goals. My admission to MIT with a scholarship had given them confidence that my efforts produced results and they wanted to help. One afternoon, I remember, they called me into their bedroom to tell me "something important," as my father put it. He stood up on a chair by the icon-holding cabinet, hanging high up on the wall of their bedroom, and opened a little drawer at the bottom of it. He took out a small bag and untied the string around it. It was a bag full of gold sovereigns. I was dazzled by the glitter of gold and my mouth dropped open. I had no idea they kept anything but some crosses braided from palm leaves and some dried up flowers from church ceremonies along with their wedding crowns.

"These will help with your education," my father said, pouring a few sovereigns on the palm of his hand and jiggling them. "It isn't much, but we'll do what we can, and God and your work will help you to make it in college."

"You'll be fine and do great," my mother said and held me close to her.

I was moved to tears. I always knew my parents were good providers, but I never thought that they would go as far as to part with the money they were saving to build the house they had hoped for all their lives. I expected an allowance from his monthly salary to give me a start in life, but not such generosity.

"Thank you," I said and hugged them. The three of us stayed hugging each other for a while.

When I first broached the subject of going to America, I had been a little worried that my mother might have second thoughts and wouldn't let me go. But I shared my ups and downs with her and she came around. She was a dreamer and an adventurer at heart, like her brothers, and wouldn't prevent me from realizing my dream. My father was a logical man, and I knew he would come along, if the enterprise were to our advantage. When he saw that colleges, Mr. Pateras and many others were going out of their way to help me, he decided that the project was good for everyone and was ready to back me up. My mother and I could convey meanings without words, and she knew how thankful I was to her. She smiled blissfully and watched as I hugged my father.

The Bank of Greece issued its preliminary decision on the amount of currency I would be allowed to receive abroad from my parents, and it was meager by any standards, but it was just enough to make attendance at MIT possible. Now that I had the Student Visa and could work, I would find something to do and earn my keep. I had no idea what that might be, but neither did I have any doubt that I would survive – somehow.

Time was getting short and my ship's schedule was still up in the air. Finally, Mr. Pateras' secretary called and asked that I come to his office for another meeting with him. When I got there, she was very busy and I had no chance to get any hints as to what kind of news was awaiting me. I went in to Mr. Pateras' office, but he didn't ask me to sit down, as he had done before. "I thought that I could send you to America with one of my ships that is going first to Antwerp, Belgium, as I told you, but the plans have changed and I'm not sure that the ship will go to America after that. It may, but it also may turn right back and head for India through the Suez Canal. That wouldn't be good for you." Here he paused and looked at my downcast face. "Here," he said and thrust a sealed envelope toward me. "Take this to the address shown on the envelope; give it to Thomas who works there, and bring the envelope he will give you back here, to me." I took the envelope from his hand while in a daze, but I felt that, in spite of all these difficulties, this Mr. Father wouldn't leave me in a lurch. I thanked him and left.

The address wasn't too far away from his office in downtown Athens, so I walked there as fast as I could, short of running. What if Thomas was sick today? What if Mr. Pateras was trying to send me on another ship that might get stranded at some other port that he hadn't counted on?

It occurred to me that I should start preparing again for the Polytechnic exams, because I had forgotten about them for a while. But, could Mr. Pateras find a ship that would leave Greece after the exams at the Polytechnic? And if he did that, wouldn't it be too late? Besides, beggars cannot be choosers. I would have to commit to go or stay; there was no way I could do both It cannot happen that way, I kept thinking; it cannot go that way. Maybe, I would have to take a chance and go with the ship, and if it turns back and goes to India, I lose; but if it continues on to America, I win. Do they allow students to register late at MIT? A fifty-fifty chance is better than no chance at all. In this shadowy, befuddled state of mind, I got to the address marked on the envelope, entered what seemed to me like a commercial transport business office, found Thomas sitting behind a desk and gave him the envelope.

"Mr. Pateras told me to give you this," I said, hoping that he would know what it was all about.

"Yes; he called me. Please, wait a couple minutes and I'll give you an envelope to take back to him," he said with a smile.

Things were looking up, or I had entered La-La-Land and was playing a stooge. No! Things were going well. Thomas is working, and Mr. Pateras is at the controls. What more could a person ask? I asked God to help me.

"Take this to Mr. Pateras," Thomas said and handed me another sealed envelope. "Mr. Pateras is a fine man," he added.

I agreed with him, thanked him and started on the way back, thinking about the meaning of these messages I was carrying back and forth. Could a couple of sealed envelopes and some accidental connections shape my future? Where did this Mr. Pateras come from? What if I hadn't known anything about "soap"? How did it happen that Tony Condaratos was standing outside the administration building of my school in Athens, Greece, at the time that I was passing by, when he hadn't been in the school for a year or more? I was walking as fast as I could, thinking of the many coincidences that had brought me to that moment. Was God having something to do with all this or were all these events the random order of the universe?

I gave Mr. Pateras the envelope. He opened it and examined the contents. "As I told you, your arrival in America in time for your studies with my ship cannot be guaranteed. For this reason, I have decided to buy a ticket for you on the regular ocean liner, the "*Nea Hellas*," that leaves in three weeks from Piraeus for America. You'll be in America by mid-August. Will you be ready?"

I was dumbfounded. I hadn't expected this kind of generosity from a stranger. "Thank you, Sir, I'll be ready," I mumbled and shook his hand.

"Well, not yet," he added and sat down. "Hear me out, first." I sat down to steady myself. "I'll pay, as a gift to you, half of your ticket, and your father can pay me the other half in several payments over the course of a year. This is the ticket. Take it. Tell your father what I told you, and let me know if he accepts my terms." I thanked him again and promised to inform him of my father's decision within a day or two. "I hope he accepts, and you can go to America, soon. I hope you'll do well in school."

"I'll do my best, Sir," I said with conviction.

My father accepted the terms of Mr. Pateras' generous offer. He was very impressed by a stranger's generosity to us and, as I found out later, he paid his half of the ticket as he promised.

I was ready for the trip that would change my life forever. I had steered my ship with skill and hard work with providential help, to overcome countless obstacles placed on my course from within and outside myself. So many people had helped me achieve my goal that I would be an idiot to believe that people didn't care. And when my own resources were not enough to do the job, I believe that God had found a way to help me out. As they say, God works in mysterious ways . . . I felt blessed and lucky and capable, ready to sail for America, even though I was scared to death of all the problems that remained unsolved.

47 • Emancipation by Confrontation

I have learned over the years that when one's mind is made up,
this diminishes fear; knowing what must be done does away with
fear.

Rosa Parks

It was a hot summer day in July of 1953 when I saw professor Mazis for
the last time. I had invested a lot of my energy preparing for the exams at
the Polytechnic and before I focused on the American college search.
When I had secured my college admission, I was still planning to take
the exams just to prove to myself that I could pass. Now, I had neither
the energy nor the focus to do that. My plans had changed and I had
many loose ends to take care of. I was in a different place. But taking the
exams became a moot point when I found out that the ship that Mr.
Pateras had put me in was leaving in early August and the Polytechnic
exams were in September.

I wanted to tell professor Mazis about the opportunity I had to study
abroad at a top-notch school and inform him that I wouldn't be taking the
exams for the Polytechnic, which, I knew, had always been the goal of
his teaching. Whatever else one might say about Mazis, the man had
invested all he had as a teacher to prepare us for higher learning in
science and engineering, and I didn't want him to feel that going to an
American college was in any way a waste of his effort on me. I was
supposed to be one of the horses he had in the race for the Polytechnic
and I wouldn't be there; but I would be racing at another place, striving
for the same goal, excellence in science and engineering.

There were, however, other, deeper forces working their way in my
psychic underground, which I refused to acknowledge at the time. I was
the top student at the top high school in Greece and I didn't want anyone,
but especially Mazis, to think that I chose to leave Greece because I was
afraid of failure. I was as afraid of the Polytechnic exams as I had been
on every other test I had to take, but fear never stopped me from doing
what I had to do to achieve my goals.

As I considered the decision I had made, I thought it would be
helpful to seek Mazis' approval and thank him for all he had done for our
class and me. I was hoping that he would congratulate me for the
opportunity I was given, approve the decision I made to study abroad,
express his hope that I would return some day and help our country and
send me off with his blessings. Yet, I was a little apprehensive and tried

to calm myself thinking that I wasn't his student anymore, and what he thought wasn't critical to my plans.

I set up an appointment with him, at his home, and went to see him. He showed me to his living room and offered me a seat on an armchair facing him. He crossed his legs as he always did in class and crossed his hands in front of him, as he had never done in class. He was wearing a wrinkled shirt with short sleeves, gray pants and slippers without socks, so I finally could see that his allegedly wooden leg was made of flesh and bone. It was the first time I had seen him without a suit and tie on, and I thought he was shorter, less imperious, frail and almost approachable. After giving him the facts about MIT and the scholarship they had offered me, "an unprecedented action for MIT to take for a foreign student," I added, I thanked him for the superb education in physics he had given us.

"Are you going to take the exams at the Polytechnic?" he asked.

"I had planned to, but there is no time to take the exams and be at MIT on time," I answered in a hurry.

"The Polytechnic is a great school. You are a good student. You should do well," he snapped back.

"I think I should go for studies in America. MIT is the best technology school in the world, and I got a scholarship there," I repeated, without hesitation. My gut sounded the alarm, and I felt tense. What was he doing? Why am I here? How the hell do I get out of this? His eyes were screwing with my mind. They were telling the story of a traitor who abandons his comrades in battle.

"Why don't you take the entrance exams at the Polytechnic, and then, if you fail, consider your options."

I knew that he would ask some tough questions, but I was startled just the same. "I would like to do that, Sir, but there is really no time to do both. By the time I get done with the exams and preparations for the trip, MIT will have started, and I'll have no time to adjust, to get my bearings, get used to the language. I don't even know if I could register late," I said, almost pleading with him for mercy. I wanted to get out of there, but I just couldn't. It felt as if I would be leaving a battlefield, and I couldn't live in peace with that.

"What is there to prepare? Besides, you can be a week or two late . . . what's so terrible about that? You are a good student and you'll catch up." He stopped as if to gauge the effect of his words on me. He must have felt that my resolve was waning, so he pushed his advantage, without losing eye contact. "You've been preparing for the Polytechnic for six years . . . Are you going to skip the exams because you haven't got an extra couple of weeks to achieve your goal?"

I felt under attack. "I realize, Sir, that it is not quite logical, but there is also the problem of transportation. Somebody helped me pay for the fare and the ship I have a ticket on a ship that leaves in August – weeks before the Polytechnic exams. Besides, I'm not focused on the exams now; I'm planning to study in a foreign land, with a different culture and in a language I hardly understand. I have to find some additional funds by working at the school, practice English, finalize the approval for taking currency abroad, arrange for a postponement of my military obligations . . ." I stopped abruptly, catching myself in my miserable defensiveness. He knows I'm afraid like everybody else, I thought, but he doesn't care. He is threatening to find me guilty, and I'm standing here before him, offering a lame defense. Why am I doing this to myself? My anger was growing because he was extracting more than his pound of flesh.

Mazis stared at me as if I was a small creature looking for a hole in the ground to dart into it and save itself. "You sound like a person who is running away from danger toward a safe heaven."

His words piled like boulders on my back. "I would like to take the exams, but it seems unwise to wait . . ."

"You have no reason to be afraid. You are needed here to help build a better nation. You must summon the courage and take the risk!"

I stood up and faced him calmly as I had never done all the years I was his student. "Thanks for your advice, professor Mazis," I said, staring at him and drilling right into his soul. "I have always dreamed of going to America to study, and now that I can, I will."

A cloud settled on his face. The steely look in his eyes faded and liquid sadness drifted in. I felt he had judged me according to laws he had discovered in a lifetime of striving for excellence and found me guilty of breach of contract to him and to our country.

"I hope you made the right decision, but I feel . . ." he started to say as I stood up to leave.

"I know I did," I cut him short. He looked at me with resignation as he walked to the door and opened it. I said, "Goodbye, Sir," and left.

My gut was churning. 'The courage to take a risk?" That's what Kitsos had been talking about, and what I thought I was doing by going to America with the meager resources I had. Mazis was questioning my courage? I felt like turning back, facing him and punching him in the nose. I felt pity for myself as I walked the streets I had crisscrossed so many times laughing and shouting and cracking jokes with my fellow students after a busy day of classes. Mazis had tried to sink me, and came close to succeeding. I stood firm, but I was too needy of his approval. He wanted as many of his students as possible to succeed in the exams. He had so many horses in the race and was loath to lose any of them after all these years of training them. Horses. That was the problem – he didn't see me as a unique individual with his own strengths and weaknesses; he saw one of his students doing something he didn't like and did his best to redirect him. He would have done the same thing with any other of his students. Why? I kept turning that question in my mind and all sorts of spiteful thoughts came to me. I had heard rumors that Mazis was publishing a book and working hard to secure a professorship in physics at the Polytechnic or the University. Wouldn't it help his candidacy, if he managed to have as many students as possible to take the Polytechnic exams and succeed? I didn't want to go there. I wanted Mazis to stay the giant I had made him to be, even if a tad quirky. But he was not a giant; he had become a human being. A schoolteacher wounded by one of his students has a right to be bitter for a while. He certainly cared and was hurt. He struck back at me because he was hurting. What else does a great teacher have to show for his life's work besides the noble deeds of the students he nurtures? And what is nobler than the greater good of the society one knows and loves? The more I saw the situation from his point of view, the less angry I felt. You cannot stay angry with your tormentor when you feel his pain; not when you see him in a wrinkled, short-sleeve shirt dragging his slippers on the floor. He's not looking down at you from above and judging anymore; he's looking at you and pleading for help. He was right, but I had to pursue my goals in my way and also be right. A wave of calmness swept over me. It is OK to be myself. It is OK.

A new world of adventures, challenges and learning was opening up for me – why shouldn't I go after it? I thought of the many benefactors of Greece, including the founder of my school, Ioannis Varvakis, who left Greece and then came back to help build its institutions. And wasn't it patriotic to study at a top university while planning to come back and help my country, if they would have me back? Why did he not see all that? Mazis was a great teacher, not a great visionary. He must have forgotten that many of the Greeks who helped the country gain its freedom and advance had studied abroad. Why didn't he even congratulate me for winning a scholarship, or for anything I had ever achieved in his class? Didn't my achievement fit his curriculum vitae? And suddenly, the compassion I felt for his struggle seemed to cancel out my resentment and I didn't care what Mazis or anyone else thought. I did as my reason and my heart guided me to do and I stood where I wanted to stand. I felt as if I was rebalancing myself from a sudden blow. Mazis had found a way to teach me a lesson, even by his brutal insensitivity.

Perhaps, he learned a lesson as well from my stubborn refusal to bow to his will.

Now, more than fifty years later, I have no doubt that I made the right decision. I moved on with my studies abroad, and my visit to Mazis was superfluous. I didn't go there to tell him the good news I had; I didn't want to ask for his advice. I just wanted his authoritative stamp of approval for what I had decided to do, because I was an insecure boy trying to grow up and be a man. I don't know if Mazis helped me or hurt me in that meeting; but I do know that I felt less need for approval after that: if there was growing to be done, I would have to do it without a license. Nobody shows us how to grow up. Nobody can make us worthy. We live our lives doing what we judge to be worthwhile at the time and we either pay or get paid for it. That's how it has been and will always be. Sometimes, a loving God lends us a hand and we ought to be thankful for that.

48 • All Aboard for New York

New York is that unnatural city where every one is an exile, none more so than the Americans.

Charlotte Perkins Gilman

It was time to leave home. I had done what I needed to do in Greece and was ready to open a new chapter in my life. I was sad to leave my parents behind, but I took some consolation thinking that I would return a college graduate and find them happy and proud of me.

Leaving my eight-year old sister, however, was very painful. By the time I would be back, she wouldn't be a child anymore. When I saw her again, who knows when, she would be a teenager or a young woman, and I would have missed being there to support and guide her and enjoy her company. She was the one person that I loved unconditionally and felt guilty about leaving behind. She was there at the pier, waiving her goodbyes with her little arm. I knew this uprooting would be hard on both of us, but I had to go. I needed to be free to explore and find out what I could dream, and do, and be.

Many years later, when people would ask me why I left Greece, I would say that I felt both the attraction of an American college education, the adventure of exploring a new world on my own and the push away from an environment of constraints and limitations of various kinds. I no longer wanted to live under the supervision of my parents and, if I stayed in Greece, there would be no other option. I was tired of bowing to government bureaucrats like a serf, and I would have to keep doing it, as most people did, if I stayed back. I was tired of dropping names and using "pull" to get anything done or to be heard by anyone. I wanted to find out if I could make it in a place where no one cared about my relatives and my background, only my accomplishments and what I could produce.

My disappointments with girls were, in a way, fortuitous, I had no ties to hold me back outside my family. So, why did I leave Greece? In one word: to seek my fortune, like every other immigrant, I suppose, though at that time, immigration was the last thing in my mind and the fortune I was thinking of wasn't riches but learning and discovery and service. I wanted to get out of the familiar routines, experience the world anew, succeed in some worthwhile way, and come back to work and advance my career and the common good of society.

So, I hugged and kissed my loved ones and went aboard the *Nea Hellas*, an ancient ocean liner, making one of it final voyages to New

York. I stood at the balcony on the stern of the ship and waived to those I was leaving behind for as long as I could see them. And then, I was alone at sea in a strange world.

I had eighty dollars in my pocket, a couple of addresses of people who knew people, who were connected somehow to distant relatives and could help me in time of need, and a few mementos. My belongings came in two cloth-covered suitcases that my parents bought for me before I left. I had a bed in a cabin for four people, four stories down, in the bowels of the ship. It was dark down there and musty. My cabin mates were three Greek old timers, returning home to America after seeing their relatives in Greek villages. When I lay down to sleep, I could see my cabin mate's false teeth bobbing up and down inside a glass of water on the nightstand that separated our beds. I didn't mind because I was finally on my way to making my dream come true.

I enjoyed every moment I was on the ship, but I had to be careful with my money. I watched the games other people played, but I couldn't afford to participate. When we made port in Naples, I got outside and couldn't resist buying a leather wallet. I would have bought a fountain pen instead, but for the fact that in examining it, I saw that it was not a Parker pen, but a P.ARKER, and I stopped short.

When we were in the middle of the Atlantic Ocean I got attracted to a game of horse racing with dice on the deck of the ship. It seemed probable that I could win something, so I put in a few dollars. I lost and quit without much ado. My funds were getting very low. I became friends with a couple of young Americans and we had some fun talking and flirting with girls. They would go to the bar and drink, but I couldn't follow, since I couldn't afford to pay, or afford to reveal the sad state of my finances. I had no idea how I would survive for a month in a strange country with the few dollars left in my pocket and a couple of names of distant relatives and acquaintances.

My father had dug up some distant relatives whose descendants lived in New York, and they were supposed to meet me as I came off the ship. I kept thinking about that, worrying about their being there, about recognizing them, communicating with them, asking them to stay with them for a few days and then moving on to Boston and waiting somewhere until the school opened its doors to the new students.

One day I said "goodbye" to one of my American friends after a good brisk walk around the deck, and he said, "I'll see you later." I thought he meant a few minutes later, on the spot where we were standing before I left. I went down to my cabin to change shirt for the evening and came right up to meet him. I waited for an hour, but he didn't show up. When I saw him later that evening, I asked him if he had forgotten about our meeting, since he didn't show up. It took him a few minutes to explain to me what "I'll see you later" means. And, I was, once again, aware that my English was very poor. I studied some more, and tried to speak as much as I could, but I had a lot of trouble, making sense out of what others were telling me.

The ship stopped at Halifax, in Nova Scotia, Canada, and I got out to see the harbor area. It was a foggy day, moody and mysterious, but I knew it was the New World and I loved it. To this very day, Halifax means some kind of arrival, a harbinger of good events to follow. I spend a few more dollars buying some memento of having been there, but I don't remember what it was. Every time I felt that I was going to find myself penniless in the streets, I would remind myself that I had a lot of street smarts from the living in *Neos Kosmos*. I would take care of whatever contingencies arose. I was free, and responsible for all my actions and their consequences. I trusted my resourcefulness because I survived strife and deprivation; and I had faith that God will provide, somehow, if I couldn't.

The ship docked at Hoboken, New Jersey, on August 13, 1953. I had now entered a realm of fantasy and my memory is almost as hazy as that of a dream. I thought that the city was bustling with life in spite of its craggy appearance. I stepped on the earth and took in all the noises, the smells and sites of the city with inexplicable joy. I stared at the miserable buildings scarred by age and marred by smoke and abuse all around me, but I saw the pulse of industry and the vigor of development. There was no gold on the streets or on the sidewalks of Hoboken, but I glanced at them to make sure. I didn't know it at the time, but I found out later that Hoboken was thought to be the armpit of America. It was a city of hard work and misery; it came to life when ships touched its piers, only to drift back into the despair of poverty and oblivion after the ships left.

I held a sign with my name, and the people waiting for me recognized me and came to meet me as soon as I had cleared customs. They were cousins, they said, distant cousins of one of my father's cousins, who had come to America decades earlier and was gone now, "God bless his soul." They were openhearted people, curious about finding out what kind of a creature a Greek from Athens, Greece was. The young man and his two sisters told me that they would take me to their home in the Bronx, where I could stay for a few days, before I left for college in the Boston area. I was very thankful for their hospitality and very glad that I had a bottle of cognac as a gift for them. I can hardly remember what they looked like, but I know that the two women were attractive and I wished that I wasn't a penniless guest in need of shelter from kind relatives.

The way to New York City was more of a picture show than a trip. We were going in the subways under the Hudson River, on buses in downtown Manhattan, on elevated trains in the Bronx. I couldn't believe that there were subways as long as those we took. I stared at the wide streets filled with busy people as if I was watching novelties at the display window of a toy store. I clutched the posts on trains, fearing that we would certainly go off the rails any moment now at these high speeds with screeching noises and side to side swaying beyond anything I had experienced on street cars or trains back home. My cousins wanted to know how their relatives were doing, but I didn't know any of them, so I couldn't tell them anything new. They wanted to know why I chose to study at MIT, and what I was going to study, and how I was going to pay for my education. I kept gawking at the people in the trains and the bus. I had never seen so many black people. And, I had never imagined that black women would wear lipstick like white women. I just couldn't figure out why I was so stupid as to never have imagined that. And, then we got to the Bronx, and I couldn't get away from the garlic smells that permeated the very bricks of the buildings. They told me that garlic was the staple of Porto Rican cuisine, and there were plenty of Porto Ricans in the Bronx. I couldn't understand what Porto Ricans had to do with America and didn't dare start complex conversations in English because I would get lost, or in Greek because they would. I was good in Geography but when you cover the whole world, it's easy to miss an island or two here and there.

My "aunt" was a strict disciplinarian, and gave me some rules to live by while in her home. She wanted me to be present for dinner, or tell her if I couldn't make it; she wanted me to keep my things all together and not spread them all over the house; and she wanted me to take my shoes off and wear a pair of slippers she provided as soon as I entered the apartment. My cousins laughed the whole thing off as soon as my aunt was out of earshot. They called their mother "the sergeant" and wanted me to look upon their mother's disciplined approach to life as a clumsy expression of her affection. I cannot remember meeting my cousins' father. He was either dead or working nights and sleeping during the day.

All three young cousins were hard working people, but they never seemed to tire of wanting to show me their beloved city. They took me to Coney Island and showed me its famous roller coaster. They told me that it was the biggest in the country, and would take a lot of guts to take a ride on it. I bragged that I wasn't afraid of things like that, and they readily paid for my ticket, and we climbed aboard. They had a ball watching me scream and nearly faint and worse as we fell down precipitously and I saw my short life pass before my eyes, including my very brief stay in America. I was glad to survive the ride, but it was the first and the last time I took a ride on a roller coaster.

Seeing that I had survived a serious ordeal, I felt giddy also, and started teasing the two women because they had been screaming even louder than me. Before I knew it, we were all laughing at everything and making fun of each other. When we calmed down, they introduced me to hot dogs and told me to remember from that time on that I had eaten Coney Island hot dogs, the tastiest food in the world. I thought they were delicious with all the condiments on them, even though I had no idea what they were. I forgot a lot of things about New York, but I never forgot the Coney Island hotdogs.

My cousins' Greek was passable, but they spoke it with a heavy accent that required my close attention to decipher it. When they hit upon a word they wanted to say but didn't know in Greek, they would give me an English word and watch my face to see if I could work with that. When they saw a blank stare, they searched for other words and tried them on me while I gave them various Greek words, hoping to hit upon the word they were looking for. When they found the word they had been looking for they would try it on for size, for emphasis, for feeling and we would all laugh, making fun of one another. It became a two way game, because more often than not, I was the one who stumbled on more words then they did. That game was a good way to expand my vocabulary and improve my pronunciation.

Next, they took me to Radio City and introduced me to the show of the Rockettes with the unbelievably well formed ladies dancing to the music of some of the best-known American songs. Outside, at the plaza, I saw the statue of Atlas, holding a golden globe and told my cousins all about him. The grand hall, the dancers, the familiar music, the bustling rivers of humanity flowing on the grand avenues and the silhouettes of the skyscrapers in the distance came together and I felt the pulse of the great city of New York.

After Radio City we went to an amazing Automat and had apple pie and coffee. George, my male cousin, was some kind of trades' worker in a shipyard; Zoe, one of the female cousins was a secretary and the other, Kiki, was a college student. They didn't talk much about their jobs, but they wanted to know all about the work of all our relatives in Greece. They understood that I was a bit confused by the environment, and if one of them were pushing me too hard, the other two would stop him or her and defend my rights to ignorance. We became a group, a kind of community, apart from the nine million other people of all colors and ethnicities surrounding us. Nights, I would lie in bed and try to convince myself that I was in New York, the city most people in the world dreamed of visiting some day.

One day, thinking of all the happenings in that cosmopolitan city I was missing by hanging around the house in the Bronx all day, I decided to go to Manhattan and find out first hand how the city works. I got some directions on trains and subways I would have to take to get there and back, and headed for the "Elevated," as I was told. I have little recollection of the places I visited, or how I got there, but I do remember that when nighttime came and I decided to get back to the Bronx, I had no idea what train, or subway, or bus to take to get there. I asked for help from a policeman and he was very kind and told me exactly where to go and find my trains, but I could capture, remember and decipher only the first four or five words he uttered. So, I went up the stairs to get to the opposite direction of the subway, but what do I do then? I couldn't put it together. It dawned on me then that I would gather the information in segments: I went form one policeman to another and another and collected a few words from each of them, until I had enough to piece together a coherent message and take action. I got back to the house in the Bronx late that night and had to explain my misadventure to my cousins and my aunt. My aunt gave me a lecture on the perils of bullheadedness, and the cousins had a ball imitating my dazed search for the return home. I knew how unprepared I was to enter a major academic institution bustling with people, but instead of crying about it, I joined the party and laughed my head off as well. Now that I was in America, I would make it work somehow, no matter what.

I stayed a week with these very generous and fun loving, distant relatives. They were hard working people without much to spare, but they gave me a home and a glimpse at the American life that I will never forget. I think of them with gratitude and pray that their lives unfolded in the ways they were hoping. I was too confused at the time to be properly thankful and appreciative. They suggested that, if I had no other place to stay, the Boston YMCA would probably be the safest and least expensive place. They took me to a bus station, and after thanking them and giving them a warm Greek hug, I was on my way to Boston.

I had an address and a telephone number in my pocket, but I knew next to nothing about the people I was asked to contact, so I wasn't eager to do so. I can't remember how I happened to have that contact, but there it was. They lived in Cambridge, not far from MIT, and they were apparently willing to help. But, I wanted to get myself established first, before I called them.

Part Three

College Student and Steelworker in America

49 • Hot Dogs or Bust

"Chance is the pseudonym of God when he did not want to sign."
Anatole France

I managed to find my way to the Boston YMCA on Huntington Avenue with my two suitcases and get a room, the first room I could call totally my own. I was alone in a big strange city, in America, with twenty dollars in my pocket and close to a month stretching out before me without school, and no "room and board." I first became giddy as if I had to get past another obstacle in a new game I was playing. Then, I calmed down and felt the weight of the rock I would have to push up the mountain all alone for the first time in my life. I had no idea where I would find food, how much it cost, or if I would be able to eat it. I spend the night in my room, thinking of going out, but not daring to do so. For dinner I munched on some candy my cousins had given me for the trip. But the next day, at lunch, I stepped out into the street looking for a place with food. There was a little hole in the wall food place across the street, so I went there. Immediately, I recognized that they were serving hot dogs and relaxed. I approached the counter, looked the man straight in the eye and said with bravado, "Hot dog."

The man picked up the bun, split it, grabbed a hot dog from the grill and dropped it on the crook of the bun in his hand. ""Ketchup, relish, mustard?" he asked, looking now straight at me.

I had no idea in the world what he was asking me to do, but whatever it was I felt as if I needed to defend myself, and stuck to my guns: "Hot dog!" I repeated with more emphasis this time.

The man looked at me holding the hot dog at his side, as if he was ready to throw it at me. He asked me slowly again what I wanted on it.

I said nothing, but reached out to take the hot dog from his hand the way it was. He gave it to me reluctantly, as if he was a relay runner who suddenly changed his mind about passing the baton to his teammate. I thought he didn't trust me and wanted to make sure that I didn't reject his offer because I wanted some other food that he couldn't provide. I gave him one of my two tens, and I took a bite lustily, trying to reassure him that the food was fine. Then, at my side, by one of the stands, I saw somebody pouring tomato paste on his hot dog before taking another bite. I remembered that this was precisely how we ate our hot dogs at Coney Island with my cousins, and I nearly emptied the ketchup bottle on my hot dog. Since ketchup was free, I liked it even more. The thought occurred to me that, if I had to, I could live on free ketchup for a while.

The cook behind the counter saw what I had just done, and stared at me with utter contempt. I bet he was saying, "Look at those damn foreigners – they don't know enough to ask for the kind of food they want!" I just hoped that he didn't hold a grudge on me because I was planning on a steady diet of hot dogs for days to come, and, as far as I was concerned, he was the only provider around. What else could I risk buying with my few, precious dollars and my total ignorance of foods in America?

Like all prudent explorers of strange lands, I wanted to find out as much as possible about the environment I was going to live in. I tried to visit the MIT campus but got lost in the Boston subways. I kept asking for directions, but I could only understand a couple of words from every answer they gave me. The Boston accent was an added obstacle to understanding the language. It took me several wrong moves to finally sort out "Boylston" from "Boston" and years before I could grasp that "Havel" was "Haverhill," or "Wooster" was "Worcester."

When I finally found myself at MIT, I was struck by the stark presence of the place. Other than a great dome over the main entrance, everything seemed ordinary and efficient. Brick buildings, concrete walls and grey warehouses weren't worthy of admiration. Kresge Auditorium, the MIT Chapel, the Hayden Library and other noteworthy structures were later additions that gave the grey character of MIT a graceful distinctiveness. I saw the steel Quonset huts at the end of the field on the west campus, but I didn't know then that they provided housing for married students, many of them veterans of the Korean War, on the GI Bill. Behind the main buildings, I found the antiquated, wooden structures where many of the technological innovations that contributed to victory in WW II were made, but I had no idea what they were. I was in no condition to judge MIT, but I felt the greatness of the institution was not reflected in the drab appearance of its facilities. I found out that the earliest I could move into Burton House, an ancient-looking dormitory at the end of the western campus, was about three weeks away.

I ate hot dogs and added apple pie to my menu at a cafeteria, close to the Y. I was running out of money, and my first bank check wasn't due to arrive for a month. I had no idea where it would arrive, and how I would be able to get it. I couldn't pay for more than a couple of meals, and I couldn't stay at the Y another week without some income. I took some extra sugar cubes from the cafeteria since they were free. The sugar and half the hot dog bun I had for dinner would be next day's breakfast. I tried to read a newspaper at the Y, hoping to find a job I could do and earn some money, but I had trouble understanding what I was reading. In my room, I tried to imitate the sounds of words I heard around me by sounding them out. I couldn't quite bend my mouth in such a way that the word "bug" could sound different from "boog" or "bag" or "bog," and the word "uncle" different from "ankle." I still have a little trouble, fifty years later. I lay in bed and listened to the radio.

I felt that I was thrown into the harbor of Eleusis sinking once again, but struggling to come up did no good this time. No one recognized me, and no one would know what happened to me for weeks or months, if I happened to disappear from the face of the earth. I had no problem being alone, but the thought of being lost, invisible, unknown to all, shook me. I decided to carry my passport with me as I went around the city. I had to become part of the world. I had to barge into this new world, somehow. It never occurred to me to ask for help from any office at MIT. They didn't know me; why would they help me? I made the call to the family whose name I had been given by my mother. I didn't know who those people were, and I cannot remember how my mother got their name, but they were the only link I had to the world around me. I heard the foreign accent and breathed a sigh of relief. I started talking to the lady on the phone, in Greek. For a moment, I thought that Mrs. Carline Barlas was more relieved to hear Greek on the phone than I was. I introduced myself, and she said they had been expecting a call from me. She invited me to her home for dinner, and told me how to get there by bus. She and her husband had a lot of Greek friends and relatives and they all converged to their home and welcomed me as if I were a long lost relative. And by the grace of God and the good heart of some of my compatriots, I entered the American society and I didn't feel lost anymore.

50 • The Greeks of Darbury Room

No matter the nationality, no matter the religion, no matter the ethnic background, America brings out the best in people.

Arnold Schwarzenegger

My newly found Greek friends asked how I was doing for money, and I told them I was running out, but I was willing to work. Three or four of the men got together, and argued for a few minutes about my situation. One of them left the huddle, made a phone call and came back to report to the rest of them. They broke up and approached me. They had found a job for me as a busboy in one of the high-class dining rooms in town, the Darbury Room, in Copley Square, downtown Boston. They asked me for my Social Security Card, but I didn't know what they were talking about. No problem. They would take care of it after I filled a form. It would take a few days, but I could start work next day, if I wanted. Of course, I wanted. They gave me some money for my rent at the Y and for food, and said I could repay them later. They were poking their noses into my business and I thanked God for that. We celebrated their effective solution of a problem with a toast. My being a Greek made me familiar, if not exactly family, and they were doing what was expected of relatives.

They were all hard working people, waiters, cooks, Maitre Dees and service providers. They were all friends, and relatives, and knew the restaurant business like the palms of their hands. I had no idea that the Greeks in America were into restaurants! I didn't think that was something the people in Greece knew. Mrs. Barlas' husband, Tom Barlas, was a shoeshine shop owner and the master shoe shiner in the place. He was a very quiet man. I don't think I heard him utter more that a dozen sentences, in the couple of years I used to visit their home as a guest. But he was a congenial host, eager to make his guests feel at home. Mrs. Barlas never told me what kind of a store her husband owned, until I had been around for a year or so. She was a good hostess and proud of her home, which she always kept as pretty as a dollhouse. She looked after her two children with enormous affection and was involved in every aspect of their lives, as most Greek mothers tended to do. Her dream was that her children would go to college someday, perhaps MIT or Harvard, and thrive in the world. She was about fifteen years younger than her husband and had met and married him when he visited Greece looking for a bride to bring back to America. She had wanted to leave Greece because there was no future for her there, and she didn't pay much attention to the details of "with whom," or "how." In time, I gathered that she wasn't happy, but she was content, and her being a mother, apparently made up for whatever her marital relationship may have lacked. It took me months to figure out all these details, and when I did, I made sure to never allow myself to take the slightest advantage of that knowledge. I was a grateful guest, and offered her and her friends a window into the world of ideas and the student life, which she and the others appreciated and were glad to have. I think that they were all thinking of their children going to college, and I was a kind of link to what they hoped for them.

Next day, I went to work for the first time in my life. At Darbury Room. Nick, the Greek Maitre Dee, was expecting me and greeted me with a warm handshake, not a Greek hug, which I took to be a way of maintaining a distance between management and staff. He told me that my salary would be twenty-two dollars a week, for seven hours of work per day, from two to nine thirty with a half hour for a break, unless I worked overtime. I would also get tips as a percentage of the tips from the waiters I served with, and I could eat dinner free.

I met another busboy, Chester, and the two of us were assigned to serve four or five waiters. Chester was a little uneasy when he realized that I had trouble with English, and asked me if I had worked in restaurants before. When I told him that this was my first such experience, he slapped his forehead with the palm of his hand in despair. I suppose, he thought he would have to do most of the work. I thought he should have been called "busman" not "busboy" because he was a man in his late twenties or older, but I said nothing.

Darbury Room was dark, hard to tell what was happening in the far reaches of its walls, a cave for the "Haves" to escape to and be served drinks and dinner by skilled "Have-nots." Conversations blended into a steady drone that muffled the bustle of glasses, plates, silverware and the shouts and curses of displeased waiters and angry chefs who had their cordon bleu rejected by dainty ladies and their steaks by fat men who knew their "rare" well.

I had always thought that manual laborers and service workers, who had to use their physical abilities for routine, repetitive work, were unhappy with their lot, but I began to doubt that. Most of the people I worked with at the Darbury Room seemed satisfied with what they were doing. They weren't losers and had no desire to be pitied because of a lousy hand that fate dealt them; they had no regrets for the decisions that got them to that place. They were proud to work at Darbury Room and bragged about its elite clientele. They cracked jokes, played tricks on one another and were quick to spot weaknesses or flaws and pick a slur to make fun of those having them, until the frequent use took the sting out of any offence and made the offender look like a dolt. Most of all they poked fun at their customers with the ingenuity and humor of masters in the art.

Mike was one of the most creative such artists. He looked like a wrestler and spoke Greek with what I would now call a Greek hillbilly accent. Though I was mostly lost and couldn't remember all the names of the things I was supposed to handle and maneuver around, Mike told me that there were only two things that I had total control over, and was totally responsible for: butter and ice water. "Within a minute after the customer sits down, you *must* bring a glass of water with ice in front of him and a dish with butter." Mike emphasized the rule by repeating it several time like a mantra. "You *must* keep both the glass and the butter properly supplied throughout the entire dinner. If you don't do that, you're messing with *my* bread and butter, and I'll have your ass for that," he said, looking at me as if he was delivering an ultimatum to an enemy in the battlefield. This was all in Greek, so I got the message without ambiguity. He told me that his tips were dependent upon what I was doing as much as on what *he* was doing. We had to work together, he said, or I didn't work there. I told him that he could count on me for these two things. He said that he better count on me for everything he asked me to do, but I made no verbal commitment to that. Before we ended this indoctrination session, he told me that I would get ten percent of the tips he got. "So, the more I get, the more you'll get."

Later I found out from Chester that the name of the game in that reward system was to find out whether the money your waiters gave you was anywhere near ten percent or one percent of what they got. Chester spent more time watching the waiters pocketing tips than serving butter and water. But, he was an old hand at busing and he could perform his necessary tasks with his eyes closed. And I was in no mood to check up on anything – all I wanted was food and a few bucks to pay the rent at the Y.

Working at Darbury Room was never dull. There was always something new happening in the kitchen, or at the dining room, or at the bar, or outside. The hatcheck girl's boyfriend threatened to barge in and beat her up, but the Maître Dee called the bouncer from the adjacent nightclub bar and the boyfriend was ejected. The hatcheck girl was terrified, and we had to send her home in a taxi with one of the barmaids from for company. I was learning about people and their ways, so different from those I had known.

The waiters were always finding something to argue about, something to curse at and something to do for one another that helped them get through the night or annoyed them for a while and kept them awake. Harry, an old Greek waiter was a family man, and didn't put up with any kind of games and teasing. "You let me be, and I'll let you be," was his mantra, and everyone seemed willing to accept it as a good work rule, but respected it only when it pertained to the "Old Greek." He and Mike quarreled regularly, but always found a way to patch up their differences. And when they couldn't, they appealed to Nick, who straightened out whatever mess they were in.

Waiters and busboys moved with precision from table to table in their assigned areas, like dancers executing a routine they had rehearsed many times before. I learned how to set up the tables, where to stand to fill the glasses of water, and how to serve butter on the plates, and how to remove dirty dishes, and smile when I wanted to crawl under a bed and never be seen in that dungeon again. The whole idea was for me to do my job without ever being noticed. I was back into my invisibility mode.

As the waiters passed each other on the way to the swinging door to the kitchen, they lifted up their trays and made themselves thin and tall like ballerinas standing on their pointy shoes, and never touched one another. I was always expecting a collision, but they were very rare. They made sure I was nowhere near the swinging door when the room was busy. Mike, who thought of himself as my boss and my mentor was the clown of the lot, and couldn't resist "sticking it" to the "fat cats" because they deserved it and never knew what was being done to them, anyway. He had a particularly nasty way of showing his distaste for the upper class of Boston – politicians and financiers of all kinds.

One evening he took me aside and told me to watch him silently but say nothing while he reeled off his wine list at the table of half a dozen high-class clients. So, I performed my duties and stood by, as Mike started rattling off the Champagnes and the Pinot Noirs and the Sauternes and the Bordeaux and all of a sudden, Scatasi Nafas, Red, a "vintage wine," urging others to eat shit. I flinched, and Mike's eyes pinned me down into my dull expressionless face. He went on with his list, which was authentic, but for the next foul Greek word.

I waited for the customers to choose their wines. I waited for one of them to take a risk on something new and ask for one of the vintages fabricated in Mike's sick mind.

"What would you do, if one of these people asked you for Scatosi Nafas, Red, like you were peddling?" I asked Mike later that evening.

"They never do," he said and hurried on.

"But, what if one of these people had visited Greece and learned some of the foul words you were throwing around? What would you do, then?" I insisted following behind him.

"Nobody does that. Even when they know, people convince themselves that what they know isn't what they just heard. People are good at lying to themselves. Besides, if one of them asked me about one of the words I spoke, I would change it enough to match some damn wine from somewhere in this godforsaken world."

"What can possibly . . . "?

"How's Santorini Red?" he burst out. Then, almost lamenting what he felt was the reality of the situation, he said, "I sure wish the hell somebody would challenge me . . . There's so much bullshit around."

I thought Mike was weird, but I hadn't met some of the other masters of the craft, yet. Luigi, the Italian maestro, was very particular when it came to serving the food, and Mike told me that the chef "hated his guts." The dishwasher said that Luigi was a psychopath masquerading as a nut. I didn't hear the dishwasher's comment when he made it because he was bent down, scrubbing the sink. The others called him "Scrubs," but never to his face. He was always bent down, bent because of a "broken back" from an accident, or from forty years of scrubbing dishes clean, or from arthritis, or from all of the above – no one really knew for sure.

It took hours to put together in my room at the Y the bits and pieces I am relating here, like it was a homework assignment in comprehension from my Darbury Room teachers. Mike said that the chef's name was Marcel, and advised me to stay out of his way. "He doesn't like waiters and hates busboys." I kept my distance, but there were times when I had to get stuff from the kitchen for the waiters, and Marcel didn't like that at all. I thought he might attack me for no reason I knew. I assumed that he thought it beneath himself to deal with the riffraff in the place.

Once, I had to go into the room-size freezer in the kitchen to get two steaks that Luigi told me he had saved for a special customer and give them to Marcel. While I was fumbling to find Luigi's steaks in the freezer, Marcel saw me in his domain and slammed the door shut on me. I felt a slap as the icy compressed air hit the left side of my face, which was turned toward the door. My ear crackled and I felt a dull earache deep inside my ear. With my history of earaches, I was happy that it was my left ear this time, so it could stand taking some beating. Years later, a doctor told me that my eardrum had the same purplish coloration that he had seen in the eardrums of divers who were near underwater explosions.

I got out and complained to him. He was furious and told me to "get the hell out of his business." I shook my head at him and went around the corner, out of his domain. Luigi was back there, busting his gut at "the little Greek moron." I should have known that waiters don't get to choose what steak goes to which customer. I was ready to tangle with Luigi, but I held myself back. I had to fight by mocking, ridiculing, laughing, not with my fists. Somebody told me later that Mike wanted to beat the crap out of him for making fun of his compatriot, but a couple of other waiters restrained him.

As the night progressed, the workload usually increased. One night, a customer had ordered a rare steak but instead he got one that was well done, and Mike had to take it back and order a new steak. He was very busy as he came back from the kitchen, carrying the plate with the rare steak, and had to rely on me to take it back to the customer and ask, if he was now satisfied. But, what are the words for that? I took it back trembling with fear. What if he wasn't happy with it and started complaining to me so that I could fix the problem?

"Is OK?" I said as I placed the plate before him.

The man slid his knife into the steak. "Good!" he said, and I breathed a sigh of relief. Then, as I was about to retreat, he asked me something that sounded to me like a question about my nationality, but I wasn't sure, so I smiled. "You Greek, yes?" he asked again.

"Greek, yes," I said. And then, for whatever reason, my mouth made a noise and I defended my presence in this country. "I am student in MIT, September of course," I said, treading very gently upon this *terra incognita*.

That's all the man wanted to know. But, I stood beside him sweating and praying that there would be no other direct question to me. Mike was going crazy with his signals, wanting help with all sorts of things. I asked the customer to be excused, cutting him off in mid sentence. I had no idea where his sentences began and no clue where they ended, so any point was as good or as bad as any other to withdraw.

"A new napkin for the lady over there." Then, "More water on table number four; the blond bombshell." I saw a woman looking at her stained napkin, rushed up there, yanked the napkin out of her hands, said a lame "excuse me" and run to bring her a new one. There were more customers, with more orders. I began to suspect that Mike and the others were using more English idioms to confuse me. "Bombshell?" Where did that come from? I had to learn a lot, but some things couldn't be explained.

An older lady with blue hair wearing an evening dress with sparkling sequins received her steak from Mike, cut a small piece at the end, tasted it and then put it back on her plate and looked at Mike with great disappointment. "I ordered rare, Mike; I said rare three times!" she complained.

Mike stood at attention with hands crossed, jaw dropped and eyes wide open in dismay. He looked crushed. "I'm sorry Mrs. Bradley. My fault. Please, give me five minutes. I'll have the best rare steak in Boston for you, just the way you like it," Mike said, bowing apologetically, and sliding the plate away from her with a magician's sleight of hand. He pirouetted to the kitchen and plunked the plate down on the table the staff used for eating their dinner. "All yours, guys! The old witch turned up her nose at this." He turned the corner to the kitchen. "We got to do it all over, cookie!" he called out to the Chef's assistant. "Filet, raw like a monkey's ass!" he ordered, and rushed back out.

"It's all yours, little Greek," Luigi called out to me.

"I don't eat leftovers," I said with disgust. It was a pity to let a steak like that go to waste, but I couldn't quite get myself to eat from someone else's plate. Besides, I didn't like Luigi, and I resented his attitude.

"Slice out the corner and eat the rest," Luigi insisted. "It's the best damn steak you can buy in Boston!"

I just shook my head and walked away. I didn't want to do what Luigi wanted me to do. I recognized my childish rebelliousness and I was troubled.

Chester showed up just in time and took Luigi's advice, just as Harry claimed half of that steak. I watched them dig into that meat from a distance. The dowager hadn't even taken a bite out of the steak; she just cut it at the edge and rejected it outright. Mike said that she was the widow of an industrialist. Her husband was a great tipper, but she was stingy and wished that she got her rich ass out of his dining room for good. I wondered whether he had engineered the entire incident to achieve that end, or the mistake had nothing to do with him, the lady was a great tipper and he was telling me the story to reduce my expectations for that night's tips.

One evening, when the flow of diners had stopped, and I was relaxing and calculating in my mind the money I had coming in tips, Mike nudged me. "Customer wants you in Table Two," he whispered.

I saw a man waving his hand at me. A Blue Pinstripe Suit and Red Tie. I started walking to my doom. This wasn't my domain. Butter and ice water, was what I did. They had their ice waters and their breads and their butters, and that's all they had a right to ask of me. The Blue Pin Stripe Suit was talking to me. I nodded and smiled, but I understood nothing. I was a pillar of salt. I sensed that he wanted me to do something for him, but I had no idea what. He gave me a twenty. He said something that sounded like "packapallmals," but I couldn't make out the meaning of the word. I knew I had to go in the direction he pointed. But, what would I do there, in the shadowy outer edge of the room? He was now talking about me to the others. Were they laughing at me? Not quite. A beautiful dark haired woman with bright, glistening lips glanced at me and smiled sympathetically, as if she understood my plight. Just discussing me, I thought. OK. I started walking toward the dark area of the coatroom.

"He wants thing here," I said to the hatcheck girl, pointing back to the man who sent me. I was sweating. She looked at them and recognized the man. He made the motion of smoking a cigarette.

"Here!" She gave me a pack of Pall Malls and change for the twenty in a plate. "He smokes Pall Malls. We share the tip afterwards, OK?"

I was glad to be alive, and perfectly willing to give her anything she wanted. I took the pack of cigarettes back to the man, hoping there would be no further discussion. He thanked me and smiled. He said something to me, and I smiled some more. I said "Thank you," but I didn't know why. Then I saw the five-dollar bill he left on my plate.

"Keep the change," he said amiably. He looked at the others around the table, and they all smiled or laughed at me, with me, for my situation . . . I didn't know why, and I didn't care. I made a turn and went back to leaning at my spot, up against the wall where it was safe.

"Nice work," the hatcheck girl said, as she pocketed the fiver and gave me two dollars and fifty cents.

Later at night, when the few customers left were drowsy and mellow, drinking their Drambuies, or grasshoppers, or over the rainbow drinks, Mike would go into some kind of reverie, leaning up against the wall as if he was waiting to be called for some other higher calling. No one wanted his services anymore. He was bored when he wasn't overwhelmed with work. Now, all that was left was the hope of a few extra-generous tips from the drunks.

When all the customers were gone we cleaned up the tables and went to the kitchen for snacks. The waiters counted their tips, all by themselves. Chester and I thought it was unfair to us, but there was no appeal process there. They gave us what they claimed was ten percent of their take. It was about five to ten dollars every night. Not bad for a starving youth recently brought across the world to the land of plenty.

Some days, when we had to work overtime and they gave us a half hour break, I would take walks in the Boston Commons, snapping a few pictures with a Kodak I borrowed from one of Mrs. Barlas's relatives to send home to my family. Most days I would sit at a bench near a pond and watch the swans sailing by. I had never seen black swans and was surprised when I saw a couple of them. The white swans didn't seem to notice the difference. I remember that a couple of days later, I was sitting at my bench, when a group of black children came by. They were cavorting around the bronze statue of Paul Revere on his horse. Their shouting and running around were a welcome diversion from my usually nostalgic reflections. I forgot about home and how alone I was and was going to be for many years. I got up and called out to them to come and help me out. I asked them to gather around the statue and joined the group, while a passerby took our picture. The kids were curious about my awful English and my heavy accent, but they never mocked me. I enjoyed talking with them and explaining to them what a Greek from Greece was like. They seemed to understand what I was trying to tell them with words and gestures of all kinds and a stick to draw some shapes on the dirt near the statue. I wanted the picture to send home; I wanted my family to see that I was alive and getting along with all sorts of people. If I could be laughing while posing with a bunch of black kids around a bronze statue, I must be doing great in America. Wasn't I?

I learned from Chester about the Lucky Dollar lottery they had in Boston at the time. The newspaper published a set of "Lucky Dollar" numbers and, if you had one of those lucky numbers, they gave you a hundred dollars for it. This is America, the land of plenty, the generous country with a golden heart, if not golden sidewalks, I thought, and deduced that the odds may be better than they would have been back home. I started looking up the numbers. I converted all my money into dollar bills, wrote their numbers down and, after work, starting in the bus when I left work at night and continuing the process in my room, I would judiciously check the numbers, hoping to get one of the Lucky Bills and double my fortune. It didn't happen; but the game was fun to play, and I needed a little more hope from fantasy than reality could provide at the time. I would go to sleep in my closet-size, YMCA room, without a care in the world.

Working at the Darbury Room gave me confidence that I could survive on my own, if I had to. And that confidence spilled into my attitude toward MIT. By that time I knew enough about the school to be aware of the high expectations it had of its students and be a little afraid of being a student there. But if I could make it as a busboy, a job that I knew nothing about a month ago, why wouldn't I do just fine in the academic environment that I had prepared for all my life? I prayed and steeled myself for the beginning of my college education. I said goodbye to all the guys at work and they wished me well. Back at the Y, I packed my stuff on the car of one of my Greek friends and headed for MIT.

51 • MIT for Dummies

Heaven is high, Earth Wide. Bitter between them flies my sorrow.

Li Po

When one burns one's bridges, what a very nice fire it makes.

Dylan Thomas

I have written and rewritten about the way I felt the first few months I was at MIT, an ocean and half a continent away from home, but I can never get it right. The words change, the metaphors shift but the expression of feelings is as elusive as ever. So, I take some of these notes I made from time to time and attach them here, trying to loosen the hold of sadness and remove the bitterness I felt as I struggled to adapt to the world I had sought so ardently:

I am alone in my dorm room at MIT studying as hard as I can and keeping an eye on the night that hugs my window. Four floors below, a streetlight breaks up the darkness. I am sitting on a regulation chair, before a green-topped regulation desk, staring and despairing at the assigned books. Across the football field, cheers and jeers have been chilled by the November frost, but the giant ketchup bottle peddling Heinz 57 still spills its river of red neon sauce. The city spreads its edges out and up, leaving only faint lights behind. Cambridge has gathered ambitions from all over the globe. My job is to take in all the knowhow I can from this mother lode of expertise. The people I left behind are limping back, demanding to be recognized. I know them, but they don't know me anymore. I am a stranger here too. I am surrounded by nerdy Americans with foot-long slide rules dangling from their belts, perfumed Frenchmen who have no interest in mixing with anyone, Muslims from Pakistan, Iran and all the Stans in the world, kneeling on their prayer carpets and looking serene, Indian survivors of cobra bites burning incense in brass bowls and reciting the Kama Sutra, and Greek head cases bragging about their ships and factories and sports cars or wannabes like me, pinching pennies to make it. Everyone speaks English, but I understand close to nothing. Classes have just started and I am already behind. I would give a lot even for misunderstanding the English language. I feel lost. I am plagued by doubts and climb out of my window to the fire escape ledge.

These four square feet of ironworks belong to me and to the night. Here I can sit alone and shrink the miles of ocean to my home in beloved Athens. The couple of months I have been away from home weigh their heavy days inside me. I depart from Piraeus by boat over and over again, as mother, father and sister wave their last goodbyes. It was done – why must it be undone so many times to be forgotten? Thousands of arms are moving up and down waiving goodbyes, like a multitude of upended beetles kicking the air in despair. I feel a tear of regret, and the red sauce across the way turns muddy. I hold on to the memory of the Attic sky, as it was burnt in my heart the day I knew I would be leaving home. "You'll be going on a long voyage," a gypsy up on Philopappou hill of Athens had told me. I kept my eyes on the blue of the sky, smiled and gave her a tip. There is no escape from this room. Did I forfeit my claim to happiness when I left behind my people and all the futures rooted there? I will always wonder. I have pawned all pliant dreams to pay for a stake on this uncharted voyage. I have to make it work.

I wipe the tear off and study carefully solutions to the math problems for tomorrow's exam. Calculus is not a problem if you know algebra and can pick up the scent of the unknowns. I do know algebra and can sniff what needs to be found in Greek or in English, but philosophy . . . that's another matter. I take Plato's *Republic* and give it a glance. The English book feels ten times heavier than it did in Greek. There is no way that I can read fifty pages of it in English, but I remember that justice is a quality of the soul, not a social convention and a few other bits and pieces of wisdom from my high school class, when Professor Xifaras was delivering his lectures on Plato. They'll have to do.

I have met up with Tony at MIT, as we had planned in Athens. We are trying to orient ourselves and avoid talking about home. Tony looks dapper and is looking for girls in his desirous but disinterested way. He believes that if you show you are interested in a girl, you've lost her. "Stay cool and look bored," he advises. But isn't that disingenuous? He recoils at the use of the word. "What do you expect me to do – tell a girl I just met that I want to make love to her right now? Right here? You have to act indifferently, or she'll think you are a sex maniac out of some asylum." That's not what I meant, not what I meant at all. I'll have to learn from experience or by accident, somehow. "We should go to one of the acquaintance-dances they have every weekend," he tells me. I have no money, no language and no time for dates. Not yet. Then he comes up with a bit of wisdom that gives me food for thought. "Girls are human beings and want the same things that we do," he says and turns my existential applecart upside down. I had thought girls had different interests, but now I see his point: we are all made of flesh and blood, and, therefore, similar desires. Better go slow here and think more about such weighty matters.

We usually find some diversion, like the TV at the lobby of the upscale Baker House dorm, to stave off remembering. Rene from San Salvador is slouched on an armchair eating his paper napkin, his "after dinner dessert," he tells us. "Clean, white paper is good, no?" He really means it, and we realize we've come across another head case inhabiting the realm.

I found out that Tony Condaratos was staying at Baker House and paid him a visit soon after school started. We hugged each other and I thanked him and got all the details about the way he got Professor Chalmers to reevaluate my application. He said it was all due to my hard work and the strong package I had put together. I thanked him again for his interest and his efforts.

Somebody knocked at the door and asked if his desk lamp had arrived. Tony assured him that it would arrive within the week and the guy left. Tony smiled and pointed at the neon lamp on his desk. "I sell these and make a few bucks for some spending money," he said. It had never occurred to me that one could go into business from his dorm room, but I thought the idea was wonderful and wished I could do it too. Tony asked how I was getting along and I said "fine," not wanting to pile any more cares on him. "Listen," he said holding me by the shoulder as I was leaving his room, "This is America and everything will be fine." He laughed in such a gregarious way that I couldn't help but feel uplifted. "Let me know if you need any help, OK?" I was so moved and I didn't want to talk. I shook my head. We agreed to get together sometime soon and I left.

He was a year older and we didn't get together for a long time. I saw him a few times when he joined the Greek crowd. We had some good times together, visiting the Greek Church in Boston and dancing with the girls. Many years later, I visited him and his wife, at his home in Washington DC, when he was working for the United States government and I was on a business trip for Honeywell. We got to renew our friendship and discussed the experiences we had after leaving MIT, and our plans for the future. After graduation, Tony went to Greece to practice as an engineer in a power plant. He wanted to live like a Greek, he said. He had found out that the people around him were acting irresponsibly and had no interest in teamwork. "It's a dog-eat-dog world in our homeland," he said. He had returned to America disappointed from his Greek work experience. "They don't want our help," he said, sadness clouding his face. I thought of Mazis and his harping about helping our country, but I said nothing. I mentioned that another Greek from MIT had returned to Greece as a director of the government's nuclear facility only to return to MIT disappointed with the corruption that permeated every level of government and the professions. The news didn't help Tony. The man cared about the homeland. Tony said that he was enjoying his government job very much. But, it was clear to me that he was a restless man and was always looking for other things to do. He told me that he had written a book on Santorini with archaeological evidence showing its links to the ancient continent of Atlantis and was thinking about going back to Greece again and teaching engineering at the newly established University of Patras.. When I visited Greece many years later, I found out that Tony had become an executive for a major hospital in Athens and was as always hopeful, persistent and forceful. Tony Condaratos was great friend to all the people who knew him – "all heart," as the Greeks say and filled with dreams and dynamism.

> Many of the foreign students hang out at Walton's cafeteria across the Mass Avenue entrance of MIT. It is an easy way to forget the grind of schoolwork for a while. We are getting to know each other here. I have met some Greeks and wait for them here, as I watch faces of strangers get muzzled by coffee mugs, mugs staining the dappled white Formica tabletops, breaths and voices breaking up the lingering cigarette smoke – all rituals of pagan cultists praying for empowerment through various notions of success. The din of foreignness in accents, languages, colors, dress and manners is soothing. I realize that I have to work hard to become a foreigner and I get ready to laugh at myself when I see Miltos and George coming.

Tony Hambouris and I were surprised to find so many foreign students at MIT. Walton's cafeteria was like a junior chamber of the UN assembly. Here the world comes together to commiserate and make comparisons between the old country and this strange country we have flocked into but cannot put in a bin and label, yet. There is a thinly veiled affinity among foreign students, and we get to know many of them. We just join the discussions that go on at the tables and proceed to debate any issue that is on the table. First encounters feel like reunions. It seems that the foreign accents make us more comfortable. Raj is as forlorn as any Greek I know, so he's always present wherever we clump together. I think he meditates because I've seen him stare into the night without moving for long stretches of time. I don't know if does him any good. He complains about the cold and is always on the prowl for a girl to go out on a date. We asked him in what caste does he belong and he said he was a Brahmin. His father is a judge in India's supreme court, but I have never seen him put on airs toward anyone around us, including some other Indians who admitted to us that they are "untouchables." We thought hey were a bit haughty. I suppose, if you are a Brahmin and make it to MIT is not a big deal, but if you can do that from the untouchable caste, you've got to have a lot going for you. Raj refuses to pay attention to these things.

Nobody knows what George will bring up for discussion, and everyone knows that Miltos will talk about the rich Greek students at MIT.

"The rich have pockets but no hearts," says Miltos, puffing on a cigarette.

"Not all of them," I protest, thinking of Mr. Father. "It's not right to assume that every ship-owner is a horse's ass like Zaharias, or as weird as George."

"You think I'm weird?" George asks with genuine surprise, even though we have told him countless times.

"Yes, George, my friend," says Tony and smiles at him. "But, you are also very nice."

"And, let's not forget that you're crazy and angry – a bad combination, if you ask me," Miltos chuckles as he teases him.

"He's had a hard life, right Milt?" I pile on Miltos' affectionate sarcasm.

"Everyone is something he wishes he wasn't," Raj says, as if the thought had reminded him of something forgotten long ago.

"What are we?" I ask, pondering his wisdom.

"Insecure, insensitive, moochers, girl-crazy dogs, tech tools . . . take your pick," Tony offers a response that includes all of our sins.

"If we knew *that*, we wouldn't be here," Raj says, but doesn't explain. No one asks him to explain because the answer might be obvious and he would look stupid.

"Hell, everyone must also find something to be proud of. What is our thing? Not money or a famous family, that's for sure," Miltos says in earnest.

"I thought it was intellectual superiority," I say, "but that was before we came to this hellhole of intelligence freaks with monstrous IQs and scads of accomplishments. Where the hell do they find the time to learn about Fermat's last theorem and Veblen's *Theory of the Leisure Class*, and work in hospitals, teach the poor, start businesses, or hook oscilloscopes to radios? I have no idea," I protested, dropping a couple of the new names I had learnt from Howard, another dorm resident with knowledge to spare.

"Everybody is in the middle of some heap or other," Tony philosophized. "I'm going to use engineering to go into business. That's where I'll end up. Something that involves taking a risk and puts luck in play."

And we filled the cracks of the day with idle conversation and hard work, with problem solving, emotions, memories and dreams. We had few answers – they were always hard to come by when we were learning more about the world every day. But we made every day count for something, as if it was a sin to let it slip by without learning.

"So, can you spare twenty bucks for your poor old buddy here?" Miltos asks George, continuing a conversation that had probably began hours ago.

George opens his billfold and looks inside. "No cash," he says, "Only checks." He looks at Miltos searching for a response. "Alright, I'll buy you dinner, if that's what you want."

"Thank you. That and some cigarettes, if your budget allows," Miltos says.

It is dark when I go to Tony's room, to see how he is doing. No. I want to make sure that he hasn't discovered some way to do a lot better than I'm doing without letting me know of it. He understands what is going on around him. Donald, his roommate, is a Korean War veteran on the GI Bill, and they are having long discussions about the Truman Plan that saved Greece and the existence of God that will save the world.

I find out that Bud, the guy who is in the single room across the balcony from Tony's room, is an heir of the Heinz family fortune. "The ketchup bottle people," says Tony, who already knows a lot about the American culture and translates a few words for me now and then.

"He drinks all night and sleeps all day," Don, the veteran, says, voicing his disapproval.

"Nehru's nephew is three doors down from your room," says Mitko, another resident of the dorm. Mitko is a Bulgarian, a gossip par excellence with a knack for math. He knows where my room is, but I have no idea where his is. He had just poked his face in the room and had no problem socializing. "Raj said that he's got a Sikh body guard, turban and all, just in case there is any trouble here." I wonder if I am the only person in the dark.

And then the conversations turn to the careers we plan to pursue. I understand a little better what is going on. Donald is in electrical engineering and he already knows a lot about radios and telephones. He has made electrical devices, solenoids that operate water valves, knows how to connect oscilloscopes to amplifiers and how to hook up an alarm bell to a photoelectric eye to detect intruders. All I know about electrical engineering is that if you plug copper wires that have no insulation into an electrical outlet, they will kill you. All I know about electronics is that, if you look behind a radio through the peepholes of the cover, you can see the vacuum tubes glowing with little faint, reddish lights. I have to rethink my career plans. A few months later I will conclude that I can understand mechanical engineering better, because I have touched machines and breathed machine oil and I'll have a better chance to compete there. I will switch my major to mechanical engineering and be content for a while. I will find out later, that in spite of having done well as a research engineer and advanced in the ranks, inventing products and building various devices, I wasn't cut out to be an engineer. I couldn't care that much about how things work. I would play on a strong bent toward human relations and succeed an organization development consultant then as a teacher, a writer and an amateur theologian. I knew from those early days, listening to some of the other guys that there would be changes.

But for now, I'm having trouble connecting nouns to verbs, adjectives to nouns, and yawn to hide my ignorance. "Exam tomorrow," I announce and leave the gathering. I go to bed and fall asleep trying to convince myself that I belong here. I heard Jerry through clouds of sleep when he returned from his excursion to downtown Boston with a bunch of other guys. I dreamt of Radio City's dancing girls in the nightclubs of Boston's Scollay Square.

In the morning, like my father, I thought of all the money I made by staying home rather than carousing. If you have only a couple of dollars to your name, necessity, not free will, guides your morals. I grabbed a handful of cornflakes in the dining room and run to the classroom.

52 • The Psychopathology of Our Exams

As I approach the cavernous drafting room where the exam will happen to us, I feel my insides churn. This sixty-minute ordeal with two hundred bleary-eyed faces in various states of shock waiting for torture to begin will always haunt me. Proctors are prancing the aisles; my sweaty ass is glued to the tall stool, and my eyes search the inanities left on the desk's pressboard top. It is in this room that I'll be asked to give my solutions to the problems of the world. The professor is lodged behind an ancient desk at the head of the class, under the clock, guarding time and the exam booklets with his life.

There is time to review one last theorem, check one more proof. They won't bother with proofs of theorems – they're taken for granted. But nobody can tell what an MIT professor will do. They don't follow the beaten path. I see a paragraph that I cannot remember seeing before. How could I have missed it? It bulges with significance, and I try to grasp it. It is too late. I feel like a leaf holding on to the tree branch, against the strengthening breeze. I must make the effort, so that failure will come with inevitability and without excuses. I must be able to say to myself, "I did my best."

Tony sits close by, and asks me if I know the definition of a logarithm in chapter four. I tell him that the test is only on the material of the first three chapters.

"Not so; we have one through four, and logarithms are definitely included," comes the thunderous voice of the guy in front of us.

Tony is about to have a fit, and I have no idea what the mathematical definition of a logarithm is. We hate people like the guy in front of us. They make it their business to break others, and bring the class average down. Other misanthropes refuse to give a hand to their fellow students when studying for exams, because they want them to drag the class average down. I had never met the monster of the class average before. It sets brother against brother and breaks up groups. But, you can't get too angry at that beast. It makes sense in this madhouse. Teachers don't know what students can handle. The problems they give in an exam could be trivial or unapproachable. The class average will divide the sharpies from the dolts. A couple of years later, in a thermodynamics exam I took, the class average was seventeen out of a hundred. I got the top grade in the class with a forty-four. I give Tony a brief definition of the logarithm as far as I can remember from high school: the logarithm of a number to a given base is the exponent of the power to which the base must be raised to give the number. The guy in front is explaining the difference between common and natural logarithms to another muddled brain. We have no idea what is going on. The guy in front of us is chuckling at the confusion.

"Are you ready for the offering?" the proctor's eyes search our souls. I hope they ask something I can understand; something I know, and can express well enough to get over this hurdle. It is a humble prayer. No hard words, God. Please, no subtle formulations.

The exam books are handed out and the noisy room sinks into silence. Only the nearby proctor's steps pound the floor. It is Cerberus drumming the nails of his paws to pass the time outside the gates of hell. You set down anything that can possibly help you, including your name, address and serial number. These are the times when the body mutates. It gets sucked into the skull, and the only muscles left intact are those of the hand that holds the pencil. Everything I have flows through the pencil's lead. If this lead breaks, my system will crash. Legs and body will have to be grown all over again to move the system to the front of the room where the pencil sharpener is located. I answer the questions without having to think long or hard. You either know by now, or you don't. Some students write fast without stopping, while others chew their pencils and stare at the ceiling. There is no telling who knows and who has no clue. Everyone in the room was at the top or near the top of his high school class, but some of them are monsters of intellectual power and others are just good students. Some want to be here real bad, and others are here for a hundred different reasons that even they don't know yet.

I write down what I know, the way I think it should be written, until I run out of paper. I raise my hand and the proctor approaches. I am ready to speak. "Do you have to give me a shit of paper, Sir?" a sentence is born out of my mouth with the best of intentions and many unintended consequences in English syntax and propriety.

The proctor stares at me for a long while, looks at my paper and hands me another sheet. "I don't have to give you anything, but I *can* give you a *sheet* of paper," he says and retreats.

How long before the clock drops down from the hook on the wall and this universe of discourse is obliterated? So many pages, so much effort and so little meaning, when it comes down to it . . . If we continue doing this for a few generations, a creature would evolve with a five-cubic-foot cranium and one hand that has the precious opposable thumb and a finger to hold any instrument, any tool the brain wants. No legs, no torso, not even a penis; just the stunted hand, the huge head with a shrunken liver, heart and lungs and all the rest of the apparatus absorbed and kept under bone and frowning brow. We'll reproduce in vats with the DNA from our breath. One more problem to go, and then I'll hit the dinning room, eat and hope for the best, or doubt and spend a couple of sleepless nights trying to undo the past.

A voice is heard from the back of the room.

"I cannot stop just because you say so, Sir!" a loud protest that forces everyone to look in the direction of the shrill voice. We see a proctor escorting a student out of the room. "I have a condition!" the student is shouting. They are too far away for me to make out their faces.

Tony looks at me. "Zaharias is throwing a fit!" he says and goes back to working on the exam. I stare into the unknown. Tony gets done and hands in his exam.

There is no point in prolonging the ordeal. I turn in my paper, also, and walk out of the cavernous hall. I am empty.

"How did you do?" Joe asks as we get out of the building.

"I not know; better I thought."

"Did you answer part three of the fourth problem?" he insists.

"Two alone parts," I say, annoyed.

He looks at me with a strange sadness. "I'm afraid there were three," he says.

I want no further discussion of the exam, or any other damn thing about classes. I retreat, as if I lost a battle in a war that I forgot I declared. Joe is a nice guy, but MIT marks the end of his search for status in the society. He has all the main questions of the future settled, and I'm nowhere near there. MIT is the beginning of my adventures and explorations. I have other things to do, many more trials to put myself through – work for the summer, residence requirements, a place to stay, no family to call upon if I get sick, no money, military service pending, choice of the right career for practice in Greece, sex, relationships, dreams of doing something to justify my existence on earth . . . Instead of one hundred, the top grade I can possibly have now will be ninety-two. The earth is still going around and around without ever wobbling because of the problem I missed.

At lunch we are trying to decipher Zaharias' protest during the examination when he saunters into the dining room with a tray full of plates and bowls. Zaharias was the only fat Greek student I had seen in a long while. Some of us were slim because we were hungry; the rest were rich and knew better than to let themselves get fat.

"What the hell came over you?" Miltos asks.

"Were you truly in distress," asks Raj politely.

Zaharias smiles beatifically as he shovels the meatloaf in his mouth. "That bastard caught me as I was asking Dimitri a question of clarification. I told him about my condition."

"What kind of condition?" Miltos is like a hound after a fox.

"I have a mild form of *glossolalia*, a psychological condition that makes me say things I don't mean."

"Are you sure you haven't got *pseudologia*?" I let go the words disgusted with the man. "You were lying . . . weren't you?"

"Great word!" came Mitco's admiring input. "Telling lies, right? The whole world is crazy!"

Zaharias looks at me and cuts us off, waving a spoonful of mashed potatoes to our faces. "Listen you guys: I was cheating, alright? I was cheating and I told the proctor something to get him off my back," he says surprised at our naïveté and consternation. "You guys don't know how this country works. Tell Americans that you got a psychological condition, and they'll let you get away with just about anything. They don't want to be responsible for endangering your psychological health," the words were barely understandable in his relentless, nonstop eating with a full mouth. He has no idea of his pathology. He thinks that Americans are idiots. He believes that we would approve of his sick excuses, admire his creativity and help him escape any ethical boundaries.

"*Glossolalia*, my ass!" Miltos said with contempt. We all got up. "They'll get you Zaharias, mark my words. They'll get you!" and he left. A couple of minutes later, only Zaharias was left at the table, still tearing into the meatloaf, all alone as if nothing had happened. The earth was still going around and around as always.

53 • Coping with Loneliness

Courage is not simply one of the virtues, but the form of every virtue at the testing point.

C. S. Lewis

Christmas came and everyone who could get out of Burton House did so. They were in a hurry to leave and shouted their goodbyes and their Merry Christmases on the run. There were jokes and laughter in the hallways and bags, lots of bags everywhere, and the stairs were ringing with yells and triumphant cries reminiscent of the jubilation at the end of the war. After that, silence rushed in like a mountain of water to fill the hull of a sinking ship. But we are still here – those of us who have no plans to go anywhere any time soon. Tony, Mitko, the Bulgarian, Raj, Miltos, Tariq, an Iraqi chemical engineering student Tony has befriended, Howard, the Brooklyn Jew and fellow explorer of the mind and the world, all shipwrecked sailors stranded on this barren shore, people of faith and agnostics, singing strange songs of longing and return in the showers, looking for rescue. Emptiness heightens the expectation of a hopeful echo. We'll argue and agree and play cards and drink and laugh at happy people and brag about achievements and success, but we'll never reminisce. Not in public, anyway. Not on this joyous season!

I'm looking forward to spending Christmas day at the Barlas' home with a great turkey dinner and lots of Greek delicacies prepared by Mrs. Barlas. I'll pay for it with full participation in discussions of the restaurant business in greater Boston and the prospects little Greek children have for big New England Colleges. Actually, I have missed the people who helped me when I needed help. A few of these immigrants will be there as usual dealing and wheeling with facts and fictions, chasing dreams, and making deals, building nest eggs and college funds and working their day and night so they can belong. Immigration is the blood transfusion America gets to keep itself invigorated.

In the meantime, I got a job cleaning rooms, making beds and emptying wastebaskets at the dorm. I am a little worried because I may have to spend the entire Christmas vacation just reading Shakespeare's *King Lear* and writing a six-page paper on it. I have to do it, come hell or high water. Every day I devote at least three hours to reading with a dictionary by my side, keeping notes and sounding out the words that I've never heard before in my life. Every now and then I flip the pages I have read and count them with a certain pride. The paper – how am I going to write a paper with my first year English? Keep busy.

Evenings, I argue with Howard about the existence of God as far as my English will permit. He says that my cosmological argument will not stand the onslaught of science much longer, and tries to tear it down. I find out that trying to prove God's existence based on the existence of a finely tuned universe out of nothing constitutes "the cosmological argument." I have no doubt that he is wrong. He says he doubts everything, and I learn that everyone is entitled to his or her opinion. Not that I don't have my moments of doubt, but God exists and doesn't mind one bit about my doubts. He may even like to watch me struggle with my doubts.

"I got a job, and earn some money to pay for my many needs," I write proudly home. "I miss you all, and send you many kisses and special hugs for my little Vassaki." My mother says that Vasso is doing fine, but she hasn't written a word to me. I wonder why, but I don't want to search too hard for the reasons. I escape the onrush of ruminations to maintain my sanity in this hollow hull of a building. The Muslim student squats on his little carpet and prays every noon when I go by.

Mitko is nowhere to be found. Tony says that he found an older woman and is shacking up with her. We are both silent for a while, trying to imagine the tryst of the lucky Bulgarian.

Jerry, my Jewish roommate told me that he planned to ask a girl he has known since fifth grade for a date. I wished him good luck and Merry Christmas. He smiled and wished me Happy Hanukah. I didn't know enough to get either his joke or my mistake. I had no idea what "Hanukah" meant but I never suspected that he would call me names.

On Christmas Day, I went to the Barlas' home for dinner. Mrs. Barlas took me aside and said that they had invited Mike and his wife to come for dinner, since he and I had worked well with each other at the Darbury Room. Mike arrived soon after that and proceeded to tell all of them how I had managed to survive in the jungle of Darbury Room under his protective guidance. I told a few Greek jokes and had everybody in stitches. Mike did his best to appear as my mentor, and I let him. I had so many mentors that I stopped counting. As they say, "it takes a village."

They were all happy to see me doing well and wanted to know how I was progressing in school. When I told them that school was hard but I was doing OK, they urged me to keep at it and take the pain. "There's no free lunch in this country," everyone agreed. Tom Barlas came out of his splendid isolation, leaned forward on his recliner and said, "Ain't that the truth! Nobody gives a damn about you . . . only they want something . . . You pay, is all."

We took our seats and waited. Mrs. Barlas and a couple of other women brought the food to the table. We must have been about a dozen adults all in all and about as many children in an adjacent room. I stared at the variety, the quality and the amount of food that was prepared. Was I one of the people Tom Barlas was talking about? This was a shoe-shiner's home, and the food was fit for a king, I thought. The atmosphere in the room was festive. We forgot the daily cares and troubles and gave every moment a chance to flourish.

"Isn't that a great country?" someone said. Everyone raised his glass of retsina wine.

"Merry Christmas to you all!" Tom Barlas said.

"Stin iyia sas, to your health, everybody," I said along with the others.

Ever so slowly, I'm getting used to the deprivation of contact with the people I love. The school's demands pushed me away from all other needs and landed me in the middle of a battlefield to defend my intellectual survival with all the skills and talents I had. I think that Calculus is going to give me an A or B. Physics is hard, but Mazis did a good job of teaching us the fundamentals, so I should do well. Chemistry will always be a problem for me, and I will only try for an average grade. I did well in Plato's Republic with some help from Joe in the paper I wrote on the allegory of the cave, and if I can manage a fair grade in the Lear paper, I could end up with a B in Humanities. Wouldn't that be a joke on the Institute? I have no idea how I'll be able to read a play by the master of the English language and write a paper that makes any sense. Tony and Jerry have promised to give me a hand with grammar, syntax and spelling, if I provide the ideas and the rough draft of the paper. I thank them for their help and go to work, trying to grasp some meanings from the text. My job was tedious and boring, but the few extra dollars I made allowed me to have dinner at the *Omonia* Greek restaurant once in a while with my friends. After Christmas, I got a job doing data reduction with a Marchant calculator at a Civil Engineering lab along with a couple of other guys. We were never told what we were calculating, but we figured that we were doing stress analysis calculations to assess the damage various structures suffered after a nuclear bomb blast. Having learned the routine and the rewards of work, I began searching for a more challenging position.

Around that time, several of us started going to the International House, in Harvard Square, to meet American girls who wanted to meet foreign students. Gathered under one roof, dozens of us thrown together by the winds of fate and our intractable ambitions, we constituted an array of interests, skin colors, languages, cultures and mentalities that the college girls in the area found fascinating. Still, there were four or five guys for each gal, so the competition was fierce. I made up stories based on my experiences that I thought would get me some respect from the girls hunting for the bizarre and the weird. The images I formed in my mind had to distort the real world and make an artifact out of it, so I could laugh at it like the fox in Aesop's tale that scoffed at the beautiful grapes it couldn't reach. But, most of the time I just sat in some corner and observed and imagined.

The Mistress of the House dressed impeccably in a dark blue evening dress and wearing a necklace of pearls and a smile, spends a few minutes with every cluster of visitors in her abode and moves on, as if to pollinate every flower and every thorn in her domain. The foreign students have talked to each other long enough. We need her to stir the pot. She will come to us, I know, and she will be as sweet as any hostess can be. Piano music drifts lazily around, spun from the fingertips of an American college girl with long, golden hair. Assorted cosmopolitan admirers surround her. She's out of sight and out of reach because I'm out of touch and out of my head. I move on and find the German baron, who has declared his impatience with imbeciles, and spouts categorical pronouncements of Kantian morality. A black American woman's bright black eyes send prayers up to heaven as she digests the baron's offerings. Tariq, our Iraqi friend, explains to a couple of women the contours of the Arab world back in the glorious years of the Abbasid Caliphate in Baghdad. The American women, eager to get to the soul of the world's mysteries, listen and gear up for questions. Will they ask about Saladin and the Crusaders, or will they play it safe and ask what was all that about The "House of Wisdom," in Baghdad? I suspect that some of the "college girls" around us are secretaries who don't give a damn about Kant or the Caliphate, but want, instead, to meet European aristocrats, Asian potentates and Arab oilmen. I have become a paranoid trying to make sense of the world around me and entertain myself.

I move on. Most Americans are delighted to catch a foreigner's mannerisms, as if they were ripe fruits falling off a tree. Tony helps them execute such maneuvers gracefully.

"Do you really lift up your head and move your neck backward when you want to signal 'No'?"

"Sure. You also make a clicking noise with your tongue, like this: tsuh-tsuh-tsuh . . . Saying "No" is a very delicate maneuver, in Greek."

"Really? I had no idea."

"Sure. Do you go to school here?"

Conversations can get complicated as easily about trivia as they can about the phenomena of the quantum world. Some of us invent new mannerisms, bizarre ways of interaction, grimaces, contortions, all kinds of distortions to impress the girls and engage them, fascinate them, hold their attention, get to first base, score.

Music from a hi-fi fills the living room. Raj is dancing with a stunning black beauty, and Tony watches transfixed. I'm tired of thinking and imagining and observing. In the end, you have to check out of your thoughts and your dreamscapes and jump into the mess of life like a parachutist. I ask one of the women sitting on the couch for a dance, and she gives me her hand. Then she unfolds and rises and straightens and stands about a foot over my head. We dance and look blissful in spite of the fact that I'm sweating like a pig because my head is tucked between her breasts and I'm suffocating of embarrassment. The earth kept going around and around even when the music stopped and I got off the merry-go-round in a hurry.

And so, with hope in my heart and a few extra bucks in my pocket, I started looking for a girl who would want to be with me as much as I wanted to be with her.

From posters I learned that there were acquaintance dances sponsored by the school's many organizations. The concept was attractive, but I had no idea how it works. Who acquaints whom, and with what? "You just meet girls," Raj said, and went on talking about the benefits of these dances. I thought it was time for me to try my luck there. I went around the room eyeing the dancers, the talkers and the dreamers. I approach a beautiful girl, thinking of the sentence I'll speak when I ask her, but someone else cuts in front of me and beats me to it. I hate this lack of facility with the language when I need it. I withdraw, and let myself drift into a reverie. But, it doesn't last long. I see two black girls talking to each other. One of them has a serene look that attracts me. The melody of a song of black sirens comes to mind but she doesn't fit the fantasy; she dwells in the loftier parts of my mind. I will take a chance.

They are playing *Stardust* and we glide on the floor as if we had practiced this routine for a long time.

"You are good dancer, Sandy," I say, trying to look into her eyes, which are playing hide and seek with me.

"You got style," she said. "Do you come here often?"

"Me the first time."

"Me too. I came with my girlfriend." We said nothing for a while. "Where do you come from?" she asked.

And I talked about Greece, Athens and all that I was proud of, and she talked about her studies in nursing and her work at the Mass General hospital. It seemed to me that she had slowed down her speaking so that I could understand her better. I offered to take her home, but she was with her girlfriend and she said that wouldn't work. I took her phone number and said that I would call her for a date. She smiled.

"If you like," she said.

"I shall like."

Back at the dorm dance, sponsored by some dorm committee on the first floor, students were getting drunk in droves. Guys were coming out of the great hall staggering in the lobby. I had never seen so many drunks in one place. Upstairs, I bumped into Doug and asked him if he needed any help to get up off the floor and go to his room. I had cleaned his room several times and picked up his empty bottles of gin, so I knew why he was helpless now. "Can't stop, Greek. Can't handle it, and can't stop," he moaned, holding an empty paper cup close to his chest. I felt sorry for him. I couldn't have imagined anyone admitting that he couldn't stop doing what one was free to do or not. Besides, where I came from, it was a sign of weakness to get drunk. I had given him all the advice I was able to give, so I moved on, thinking of the evenings I used to stop by with my high school buddies for beer and tyropita. One beer and out. Nobody ever got drunk. Nobody wanted to get drunk. Here, however, we all learned how to drink to get drunk and forget the stifling load we were pushing every day uphill. But, we could and did stop. Doug got worse. A time came when Doug moved all his furniture into the shower room.

"Has he lost his mind?" I shouted, and burst into the bathroom to save him, or laugh at him, or cry for him, I didn't know what. The shower was coming down hard on his reclined body and his books.

"His girl sent him a 'Dear John'," Donald said, as he stood by with arms folded in front of his chest and stared with pity at Doug. I didn't know what a "Dear John" was, but I knew Doug was in pain. He had transcended to another realm. His eyes were shut, and he held a wet *Tropic of Cancer* with one hand flat on his belly.

I thought of Sandy, yearning for another person to be close to. I wanted to talk to someone about the way I felt, but no one else around would do. So, I called her and went out with her on a date, my first date. She lived somewhere in Roxbury, in one of the housing projects, where the streets were dark and empty. We took trains and busses and went some place to eat and talk. Sandy was a kind and welcoming person but there was no way she could understand the heartaches of a lost Greek, and I was far away from touching the wounds that seared the hearts of the black people in America. We were survivors on rafts moving in the same direction, but miles apart from each other.

I had other dates with girls, but I couldn't find a person who attracted me enough to establish a relationship. There were too many unsettled things in my mind and a relationship requires a sense of permanence that I didn't have at the time. I even managed to find a girlfriend at an acquaintance dance, after I moved out of the dorm in the second year. She was a college student from a small town, lost in the chaos of the city and held on to me because she was looking for a guide. I thought I could help her find herself, but I was ignorant and condescending. I was a survivor, hardened by my recent struggles and proud of my little victories. I couldn't be of much help to anyone at the time. After we went our separate ways, I realized that I wasn't very kind to her. She was devoted to me, but I had nothing to offer her, because I could not respond to her feelings. So that relationship was doomed from the start even though it lasted for several months. She gave me what little she had and I took it and gave back the little I had. The difference was that I knew we were not going to travel together for long, and she was so full of hope that someday we would set sail for a lifelong cruise.

54 • Chess with Checks and Balances

Sometimes George would come by and ask anyone around if he wanted to play a game of chess. That was the way George said "hello." He was a good player but he could be beaten, if he was distracted. We knew how crazy he was about chess and sports and antique cars and cameras and who knows what else, so we would try to get him talking about something else, rather than playing chess with him and lose. George must have been in his late twenties or early thirties, but he behaved like a restless teenager, excited about the things he liked, outspoken about topics of interest to him, oblivious to the dynamics of social interactions around him and very unpredictable. He was skinny, I would say, skeletal, with thick black, myopic glasses that usually drooped down his nose and straight hair in tufts like Hitler's.

One night Tony, Raj, Mitko and I were listening to George telling us about a Monte Carlo race that he had tried to enter but didn't qualify for, when Miltos showed up and said that he was having money troubles. He wanted borrow a few dollars, until his next remittance form home. Raj said that he had given what little extra he had to Mitko. Tony, Mitko and I had no money to spare, but George was always loaded, so Miltos asked him straight up for a loan of fifty bucks for two weeks. We all knew that fifty bucks was peanuts for him, but, when Miltos asked him, he jumped up from his chair as if electricity had run through his body.

"How much money have you got on you right now?" he asked, pointing to Miltos.

Miltos took out of his pocket a few bills and counted them. "Seven bucks, is all."

"I'll do better than loan you fifty," George said without hesitation. "I'll *give* you a hundred bucks, if you can beat me in a game of chess, right now!"

We stopped talking. "I just want a damn loan," Miltos protested.

"Take it or leave it; make a hundred, or lose your seven, that's the bet," came George' swift challenge.

Miltos stared at his opponent gauging his seriousness. George waited standing. "All right! Get the damn board, you guys," Miltos said and threw his bills on the table.

George took out his billfold and looked inside. "I have no cash."

"No problem," said Miltos.

The game began with George attacking, and Miltos having his hands full, defending his pieces. A few moves later, Raj opined that Miltos had "a strategic advantage and would dominate the game to the end." George became agitated. He protested the interference and threatened to quit, if "the psychological warfare" continued. Raj took a few steps away from the table, as if to show his utter disinterest in arguments and conflicts of any kind. The game went on. George was cautious and taking his time now. The worse his position got, the longer it took him to move.

"If you play as slowly as you do," I protested, "we'll grow beards by the time the game ends."

"It's checkmate in three moves," Miltos announced in a somber tone. We looked at each other, puzzled. None of us could see how that would be achieved.

"Bullshit," grumbled George. He loosened his tie and concentrated on the board. He scrutinized the positions of the chess pieces on the board, murmuring arguments for his strong defenses. Everything was as he wanted it to be, but he was distracted. He told Miltos that he was full of crap and moved one of his pieces. It was a fatal mistake, and we all burst out with a cry of utter disapproval. George immediately saw the error and put his hand on the piece intending to take back his move.

"No way!" came Miltos' thunderous command, and he slapped George on the wrist.

George withdrew his hand, looking like a dog with his tale between his legs. Miltos took George' bishop and the game went on, but the error had changed the situation on the board.

A few moves later, George gave up in disgust. "It took you more than three moves!" George protested.

"Sorry!' Miltos sneered.

"Is there any rule for that?" George asked, but no one answered him because he knew the rules of chess better than anyone around. His normally pale face turned red and his neatly parted hair dangled down on his forehead touching his glasses. I thought that Miltos had intimidated George with his bold announcement, but I said nothing. No one did.

Miltos checked his watch leisurely.

"Double or nothing!" George howled now.

We looked at each other, dumbfounded.

Miltos remained calm and reflective. A hundred bucks would more than cover his needs. He was satisfied. He got ready to gather the bills, but George was furious. Before Miltos could reject the proposition and touch the money, George shouted with the urgency of a drowning man. "Four hundred bucks for all you have," he shouted.

Miltos hesitated. He was reluctant to play again, but didn't want to drop out either. He smiled, straightened himself, and a new game began with a rattled George and a cool and confident Miltos. George was first to comment about the game, and then I said something, and Tony said something else, and George protested that there was too much interference for him to concentrate. He pulled back for a moment but he didn't quit; he kept on mumbling the names of pieces and their possible moves to himself, and Miltos kept his cool and found a weakness in his opponent and capitalized on it.

"Sorry, George," Miltos said, and moved his queen. "Check!"

It took George just a moment to see that it was a checkmate. He cursed something awful, and then stopped abruptly. We waited for someone to make the next move, someone to say something and end this unseemly contest. George stood up and shouted, "I bet you eight hundred bucks for what I owe you what's on the table." He thought for a moment, and added, as if talking to himself, "My luck's got to change!"

"Stands to reason," Raj said, faking conviction and sympathy.

"You need a roulette for that," I added, trying to understand why George wanted Miltos to be totally broke, and why was he talking about luck in chess when he knew better.

"Are you sure that this is what you want?" Miltos asked.

"Absolutely."

And so the final chess game began and, as with all the previous games that night, it ended with another loss for George. He was devastated now; his shoulders were drooping and his face had lost all color. His hair kept falling over his forehead and he kept shoving it back up with his hand. He was the better player, but no matter how hard he tried he couldn't focus on the task that night. His reason was crippled by his raging emotions. Could one remark of a needy student destroy the confidence of a man more than five years older? I felt sorry for George. By now everyone was on his side.

"I don't have the money with me," he said to Miltos. "I'll pay you tomorrow."

Miltos stood up. "A bet is a bet, George," he said with authority that surprised everyone. "You pay me now . . . by check." We all knew George always carried a checkbook with a hefty balance. He was the go-to guy for a few bucks in an emergency and he had bought dinners for most of us when we were down and out.

George was taken aback. "OK, if that's what you want," he said quietly. He took out his checkbook and wrote a check to Miltos for eight hundred dollars.

Miltos reached out and took the check. He scrutinized it, as if to make sure everything was in order. Then, without any comment or even a single word, he stared at George and with a rapid move he tore the check in two, and then in four, and then in little pieces, and tossed them in the wastebasket. "It was fun to play the game and win," he said. He picked up his seven dollars and shoved them into his pocket.

We were in shock. George turned to leave, but Miltos stopped him. He scooped up his seven bucks from the table and put them in his pocket. "George," he said as calmly as he could, "can you let me have fifty bucks for two weeks?"

George reached into his pocked and pulled out a few crumpled bills. He counted fifty dollars and gave them to Miltos. "Two weeks," he said as if that was the best he could do.

"Thanks, George. I really appreciate this."

Next day we told the story to all the friends we had, and they told it to their friends, and the story became a topic of conversation and a kind of legend. They were both likeable and memorable people, but neither endured the rigors of MIT. Miltos left school for personal reasons, probably financial distress being one of them, and never graduated from MIT, as far as I know. George stayed around school for some time, and we all became his friends. He drove an Austin Healy sports car and later a Mercedes SLR with doors that swing up like an eagle's wings. He invited everyone he knew to ride with him, go places, do something fun with him. Most of us took at least a ride with him and did something we liked, because we wanted the thrill of speed and flash and because it was hard to say "No" to George. He was a terrific driver, was never distracted when he was at the wheel of a car and you never knew what surprise he was going to come up with next.

55 • A Fool's Errand: Photoshoot for a Roadkill

If I were following a chronological order, I should go on with my story, telling what happened next and then next after that and so on. But, my memory has its own rules for ordering events and imposes them upon my writing. When I remember George and Miltos, the order of time gets upended and their participation in some other events comes into focus. So, I jump ahead a year or so, to relate these two events before I pick up the thread of my story's tenuous timeline again.

Tony and I had moved out of the dorm in our second year, and many of our friends, Greeks and other foreign students like Mitko and Raj, would hang around at our living room playing cards or chess or listening to music or arguing about the ills of school life and the world.

George stopped by our place one night when Tony and my other roommate, Dimitri, were out working, studying at the library or chasing girls. It was getting late and I had waited long enough for them to get back and play some cards or hang out for a while. More importantly, I wanted to find out if I could borrow a few bucks to buy some groceries. Without any introduction, George asked me if I wanted to take a ride to New York with him. He said he wanted to look at the new Mercedes SLR sports cars. The snow was melting and the smell of spring was in the air. A long weekend of studying and boredom was fast approaching, and a trip to New York for a couple days seemed like an adventure. I left a note for Tony, jumped in the Austin Healy and off we went. I was eager for exploration and thought George would want to show me some of the wonders of the city he knew so well, like the Empire State Building and the Brooklyn Bridge, some museum or other, or that he would want to stop at his family's Park Avenue apartment, and I would get a glimpse at the life of the people in the Greek ship-owning class. I told him that I had been to Coney Island and Radio City, thinking that he would praise my knowledge and want to add to it, but George was aloof, even derogatory. "These are sights for the hoi polloi; stay away from them. He advised me totally unaware of his putdown artistry.

I was hungry and was hoping for a good meal. George always paid for the food when he asked you to go riding with him, and that was an additional incentive to take the trip because I was broke. I was hoping that, if the trip went well, I would be able to ask him for a few bucks to get by until the end of the month without having to undergo an ordeal. But, as I have already pointed out George wasn't all there at all times, or *I* wasn't – hard to tell when you get mixed up with people who don't act the way you and others have acted in your past life. By the time we got to New York in the early morning hours and headed for the Mercedes Benz dealership in downtown Manhattan, I was famished and said so. He showed no interest in stopping at a restaurant for something to eat.

The lights were blazing in the showroom of the dealership, and George got out and went from window to window, staring and making all sorts of observations, until he had covered the entire length of the glass wall of the dealership and had pointed out to me all the fine details of every car in that showroom.

"Let's go," he said when he was done.

"Go where?"

"Back to Boston."

"Don't you have a home somewhere around here? We can stop and relax for a couple of hours."

"Relax? You don't want to relax now. Wasn't that a great car? Isn't that an exciting machine? Let's get going. I feel like driving some more."

I told him that we had to stop and eat within an hour or I would never speak to him again. I don't know if I meant that because George was a person to dislike in spite of his eccentricity, but I was hungry and I needed nourishment.

We headed back at the same breakneck speed at which we came down. I was thrilled to travel at one hundred and twenty miles per hour in a tiny sports car. We stopped at a roadside restaurant and I had hamburgers and French fries for breakfast. George said that I had earned my keep, so it was his treat. I laughed. Coming out of the restaurant, I told George that if it had to be my treat we'd be washing dishes in that restaurant's kitchen to pay for it. "I know you don't have much money, but you are a good friend," he said as we came out and watched the dawn edge the night away. We got back in the little tub and hit the road again at 117 mph. That was as fast as I had ever gone or would ever go in a car. The road kept unfolding beside me with a hiss too close for comfort. I realized that I had to trust George much more than I trusted him. He is a damn good driver, I kept thinking, my eyes shifting like windshield wipers from the road to his face and back to the road again.

A few miles after that, there was a thud and George slammed on the brakes. We looked at each other to affirm our non-interference with the workings of the machine. We got out and looked for damage. A little gray rabbit lay mangled beside the car. George stared at the dead critter for a long minute and then went into frenzy, getting his camera from the car and shooting shot after shot at the dead rabbit. He must have taken dozens of photos from all angles and at various distances and with various settings. He thought he was a good photographer, and was always prepared to capture the essence of reality in the unexpected and the bizarre. I wanted a picture to send home, with me looking at the rabbit, but he wouldn't consent to take one, unless I agreed to hold the rabbit by the ears. Later I got that picture for home and several others to remind me of the trip to New York, as if there was a chance I would ever forget. All the photos were blurred, out of focus, tilted, out of context, like the memories left from the way we lived our lives in those days. We left the rabbit by the side of the road, buried in a shallow grave with a little dirt scraped by our shoes piled over it.

What was that trip all about? My friends seemed bored when I told them about the rabbit. They didn't see anything remarkable; nothing was funny; nothing was sad enough to mourn. There was no big story, but there was living and dying. There was danger and thrill. Something of consequence could have happened. For a man who had lived his life pursuing one goal after another, this pointless exploration should have no value. I expected nothing in particular; it was an experience without any goal. It was like fishing without a goal to catch fish. Fishing has value even if no fish are caught. It had been a long time since I felt the sweet waste of time during the summertime in Eleusis, and the New York trip with its roadkill its SLR, its dawn and its danger felt almost as liberating.

We saw a lot of George the year after the trip to New York. We hardly ever had anything to do with Zaharias anymore, but we wanted George to be part of our group, not only because he bought us dinner and lent us money sometimes, but mainly because he always said or did the unexpected. George was a very smart man, but his great need for acceptance and approval blurred his judgment. He had left MIT once, before we were there, for undisclosed reasons and finished his Bachelor's degree at Worcester Tech, though he was embarrassed about that and mentioned it only once. When we met him, he had come back to MIT as a graduate student because he wanted to be a Naval Engineer and MIT was the best school for that. Yet, we never saw him study, or carry any books, or talk about any exams. He knew a lot about cars and ships and cameras and racing and chess, so everyone assumed school would be a breeze for him. But MIT is a strange, weird world of wonders that distorts reality and challenges you to adapt to it or perish. Years later, when I learned a few facts about Einstein's theory of General Relativity, I came to believe that MIT was tucked into a trough of the space-time continuum and had its own brand of reality. George never adapted to it. An education at MIT is a test of one's ability to adapt to change, absorb blows to the ego and cope with the ordeals of learning so one can reap the rewards of success with equanimity. They say affectionately that

"Tech is Hell," but they mean it is also Purgatory, Limbo and Paradise, depending on the day. Many students succeed though a few do not. George left school for the second time without the degree he so desperately wanted to get. We were all sad, but we knew that George was afraid of the school itself and that in the end, his fear won out.

In some ways, George was one of the lost souls in the community. He gave what he didn't need, couldn't find what he needed and we took from him what we could until he faded away. As far as I know, he never flunked any courses, but just the same, he dropped out. I wish I had been wiser, to help him find the kind of person he wanted to be. I didn't know then that I had to spend years experiencing the hardships of life before I could help myself, let alone anyone else.

56 • Light Bulbs Make Good Hammers

"Ask, and it will be given you; seek, and you will find; knock,
and it will be opened to you."

Matt. 7:7

At that time I was drowning in debt and could think of little else beyond
making ends meet. The money I had earned from my summer job (I will
say more on this, below) was gone. I had spent some of it to buy my first
car, a 1949 Plymouth, and the rest of it took care of my living expenses
for a couple of months. I had told my parents that I would need less
money in the second year, to ease the burden on them, so they had
reduced their monthly stipend. My plan was to get a part-time job and
make up the deficit; but the courses I was taking as a sophomore were
very demanding and I couldn't handle a part-time job. I had to rely solely
on the little money my parents were sending and drastic cuts on my
living expenses, which included rent for our apartment, food and gas for
the car. (I named the car Zaimis, after a Greek revolutionary hero from
the War of Independence, in 1821 and thought of it as the tangible proof
of *my* independence.) The result of my miscalculations was that I would
run out of money in the second or third week of every month and I would
have to borrow from friends to make ends meet till the end of the month.
Most of the money I would get from home would now go to pay my
debts, and I would be broke again. I was disheartened and had to resort to
all sorts of maneuvers to survive. I would mooch from George and other
friends who could afford an extra meal for me at a restaurant, or a few
dollars till the end of the month. Most weekends I would visit Tom and
Carline Barlas and eat a good dinner there. Sometimes, Tony and I would
visit one of our Greek friends working at the Graduate House cafeteria
and he would serve us an extra-generous meal, which was good for a
couple of days, counting what we stuffed in our pockets. On
Thanksgiving and Christmas, when most students had left for home,
there was extra food left over and less supervision and we would carry it
in trays from the kitchen back to the apartment and have enough food for
a few days.

When I had some money for groceries, I would buy a pound of
sirloin steak from "Stop and Shop" and flatten it with a light bulb – I had
no hammer – until it was about a quarter of an inch thick; then, I would
cut it into four pieces and store it in the refrigerator to provide myself
with meals for four days. I think that the knowledge of having secured

four meals gave me some peace of mind and I could relax for a couple of days.

It was about that time that the ceiling in my bedroom started to leak drop by drop in a steady drip by my bed. I placed a wastebasket to collect the rainwater and waited for the super to come and fix it. The steady echo of the drops felt like hammer blows inside my head. I would close my eyes and dream of driving Zaimis on long straight country roads in Louisiana or Alabama with windows open and the radio blasting triumphant songs. The illusion of independence persisted, even as I started missing classes, sleeping during classes and slipping into the dark labyrinths of lassitude. When my grades for the first semester arrived, they told a story of declining performance. I was on a trajectory for failure and I became afraid. My only consolation was that I hadn't flunked a course yet.

George was usually unaware of the emotional state of anyone around him, but he did think fast and unconventionally when you nudged him into reality. Sometimes he made unexpectedly helpful remarks and never knew it. One day, as I was discussing the perennial lousy state of my finances, he turned to me and, in his characteristic impetuousness said, "You should stop bitching about being broke, swallow your pride and get a damn loan from the school." He fired his words at me without hiding his irritation.

I wasn't used to him talking like that to anybody. "What the hell are you talking about, Georgie?" I countered, ready for a showdown.

"They give loans to students like you. Go get one." He said this as if it was a trite bit of information provided to a client by some accounting firm.

"They give loans to people who have no way to pay them back? Are they nuts?"

George looked at me and saw an ignoramus from the hill country of Greece. "This is the American way! When are you going to figure out that this is the *New* World? You borrow now and you pay it back with a little interest later. Everybody wins."

"What have you got to lose?" Tony said.

The eccentric and the pragmatic advice I got made me pause. I said that I would think about it.

A couple of days later, I got a letter from Professor Chalmers, the Advisor to Foreign Students who was instrumental in my coming to MIT, asking me to go and see him at his office. I was very concerned that they had already taken my scholarship away and he was just going to inform me of that fact. Mr. Kizilos, you're done here. Good luck to you.

I couldn't stop thinking of the worst that could happen: expulsion and return to Greece humiliated.

I went to Professor Chalmers' office the next day. I met his secretary in the waiting room and she informed him that I wanted to see him in response to his letter. He told her to send me in. I knocked at his door and entered his office hesitantly.

"Come in, young man," he welcomed me with a joyous smile. I responded with a meek greeting, confused by his attitude. I thought I was going to a funeral, but instead I walked into some kind of reception. What is he up to? Is he letting me down gently? It won't work – I'll have my pain raw no matter what.

"Sit down, sit down," he said and picked up a file from his desk and studied it. "I see that your grades weren't so good this last semester. Is there some problem?" He waited for me to answer. "We are here to help you deal with problems. It's what we do."

"I'm hungry, Sir," I blurted out without any introduction. "I don't have enough money to live on. I made some mistakes . . . "

"You're hungry?" he burst out loudly and leaned forward as if someone had stabbed him in the back. "You should have come to me sooner. No reason to be hungry, Mr. Kizilos. We can help you. The School is on your side. Lean on us."

I couldn't believe how hurt he was. It seemed that he was feeling my hunger.

He opened a side drawer in his great desk and taking out an envelope said, " A great lady in Boston has established an emergency fund for foreign students." He counted some bills and returned the envelope to his desk drawer. "Here are a hundred and fifty dollars for you to spend getting some good food right away and covering any other needs you have now," he said and handed me the money. "I don't want to hear that you are hungry again. I want you to go to the bursar's office tomorrow and take out a loan to cover your needs. I will call and arrange for it."

"I cannot pay it back, Sir."

"You will, when you earn money after you graduate and find a professional position. But till that time comes, you will have the funds you need to function well. Your job is to do the best you can in your classes."

"I will," I said and shook his hand, thanking him for coming to my rescue again.

That evening I went to the Omonia Greek restaurant and had a rack of lamb with red sauce and rice and drank retsina, toasting the generosity of professor Chalmers, MIT and America. I thanked God for another providential assist.

I took out a loan and managed to continue with better performance till the end of the school year.

I paid the entire loan I received from MIT in the first six months after I got my first job as a professional engineer, at the Griscom Russell Company, in Massillon, Ohio.

57 • On the Road to Augusta

There is only one good, knowledge; and one evil, ignorance.

Socrates

For Easter vacation that same year as the incident I recounted above, Tony, Miltos, Dimitri and I decided to head north into the forests and seashores of New England. We packed into Tony's car, an old 47 Ford he had bought with some money a relative of his had sent him as a gift that first summer, and were off toward New Hampshire and Maine and beyond. We were jubilant to have made it as far as we had for a year and a summer and all we wanted to do was enjoy the ride going north into the evergreens and the sea. Dimitri had found a brochure that promised a good time to any able bodied youth who made it to the Festival of Friendship in Augusta Maine, so our default destination became the Festival and we all talked about the girls waiting for us up there and the fun we would have dancing, drinking, eating and cavorting with them. We had enough money for gas and food on highway diners, but not much more than that. We entered New Hampshire and passed by Lawrence where America's textile production had reached its peak and the working class had felt its union power decades ago, and we headed up past Haverhill where Greek immigrants had set roots since the beginning of the century and from where many Greek American college students hailed. We stopped at Portsmouth, New Hampshire, and stood on a bluff and gazed at the astounding complex of islets and bridges and cranes and ships all painted on a mural of gigantic proportions and hung from the sky for our benefit in memory of those who labored and sweated to make it a great harbor once.

"Human beings can build wonders!" said Dimitri, puffing on a cigarette.

"When they are not killing each other," came Miltos' obligatory opposition.

"Lots of blood and sweat out there," I said.

"Enough chit chat, guys," Tony intervened. "We better hit the road, if we are going to make the Festival."

And off we were, going north on highway 218 and then on 27, further up toward Augusta, toward the pole, toward some kind of Eldorado. It started to rain and we became quiet, as if the opaqueness that descended all around us required contemplation and respect. The lull of the engine was hypnotic, but Miltos was in charge of keeping Tony awake and would shout something outrageous like an insult to all of us, or a curse upon all capitalists, or imperialists, or cannibals every few minutes. We travelled for one maybe two hours in this mode of limited awareness until the rain stopped and the sun came out and we started singing Greek songs about girls with green eyes and long flowing hair on their shoulders, or black olive eyes and long black braids down to their waists. We were dreaming again. The forests hugged the road and everybody wanted to stop at a clearing and relax for a while. Tony pulled the old black beetle of a Ford car on a little rest area by the side of the road and we got out. We went some distance into the trees, found a clearing in the woods and lay down on the grass under the sun that God had sent us to enjoy. We were happy frolicking and shouting in Greek and teasing each other about the girls we would meet and how we would behave and laughing merrily along.

Suddenly, a large man with a red hat burst out from a nearby thicket holding a riffle and pointing it at us. "Get the hell out of my land you goddamn foreign bastards, or I'll blow your brains out," he shouted.

He was trembling with anger without any cause from us. We were stunned. No one moved. We just stared at the man. We had no thoughts, no words, no motion left in us. His howling anger wiped out all the life we had.

"Get!" the man shouted waving his riffle from us toward the exit of the clearing.

We looked at each other and, without words, agreed that there was no way to reason with that man. We picked up our thermos with coffee and a paper bag with a couple of sandwiches we had planned to enjoy eating in the woods and beat it out of there. We had seen the ugly face of America and wanted no part of it. We got in the car and sped away.

I think that Tony was as shaken by the encounter with the bigot as the rest of us but didn't want to show it. His attention wasn't on the driving. We hadn't gone more than ten miles when he cut the wheel to the left to avoid a pothole, overcorrected, veered to the right and the car skidded past the soft shoulder and came to rest on a muddy ditch just below the shoulder. He tried to rock the car, but only managed to get it deeper in the black muck. We got out and tried to push while he revved up the engine, but we only managed to get mud all over us.

"Bad luck," mumbled Dimitri.

"Sorry, guys," Tony said in contrition, "I was trying to avoid a pothole. Stupid maneuver!"

"We have to get to some gas station and get help," I said looking around at the interminable, deserted highway.

"If they don't chase us away with bazookas . . ." Miltos mumbled to himself.

A truck was passing by at that moment and it slowed down. The truck stopped, and we all held our breaths. The driver got out and sauntered to the edge of the shoulder as if he wanted to get a better look at the car. "She's pretty deep in the mud, isn't she," he said.

"We didn't realize the shoulder was so soft."

"It's been raining for days on and off," the man said as if he wanted to exonerate our driver from all guilt. "I'm gone to have to get a chain to pull you out," the man said, looking at each one of us in succession. "I'll be back before you know it. We'll pull her out of that mess." And he got back in his truck and was gone.

We looked at each other asking each other without words what to make of this. Was he coming back? Would he come back with help, or with hatred?

Dimitri was the first to venture an opinion. "He seems like a do-gooder," he said without much conviction.

"This is America, guys," Miltos weighed in. "He'll come back alright and will pull us out, and charge us an arm and a leg; we are in need and he provides a service without competition." He paused. "Capitalism in its ugliest form," he delivered his prognostication with aplomb.

"I don't think he's coming back," I said, feeling the gloom of abandonment. Back then, I used to start with gloom rather than wait for a lousy outcome to hit me. I could have saved myself a lot of premature sadness had I been able to reason better.

We waited for the truck with anticipation. We gathered our money and decided that we could pay him or someone else $50 with enough left over for gas to get back. Fifteen minutes later, we saw the truck coming toward us. Our spirits lifted. I was very happy to have been wrong, once again. The driver was alone. He dragged a chain out of his truck with some help from Tony and Dimitri and hooked it to our car. He made sure the chain was tight and got back in his truck and slowly started inching forward with our mud-mired Ford behind. The chain held. We watched the car creep up the side of the shoulder like a reluctant beast yoked to the chain and dragged to safety. We held our breaths as the driver did his job with expertise. It seemed that he had done this a thousand times before. The car was back on the road, dripping muck, but otherwise intact. Not a bad way to drum up some business, I thought.

The man got out and we helped him pull the chain and store it in his truck. We thanked him for rescuing us.

Tony approached him. "What do we owe you, Sir, for your work?" he asked with as humble a tone of voice as anyone could have produced. And, he meant it.

"Oh, nothing," the man said. "I just wanted to help you out."

Miltos stepped forward, closer to the man. "We appreciate your help, but we would like to pay you for your labor," he said with a businesslike efficiency of a man who wants to pay his bill as a matter of pride.

The man glanced at him. "If I was stuck in your neighborhood, wouldn't you give me hand?" he asked.

Miltos stepped back. "We really want to thank you, sir," Tony repeated.

"It's OK, boys. Like to help strangers in trouble." He climbed up to his truck and before shutting the door, he said, "Where do you boys come from, anyway."

"Greece," we said with one voice. "We're going to the Festival, in Augusta."

He was troubled. "Sorry, boys, but they called it off yesterday," he said, his face showing sadness. "The field was all mud." He shut his door and lowered the window. "Greece is far away," he said as if talking to himself. Then he smiled. You guys are young and we want you to have fun, anyway. Augusta is a nice town. Go to "Lorna's Bar and Grill" and have some fun there. She's also got the best hamburgers in town." He made a U-turn and stepped on the gas. His arm was out of the window, waiving at us.

"What a guy!" I said with admiration.

"Weird!" said Miltos.

We started arguing as we did on anything that had room for alternative explanations. In the end we came to the consensus that we had seen two sides of the American psyche, and the more I have thought about the man with the gun and the man with the heart of gold the more I that consensus made sense. That's America, the best and the worst there is. America is the world, after all, how could it be anything other than that? But, America, sometimes, lifts itself above the normal state of existence and surprises the world. When that happens, it is a moment of wonder and a great privilege to be a U.S. citizen. The rest of the time, it makes no different which flag you salute.

We never got to the Festival, but we did visit Augusta briefly. It was a nice city with welcoming people, but we were tired and couldn't afford to stay in a motel. We had a good dinner at "Lorna's" and headed back to our base. We had begun working on the puzzle everyone works on sooner or later after living in America for a while. What is America like? Ask me on a good day, and I'd love to tell you.

58 • The End of the Beginning

I finished my essay on King Lear, managed to get enough down on the exam papers on the pre- and post-Socratic, Greek philosophers, did just fine in the calculus, physics and chemistry exams and did what I had to do in projective geometry. When the first semester grades came in the mail, I found out that I had made the Dean's list. I couldn't believe my eyes. I was standing up and was still in the game and in style. What a relief! I concluded that my rate of learning the language and my ability to adapt had helped me achieve my goal. "Born in the clinic of Dr. Mayakos," I chuckled to myself, thinking of the boost in self-confidence I used to get from that fact in my early years. Then I found out that Howard had blasted past the Dean's List to the High Dean's List and my faith in what I had concluded was reinforced. I was smart enough to compete here, but I should never brag too much about my smarts. Some people just got it without having to try very hard. It was awesome, God bless them. Jerry was no slouch either. He was in the High Dean's List and got a PhD in Food Technology some years later. He joined the Agriculture Department of the U.S. Government and played a key role in the development of the process for making instant mashed potatoes. It never occurred to me, until many years later, to ask whether all the people with the monster IQs did great things in life, or not, but I believe that most of them did. There are many good performers and some goof offs even, who do many good, even great things, as well. What matters is doing your best, no matter how inadequate that is for some fields of competition. I was satisfied that I did.

The second semester was even more intense than the first, but it seemed to go by faster. I knew better what to expect and had developed ways to cope with the problems that came up. I was weary of living a hand to mouth existence, borrowing from my friends regularly and have to pay it back from my monthly stipend, only to run out of money again and have to borrow from someone else. I started looking for manual work that paid well, even if it was far out of Boston. The final battle of the first year exams at MIT was fought, and the war ended. All sides won something. I got out of it with all my courses completed and my body parts intact, and MIT protected the integrity of its grading-for-knowledge system. There were casualties, like the ketchup-fortune heir from the dorm along with roughly one hundred out of the nine hundred of us, who didn't make it. Doug couldn't stop drinking and left quietly before the finals. I never found out what happened to him. I didn't make the Dean's list the second semester, but I passed all courses with respectable grades.

My English was much better now, but my grades were lower because I didn't spend as much time studying as I had done before. I could understand most of what I heard, and I was able to say most of what I needed to say. I would always ask for the meaning of a word I didn't know, not caring about showing my ignorance. I would also ask others for help with the correct pronunciation of some words, and learned to live with my accent. I have always wished that I could get rid of it, so I could pass as an American born in America and blend with the common man and relate to others without a lingering question of my trustworthiness some people, especially people in the hinterlands with little contact with foreigners, seem to hold onto. I began to read more and fell in love with the English language because it took on words from every language its immigrants spoke and made them its own without any apologies or prejudices.

Our little Greek colony, enhanced by nationals from other parts of the world, was always doing something that was fun and took time to do. We took long rides in all the little towns around Boston and visited Cape Cod, where Tony and I got stranded on the rocks far from the shore at high tide and had to scramble to get back. The workload kept increasing and I just couldn't focus on it and my job at the Civil Engineering Lab and the fun and games of my gang of friends. I dropped the job and started pinching pennies again.

As soon as the exams ended the Greeks with the bank accounts left town for their summer homes on the Aegean islands and trips to Paris or Rome, or safaris in Africa. Dimitri said he was going to spend some time at his father's factory learning the business, but he also planned to visit his aunt in Switzerland. Zaharias and George and Paul Anik were going to New York and to points around the globe after that. Tony was going to tough it out in Cambridge with a part time job. I envied the guys who were going to these magical places and would no doubt have a chance to get back home and see their families again. I couldn't afford to do that. I didn't manage to get back home until twelve long, interminable years had gone by. The link with my birthplace was broken and would never be fixed again. I became a stranger to my home because that was the only way I could survive. And every summer I saw all the rich foreign students return home, I would experience the longing for my people. I learned to cut off this feeling of wanting to return before it had a chance to grow and choke me.

I was ready to leave Boston with a bus ticket and five dollars in my pocket, borrowed from Tony. There was a distant great uncle of my mother in the Chicago area, and I was planning to go there and ask for his help in getting a job. I wanted to earn enough money, not only to survive for the summer without remittances from Greece, but also to have some left over to supplement my expenses when I got back to school in the fall. Tony asked me what I would do if I couldn't find a job. By that time I had learned enough American expressions and was itching to use them. "Punt!" I said and watched Tony scratch his chin pensively, not about the meaning of the expression, but rather about my uncertain prospects.

But, the truth is that my worries were dwarfed by the excitement I felt, striking out into the unknown by myself. I was broke and alone in a strange land, but I was healthy, street smart, highly motivated with a "can-do" attitude that wouldn't quit; I had principles tested by experience and faith in a God who cares. I knew that I was good at sorting the wheat from the chaff when sorting out alternatives to problems, and I could make decisions that produced good outcomes. I was ready and willing to face the challenges that no doubt would come. I was headed for the steel mills of East Chicago. I should have been more worried than I was.

59 • Steel Town Blues and Highs

The way to love anything is to realize that it may be lost.

Gilbert K. Chesterton

I'm done with Boston for now. Turn the page and follow me through the hell of days in the highways and the tunnels dug into the night by bus and car lights. I'm headed for the steel mills of Gary and East Chicago, armpits of America's labor body. People told me that these places need laborers and pay good wages. They pay double for overtime, and I'm ready to go after any job like a bulldog goes after meat.

Night creeps in. The bus plows on the highway with a relentless drone. "Clearfield! Half hour stop," the bus driver announces and pulls the handbrake in front of *The Crystal Clear Cafe*. Bodies rise from the shadows around me. The stench from the men's room sneaks outside and assaults us. We wait for our turn taking shallow breaths. I think of Howard expounding glibly that a list of mankind's great inventions will certainly include indoor plumbing. We next take to the counters in the diner and wait for the waitress or the short order cook to get to us. One hamburger and a cup of coffee at the Clearfield Café will have to last for the rest of the day. I'm left with three dollars in my pocket.

"You going far?" a man on the stool next to me asks.

"East Chicago," I say.

"Got a job, yet?"

"No. I will get one, in first order."

"Don't count your eggs before they hatch."

It was too early in the morning for surprises. How many of these damn expressions does the English language have, anyway? Probably, as many as the Greek language, I thought. "I will find for certainly in the steel mills something, restaurants, construction also."

"Good luck," he sneers and leaves.

I should have saved a few dollars to see me through this transition period. "Save." I remember telling my father how I would save some money, so I wouldn't need help for the summers. He thought he would be comforted by that "Save." The people crawl back into their shadows and the bus rolls again. No one has taken a seat near me. The ride lasts forever. The steady hum of engine and rubber on the road isolates and lulls the mind into reveries. I'm a great Greek poet composing the *Ode to Clearfield*, my *magnum opus*, while sunbathing in Tahiti with my bikini-clad girlfriend frolicking in the sand. I'm looking for an answer to what makes millions of workers go to work every day without rebelling against the lousy lot life and circumstances dealt them. Are there any bus drivers whose childhood dream was to drive a bus when they grow up? Society entrusts them with dozens of human lives, but pays them very little, compared to used car salesmen or bureaucrats wielding rubber stamps. Bus drivers are not looking for adventure; they are not doing their job as a way to a life of learning; and they don't get their jollies confined for hours on sweaty driver seats. What do they know that I don't? I make up answers, but I cannot fit the pieces of the puzzle together. In the humanities classes we talked a lot about Truth and Beauty and the Virtues of Aristotle. Now, Truth and Beauty have become gargoyles that contemplate the irrational, the random and the bizarre.

Night has settled down. Some passengers get off and new ones come aboard. A woman with a baby takes the seat in front of me. The baby cries, and she offers her breast to it. The baby is hungry because I can hear its lusty sucking, cooing noises over the steady hum of the bus. I think again about the knowledge I need to draw from this expedition to the sweat-lands of America. The mother and her baby are in the mix of answers, or questions, I am too drowsy and cramped to think clearly about anything. How long before we get to the Promised Land? Night creeps everywhere now. I'm hungry, but I still have three dollars in my pocket.

The air rushes in from the open window. Through holes of dreams I see the outskirts of hopelessness. It is only a summer. Fires burn unchecked from smokestacks like tongues of mythical beasts struggling to articulate a message. Uncle Orestes lived in the moment when he was young, but ended up living in the past when he was old. He thought Africa had the answers, but all he found there were more questions. How much of what is can be allotted to futility? Smog and fog blur the outlines of factories that crouch in the dark. All lights are yellow, like halos of unseen saints. The Steel Town lies comatose on the shore of

Lake Michigan. The smell of industry, a blend of fumes from oil on steel and the debris of coal and lime and sulfur engulf me. I take it all in as if it could have a hidden meaning for me. Those who haven't shed sweat and felt pain from work can afford a romantic view of labor. I was looking out of the window, absorbing what I thought was a town made of nightmares. The deceptive tranquility, the silence of desolation, clouds of steam glowing red near the ground, cranes perched above mountains of coal and limestone, the entire complex machinery and structures of might and misery bundled tight on this town overwhelmed me.

"East Chicago! East Chicago!" the bus driver called out and stopped at the Greyhound depot, next to a *Speedy Laundromat* and the *Fill It Gas* Station. Across the street there was a hamburger joint and a red neon sign with *Liquors* writ large next to a yellow sign of a pedestal glass. I knew that this city had a lot to teach me, but I didn't know what, yet.

I got off the bus and walked toward the blue neon lights of *Summit* and *Rooms for Rent*. The streets were littered with crumpled paper cups, newspapers, cigarette butts, spilled liquids and rubbish that moved at every puff of breeze. I passed a doorway with a small sign that read *Bingo*. The lights were turned off and I had no idea what bingo was.

I signed for a room and the clerk said, "Three Dollars." I picked up a key with a wooden tag. "Four sixteen," he said and pointed to a corridor. The chairs the bedspread the walls, everything in the room had large, reddish flowers and greenish leaves on it. A mad decorator with intent to obliterate beauty once and for all had been let loose in that room. I took off my pants, drew back the sheets and left the world.

Early next day, I appeared at the house of my mother's distant uncle and was welcomed into their home. Uncle Vagelis Lascos was a big man, loud and volatile, with the temperament of most of the Lascos people in the family. He was a hard working owner of a diner who had immigrated to America in the early part of the century to work and raise a family. He had a very quiet and welcoming wife and two daughters, a little older than me, who were curious and kept probing me with questions about everything Greek and everything related to college life. They offered me a room at their home until I was settled, and my uncle told me where to go and get a job at Inland Steel, the biggest employer in the East Chicago area.

Years later, after I had worked in the steel mills of East Chicago for three summers, my view of working people changed from politely ignoring their existence to embracing them warmly. I saw why people who never got much education and didn't pursue intellectual work are often, rightly called "the salt of the earth," and why so much of what makes life worthwhile comes through the work, the courage and the generosity of blue collar workers. I experienced this reordering of my values when I started laughing at the jokes they told to pass the time, the crude ways they invented to make sense out of the grind of work and the meaningless foul words that spiced their speech. It took me a couple of weeks after I got back to school to clean up my language from the four letter words I used all summer long at the steel mills. These words were spoken at the mills among people bound together by trust, not hatred. The "fuck" of the steel mills had none of the poison it carries in other venues. Even with the hook of anger, four letter words among workers who labor for their living never cut to the bone.

Though a greenhorn, I started offering suggestions on work improvements and found out that my coworkers listened and used some of the solutions I came up with. Of course they would tease me and call me smartass and even be defensive sometimes, but they were not too proud to follow some of my suggestions. Some of them were too scared to do anything other than what the foreman told them to do and paid no attention to me; but sometimes I did get through.

I came to admire Jake, the steel worker with the eighth grade education, who headed the crew of one of the pickling lines for cold rolled steel, where I worked that first summer, after my freshman year. He could do the job with the most motivated crew in the mill, faster than any other crew, and with the least scrap waste. When Jake sat at the operator's seat, high above the 300-foot long Mesta Machine and the rest of us were at our posts that monster of a machine obeyed like a hundred yoked oxen. Jake worked the controls with levers and buttons of many shapes and colors, and we fed hot steel coils through the behemoth's mouth, to press them down with its massive steel rollers into thinner gauge and harden them and drive them screeching and steaming into the belly of the beast, which was a two hundred-and-fifty-foot long tank like a sewer tunnel, only filled with acid to temper the steel and coat it and make it into the sheet metal needed for making cars, refrigerators and every other little monster that our society needs.

Jake had been a steel worker for thirty-eight years and had a thriving family life. He was not an average man. He was a member of the elite, as far as I was concerned. He had the respect of his peers and deserved it; the bosses consulted him every time they had a difficult order to deliver to a customer, or when they wanted to make a change in the process and the equipment. He was a stickler for quality work, but he was also flexible when it came to helping any one of us do the work our way.

At first I was the only laborer pulling scrap, but halfway through the summer, they hired another man to work with me and take over after I left for school. Calvin told me he was thrilled to get his job and planned to make a career out of the mill, advancing to better and better positions and making more and more money as the years went by. He wanted to have a family and he thought he could afford it after a few years in the mill. He was black and, at first, cautious with a foreigner like me. Getting to know Calvin made me think that my foreign accent and his skin color were somehow equivalent. Calvin was strong and smart, but he couldn't afford to take chances when it came to following the bosses' directions. He liked his job and didn't want some crazy foreigner messing it up. He was a little older than me and from another world, but talking about our different experiences we found that we had a lot in common and got along very well.

When Calvin showed up we took turns doing our job at the pickling line. Several workers were busy lining up coils for the machine, checking the orders to set the parameters, get the coil into the feeder rollers, check the oil bearings, the strength of the acid after a few runs and so on. Calvin and I removed the scrap from the beginnings and the ends of the steel coils after a huge blade cut them off. Then the "joiner" would join the pieces together and, if the joint was good, he would signal Jake to start the coil rolling. The newly spliced coil would plunge into the acid tank and travel at thirty miles an hour with deafening noise. If the joint was bad, Jake would curse the coil and the "joiner" and everybody else responsible until his fury was exhausted and he was ready to begin the grind again. There would be no letup until the joint was "good" and the coil rolling.

It normally took three minutes working and three minutes watching the other guy work. I thought that it was a wasteful way of doing the job, so I started reading *The Cane Mutiny*, three minutes at the time. Calvin watched me horrified. He was afraid of what the bosses would say if I was caught reading a book. Jake didn't mind as long as the work was done right and, I thought, if Jake is happy no boss would care either. Then, Calvin and I had the night shift, and the boss traffic was very quiet, and it seemed to me that this routine of three minutes on and three minutes off was too wasteful to continue it. Calvin had nothing to do for his three minutes off. So, I proposed that he work for four hours straight, while I found a spot behind some stacked machinery parts to read or sleep and then we switch. Calvin freaked out at this. He wanted no part of such radical departure from the routine. But, the inefficiency was gnawing at me, and I went on reasoning with him quietly, until he agreed to try it. He could work his four hours and then stand nearby and watch me, if he didn't want to go somewhere and relax. To put his mind at rest, I told him that if any question came up while he was on the job, he could say truthfully that it was my idea and I convinced him to go along. So, Calvin and I, without any official sanction, changed the workflow and no one was ever troubled by it. Calvin couldn't believe that he was free to sleep for four hours while he was getting paid. But the joints had to be "good," which meant that all of us had to do our job very well.

But, it wasn't always so quiet and peaceful. When the machine went down and the whole crew was struggling to check and fix the malfunction of the Mesta Monster, Calvin and I were, literally, slaving in the pits. On one of these midnight breakdowns, I was told to go down a pit, under the steel drum rollers, to find out if there were any fluids leaking from the countless hydraulic lines crowding the space. The pit was like a tomb, dripping with moisture and the floor was wet with pools of dark oil mixed with water. The smell of grease was overwhelming and I thought I would choke. A rat was caught in my flashlight beam and scampered, sloshing on the muddy floor past my boots as I advanced. I was repulsed by the disorder of tubes and hoses and debris. I heard no telltale dripping and saw no ripples on the pool of oil on the floor, so I concluded that there was no leak and got out.

When the machine went down, Jake and the rest of the crew lost money, because they made more, the more they produced. Calvin and I were straight wage laborers, so we didn't lose anything other than some time for sleep or reading. Jake would come down from his perch and check the Monster's critical parts himself, giving directions or making suggestions to members of his crew. He was never rattled, though he was angry at the cosmic forces of mayhem and mischief that cause such problems. The guys in the crew followed his lead and worked hard to fix the problem, helped by the crew of mechanics that rushed to the trouble spot and stayed on it until the job was done.

Sometimes I would be taken off the line and assigned for a few days at some other job. Once, I was in a labor gang sweeping the floor of a warehouse. I was given an area by the pusher and told to work as fast as I could and clean it. When I got done, I sat down admiring the sparkling clean floor and reading a piece of a newspaper I picked off the floor. Sometime later, the pusher showed up and came straight at me huffing and puffing.

"What the hell you trying to do to me, boy? You want to get me fired?" he shouted at me.

"What did I do bad?" I protested.

"You think we pay people to read newspapers here?"

"You told me to clean floor good, and I did such. Look! Clean!" I defended myself.

"You get back there and work that broom nonstop or you go home and play with yourself, boy. Hear?" Then, by way of an explanation, he added, "If one of the bosses sees you reading rather than working your butt off, he'll have my ass. Get it?"

"Yessir!" I said without hesitation.

And I went back to work, moving that broom as if my life depended on its perpetual motion. When the floor was sparkling clean and all the dirt dumped in the garbage can, I would tilt the can down and empty whatever I had put in there, and spread it all around, so I could keep working hard, cleaning the newly dirtied floor. I just couldn't stand working leisurely.

"Good work, boy," the pusher congratulated me when he stopped by next time. "You're sure a good learner."

I just smiled and went on sweeping.

60 • But for Luck or Providence

When I wasn't working I would be at my uncle's home watching wrestling on TV, or hanging out with some Greeks I had met at work or at my uncle's diner. On a couple of occasions I went to the nightclubs of Chicago and Cicero with these friends and caught a glimpse of the seedy side of America. One evening that first summer I was there, I remember that there was a Greek wedding and I was encouraged by my cousins to go and have some fun. I had my car by that time and I drove it to the parking lot of the reception hall. There was a lot of food and plenty of drinking. I had a glass of wine and a full plate of roast lamb and decided to go. There were some young people staggering out of the hall drunk and I was repulsed. I got back to my car in the parking lot and backed up to maneuver out of my stall. Unfortunately, I hooked the front bumper of the car behind me. I was about to come out and check the damage when a guy opened the passenger door of my car.

"Don't try to get away, friend," he shouted at me holding the door open. "You're stuck, and I got you."

An ugly, defiant rush of energy overwhelmed my thinking. Some other entity got control of my being and was executing my movements. Instead of getting out and checking, or negotiating, or arguing or fighting with that obnoxious lout, I shifted the car into gear and started rocking the car to unhook my bumper from his and get out of there.

"You cannot get away, buddy!" the man insisted.

And I saw myself banging his car back and dragging it forward with force, while he still held on to the door of my car risking a blow to his body.

On the third or fourth try, I disengaged my car from his and sped at screeching speed through the parking lot out into the street and then the highway. I was racing at high speed and didn't hear the police sirens behind me. I wanted no part of an encounter because I had only a permit and no insurance yet. The sirens got louder and I became afraid. I stopped the car when I caught the flashing lights at the rear view mirror. I must have been in a chase without knowing it, because the cops approached my car with guns drawn and when I got out they manhandled me and loaded me in a paddy wagon and took me to the police station.

It was quiet now. I felt calm and safe there. They asked me to give them my belt and whatever was in my clothes and put me in a jail cell. I was the only prisoner there. When I realized that I was arrested, that I was in jail, I became anxious and started thinking very fast. I asked why they had brought me to the police station and was told that my offense was "reckless driving," which I took to mean driving without acknowledging the presence of the police. They asked me if I wanted to call anyone and I gave them my uncle's name. That was a very smart move, because everyone there knew my uncle's restaurant and some of them dropped by for a coffee and donuts or a "small steak" now and them. The policeman behind the desk smiled when he found out that I was a nephew of Vangelis Lascos and a foreign student in Cambridge, working at Inland steel for the summer. I imagined being taken to court and accused of a crime and found to be guilty and rotting in jail before being deported. How much time would I have to spend in jail? I asked when they would take me to court, but the policeman said that he wasn't sure how long it would take. I felt that because of that one streak of madness that had taken over my mind, I had flushed my education, probably my career and my life in America down the drain. The hours went by as I waited for a word from someone who could tell me what would happen to me. I was numb and dozed off on the only chair in the cell. I heard the heavy footsteps of the policeman from the desk approaching.

"It's all over now," he said in a pleasant tone of voice. "You can go home."

I thought he was part of my nightmare. A joker sent to torment me. I looked at him in disbelief. He opened the door and we walked back to his desk where he returned my stuff to me. "Did you contact my uncle, Mr. Lascos?" I asked. It was like asking a magician how he performed his trick.

"Oh, we don't want to put our college boys in jail, now; do we?" he said and looked at me with a relaxed smile as if he was welcoming his wayward son back home.

"Thank you," I said and meant it more than at any other time I had uttered these words to another human being.

I thanked my uncle for straightening things out with the police and assured him that I would never embarrass him again.

The second summer I was in the steel mills, I was asked if I wanted to stay at my uncle's house again and save some money for school. I didn't feel all that comfortable without much privacy there and I didn't want to be a burden on them again, but I needed to save as much money as I could, so I accepted the invitation.

I had been a guest for about a month and I felt that I should do something to help and express my gratitude. My uncle's diner attracted a lot of working class people from the mills and the surrounding businesses and he was very busy on weekday evenings. I would stop there sometimes for a good steak after work and I knew he was shorthanded. I thought that I could give him a hand now and then.

One afternoon after I had just finished my day shift, I stopped by the diner and offered to help him that evening.

He was a little taken aback, but he welcomed the offer. "Sure," he said, "You can start right now. I show you what you do." He reached under the counter and gave me an apron to wear. My uncle was a big man with a big belly and the apron looked a little too big for me, but I took it and wrapped it around my body like a robe. I felt like a butcher about to enter the some bizarre rink. I started to pick up some empty dishes that lay on the counter, but my uncle stopped me.

"You've got to put on the hat!" he said, as if that was something anyone should have known.

I laid down the dishes and stared at him as he approached me holding a huge, white, chef's hat in his beefy hands.

"I don't need that," I said, shocked by the image of a short little guy my size, weighted down by the massive topper.

My uncle smiled. "You can't work without the hat," he said, as if he only wanted to let me into the secrets of a cherished profession. And he took a step closer and offered me the hat like it was a crown on a silk pillow.

I looked at that monstrous hat and saw an unbending will reflected in his eyes, the Lascos' stubborn determination and I backed off. "I want to help, but I cannot wear that hat," I protested. I just didn't want to obey. "Let me put on some other hat," I tried to negotiate.

My uncle turned his back to me and moved away with the hat, shaking his head.

"I'm sorry," I said, and got out of the store.

Later that evening I told my aunt and my cousins that I would be moving out in a day or two, at most. I don't remember if my aunt and my cousins tried to get me to change my decision. They probably did, but I couldn't do that, then. I cannot remember talking to my uncle, or even if I tried to talk to him. I know that I thought of the many times my uncle had helped me, but I couldn't abandon the stand I had taken. I don't know what deep, lurking emotions blocked my rationality again and produced such an outlandish decision at that time, but they did. I knew I didn't like the laughable figure I would cut and told myself that this was the reason.

Later, much later, I realized that fear, not just vanity nailed me to such obstinacy. I was afraid that if I obeyed my uncle's demand, I would be subservient to him. I felt that I would never be myself again. I was the little boy who disobeyed his father's direction to hold on to his hand in crossing streets in downtown Athens and ran through deadly speeding cars and streetcars getting nearly killed. I was the grade school student who accepted daily punishment, rather than obey the teacher's commands. I was the worker who was told to shave when I showed up for work at the snack bar of the graduate house at MIT and refused to obey. I needed the money from that job, but I told the short order cook he could shove it and walked out. And I was the driver, who lost his head and took off from the scene of an accident in a parking lot while carrying no insurance, and was caught by the police and almost lost his right to get an education and have a decent place in society. After I left my uncle's home, I was depressed. I didn't like the way I had behaved toward him. I owed him a lot and now there was no way to pay back my debt to him. Later, much later, after many more such irrational outbursts of pointless rebellion, I learned to control myself and hold on to my humanity. The gratification that comes with rebellion can feed the monster within and I just couldn't afford it.

The next day, I found an efficiency apartment next to a couple of Puerto Rican workers at the steel mill, who became my friends for better and worse.

As I said, I had a car, but I had not been able to get a license and registration yet. I needed both, so I could drive back to Boston. One of the Puerto Ricans said that he had some old registration plates and we could put them on and use the car, rather than let it go to waste. I was uneasy about doing that, but I needed the experience, if I was to pass the driving test and I wasn't sure that it would be a serious offense if, by chance, the discrepancy of invalid plates was discovered. And so, one of these amigos mounted the plates and he and I drove the car around town. I was taking a course in Economics at Indiana University that summer and I was going to class one evening when I ran a stoplight. I got flustered and tried to get away from that corner, so I paid no attention to any other stoplights that I might have passed. I heard a police siren, but I couldn't see a police car, so I figured it might be wise to get away from that spot and escape any police encounter that was taking care of someone else's problems. Then I saw the flashing red light of the cruiser behind me and knew that I was the culprit the cop was after.

The state trooper approached me and asked me where I was going. "I'm taking a class in Economics at the University extension."

"Do you know that you ran three red lights?"

I did and I didn't, so I said, "Three?"

"You most certainly did. And, you were speeding – twenty miles over the speed limit. Did you know that?"

I said nothing. I prayed real hard that he would not ask me for the registration, which would compound my crime. And, since I had only a permit and no license to drive, I prayed for protection against that evil, as well. There would be no uncle to lean upon this time, but there would be jail time. My mind was racing to construct a story to get myself out of the mess I was in. He thinks I'm guilty of all these driving violations, but oh boy, is he going to be surprised when he finds out that I have no license and no valid plates. Should I pretend that I am a stupid foreigner who didn't know any better? I didn't think it would stick; and it just wasn't right.

"How would you like to appear in court on Monday morning?" he asked in a conversational tone.

"I would prefer no," I said in all honesty and in total confusion.

"You would not prefer!" he repeated mockingly. "How much money have you got with you?" he asked, staring at me intensely.

I took my wallet out of my back pocket and pulled out my cash. "Two dollars, Sir," I said, and showed him the two bills and my wallet, embarrassed at my lack of resources. I prayed that he would not take my wallet and see the yellow permit and discover what else I was lacking.

He took the two dollars and looked at me with the sympathy of an older, wiser man. "Buddy, you are in ba-a-a-ad shape!" he said and pocketed the money.

"I am sorry," I said sheepishly.

"OK. You can go, now. But drive carefully, will you?"

"Thank you," I said, and looking up at the clear bright sky, I added, "Lord!"

I drove off slowly and prayed for wisdom. It seemed hard to win doing either the right or the wrong thing. It was a commentary of the human condition. I was an engineer and had no license to rampant philosophizing, but philosophizing was what I loved to do when I was away from the rolling mill and roamed free in my dreamscapes.

61 • Slim Takes the Stage

"I put on my hat, change into my safety shoes, put on my safety glasses, go to the bonderizer. It's the thing I work on. They take the metal, they wash it, they dip it in a paint solution and we take it off. Put it on, take it off, put it on, take it off, put it on, take it off . . .I work fro seven to three thirty. My arms are tired at three o'clock. I hope to God I never get broke in, because I always want my arms to be tired at seven thirty and three o'clock. "Cause that's when I know that there's a beginning and there's an end. That I'm not brainwashed. In between, I don't even try to think."

Studs Terkel, in *Working*, quoting Mike Lefevre, Steelworker

The stories above are just a few examples demonstrating how much I learned about myself living in a steel mill town. Every situation I found myself in seemed to contain some insight into the kind of person I was. In later years I came to think of the steel mills as "the other university" I attended. I could tell many more stories that have helped me guide my life, but I have already done that in other books. Yet, I cannot resist mentioning Slim, the master electrician who worked in the electricians' crew that I joined one of the summers I worked in the mills.

The first day I got to the electricians' crew site that summer, the foreman tested me for my ability to work up high. He asked me to climb up a hundred foot spiral steel staircase that stood far apart from the steel frame of a big tower. When I stopped about fifty feet up and clutched the center pole of the staircase and wouldn't let go, the foreman called out "Yooooh!" and ordered me to get down and pronounced me "the ground man" of the crew.

I had seen Slim moving about in the few days I had been with the electricians, but I hadn't seen him do any work. While most of us worked hard at our jobs, Slim was chitchatting with other workers and the various bosses checking on our progress and laughing at his own jokes. When he was alone, he read the paper behind the steel lockers arrayed at one side of the huge warehouse we were wiring. I didn't think much of him, his goofing around or his goldbricking. Yet, no one seemed to mind it. My fellow workers were very tolerant of Slim, even respectful, I thought.

"Why isn't Slim pulling his weight around here?" I asked one day, puzzled by what I thought was a double standard.

My comrades laughed. "Oh, Slim is a hard worker, alright, but you have to catch him doing it," one of them said cryptically. They know he is lazy and there is nothing they can do because of some stupid seniority rule or some other protectionist union regulation, I thought.

I was a greenhorn and had no business giving anyone the third degree, so I shut up and waited to catch Slim in the act of actually working.

One day they told us that we had to install a heavy cable between two towers about two hundred feet apart. The towers were connected with two parallel angle steel bars, braced for strength diagonally with flat steel bars, every three or four feet. This flimsy looking, steel bridge was a hundred feet up in the air. The cable would have to be hoisted up there and fed through rings on the steel bars to stay down. It was then that I saw Slim don his gear, strap one end of the cable from his belt and start climbing up the tiny ladder of one tower. Everyone else was on the ground looking up at him, as he stood erect up high with clouds and blue sky for background. He was the ancient philosopher's wingless creature only now he had a long black tail coming out of him. He started taking steps one at a time on the angle bars. The sight of a man working up high was both riveting and horrifying. I saw Slim bend down and feed the cable through the rings. He made his way carefully, methodically, from one end of the aerial gangway toward the other. We could see one-third of his boot's black sole from the ground, because the steel angle bar wasn't wide enough to cover the width of his boot. Slim was like an apparition sliding along the two thin lines of solid matter and the sky. I would have not been able to do what he was doing, if my life depended on it. There wouldn't be any cables strung up anywhere. Was my ability to solve second order differential equations more life enhancing than Slim's ability to work up high?

"Some goof off, eh?" one of the electricians whispered in my ear, as I was looking at the sky walker.

"Can you guys do that?" I asked.

"We might be out of work, if we didn't have Slim with us," another one said.

"We've had some guys who tried to bite more than they could chew and froze up on the rafters. Slim had to get up there and talk them down."

A few days later I approached Slim while he was reading the paper. I told him that I couldn't work up high and admired his ability to work so freely up there. He told me a couple of jokes and laughed his head off. I laughed out of respect for his fearlessness, but I wished he took me more seriously.

Then, I asked him if he ever thought of death when he was working up high on a job.

He turned a page of his paper and seemed interested in whatever was there.

I didn't think he planned to answer me. "See you around, Slim," I said and started to leave.

"Hey, ground man," he called after me, putting the paper down. "You don't think of death when you do what your gut tells you." He paused as if he was reluctant to go on. "You don't want to live some other guy's dream," he said seriously. Then he burst out into a hearty laugh and added, "or mess in his shit."

I made an effort to laugh, but I wasn't sure I should.

"Remember when you are a professor in some fancy college out East and kids want to know what's the purpose of life. Tell them to come here and we'll show them meaning up high in this lowdown world."

"It's more than I got working on the pickle line," I said and smiled at all that wisdom he was spouting.

And so, I learned about the "common folk" the only way that this knowledge can be extracted from the bedrock of life: by living in the real world and seeking answers that make sense or make you want what you know is your thing.

As I was leaving, I thought of my critical attitude on Slim's behavior and remembered that I was working only four hours a shift at the pickling line and never was critical of my own behavior. What a hypocrite I was! How could I be so damn blind? Besides being hypocritical, I was angry and ungrateful and selfish, a cheat, a rebel and a fool. I hated all the flaws I was finding in myself, and how they kept recurring. Why couldn't I get rid of them once and for all? It took time to learn that Sin, unlike Teflon, sticks.

62 • Struggling Against Chaos

Chaos is a name for any order that produces confusion in our minds.

George Santayana

The steel mills of East Chicago had been good for me, so two Greek friends I had met on my junior year, Ted and Leo decided to come along and find jobs there when I went back for the third summer. I immediately went looking for work at the mill, got hired and was assigned to the electricians' crew, as I have already written. Ted and Leo wanted to explore the job market before committing to the mill and took their time in getting to the hiring office. Unfortunately, by then the mill was going through uncertain times and hiring was frozen. They continued looking, but they had trouble landing any kind of work. I had been working only for two or three weeks when the steel workers went on strike and everything came to a standstill. All three of us sat around the apartment we had rented and moped all day long.

I was passing the time at the Greek coffee shop when I met Nick, a rough looking Greek man in his thirties, who told me he had been a tailor in Greece and was looking for work as a painter around there. He was always looking furtively around him and appeared to be very anxious, especially around men in trench coats. It took me a couple of days to discover that he was a sailor, who skipped ship in Duluth and came by bus to the Chicago area looking for work. Nick spoke no English – nothing other than "Yes" and "No." He had only grade school education, but he was quite resourceful and had managed to survive well for several months. He was a great storyteller and had unfathomable optimism. He knew that I was out of a job and took it upon himself to find work for both of us.

"I have a job for us out of town," he told me one day at the coffee shop where he hang around playing a version of baccarat with Greek old timers and losing. "I told them I have a friend," he said, concentrating on his cards. One of the oldsters won the pot and Nick turned and focused on me. "Come with me and work on the toll road. The boss is a Greek and we'll paint guideposts and bridges all summer long," he said and slapped my arm to show he meant it.

I thought of Ted and Leo and told him I couldn't leave them behind.

"Tell them to come too," he urged with enthusiasm. "There's plenty of work for everybody, and we got a compatriot doing the hiring."

I told him I would let him know next day.

"I'm running out of money, so I'll be leaving day after tomorrow.

Ted and Leo thought I was nuts to trust the word of a fugitive Greek sailor and go looking for a pot of gold. They wanted to look some more around town before they could make a move. I bid them goodbye and headed with Nick to South Bend for work. We got hired by the Greek boss, found places to stay and started work the next day. I found myself in a crew, painting the guardrails on the sides of the Indiana Toll Road. After a few days, I was turned loose on painting the expansion joints on the pavement of highway bridges. That was a job for Sisyphus because I could never finish any of the jobs I started. I would paint and a car would pass over the steel joints and splash the paint away. I would go faster, hoping that I could get the job done fast and it would dry up in the hot sun, but, no matter how small the overpass was, a car come and go over my work and ruin it. I was frustrated and asked if they could stop traffic until the paint dried up, but the boss ridiculed my suggestion with a belly laugh. I reconciled myself to producing botched up products and waited for my check to come.

In the meantime, Ted and Leo showed up in town and started looking for work. The Greek boss we knew was no longer hiring and my friends weren't all that excited about painting toll road bridges and guard posts, anyway. They bumped into a congenial Greek restaurant owner and hang around his place every day looking for work in the want ads of the paper. I couldn't understand how they were able to sit and relax without pursuing the goal of finding work more actively.

Payday came and went, but I didn't get paid. I complained that I needed to get paid, but our boss was stalling. Nick understood my concern, but urged patience. Several days later the boss found me at the bar where we used to go after work and have a beer and handed me a check. I immediately examined it to find out how much my net was. When I read it I froze. "This isn't my check," I protested.

"It sure is!" the boss said, downing the whiskey of his boilermaker.

"It says 'Pay to Paul Plesh,'" I told him, getting angrier by the second.

"Just sign the damn thing and cash it," he said, as if I was fussing over nothing.

"I'm not doing any such thing," I said and shoved the check in front of his face. "I want the money I worked for. Right now," I said, standing up and ready to tangle with him. I had never been more convinced I was right than I was that time. I just wanted to be paid for my labor without becoming a forger.

He took the check and signed it himself with the name that was printed on the check. Then, he gave the check to the bartender and received the cash. "Here's your damn money," he said ticked off.

I took the money and walked out. I wanted to have nothing more to do with him after that. A couple of days later, Nick found out the reason for the skullduggery. He said that the Greek owners at the main office in New Jersey were worried that the company had too many Greeks and that might hamper its ability to get government contracts. To correct the situation they decided to diversify the workforce by giving American-sounding names to some of the Greek workers. "They are crooks," I said. Nick nodded agreement, but I knew that he would have agreed with anything I said to avoid a conflict.

A couple of days after we had that discussion, Nick told me that a government inspector had discovered that our boss was cheating on paint for the bridges: instead of painting the bridges three coats, the red oxidation protective coat on the steel, then the primer and finally the paint, he was trying to get by without the primer! Nick said that he saw our boss at the bar buying a bottle of seven star Metaxas cognac to pacify the inspector with that "gift." Another Greek worker told Nick that the inspector was offended by the "gift," and called the main office of the company in New Jersey to complain about the shoddy work and the bribe. Our boss was fired and had left town. We chuckled at that crook trying to mend his ways with a lousy bottle of Metaxas. Could he have been naïve enough to think that a government inspector would close his eyes to major theft for a cheap bribe like a bottle of cognac?

So the toll road job ended and I was unemployed again. The summer was halfway gone and I was still low on funds for the school year. I had to find another job, or I wouldn't be able to attend school. And, if I wasn't a student, how could I get my Student Visa extended? I was afraid that I would be sent back home and my entire plan for a good education and a professional career in America would come to sad end. Everyday, I would copy all possible job openings in the want ads of the paper and go looking for work in person. All employers wanted permanent workers, so I decided that I would say I wanted a permanent job since I wasn't sure I could save enough money to get back to school by September. I was turned down in every place I went because I wasn't skilled; because I couldn't get a clearance; because I had no previous work experience and because the job had already been filled. While Ted and Leo sat paralyzed at the Greek restaurant that had become their watering hole, I was out there banging my head stubbornly on the walls of drab personnel offices. I finally reached the end of the line when my list with ten jobs showed nine rejections. If I couldn't get hired, I would return to the Boston area and look for work there. I loaded all my possessions in my car and told the others that, if my last effort yielded nothing, I would head back to Boston to look for work among the Greeks or a part-time job at MIT. I offered to take them along, if they decided to return.

The tenth employer on my list was Dodge Manufacturing Corporation. I interviewed calmly sensing the inevitability of another rejection and giving all I had. The manager talking to me cut the interview short and gave me a job as a designer of fluid clutches. I could hardly believe it. It was an engineering job and they trusted me to perform it. I thanked the manager and told him I was ready to start next day. I went straight to the Greek restaurant and urged Ted and Leo to never stop looking. I got a room at an eighty-year-old lady's house in Mishawaka, IN, and worked very hard to prove to my supervisor that they hadn't made a mistake. I saw Nick a few times in South Bend where he had met some other Greeks and was hanging out at their homes. He was working as a painter, somewhere. He was very worried because Immigration had found some illegal Greeks working at a restaurant and grabbed them. He would freak out if any man glanced at him more than once and thought that not only Immigration but also FBI was after him. He suspected every stranger he saw, thinking that he might be a government agent of some kind, and like many people with little education, he thought that all people working for the government were not to be trusted. I found out from him that Ted and Leo had given up looking for work and left for Boston. Before we parted, I asked him what he was planning to do for a permanent job in his life. "Tailor," he said. I asked him if he had really been a tailor in Greece. "The best," he said. I was certain that he believed it absolutely, but I just couldn't and didn't know why.

My salary at Dodge was much higher than anything I had made before, and since I was saving every penny I could, I was able to get together a nice sum by the end of the summer. I decided that it was best to return to school and continue my studies at MIT. I told my boss exactly what my situation was and how I regretted that I had to break my promise to work there for the year because I couldn't afford to return to school. He told me that I was doing the right thing and shouldn't feel bad since I had done a great job for them. "If you want to check us out after you finish your degree, we'll be happy to consider you here," he said. I felt a great sense of accomplishment and relief. I thanked him and my colleagues for giving me a chance to be productive and bid them goodbye.

63 • Love and Laplace Transforms

Among the men and women, the multitude,
I perceive one picking me out by secret and divine signs . . .
Ah, lover and perfect equal!
I meant that you should discover me, so by my faint indirections;
And I, when I meet you, mean to discover you by the like in you.
Walt Whitman, "Among the Multitude," *Leaves of Grass*

Being deeply loved by someone gives you strength,
while loving someone deeply gives you courage.

Lao Tzu

A couple of months before I left for the steel mills in the chaotic summer of 1956 with the steelworkers' strike and the other difficulties I have been describing above, I was taking a class in advanced Calculus for Engineers. It was neither assigned nor needed for graduation, but it would help me to satisfy some of the course requirements for the Master's degree. I was planning to start and finish the Master's Degree program in one year because the Greek Navy had refused to extend my exemption for an advanced degree and every month I was late in starting my draft duties after obtaining the Bachelor's degree would add two months to my four years of service as a naval officer.

It was April and the snow was finally gone and green was showing up all around the campus. I was absorbing the new knowledge of unlocking the mysteries of nature using Laplace transforms, Bessel functions, Vector analysis and all the mathematical tools with utter delight, as if I were going through a protracted initiation to some secret society. Professor Levinson was sharp, a good teacher, and welcomed class participation, so I asked a lot of questions, trying to satisfy my curiosity and look smart, especially given the presence of a beautiful girl in class. There were very few female students at MIT back then, and most male students kept their distance from them, though I set no such artificial limits to my pursuit of girls.

I found this girl already sitting at the front of the class every time I got there. She seemed to mind her business to the exclusion of any other comings and goings. One day I got to the class feeling real good after working on the assigned problem we had and when professor Levinson outlined the answer, I raised my hand.

"I solved the problem another way," I said.

The girl turned around, and I caught a glimpse of her. In that brief moment that our eyes met I felt the desire to know her. Her solitary existence in that classroom gave the momentary turn of her head and her wondering look a special significance. She is curious about my accent, I thought, and went on with my alternate solution to the problem, hoping I was not only right but also profound. I have to meet her, I thought as the class ended. I approached as she was leaving the class.

"I noticed you taking a lot of notes," I said, having no idea what would come after that comment.

"It helps sometimes," she said without asking for explanations.

"What are you taking the course for?" I asked. I couldn't believe what I was saying; yet she wasn't taken aback. Her eyes seemed to welcome me.

" I happened to test out of differential equations."

This wasn't good news. I hadn't tested out from anything at MIT. I didn't even know that one could test out of anything. I didn't know what "test out" meant until she used the expression. I had taken that course and it wasn't easy. But, Calculus was a subject I understood well. I was sure I could hold my own, if this coed happened to be one of the much talked about, freakishly smart MIT coeds. But, how would I know? She didn't ask questions; she didn't make any comments; she never spoke to anyone, and I had never seen anything she wrote down. The only data I had was that momentary but meaningful look she cast my way. Most American male students at MIT were worried about the relational and social weirdness of the MIT coeds, but I had no concerns about that; I was only concerned with girls' looks and their intelligence. If a girl was beautiful and smart but not freakishly smart, I was in the game. There was no time to think about all the things running feverishly through my mind. Any moment now we would split up because she was headed for the main exit and I was going to the dreary mechanical engineering labs for testing bubble jet atomizers for spray cans.

"Could I borrow your notes," I heard myself say. She wasn't shocked; she wasn't even surprised. Our eyes met and I knew she wouldn't judge me. "I haven't taken many notes, and I saw you write a lot in class," I explained, defending my stupid request, even though there was no attack, not even a question from her.

"Sure; here," she said and offered me her notebook with a smile.

"Thank you." I felt betrayed by my ego. She had several chances to show me off and took advantage of none. Who was she? "What is your name?"

"Betty; Betty Ahola," she said. "And yours?"

"Tolly Kizilos." Her blue-green eyes drew me closer to her.

"I hope you can read my handwriting," I heard her say with the same soft, soothing voice she had said everything else.

Then I thought about her. How will she brush up for the exam, without her notes? And why couldn't I return the notebook to her and find out where she lives? "I can return it to you, so you can brush up for the exam, also," I said.

"My address is on the first page."

"OK. I'll see you soon."

"Yes."

At the lab, I tried to work on the design of a more focused jet, but my thoughts were dancing on that bright face and the open heart that said "Yes" and wouldn't flinch at my muddled moves and kamikaze requests.

"I met a real great girl," I told Tony when we met later that evening.

"And, if I may ask: what makes her great?" Tony asked in his smartass way.

"She is beautiful, smart and good hearted," I replied so fast that I surprised even myself.

"This is not the time to meet great girls, man," he warned. "This is the time for fast work with sexy and willing girls."

"This is not that kind of situation," I said and clammed up.

Later that night I skimmed through Betty's notes and tried to figure out what kind of MIT coed I was dealing with. I was like an explorer looking for a buried treasure. But whatever else calculus may be, it is no *Rorschach* test, so all I could say from perusing her notes was that she was very much up to speed in math, meticulous and rather well organized. I felt a pang of guilt. But, why did I care about her so much as to stoop to such a search? I closed the notebook and set it aside. The exam was coming up and I didn't want to feel that I had done well in the exam because of that notebook.

Next day I returned the notebook to her. She came to the door with a white towel wrapped around her hair.

"I brought you your notes," I said.

"Oh, thank you."

"No; I thank *you*." I was anxious. I always dreaded asking a girl for a date. "Would you like to go to the Esplanade for a cup of coffee with me?" I felt stupid and vulnerable.

"I just washed my hair," she said.

"I guess you can't go?"

"Sorry. Not tonight," she said. But, the refusal didn't hurt because I believed her. She wasn't using her hair as an excuse. Not this time. Not with me.

"Some other evening, perhaps," I mumbled already retreating.

"Yes," she said again. I gazed into her face and the eyes that gave me the same welcome sign as she had given me before.

I sat at my usual place in the back of the room for the exam and solved all the problems without difficulty. I wanted to approach Betty after class and talk with her, but I was hesitant. I was now curious to know as much as I could about her and talking would be the way. When I raised my head at the end of the hour, she had already handed in her exam and was on her way out. There will be plenty of time to talk with her and find out, I consoled myself.

At the next class, I sat behind her determined to get to know her better, something I had never done with any other coed. She greeted me with a smile.

"You left in a hurry after class the other day," I said.

"I had a meeting with an instructor" she explained.

"I thought you were avoiding me," I managed to joke.

She raised her eyebrows, as if the supposition was preposterous.

"What course are you in?" If she was in Business or the Humanities, I could breathe easier; but some fields could threaten any male ego, and I was hoping that she wasn't in one of them.

"Physics," she said, and there was a soothing tone in her voice, as if she wanted to put me at ease again. Physics was a field that could scare the crap out of anyone. But, somehow, I wasn't deterred. There wasn't a smidgeon of the smartass in any of her answers.

The class began with professor Levinson distributing the exam papers.

I had a ninety-five. It was one of the highest grades I ever got at MIT. I looked at it and felt proud of my work. But, what did she get? I nudged forward a bit and looked at her exam. "You did great," I said, looking at her paper marked with a bold ninety-four in red, at the top of the page.

"What about you?" she asked.

I had the feeling that she asked because she wanted to be friendly, not because she was sure she had the higher grade and wanted to rub it in, as I might have been tempted to do when I asked for her grade. I too had no interest in gloating now. "Ninety-five," I said without enthusiasm. And professor Levinson went on lecturing on Bessel functions the method of Stodola and Vianello for solving differential equations while I thought of Betty's quiet beauty those blue-green eyes on her cloudless face. Two people brought together from two distant corners of the world by accident or providence – it is a matter of faith, or belief, or opinion.

At the end of the class I walked with her and asked her if she would like to have that cup of coffee I had asked her the other night. "Sure," she said as if this was something we had done a hundred times before. I thought that she was interested to know me as much as I was in knowing her. She wanted to know about Athens and Greece and I wanted to know about Ely, Minnesota, her hometown in the middle of evergreen forests and crystal clear lakes. We talked about our parents and our siblings and the high schools we had attended and the courses we were taking at the time. Time was flowing by smoothly and I wanted it to go on forever. I asked her if she would like to have dinner with me at the *Omonia*, the Greek restaurant I liked. "That would be nice," she said, as if having dinner was exactly what she had in mind as well.

We ordered some lamb dishes and retsina wine and went on talking about our reasons for coming to MIT to be ground up and reformatted into scientists and engineers. I told her how I had fought to excel and come to America and about my dreams to see the world and do something worthwhile in my life. After a few minutes, I realized that I was doing all the talking and stopped. I felt guilty and short changed at the same time. My goal was to find out what kind of a person she was and all I had found was how easy and pleasant it was to talk to her.

"Here I am laying out all my dreams and you've said so little," I complained.

"But you have so many interesting stories to tell."

"It's because you are such a good listener," I protested. "You are able to pull things out of me without even trying!" And, boy, was she a good listener! She had no urge to show anyone that she was ahead of anyone, or at the top of anything. She was where she was and that was just fine with her. But was it possible to get anywhere without ambition?

"You said that you were taking a Poetry class for your humanities elective?" I asked remembering that she had mentioned that previously.

"Yes; I like literature." She waited for a long moment, but when I kept silent, she went on. "I write poems sometimes," she offered with reluctance.

"Then why come to MIT?" I pounced, reverting to the investigative mode I was used to. But why? She was no adversary; I wasn't competing against her. Sometimes I hated myself for my antagonistic style. "It must be hard going through the rigors of one discipline, especially Physics, when you want to pursue another," I offered.

"I came to MIT to study Physics for the same reason I write poetry," she said. She raised her glass and took a sip. "I want to understand God."

I raised my glass and she raised her and I taught her how to wish the best to one's friend. "Stin iyia sou; to your health," I said, and she repeated the words with pronunciation so perfect that everyone who heard her in the small dining room congratulated us by raising their glasses and drinking a little for our health and well being.

I took her hand and we walked toward my car. It was dark now, and the blue neon lights of the "Jesus Saves" sign across the street cast a tranquil glow on the street. I felt so hopeful that night, and everything I could think seemed possible. "How about going to the movies?" I asked her, still wanting to go on feeling the warmth of her presence.

"Let's go," she said playfully, as if we were kids determined to play hooky that evening. We were ready to hop and skip to the parking lot.

We found a movie and sat in the dark, holding each other's dreams and desires in our embrace. We kissed and were drawn to one another and felt the tender joys of love. It was a matter of the heart first of all, something found in the wispy places where spirits dwell, nurtured by flesh and blood into robust humanity. It was another gift of God, but we didn't recognize it until time revealed it to us. I was in love with Betty, but it would take some trials and tribulations before my sly head could catch up with the truth of my heart. The culture had instilled in me the distorted belief that a man cannot admit he is in love and still command the respect of his beloved. For quite some time I held back a little and didn't show this wonderful girl that I was totally nuts about her.

We went out a few times and got to know each other better. Then the school year was over and I had to go looking for work in the steel mills again. We were in love, but it took many years before we knew the heart and mind of the other. And, it took many more years after that to respect each other's ways and act accordingly. Anyone who believes that love is only attraction isn't taking love seriously.

64 • Decisions that Count

It was because I turned and saw,
That time, once frozen, now did thaw.
The ocean had been crossed,
My premonition was not lost.
  Betty Ahola Kizilos, "Turnings," from Entangled Thoughts

It's a very brave thing to fall in love. You have to be willing to
trust somebody else with your whole being, and that's very
difficult, really difficult and very brave.
  Nicole Kidman

Love never ends; as for prophecies, they will pass away; as for
tongues, they will cease; as for knowledge, it will pass away.
  Saint Paul, 1 Cor. 13:8

The harshness of the summer I spent in Indiana, working and looking for
work after the steel workers' strike hardened me and took a toll on our
relationship. I didn't want to feel anything or think about anything that
didn't further my overwhelming desire to find the money and get back to
school. I was angry at the world that was about to dump me on my ass
and throw me across the sea. I was angry with myself for the steel strike
and the crooked toll road boss and all the choices I made that led me to
such desperate straights. I wasn't sure I wouldn't make it back to school
and felt that I would lose Betty. I changed my address so many times that
I didn't know whether she wrote to me or not. I didn't write to her and
she all but gave up on me. But, as I have already described, my job at
Dodge Manufacturing paid me well enough so I could save some money
and return to MIT. And what a return it was when Betty and I met again!
All the troubles of the summer seemed to evaporate when I held her in
my arms and told her how much I had missed her and how much I loved
her.

  We saw each other a lot that year and helped each other any way we
could. When I had trouble finishing an assignment reading Korzybski in
linguistics, she read it and tried to make sense out of it so she could
explain to me what she read. Korzybski wasn't understandable to
anyone, but the effort was very meaningful. We took some classes
together in psychology and we found that we could work beautifully
together. She was the best partner I ever had in the common projects we
carried out, though my bad habit of being late when we had agreed to

meet at a given time was painful for her. This ability to work well together proved to be very true later in life when we worked together in the same group for Honeywell Inc., a large industrial corporation. When I was sick with the 1957 flu, she nursed me to health. And when I ran out of money, she was always there to help with some extra funds. As time passed and our relationship strengthened, I realized that she was a rare kind of person, bright and kind, whose basic inclination was to trust and give and live in the moment. I didn't know at the time that we both had some problems to work out before we could claim any morsel of wisdom. But Betty's goodwill worked on me steadily over the years and helped me to see the better sides of myself and even live accordingly.

During Christmas vacation, we went to Betty's home in Ely, Minnesota, a town cradled in evergreen forests and clear lakes. It was a magical trip where love had a chance to grow and fill our hearts. We went snowshoeing through the woods to their family cabin at Burnside Lake and we started a fire with logs and sat beside it in each other's arms and forgot about the world. We turned away from the fire and looked at each other. I saw in her eyes the love I had been looking for all my life.

"I love you," I whispered and kissed her lips. Her face was flushed, luminous, otherworldly.

"I love you too."

My worries, my cares, all the fears and defenses seemed to drain away and I was at last filled with contentment. I knew what happiness was because Betty brought it to me in her smile and the unwavering trust of her gaze. It was a time for joy. We stormed the wilderness of passion guided by love and reached the sacred woods of bliss with prayers in our hearts.

I met Dr. Taito Ahola, Betty's father and Mrs. Luella Ahola, Betty's mother, and found them to be the most gracious of hosts. Her father was a likeable person; quiet, introspective, with a sense of humor and an inquisitive mind. Right away he and I hit it off and became good friends. He had a very powerful imagination as a professional, a businessman and an inventor and we spent many wonderful hours discussing topics in these and other topics. I think that he liked me because, at the time, I was open, talkative and active, which made up for a sharp contrast with most people he was used to. We had a great time that Christmas and every time we were together. Betty's mother was a little reserved as if worried about something. Betty told me that she was troubled about me taking her away to live in Greece. She was worried that she wouldn't be able to see her grandchildren and us often anymore. One of her sisters knew a Greek-American woman who told her that Greek men take their brides away to live in Greece, and she passed it on to Betty's mother. I wish I had known what troubled her, because that was a reasonable concern and I would have put her mind at rest, instead of thinking that she wasn't happy with me.

Up to the time I met Betty and even while we were going steady, I didn't have any desire to settle down, get married and have a family. By Greek standards, I was too young to marry, let alone start a family of my own. None of my seven older cousins were married. If I married at twenty-three, after I got my Master's degree, everyone would probably think that I had to do so out of necessity. By the time I was in my last year at school, my plan had evolved to getting job with an American company that needed engineers for its far-flung businesses. I wanted to be useful and invent tools and machines that improved the lives of working people in desserts and jungles, or at least get a job for a while outside Greece and earn some money. Also, I wanted to be free to explore strange places, meet shamans and exotic women and gain experience, become wiser and have fun after being a penniless student all my life. I couldn't get myself to think of having to take care of babies and working steady every day on the same job to support them. I would have a family someday when I was in my mid thirties, but not now, not right after I finish this stint of hard labor at MIT and just as I become a free man to do as I please.

I had thrown myself into a river leading down a fork, and no matter which branch I chose to follow, I felt, that I would lose. There was no "maybe" or "perhaps" downriver. It was genuine love or freedom for me. I would have to fish or cut bait, as they say. I was approaching the fork at breakneck speed. We were close to the end of the last school year and I had still not made the final decision I had to make. Would it be "Goodbye Betty," or "Betty, will you marry me"?

I had to look for a job and get my employer, somehow, to say that they needed me so I could get an extension of my Visa and stay in America, even though the Greek Navy had been adding two months to my service time for every month I was absent. I was going to become a draft dodger and didn't like that at all. The Ministry of Defense in Greece gave extensions to many students I knew, for all kinds of reasons, but they wouldn't give me an extension to work for one year and pay my debts, buy my fare back home and stand on my feet, because I finished my studies early. If I had the funds to attend school at the normal pace rather than slave away, taking extra courses so I could finish my master's degree in one instead of two years, they would have extended my exemption from military service. They wanted me early even if that meant I would be broke and become delinquent on my student loans. I couldn't abide by the injustice and would have done everything possible to correct it. Besides, what kind of a job would I be able to get in Greece, where the best jobs go to those who know powerful people, not to those who work hard and perform best? I was tired playing the networking game I had to play when I was looking for help to come to America. I liked the life of America and the possibilities for growth that it offered. So, I decided to forget about going back home and thought about a future in America. Or with an American company somewhere else in the world.

I was very aware of the seriousness of the decision I was about to make and was determined to implement it the best way I could after I made it. I thought I could use reason to make this decision, but I was also hoping that after the end of reasoning, I would be led, somehow, to the right answer, by some unforeseen circumstances, as it had happened several times before.

Months before I reached this critical decision point I had a conversation with Tony about going steady with Betty. "She is such a wonderful person and so lovable, but I hadn't planned on settling down; I don't know what to do," I had told him back then.

He knew the plans I had for the future. He had made his decision to strike out with an American company to a foreign land and had no such problems. "You know, your situation reminds me of a story someone told me once," he said. "There is this man who goes into a forest to find the most beautiful flower for his beloved. He finds one such flower but he doesn't pick it, thinking that he will find an even more beautiful one further down the path. He goes further into the forest, and finds another flower that is more beautiful than the first, so he's about to pick that one, but the thought that he found a more beautiful flower holds him back. He convinces himself that there will be another, more beautiful flower just a little deeper into the forest. He believes that soon he will find the flower he has dreamed about and keeps walking, but when he looks up and around him he realizes that he is out of the forest and hasn't picked a flower yet." Tony stared at me with a very telling look. "You may never find another Betty to go steady with, or it may be too late by the time you do."

I remembered this conversation again, as I was trying to decide my future. Suddenly, I realized that I had created a false dichotomy. There was only one Betty, but there were all kinds of adventures and opportunities to do good things in the world with Betty on my side. And if there was one thing Betty never even hinted at was restricting my freedom or refusing to do things together. I could be as free as I wanted to be and explore the world with Betty rather be a lone and, probably, miserable wolf. I felt that she was the only American woman I could possibly marry, because she had no need to control me, or change me, or alienate me with the superiority of everything American as some people have. I decided that I didn't want to live without her. She was the most beautiful flower in the forest of my life, and I felt certain that if I let her go I would be regretting it for the rest of my life. So, I chose love.

I kneeled before her and said, "Will you marry me, my love?"

She hadn't expected the formal request, but with me back then, formalities, traditions, rites and rituals were the things you follow to seal a decision that cannot be reversed. She pulled me up and held me. "You had no chance!" she said. "From the moment I first saw you, I knew you were mine." I had thought all along that I was the one choosing, but as it turned out, she was at the controls "from the moment I turned my head back and saw you at the Advanced Calculus Class" she said.

Some time later, she told me that when she was a young girl she knew by a strange intuition that her soul mate was a boy from across the sea. "I was ten and was helping my mother with some sewing, when I said, without hesitation or any previous comment, 'I wander what he's doing right now.' My mother was startled. She looked at me and asked, 'Who is he?' With the same certainty, I told her, 'the boy across the sea that I will marry'." Betty smiled, as if surprised by her forgetfulness, "I hadn't thought about that for years but I always knew I would marry someone like you." I tried to find out how she knew. Was it a dream? Was it some kind of vision? All my life I had been looking for the mysterious and the miraculous, so I probed; but the only answer Betty had was that the thought just entered her mind, like a premonition, at that moment she described, and she never doubted its prophetic reality. Years later, she wrote a poem about finding me when she turned her head in the Calculus class and saw me. I quoted the first stanza at the top of this chapter, because our meeting seems to have been providential.

We went up to Ely, Minnesota, Betty's hometown, and I asked her father if it was all right with him to marry his daughter.

"If you can feed her," he joked with me. A moment passed and I knew there was something in his mind. "You don't gamble, do you?" he asked, and I could tell he wasn't joking altogether this time.

"I play cards with friends sometimes," I said but I'm no gambler.

"I was thinking of Nick the Greek," he said, as if he was having second thoughts about asking me.

"I can understand that," I said. "You have nothing to worry about."

That night I happened to find him watching some movie on TV where they were showing a Greek wedding and were discussing how it was customary for the family of the bride to give a house as a dowry to the newlyweds.

Her father saw me and said without any introduction, "I'll give you a car when you get married." He paused. "I hope you like that," he added.

"Thank you very much," I said, delighted by the gift that I had never expected. Who wouldn't like a car as a gift? I didn't know why he decided to mention the car at that time because I never was aware that the topic was being discussed on TV at the time he brought it up. When Betty told me that the car was my dowry, I was a little put off. I never wanted a dowry and would never accept one. If I wanted a dowry I would be fishing for it in Greece where getting one would have been some valuable house or estate for a holder of two diplomas from MIT. But getting a dowry in exchange for your accomplishments was degrading the marriage, as far as I was concerned. But, Doc Ahola had no idea of the calculus of marriage processes in Greece, let alone the intrigues of it, so the matter was forgotten overnight and later we could joke about it. Only a sensitive person would want to at least give something substantive to honor the customs of a foreign-born son-in-law. And he was a very sensitive and kind man. He wanted so much to visit Greece and learn about the culture and the ways of a people who did some great things for mankind. We became friends and went fishing together and later had some memorable dinners together to plan for our trip. He spoke slowly, deliberately, thinking through everything he said and I wanted to get to the bottom line fast, so I would fill in what I thought came next and he would look at me with patience and tolerance and go on to whatever he wanted to say next.

Betty and I were married at Saint Constantine and Helen's Greek Orthodox Church in Cambridge Massachusetts in the presence of her father, Taito, and her sister Luana, Tony Hambouris was my best man.

After we were married, I felt so close to Betty's father and so uninhibited in his presence that I even argued with him sometimes. One evening at his home, I asked how he was spelling his name and he said "T-a-i-t-o." Now, in the culture of the Greeks, names can be manipulated, and acquire all sorts of nicknames, but they all must be rooted by etymology on some basic, original name that is fixed and unchangeable.

"You mean 'T-i-t-o'," I said.

"No! I mean 'T-a-i-t-o'," he said, and I sensed that there wasn't much give in his response. But I was quite a smartass back then and didn't like to quit when I was behind. So, with unthinkable panache, I picked an argument about what my father-in-law's name actually was with the owner of the name, himself. Betty was crawling into her clothes and her sisters and brother were looking at me with horror in their eyes. I talked about the Epistle of Titus in the Bible, and Tito the ruler of Yugoslavia, and argued that clearly Taito must be etymologically a nickname of Titus or Tito and that was that. And this very self-controlled man who might have kicked anyone else out of his house, but wouldn't think of offending his daughter's future husband, put up with me until I came to my senses and gave up the battle. It took me some time though to admit that "Betty" has nothing to do with "Elisabeth," if a person says it doesn't. Ah, the differences in cultures that would come and bite me on my butt so many times!

But doc Ahola, Taito, my goodhearted and generous father-in-law died before we could enjoy his company for long. We never got to visit Greece with him, but we did take a memorable trip to the log cabin he kept for awhile on Basswood Lake in the north woods of Minnesota. He built a lodge in the wilderness up there and had a thriving business until the government declared the whole area a national park and he had to sell it. Four years or so before he left us, Betty's mother, Luella, a wonderful lady who had welcomed me in her home with an open heart and made my stay unforgettable had died, and Doc couldn't bear living without her. He had been a very dynamic man, a pillar of his community, a successful businessman and a wonderful dentist with devoted patients. After Luella's death, however, he lost his desire to make things happen. He tried to snap out of the slump, but it was very difficult for him. I tried to console him and nudge him out of his depression a couple of times, but it didn't help. "Now, it's live and let live," he said mournfully to me. He was aware that this wasn't his way of facing the world, but it would have to do for the time being. I was sad and cried when cancer struck him and he left us and still mourn his absence when memory brings him near me again. I'm also angry because so many people and things we bring close to our heart are taken away before we have a chance to enjoy them long enough.

With Betty's parents gone and mine far away, we were now alone to fend for ourselves. We had our love, our skills and talents and, in time, our children's love to see us through life's trials and tribulations. We were guided by Christian values and used all the gifts God has given us, including reason intuition and compassion, to survive, prosper and do some good in the world.

From the start, I knew that Betty and I had the same basic values, but almost opposite styles of behaving. During the many years of child rearing we avoided confrontations and presented a unified front to the children. I thought that we had a perfect marriage for thirty years. But in later years, Betty came out of the cocoon she had been in for a long time, and our different styles became clear in open conflicts. We would clash over how something was to be understood or be done, but we'd get back together when we moved on to the basic values of governing our lives. Our different styles pushed us apart, but our common values brought us together. Strife pushed us apart, but love and meaning in life gathered us back together.

I expressed all the feelings I had about every situation, but Betty's feelings had to be pried out of her; I was quick to pick up and react to every change in the environment, but she was slow and deliberate; sometimes I was reckless, whereas Betty was always careful; I was judging everything and everyone that affected our environment, but she was willing to accept many people and situations without judging them; I was intuitive, she was thinking in words; I was demanding the best of myself and others, but she demanded very little of me or others; I was expecting the most and the best, she expected very little but, somehow, she got a lot; I wanted to win doing my best, whereas she cared little about winning, but did her best and often won anyway; I held onto what I had worked hard to get, whereas she was willing to part with things at the drop of a hat. I wanted a bigger house, a better car, higher salary, but she cared nothing for any of these things. When I saw a movie or a TV show featuring a wife infected by the virus of upward mobility, I thought of myself as being both blessed with a wife that made life so easy for me and cursed with having to further my ambitions without a fellow traveler. It was always a source of comfort and frustration, knowing that my partner in life would love me with the same fervor and commitment whether I ended up working as a janitor or became the CEO of a major corporation or a Professor at Harvard. Betty is an egalitarian Sami-Finn and I am an elitist Hellene a believer in the aristocracy of the mind and the spirit. After Betty came out of her cocoon, so to speak, we discovered that we had many differences that were not easy to reconcile. I was always focused on what I was after, which is always in the future, and she was always absorbing the aura and flavors of everything around us, which are in the present. I found myself in a marriage of an ant and a grasshopper, just like the marriage of my father and mother.

When I am looking for an item to buy, I have to explore and evaluate every aspect of that item and all comparable items in a store, whereas Betty picks up the item that is good enough for what she wants and ends the search. I usually attend to one thing at a time, whereas she is always multitasking; I express my beliefs and opinions with passion and a loud voice, but Betty, "Little Voice," someone called her, is soft-spoken and no one sees her passionate side easily; I like the contest of ideas and the arguments for intellectual honesty that ensue and the combat for proving that my views make more sense than the other side's until they are proven to be so or they are demolished; Betty doesn't much care about arguing, or proving that her position is better than the other side's, or convincing anybody of anything. But, as vociferous and committed to ideas as I am, I have changed my views on many important issues by recognizing the other side's better arguments, whereas Betty seldom abandons a position she has held for a long time. I changed many of my views on the Orthodox Church, but Betty, in spite of the fact that she joined the Orthodox Church she never changed any of her Protestant beliefs. I often care about what other people will say about what I or other members or my family say or do, but Betty could care less. I do well in chaotic situations; Betty prefers settled, traditional environments, though even I have come to like the familiar places, as I grow older. Betty wants to be wherever she is at that time, but I always ask what else is there?

It would seem that we have lived our lives without our share of suffering but that is not the case. We all had serious illnesses and many occasions for worry and uncertainty. If our lives remained more or less normal over the years, it is due to Betty's stoic character. Many years ago, Betty was in an accident, which resulted in three back operations and left her with an unrelenting chronic low back pain from arachnoiditis. With patience that is beyond the norm, Betty has suffered the pain and tried dozens of ways to learn how to reduce it and live with it. I can see the pain get hold of her because she is a little more reserved as if her energy has to be focused on containing its spread. She has never used this evil to any advantage, never given an inch to the enemy that attacks her mercilessly every day. She loves and lives for the family and all the good things in the world and she overcomes obstacles, saying "it is no never mind to me." She is an exemplar of feistiness as quietude.

Our political opinions are very similar, both of us being lifelong liberal democrats, but there are some glaring differences: Betty believes that everyone can lead, and we would do just as well electing our leaders by throwing darts on the phone book's white pages as by electing them; I believe some people by virtue of talent, character, hard work and education are better qualified to lead than others. When I rebel, it is against any man's authority issuing a binding order, or making a demand, or setting a condition that limits my freedom; Betty rebels against the existence of a system, a culture, the traditions, but can accept authority's demands without rebelling. I am restless feeling confined when I do something over and over again, but Betty can stick to a group or an organization or a computer system or a pastime for decades without feeling any need for change.

Most things that trouble me are coming from the outside; most things that trouble Betty, according to what she tells me, are within herself; I blame a law, the authorities, other people, Betty; she blames herself and sometimes she rages against the system, but rarely others. I want others to be fair or, at least, to make an effort to be fair, but Betty takes people as they are and finds reasons or excuses, depending on your sympathies, why they are unfair; I often want to see the guilty punished as they are forgiven, but Betty forgives the guilty and seldom thinks of their punishment. We are both liberals, but for different reasons, I think: I like the freedom of democracy and the individual accountability, whereas Betty prefers the equality of democracy and the potential for communal and shared responsibility. None of us works for or aspires to wealth or luxury, but I wouldn't have minded some fame when I was young, whereas Betty never cared for that either.

We have similar values on the family and individual conduct. We are both old fashioned family people who like to maintain close family relations and try to live a life consistent with the morality of liberal Christianity. We believe that, above everything else, God is love and hold similar beliefs about Christ's saving grace, as well as the main dogmas of the Nicene Creed. Science and religion are complementary and there is no conflict between them because they deal with different aspects of the world. God created the world as science discloses, including the evolutionary process, but science will never explain God or the world of the spirit.

65 •The Pursuit of Excellence in the Family

As the family goes, so goes the nation and so goes the whole
world in which we live.

Pope John Paul II

The fifty-year-old story of our family will have to be told someday, but it
won't happen here. Yet, without a brief summary of our lives, my story
would be pointless. After all, when all is said and done, my greatest
accomplishment and Betty's, I believe, is the family we nurtured and
drew sustenance from. Ultimately, what matters most is creating a family
that goes on benefitting others with its honest work and God's help. And,
of course, I would say the same for the families of our sons and their
wives, and, in time, those of our grandchildren, with God's help. I
believe that, if there is a way to make the world better, it is for people in
love to nurture children who want to do good things and make the world
a better place.

The strange thing is that our family came into being without any of
us making it the purpose for our lives. Betty and I were in love, and love
wants to spread out, so we had children, and we were awed by their
existence and loved them as ourselves. We cared for them in every way
possible and guided them toward the best they could be and do in all
aspects of life. Each one of us made the effort to do the right thing and
achieve all that we could. We all fell short time and again, but we never
stopped learning from our mistakes and from each other and trying
repeatedly to do better, until some good ways became part of the life we
lived. There was never tolerance for moral laxity, no respect for making
money any which way one could, no doubting that knowledge matters,
that freedom comes with responsibility and that gratification, sometimes,
has to be postponed. We also found ways to get the message across that
the individual and the group interests must be linked because they both
count, and that sometimes one must stand up for what is right, even at
great cost. Though we didn't wear religion on our sleeves, we had no
doubt that God is a reality in our lives and the world.

I had to change some of the ways I had lived by in the Greek culture
with a different temperament, language and mode of communication,
because they didn't work here, or were antiquated or wrong; I had to
learn new ways, American ways, to be effective and express what I felt.
(No matter what anyone says, changing cultural habits is very difficult
because the change affects the entire way of behaving in society.) On the
other hand some of the ways Betty or I encouraged and the children

eventually adopted can be traced to the ways we were brought up. The making of a family gives many opportunities to discover processes and goals that produce good results, establish good habits and build a character around worthwhile values. Unfortunately, some of my flawed ways were not or could not be corrected in time and influenced the children's ways in adverse ways. I regret that very much.

To put it simply, we pushed hard – sometimes, I pushed too hard – for developing the head, the heart and the backbone. Had I been wiser back then, I wouldn't have changed the goals, but I would have changed the way of achieving the goals. I would have tried to pull sometimes, rather than only push; and I would have been more sensitive to the needs of the individual child rather than worry about equal treatment for all, or confuse their individual needs with mine. I would have been more patient, slower to anger and less overwhelming than I was.

Almost two years after our marriage, we had our first son Peter in Minneapolis. I danced at the Mount Sinai hospital waiting room when a nurse told me the good news. The other people there, who had heard me speak with an accent, stared at me flabbergasted, probably thinking that I was performing a bizarre rite demanded by my religion. I had to laugh and talk some more to put their mind at ease. I followed the nurse to the room and kissed Betty with love and a sense of gratitude. She was bathed in joy and sunshine. I touched my son's cheek and at that very moment I knew that the real purpose of my journey through time and wonders had just began. The births of our other two sons, Paul and Mark, hit me with similar jolts of joy and a sense of purpose. I saw the momentous significance of the events and felt that their existence was my immortality. Everything else I would achieve in life would come second to my love for Betty and my sons.

We came home and placed Peter in his crib, and our lives began, with devotion to our family. The fact that Peter stayed asleep for less than ten minutes on that first night and he and his brothers gave us many worries and heartaches doesn't take a smidgeon away from the abundance of joy they brought us.

I know that my life would have been incomplete without having children to love and be with. I believe that human life is not fully lived without the experience of having children of one's own or having children to be with and care for. It's the way we grow and thrive and make progress in the world. And, so, sometimes sleepy or tired, but always with a purpose, Betty and I went to work and brought home the bacon. We both had professional jobs most of the time, though I was always responsible for earning a living and Betty for making a home for all of us. Peter, being the first to arrive to greenhorn parents without any grandparents or any relatives around, had to do all the hard work of training us and breaking our old habits and guiding us into the latest methods of human relations. He was bright and inquisitive and had a prodigious memory.

Two years later, our second son Paul arrived and we brought him home and introduced him to his big brother. Paul smiled at him and went back to sleep. Picking up on my accent, Peter called Paul something that sounded to me like "pole," and I had no idea how to fix that, because its origin was my foreign accent. Paul, unlike his big brother, was a more content baby. He would stay in his crib and do his stuff and rarely bother anyone. And, later, when he did bother anyone it was usually to tell us about a new image he had seen some summer afternoon, when sunlight scattered among the autumn leaves and made them "bloody; or to inform us with a new word he had invented that a steam roller he had seen in the street was a "rollagator."

Two years after that, our third son Mark arrived and this time, I was in the delivery room to welcome him. They had neglected to ask me to be in the labor room, so the doctor tried to make up for the error by letting me be present during the delivery. Watching the miracle of birth unfold was one of the most awe-inspiring experiences of my life. A father will have to do a lot of loving to come close to the love a mother has already given by the time a child is born. For a while, Mark was thrilled to declare with great pride and joy, after every competition with his brothers, "And I'm third!" But he was as fierce a competitor as his brothers, and that happy declaration faded as his desire to win grew.

I believe that we were good parents, not because we had to be responsible, but because we enjoyed enormously playing, teaching and learning from our sons. To put it simply, being a dad was a lot of fun for me. When I got back from work and distributed whatever treats I had picked up for the boys on the way home, I chased them and hid from them and fought with them and quizzed them and read stories to them and taught them poems and made up stories that scared them and delighted them, and got them to put gloves on so they could punch each other without getting hurt and tickled them and pinned them down or let them climb on me and put a lock on my head or toss them up in the air and scare myself out of my wits and kiss them and pray that nothing would ever happen to them that would harm them. Betty would be in the kitchen cooking for us, peeking now and then to make sure we didn't maim somebody and watching us enjoy ourselves, and we would see her wearing her apron, and the knowledge that she was always present to care for us and love us and give us all she had, made life with children worth living and all the pains of work and all of life's strife bearable and insignificant.

There were countless experiences of joy and sadness of triumph and disappointment – countless opportunities to learn and grow for all of us. We were there when the boys had contests to prepare for, races to run, ribbons to win, speeches to deliver and be commended for, poems to recite, and prizes and honors to win, and plays to perform, and violin and piano rehearsals to present, and orchestras to play violin and trumpet for, and videos to conceive and produce, and laser experiments to perform, and collections of leaves and Kirlian photographs and radio shows and war memorabilia and old books to assemble, and dogs to take care of and machines to assemble and disassemble and clothes to sew and art to create and essays to write. And we were ever watchful that the boys don't blow themselves up using their creativity and their limited knowledge experimenting with gun powder and explosives, or get blinded by lasers, or jump from high branches of trees, as Paul once did, or slip and fall at ice arenas, or fall from bicycles because of acrobatics, or become too enamored with vicious ideologies and their deadly symbols, or sneak out of the house and grasp at some forbidden fruit like cigarettes or alcohol or dope or guns, or sex before it was time. We were proud to attend every one of their parent-teacher conferences, proud to be the parents of sons who made all around excellence their objective. I was as proud when Peter suffered the pain of shin splints with courage while running long distances as when he was recognized as the best student in American History classes by the best history teacher in high school. We were the first to occupy the stands for oratory contests for Peter, debates for Mark and theater shows and orchestra concerts for Paul and Mark. We were the best fan club in town when anyone of them played baseball, basketball, football and when Paul competed in soccer and track and field championships, even if neither Betty nor I gave a darn for sports in general. We were thrilled to see them explore the talents and interests they discovered in themselves as they were growing up – film-making, collecting radio show and books, computer programming, strategy games, rock-climbing, finding work and working part-time, debating and oratory, pole-vaulting, sprinting, leather-craft, piano-playing and forming lasting friendships.

We were proud of all the struggles the boys had to go through to do what they wanted to do and proud of everything they achieved. We were thrilled with their school performance, vying for the top positions in academics. They had different interests, but they achieved their goals in similar ways: working long hours, learning from others, not giving up when difficulties arose and demanding the best of themselves. I was delighted to see them feel the stirrings of love for girls and I was apprehensive as they steered their lives loaded with emotions.

There were many times of sheer abandonment to humor when, for example, Paul would do his Donald Duck and his Duffy Duck imitations or walk standing on his two big toes, while I would lie on the floor shaking uncontrollably in a fit of laughter; or Peter would grab the microphone and imitate the voices of radio show hosts from one of his countless radio shows; or when Mark would start reciting Chaucer in the original with his Old English brogue, or when he and Peter would imitate Greeks, Brits and Indians. There were jokes and cartoons and funny stories and we would comment on them and try to understand why something was good or better than something else, or what made something funny or meaningfully humorous, or not, and argue about anything and everything from every side until Betty would cast a look of disdain on me, the instigator of the games so full of fun and strife, and we would quiet down and return to normal.

We played all kinds of table games with winners and losers so that we could all learn how to deal with conflict, accept defeat without falling and enjoy victory without bragging. We knew that we were in a game, but we also knew that the game was training for life. Besides having fun, the games were supposed to teach us how to strategize and compete for success, how to form alliances and cooperate, use the rules shrewdly to gain the upper hand, take risks, develop and assess alternatives, recover from errors, put up with psychological warfare, and make decisions calmly and with self-confidence. Sometimes the pressure of competition was intolerable and we would have defections, outright refusals to continue playing, and Mom would declare her support for the weaker side to the protests of the rest of us. Overall, the boys stood their ground very well and they learned many lessons. After an intense game was ended we would talk about it, and we would now praise each one for the good moves they made or the stamina they showed, or the way they recovered from a vicious attack or how smart they were to have spotted dad's sneak attack. I felt that the boys should go into the world seeking peace and playing fair, but they should know enough to avoid malcontents and cheaters and defend themselves against anyone who tried to take advantage of them. Sometimes I wonder whether the agony of playing the games was worth the learning. All I can say is that my intention was to impart on the boys the necessary skills for coping in the world I had known. Perhaps, the world is better than what I had known, and I didn't have to be so rigorous in training them. But, I wasn't the only influence on them. If Betty wasn't there to support the boys when things got rough, I may have never decided to play the highly competitive games, like Risk, that we played. She was the cooperative, the pacific, the calming influence, and because of her presence I could represent the other face of reality.

And we were there to discipline them when they broke the rules we lived by and made us angry or guilty or glad because they had outsmarted us. In this context, the most gut-wrenching situation for me was to refuse to allow something that was near and dear a boy's heart, but not a good choice for him. Breaking the heart of someone you love and knowing he will hate your guts because he thinks that you are mean and heartless is both hard and necessary. But, there were other trying times that we went through and I will never forget. We were there to cool their small bodies down with alcohol and an electric fan so the fever didn't rise and affect their minds as they screamed terrified; and we had to rush them to hospitals, sometimes on the spur of the moment for medical emergencies and accidents day or night, and sometimes with a meticulously laid out plan for a serious illness and for operations, there to examine, even test their doctors and question their answers, looking for ignorance and incompetence so we could find the best; we were there to nurture them back to health and love them to maturity. What a ride family life was, with all the ups and downs life confronts us with, demanding we use all we got and punishing us for every flaw we have and every mistake we make until we learn and move on or lose and have to live with the consequences. Life is a serious game to be played with total concentration, and family life is even more serious than that.

My love was always given, but they had to do their best to gain my respect, which ultimately was also their own self-respect. And with a few lapses in between, they fulfilled the promise to become worthy persons with families of their own. I was never satisfied with just "good" work, never rested when they did "better." Only doing their best work deserved my final approval. And I knew first hand what was their best because I worked with them on many problems many times on many situations. I was never upset with average work if that was all one could do; but if I knew someone had a gift on a given field, I would ask for more. Perhaps, I was too tough a grader when they needed encouragement rather than criticism; perhaps I was too strict a judge and not as good in encouraging incremental progress. I tried as hard as I could to ask, not for perfection but maximum effort to the degree one was able to perform. When something was wrong, I pointed it out even as I praised the rest of the work. I disliked and still do, sweeping anything under a rug. I wanted to teach the boys that the truth is always comforting and plain and sometimes smarts, whereas hiding things is a complex, twisted process and has always been painful for me.

I remember being thankful to God that he gave us sons who were all capable of doing excellent work in many areas. How demanding would I have been, if one of the boys had some serious mental or emotional deficiency that precluded that? I hope I would have been as caring and sensitive as I needed to be and more. Of course, Betty was always there to soothe the boys' bruised egos that were seething in the corridors outside the judge's chambers. And, she was there to disapprove of my harsh tone and plead for a gentler way of communication. These were hard times for me, also. Why couldn't I just be quiet and let that wrong sentence go by in this essay? Why not keep quiet and let the solution to the geometry problem stand, even if it wasn't the most elegant one? I suppose the answer is obvious: for me too, doing good work is not enough; it should be the best I could do. And that required corrections along with approval. Doing good work is hard.

I have always believed that every human being has an obligation to add something good to the world. Doing something that helps others in some way, qualifies as such. Knowledge, more often than not, enables one to do good but ignorance and laziness and lack of caring are evils because they don't add anything good to the world. Raising children who want to add something good to the world ought to be an obligation for all parents. So, I wanted our sons to excel in anything they had to do in school, or they chose to do on their own, as Betty and I had done. I dislike lazy minds and sloppy thinking, and never tired of correcting, inquiring, directing, watching, probing and prodding, helping, guiding and most of all delighting in their achievements and congratulating them for the good work they usually did. I knew, of course, that doing one's best is not always attainable, but *trying* to do so, should always be the goal. I wasn't as sure how to put these ideas in practice as I was in principle; our sons knew that I was demanding, but they also knew that I admired all the things they tried to do well enough.

We had discussions and arguments about working after school and academic excellence and what is good art or the right thing to do and about presence at the dinner table where these and other discussions on all sorts of topics took place and the boys had to cope with me, the ogre of the castle, until they could overcome me and move onward, beyond me. We had discussions on dating and criteria for finding girls worth forming relationships with, and we talked about people one could befriend and trust and people one should avoid. We tried to help them in our clumsy ways with their budding love for girls until they could sort things out on their own. Some talked more freely than others about their feelings, and we respected their wishes. From time to time we helped them with their hobbies, and sometimes we pushed them into contests they might not have chosen. Betty helped them to learn how to write computer programs and I taught them how to analyze and comment on TV shows like Startrek. We coached them, sometimes too much, on their careers, and helped them with their choices of colleges and with financial matters and political opinions and knowledge and excellence in whatever one chooses to do in this life under God's guidance. I brought lasers from work to see the smoke form patterns, and I borrowed computers work so the boys could play games and get enthused about learning with the Plato system. Betty took them to places where they could buy their chemicals and electronics and tapes and antiques and all that their inquisitive minds propelled them to buy. And I took each one of them alone for outings to movies and museums and parks and stores with plenty of opportunities to talk about anything they wanted and cared about.

It wasn't always as easy or as rewarding to be caring parents as all these activities imply. I would be impatient, Betty would retreat and the boys would brood or get angry and shout at me or ignore me. There were times when my anger at somebody at work spilled over to one of the boys or to Betty, and I would become a bundle of nails gouging their hearts and minds; or, times when my pride and my ego would demand obedience to the way I said things had to be done, and no rational argument from anyone else would hold sway. Sometimes my fear became a stumbling block to a good relationship, and I became overbearing, autocratic, hard to live with, only to regret it later and end up with a load of guilt crowding my innards and the alienation from my family. And there were times when the boys would strike back and rebel and test the boundaries of their power and the limits of freedom they had.

I used every trick in the book to guide them to life-affirming directions and sometimes I was there to nudge them and help them or discipline them, if they strayed; and sometimes I wasn't there and they had to work things out on their own or ask for help. We taught them that one should do the right thing regardless of the consequences, but one could not avoid making mistakes and doing some wrong things. Given that reality of the human condition, consequences of actions also matter, and some consequences are downright hard to erase in this life. On several occasions I talked to them about the list of things that they should avoid at all costs because their outcomes cause untold suffering and irreversible loss for life. Among them were violations of the laws that could ruin one's life in many ways; having irresponsible sex; using drugs, drinking and driving because it could result in deaths and crippling injuries; contracting a disease that has no cure by doing something that could have been avoided; riding motorcycles which have ten times the accident rates of cars and maim a lot of people; joining groups that endanger personal freedom or the ability to think critically; enlisting to fight a war that doesn't have to be fought, and so on. We were worried when we saw signs of depression, or enthusiasm for friends that seemed unreliable to us, or signs of mood swings, or false, uncharacteristic moves and avoiding the company of others. We tried to talk about everything that troubled us and them, and most of the time we were able to help and when we couldn't, we found experts who could and did. But, if we did any good as parents, it was not because we were duty bound, but because we had fun driving this vehicle of joined lives on such a splendid journey. As I watched the boys change and develop characters of their own and become independent persons, with hearts and minds of their own, I caught myself many times feeling the joy of having done something that would outlast me. I would wonder how this miracle happened in spite of the many errors I made and the harshness of my temper, the disappointments and reversals of life that I went through and I would conclude that it was love that did the work. The boys, somehow, knew that my faults could never overshadow my love. It was a blessed family life, including joy and sadness, exploration and worry, setbacks and growth. It was all in good measure, thank God. Later, the caring and dynamic wives they chose to marry enriched our lives and blessed us with seven grandchildren. When I became an old man, I realized that we were blessed not only with a wonderful family, but also in countless ways we haven't even discovered yet. All we have to do is look around and grasp the harmony of creation; children and other miracles of goodness outnumber the evils by far. All my life I was looking for miracles as evidence of God's presence in the world. Now I know they are all around us.

Epilogue

Love bears all things, believes all things, hopes all things, endures all things.

Saint Paul, in 1Cor. 13:4

Love is all we have, the only way that each can help the other.

Euripides

As I approach the end of this excursion into our lives, I am afraid because Betty is seriously ill with pneumonia and I cannot make her well. I pray and do the chores to try to be helpful. She lies down and stares at the ceiling waiting out the fever. She doesn't move because the cough may come back and stab her in the ribs again as it did last night. She knows that pneumonia can be deadly, but it doesn't seem to affect her. I sit beside her and wonder what she sees out there in the distance beyond the ceiling plaster. Her hands are folded and she seems to be praying, but I'm not sure, because, for her, prayer happens all the time in fleeting thoughts and poems and images cast on walls and the smiles of her grandchildren or at the supermarket encountering a woman with a walker or a child bouncing a blue ball in the street. I'll find out later what she saw travelling through space and time. I'll probably dispute, or doubt, or disagree that the forms she saw on the ceiling are meaningful shapes, but I won't keep it up now. I'll accept what she tells me because, no matter what she says, the truth is exactly as she tells it in a realm I may see someday, but cannot see now.

"You have been quiet, dear," I comment, thinking that this might help her come down to my reality, and we can talk about quantum consciousness and "*Monk*" and Obama and all the things that we have talked about and become familiar with over the years. She smiles. "What do you see up there?"

"There are so many forms . . . they remind me of people and places I have come across making things . . ."

"I thought you were praying."

"Sometimes I do."

She does her praying by doing something useful, helping someone, writing a poem, cooking a lamb shank with red sauce and rice. She has faith that everything will be all right. But she doesn't see all the nasty possibilities, so she appears vulnerable to me. She doesn't feel threatened by anyone or any thing. Sometimes she'll tell me that I am a bit on the paranoid side, which has some truth in it, I cannot deny it. I love her and

I'll do anything to protect her from the meanness of other people. She is thankful that I do what I do, but she just doesn't have the existential awareness of threat from the outside world. When I am angry and shout in protest that her trusting of strangers who come knocking at our door endangers us, or her inattention to the perils of the world may cause her harm, she is calm and feels sad that I am so suspicious, so prepared only for the worst possible scenario. She is right most of the time, and I regret what I said and apologize. Sometimes I think that the world comes at me in a different way than it comes at Betty. Sometimes I think that you have to dismiss evils to defeat them.

I worry about the fever and the cough and the medications and the viruses that others may infect us with, whereas she worries about being the kind of grandmother she imagined herself to be, or struggles to hold herself together as she grieves for the many losses she has suffered over the years. Being the outside man makes me feel like a babe in the woods. Why am I not feeling dread when I ask the big questions? I have learned a lot from her strange reports of the landscape within, but my huffing and puffing about the world out there has not helped her much.

I never met anyone else with such a narrow domain of desired influence upon others. Betty's ego is sufficient to see her through the day, but makes no demands on others. And because her ego hasn't spread out, it is very difficult for anyone to zero in on it and hurt her. The slings and arrows of the world have trouble finding the target; but when they do, as it has happened in moments of my flailing anger and sharp tongue, the pain is unbearable for her. I have regretted every one of these unintended strikes and apologized, not only because I was wrong, but also because I cannot imagine the pain it causes until I see it in her desperate, hopeless look.

Once, working hard together to identify any other persons who have hurt her besides me, she admitted that there were two other people, but she had already forgiven them: one was a German woman vendor behind a newsstand counter in the Frankfurt airport, who shooed her out of her area because she thought Betty was infringing on her domain, and the other was the new president of a women's church group who decided she didn't want an independently thinking editor for the newsletter and slyly managed to remove Betty as its editor. By contrast, I can identify dozens of people who have hurt me and I have forgiven as well.

When the Tylenol drops the fever a little and her eye catches me struggling with a crossword puzzle, she will shift from meditation upon the plaster forms on the ceiling to word searches and problem solving in a flash. She has been thinking through everything she has done, slowly, deliberately, wisely, but never with a plan or calculation or any kind of organization that gives time a robust, future dimension. Betty's world is in the here and now and is focused like a laser beam upon the task-at-hand.

"Where would you like to be right now?" I used to ask a long time ago, before proposing going on a trip.

"I like to be where I am now," was Betty's answer.

"But, how are we ever going to go anywhere, other than where we are?" I would counter.

"Let's go wherever, and when we are there, I will be in the place I want to be."

What can a poor Greek with reason in his veins do when confronted by such an alien response?

In moments of intense concentration upon washing dishes or sneaking up on the relationship of Zen and the quantum world, while we are out shopping, or dining at one of our favorite restaurants, or refusing to accept any notion that time has a past, a present and a future, she'll grab some new idea and drag it into my world and infuriate me for a day, or a year or a decade, or until I scream for mercy. Sometimes, I see what she has been trying to show me and I am thankful for it. Sometimes, I'll get through to her and she'll incorporate what I said into her thoughts without giving me credit or thanks. In a world of egos crashing against each other such behavior would be rude, ungrateful – a selfish denial of credit where credit is due. Not so in the world of ego-challenged aliens and saints, not in the world that Betty inhabits a good part of the time, because there is no notice taken either for giving or of taking anything. The world has no rigid boundaries; possessions are shared; hearts are given out freely and the world is full of God's goodness and mystery, just as it will be someday.

Betty is getting better, thank God, and I can start using my head again instead of only praying and searching with my heart. She is not an alien or a saint and she isn't going to reveal to me the secrets of the universe no matter how brilliant her insights might be. But, she is a good person, better than most of us. And she is a brave person, a Finish-Sami woman.

It is late. I have talked about our lives long enough. We are both feeling that the worst of the illness has passed and tomorrow will be a better day. It is time to go to sleep and dream. I was back at our cabin by Moon Lake, sitting on my lawn chair on the dock and gazing at the tree line across the lake. The two old trees that had lost their leaves years ago, a few yards away to my left, were fading as the sun went down across the lake. The gold streaks on the water were getting scarce, going away. It was as peaceful as I had ever experienced it when I sat there. Suddenly, the trees leaned slowly toward the water and fell into the lake and were gone. I woke up, and it was morning again.

Chronology

• I was born on May 10, 1935, in The Clinic of Dr. Mayakos, in Athens, Greece, to Petros and Marina Kizilos. I was baptized with the name Apostolos, after my paternal grandfather, and had the nickname Tolis. When I came to America I called myself Apostolos Peter Kizilos, in lieu of a middle name, and adopted the nickname Tolly at the suggestion of one of my English teachers.

• September 1941 to June 1947: I attended United Educational School, a private grade school ran by the local priest, in the *Neos Kosmos* neighborhood of Athens. I was among the top students in my class.

• January 6, 1945: my sister Vassiliki Kizilos (Vasso Kizilou) was born at our home in *Neos Kosmos*, during the Greek Civil War (the Fratricides, according to Kazantzakis) that was still raging in Athens, Greece. My sister was also a top student in the same grade school I attended, and in Arsakeion Exemplary High School, in Athens.

• September 1947 to June 1953: I attended Varvakeion Model High School, in Koleti Street of Athens Greece. I was the top student in my class and received prizes from the Ministry of Education. I was also known at Varvakeion for my yearly recitation of poems during celebrations for national holidays.

• August 13,1953: I arrived in the USA, at Hoboken NJ, with the ship SS *Nea Hellas*.

• August 1953: I spent about a week in the Bronx, New York, with some distant relatives of my father.

• August to September 1953: I stayed in the Boston YMCA and worked at the Darbury Room, in Boston, as a busboy.

• September1953 to June 1954: I was a freshman at MIT, living at Burton House, in Cambridge, MA. I worked part time during Christmas vacation cleaning rooms and, briefly, flipping hamburgers at the Graduate House snack bar.

• June to September 1954: I worked in the steel mills of Inland Steel Co. at East Chicago, IN. I was a laborer, sweeping floors at a plant and as a laborer in the pickling line for steel coils. I bought my first car here, a 1949 Plymouth, and drove it to Boston.

• September 1954 to June 1955: I was a sophomore at MIT, living at 423 Marlborough St., Boston, MA. I worked part time at a Civil Engineering laboratory, making structural calculations on a Marchant mechanical calculator.

• June to September 1955: I worked again at the steel mills of Inland Steel Co. in East Chicago, IN. I was an oiler at the boiler room of the

company's power plant and, later, oiler in the pump room of the plant.
• September 1955 to June 1956: I was a junior at MIT, living at 423 Marlborough St., Boston MA. I got a loan from MIT. I met Betty Ahola in April 1956 when she was a sophomore. We fell in love and we went steady after that.
• My wife, Betty Ahola Kizilos, was born in Ely, Minnesota on January 6, 1937, to Luella and Taito Ahola. She studied Physics at MIT and received her S.B. degree in Physics, in 1958. She worked as a research scientist and a computer systems analyst mostly for Honeywell Inc. She took several courses in Electrical Engineering at the U. of Minnesota and excelled. She is a poet and an accomplished artist in photography, graphic design, silk screening and various other crafts. She has published three collections of poems and two books of children's stories. She has co-authored a non-fiction religious book and illustrated a children's book on Orthodoxy.
• June to September 1956: I started working in the steel mills of Inland Steel Co. in East Chicago, IN, as the ground man in an electricians' crew of the plant, until the steel workers went on strike. I travelled to South Bend IN, where I got a job painting bridges at the Indiana Toll Road for two to three weeks. I was unemployed for a couple of weeks, but I finally found a job at Dodge Manufacturing Corporation, where I worked as a designer of fluid clutches. I lived in Mishawaka IN, during that time. Because I found a job against all odds, I was able to return to MIT and continue my education.
• September 1956 to June 1957: I was a senior at MIT, living at 3 St. Charles St. in Boston, MA. I received my S.B. degree in Mechanical Engineering, in June 1957.
• June to September 1957: I worked at The Thermo-Electron Engine Corporation, which was started by George Hatsopoulos with funding from the Greek ship-owner, Peter Nomikos of New York. I was hired to continue work on my Bachelor's thesis, which was related to the company's work on the Thermo Electron Engine that George was developing. This startup grew into the multibillion-dollar Thermo Electron Corporation.
• September 1957 to June 1958: I was a graduate student, and a Research Assistant at the Machine Tool Laboratory of MIT, had an office there and worked on my master's thesis, "Work Piece Temperatures in Lathe Operations." I lived at an apartment on 1 Peterborough St. in Boston MA. I received my S.M. degree, in Mechanical Engineering, on June 1958, one year after my S.B. degree because I had taken extra courses as an undergraduate. Betty and I were married on June 7, 1958, at St. Constantine and Helen's Greek Orthodox Church in Cambridge, MA.

• June 1958 Betty and I left Boston for Massillon, OH, where I had found a job at Griscom Russell Company, working as a mechanical engineer in heat transfer equipment. Betty got a job at Babcock and Wilcox Company, in nearby Barbeton, OH, doing work in computer programming for power plant boilers. Sometime later she came to work at Griscom Russell Company, continuing work in computer programming. I taught Physics to night school students in Canton, OH for one semester and I was appalled at their lack of basic knowledge.

• September 1959, we came to Minneapolis, MN, where I had found a job at the Main Plant of Honeywell Inc. Betty found a job at the Research Labs of Honeywell Inc. in Hopkins, MN. We lived in Minneapolis and in St Louis Park until September 1961, when we bought our first house on Archwood Rd. in Minnetonka, MN. We would live for at least 49 years in Minnetonka, MN.

• December 13, 1960, our first son, Peter Justin Kizilos, was born. We lived in a rental apartment, at 4084 Meadowbrook Lane, in St Louis Park, MN. Peter received a B.A. degree in Psychology from Yale University on 1982, *cum laude*, an M.A. degree from the University of Michigan in Russian and Eastern European Studies and a PhD in American Studies from the University of Minnesota. He is a successful freelance writer, and has written several non-fiction books on various topics. He continues his writing career with a historian's point of view.

• October 8, 1962, our second son, Paul Taito Kizilos, was born when we were at our first home then, on Archwood Rd, in Minnetonka, MN. Paul received a B.A. degree in Art from the University of Minnesota in 1984. He worked as a marketing associate for Honeywell Inc. and run his own business near Pasadena, CA. Subsequently, he attended Hamline University and received his JD, Law Degree. He was admitted to the Minnesota Bar and practiced law for a prestigious law firm in Minneapolis. Later, he joined the Thomson Reuters Corporation and concentrated in the development and distribution of legal software to law firms around the country.

• October 15, 1964, our third son, Mark Alexander Kizilos, was born when we were living on Archwood Rd, in Minnetonka, MN. (Paul's or Mark's middle name should have been "Ahola," to honor my wife's family's name, if I had only been wiser and more sensitive at the time). He attended Columbia University and The University of Minnesota, and received a B.A. degree in Psychology from the University of Minnesota, a Master's degree in Organization Behavior from Brigham Young University and a PhD degree in Organization Behavior from the University of Southern California. He was an assistant professor at the University of Alberta, Canada, worked for a few years as a management consultant and joined the Thomson-Reuters Corporation where he reached the position of vice president in Talent Management. He left this position to assume the position of Assistant Dean at the Carlson School of Management of the University of Minnesota. He is also a published author of several management articles and a book, a management software developer and a composer of classical music, having had several of his works performed for the public.

• In 1970 I won the Bush Leadership Fellowship and the whole family spent one year in Coralville, IA, where I attended the University of Iowa and received an MFA. Degree in Creative Writing in June 1971.

• 1959 to 1970 I worked in various engineering companies in the Minneapolis area, mostly at Honeywell, where as a Senior Research Engineer, I invented the Variable Deflection Thruster (VDT). I received 6 US patents related to my engineering work at Honeywell, Inc. and developed the VDT under several government contracts, which we won competitively from the U.S. Navy.

• In 1971, I changed careers from Engineering to Organization Development, eventually becoming Director of Organization Development at the Systems and Research Center of Honeywell, Inc. After working in this field for eighteen years, I retired early in 1990, at fifty-five, to pursue other interests.

• In 1979, our family moved to Mayfield Rd, in Minnetonka, MN, before any of our sons were married.

• Starting in the late 1980s to the early 2000s, I taught courses in Participative Management and Organization Development at the University of St. Thomas, in Minneapolis and St. Paul, MN, as an Adjunct Professor. In later years I became a lecturer on topics related to religion, science and theology for church groups. Thus, my career has included being an engineer, an inventor, a manager, a writer, a book reviewer, a teacher and a lecturer.

• As of 2009, I have published five books, two non-fiction on religious topics, two novels and a collection of short stories. I have written many reviews for the Minneapolis Star and Tribune and several articles in professional and local magazines, including two articles for the Harvard Business Review.

Photo Album of

Tolly and Betty Kizilos'

Family

My grandfather, Apostolos N. Kizilos, my
father Peter A. Kizilos and I, Apostolos P. (Tolly) Kizilos.

Posing in the Royal Gardens of Athens
at three and a half years old with my signature beret.

In a hurry, after class, with my cousin, Nondas Laskos
(my right) and Andreas Manoussos, downtown Athens.

High school class excursion with professor Xifaras on the lead.

After high school
graduation, a portrait for my passport and official papers.

My mother, Marina Laskos, before her wedding.

My father, Peter Kizilos, twenty years old.

My father working in his office with his assistant.

My little sister Vasso Kizilou, at four, in Eleusis.

My sister, Vasso, likes to tease me when I visit her in Athens.

My father and mother in their home in Pagrati, Athens,
during one of my visits from America to see them.

The ocean liner *Nea Hellas* is about to leave the port of Piraeus, Greece, and I'm bidding goodbye, waving my hat to my parents and Vasso on the pier (see above the arrow, under the flag of Greece).

Two weeks after landing in the U.S.A. and just before M.I.T. started, I found a job busing dishes at the Darbury Room, in Boston.

Tony Hambouris and I celebrate our arrival at M.I.T.
Tony has always been a good friend.

Getting used to being a college freshman at M.I.T.

Betty Ahola and I, in love, at M.I.T. in 1956 or thereabout.

Betty's father, Dr. Taito Ahola and her mother, Luella Ahola.

Betty and I had this photo taken in
1958, around the time of our wedding.

Graduate student in my office, 1958, when I was a research assistant at M.I.T.,
and Betty at our apartment in Massillon, OH, where we both worked in 1958.

As project engineer with a colleague and my invention, the VDT, at Honeywell.

Standing on the marble stoop at the house I grew up in.

Betty working as a research scientist in physics at Honeywell, 1959.

The Kizilos side of my family roots: my grandfather Apostolos my grandmother Ekaterini and their four boys, Gerassimos, Stavros, Paul and Peter (tallest with a hat).

Uncle Paul Kizilos   My father Peter Kizilos   Uncle Gerassimos
                                                                       Kizilos

My grandmother Marigo Laskos, matriarch of her clan.

My uncle, commander Vassilios Laskos (barba Vassos),
on his submarine, *Lambros Katsonis,* with captain Konstas.

My uncle Orestis Laskos, poet. film director and producer.

My uncle, Commander Vassilios Laskos, captain of the submarine *Lambros Katsonis* was killed heroically in a naval battle, in WWII, 9-14-1943.

Our nuclear family, from left: Dad, Paul, Mark, Peter (up) and Mom.

High School graduation pictures

Peter 1979   Paul 1981   Mark 1982

Our family at Paul's wedding, September1990.

Our extended family, adults from left: Mark and Melissa, Betty and Tolly, Paul and Rina, Nancy and Peter with our seven grandchildren in front, Joshua, Justin Jason, Andy, Olivia, Jamie and Alex.

Betty and I celebrating our 52nd wedding anniversary at dinner

Writing, lecturing and celebrating the life of our family in my 70s.